"Donna MacM...
turning the...

PRAISE FOR DONNA MacMEANS AND HER NOVELS

"Be ready to laugh and cry. I can't wait for other books from this author."
—Karen Harper, *New York Times* bestselling author

"MacMeans writes with grace and wit." —*Booklist*

"[A] sweet, sexy, and smartly told Victorian romance."
—*Publishers Weekly*

"Wonderfully wicked and deliciously sensual."
—*Romance Junkies*

"Donna MacMeans writes with intelligence and panache . . . An author for your 'must-have' list. Don't miss this one." —**TwoLips Reviews*

"[MacMeans] grabs the reader from the onset and takes her on an unforgettable ride." —*Affaire de Coeur* (5 stars)

"...n Victorian romance with a touch of fantasy."
—*Genre Go Round Reviews*

"...what a joy to read! Truly humorous . . . Wonderful
v...ng." —*The Romance Readers Connection*

"...ginal and charming." —*A Romance Review*

"...n and fascinating tale that readers are sure to enjoy."
—*Historical Romance Writers*

"...cMeans] knows how to make the pages sizzle and
p...on readers' fantasies." —*Romantic Times*

THE
Casanova
Code

DONNA MacMEANS

BERKLEY SENSATION, NEW YORK

THE BERKLEY PUBLISHING GROUP
Published by the Penguin Group
Penguin Group (USA) Inc.
375 Hudson Street, New York, New York 10014, USA
Penguin Group (Canada), 90 Eglinton Avenue East, Suite 700, Toronto, Ontario M4P 2Y3, Canada
(a division of Pearson Penguin Canada Inc.) • Penguin Books Ltd., 80 Strand, London WC2R 0RL,
England • Penguin Group Ireland, 25 St. Stephen's Green, Dublin 2, Ireland (a division of Penguin
Books Ltd.) • Penguin Group (Australia), 250 Camberwell Road, Camberwell, Victoria 3124, Australia
(a division of Pearson Australia Group Pty. Ltd.) • Penguin Books India Pvt. Ltd., 11 Community
Centre, Panchsheel Park, New Delhi—110 017, India • Penguin Group (NZ), 67 Apollo Drive,
Rosedale, Auckland 0632, New Zealand (a division of Pearson New Zealand Ltd.) • Penguin Books
(South Africa) (Pty.) Ltd., 24 Sturdee Avenue, Rosebank, Johannesburg 2196, South Africa

Penguin Books Ltd., Registered Offices: 80 Strand, London WC2R 0RL, England

THE CASANOVA CODE

A Berkley Sensation Book / published by arrangement with the author

PUBLISHING HISTORY
Berkley Sensation mass-market edition / June 2012

Copyright © 2012 by Donna MacMeans.
Excerpt from *A Lady Never Lies* by Juliana Gray copyright © 2012 by Juliana Thomas.
Cover design by George Long.
Cover art by Aleta Rafton.
Cover hand lettering by Ron Zinn.

ISBN: 978-0-425-25083-9

BERKLEY SENSATION®
Berkley Sensation Books are published by The Berkley Publishing Group,
a division of Penguin Group (USA) Inc.,
375 Hudson Street, New York, New York 10014.
BERKLEY SENSATION® is a registered trademark of Penguin Group (USA) Inc.
The "B" design is a trademark of Penguin Group (USA) Inc.

PRINTED IN THE UNITED STATES OF AMERICA

10 9 8 7 6 5 4 3 2 1

ALWAYS LEARNING   **PEARSON**

ACKNOWLEDGMENTS

Stephen King once described story ideas as being buried in the ground. All the writer had to do was dig the ideas up. If that's the case, there were many hands on that shovel. I'd like to thank a few.

Thank you to Libby McCord and the MR-Debuts group for finding a *New York Times* article on Victorian personal ads. It was that article that initially got the creative juices flowing.

I took that article to Cassondra Murray, Jeanne Adams, and Nancy Northcott and said, "I think I can do something with this." They helped me flesh out the series concept and pushed me over some plot hurdles. Special kudos go to Nancy, who late one night uttered the words "Rake Patrol." That "sealed the deal" and provided a name for the series.

A special thank-you goes to Rene Michaels. She suggested the idea of cryptograms when I despaired that crossword puzzles hadn't been invented in my time period. As it turns out, codes and ciphers became the backbone of the story, all because of her Facebook suggestion. Serendipity works that way sometimes, adding a magical element to the process of writing. I hope you like what I did with your suggestion, Rene.

Thank you to the Romance Bandits. I couldn't ask for more supportive friends.

Finally, as always, thank you to my understanding and supportive family. It is your love that allows me to indulge in my passion.

· One ·

PATTERNS. EDWINA HARGROVE NOTICED THEM everywhere, in the design of the teacup on the table before her, in the ebb and flow of voices at the Crescent Coffee Palace, even in the grain of the wood beneath her feet. The order and predictability of those patterns formed the framework of her rather tedious life. When those sequences were broken, yielding new patterns requiring interpretation— Edwina smiled as she retrieved her brother's encrypted letter from her reticule—that's when adventures began.

Smoothing the folded stationery on the table amid the chatter of patrons, Edwina savored the thought of leaving her predictable surroundings behind, if only for a mental excursion—to unlock the secrets from the coded letter.

She had her own patterns for transcribing the code. Her journal sat to the left; a red grosgrain ribbon used to contain the overstuffed book was loosened and buried beneath the clutter. The book lay open to a page with the alphabet already inked down the side in anticipation of the coded text. The opposite page remained blank, waiting for the transcription.

Fragrant steam rose from her teacup on her right, and in the middle, she'd placed her copy of *Treasure Island*, just as she did every time her brothers sent her a letter. The pirate adventure, a favored novel of both her brothers and herself, provided the key to their code.

The transcription process required concentration, the sort one would not expect in such a public setting. Nevertheless she paused, letting the ring of spoons tapping fragile porcelain and the blended voices of the Crescent patrons dissolve into the distant cry of seabirds and the thunder of the Caribbean ocean pounding a white sand beach. She mentally transformed the lingering scent of wood and aged spirits from the once popular gin palace, now a ward of the Temperance group Women for a Sober Society, into that of imagined casks of pirate's rum. Even the current generated by the sway of a passing skirt became a gentle island breeze. Thus solidly engrained in the world of the book, and isolated from familiar reality, she bent to the task of transcribing the letter's nonsense patterns into meaningful discourse.

Soon she was lost in the tale of her brother's recent trip to a Caribbean sugar plantation. She scribbled out the English words almost as if her brother whispered in her ear. A sigh of yearning passed her lips. How wonderful it must be to see such things, to know a little of the world outside of London, to have unlimited possibilities for future adventures . . .

"Another letter from your brother?" Faith Huddleston peered down a moment before slipping into the chair next to Edwina's. "It would be so much easier if they used the King's English. I just don't understand why they make you decipher everything."

There was no explaining the unleashed joy of solving the mystery behind the coded letters, so she didn't try. She'd encountered similar skepticism and annoyance from her friends before. Reluctantly, she closed her journal, then slipped the letter into the relevant pages of *Treasure Island*. She'd finish it later when she was alone. For now, she set it aside, ready to turn her attentions to her friend.

Faith tossed a copy of the *Mayfair Messenger* on the table.

"The publisher didn't run Sarah's article on the number of birds killed for women's hats." Faith pulled off her gloves. "She won't be pleased."

A cup and saucer rattled loudly as one of the Crescent's former barmaids placed it by Faith's elbow. The renovation of the former gin palace into a tea-toting coffeehouse required more than just changing the gilt lettering on the windows. The barmaids had to take the Temperance pledge as well. The change had been more difficult for some than others. Faith smiled up into the woman's lined face. "The chamomile, please." The barmaid nodded and left.

Edwina quickly shifted through the *Messenger*'s pages, confirming the absence of Sarah's contribution, and leaving her own black smudge on each page of newsprint. *Drat!* One of these days she'd manage to use that fountain pen without getting ink on her fingers. Filling the pen with an eyedropper each morning was a nuisance, and the pen sometimes leaked, but still this modern miracle made it possible to write without a vial of ink and for that she was grateful.

While they waited for the rest of their group, she turned to the "Personal & Misc" listings in the classified advertisements. Coded messages often lurked among the forthright and sometimes humorous ads. Men sought women, women sought men, secret arrangements were established for illicit rendezvous, and star-crossed lovers exchanged messages of longing, all on the very public pages of the *Mayfair Messenger*. Edwina scanned the column for snippets of an awkward construction, or the use of numbers instead of letters, all signs of a hidden meaning. Breaking a code was as close to adventurous as her dull life got—would ever get, she supposed. Her brothers got to experience some of the world's excitement, but she had to stay behind in dreary London. A weary sigh escaped her lips.

"At least he ran Sarah's column on the Abington party," Faith continued, her eyes wistful. "She's so lucky that she's allowed to attend those upper-class affairs. The ladies must be something to see with their beautiful gowns and jewelry."

"She's not exactly invited," Edwina reminded her. "She

goes as a reporter, and an undervalued one at that. She could write circles around the men reporters if old Morrison wasn't so set in his conservative ways." But she had to agree with Faith's envy. Years had passed since Edwina had last visited the world of the truly wealthy. Revisiting such opulence would be an adventure, even if viewed as an outsider.

Faith pursed her lips. "I'd still like to attend just once. Even if I were to go as —"

"Look at this!" Edwina stabbed the newsprint with her finger. "It's in code. If you ignore every other word, the message really says: 'Husband suspects. Not tomorrow. Watch ads.'" She looked up, pleased with her accomplishment. "She's canceling a tryst."

"Let me see." Faith bent her nose toward the column. "How do you know to do that? The listing looks perfectly normal to me." Astonishment registered in her friend's eyes. "Why would you even consider looking at every other word?"

Edwina smiled, triumphant. "Patterns." She shrugged. "It's such a simple code, I'm surprised they bothered. Still, I wonder who sent it?" A smile curved her lips. "Do you think Sarah would know? Whoever placed the ad must have done so through Sarah's station at the *Messenger*."

The bell tacked over the Crescent entrance jangled with a discordant tone. Sarah barreled into the renovated drinking parlor like a steam engine puffing out of Victoria Station. Just as a steam engine is unmindful of the cars behind, Sarah took no notice of the fourth member of their party, Claire, who followed silently in her wake.

Sarah dropped her satchel onto an empty chair before she slipped into another. "Mr. Morrison doesn't believe anyone would be interested in the vast quantities of birds sacrificed for women's fashion."

"I'm so sorry." Faith patted her friend's arm. "After all your research . . ."

"It's only because you're a woman," Claire insisted, moving Faith's satchel to the floor before she lowered herself into the seat. "One of these days, old man Morrison will recognize your value and remove you from the agonies."

"You know, I dislike that reference," Sarah scolded. "There's more to the personal column than sad lovelorn ads and letters written in torment." She smiled weakly, then adjusted her glasses. "However, I hope you're right."

"But in the meantime . . ." Edwina hesitated. "Do you know who placed this ad?" She turned the paper so both Sarah and Faith could see.

" 'For my darling husband,' " Sarah read. " 'Who suspects tenderness not neglect, tomorrow awaits. Watch praising ads multiply.' " Sarah grimaced and released the newsprint. "It's not as well written as Faith's poetry, but Mrs. Bottomsly wanted a tribute to her husband."

Edwina exchanged a satisfied look with Faith, who retrieved the paper from the table.

"What?" Sarah asked, looking from one to the other. "We just print what we're paid to print. We don't edit the personal ads for content." She poured some tea from Faith's pot into the empty cup that appeared by her wrist. "No one wants to pay a few pence more for extra words even if urgently needed."

"Look at this one. It's so sweet." Faith sighed, then smirked at Edwina. "And it's not in code." She read it alone for the benefit of all.

A refined gentleman, age 25, of wealth and education, seeks the acquaintance, with a view to matrimony, of a high-minded, kindhearted lady who prefers an evening of quiet conversation and a good book to the lively demands of society. Address box 8 at The Mayfair Messenger.

"He's not a gentleman." Sarah scowled and sipped her tea. "Refined or otherwise."

"You know who placed this ad?" Faith asked, her eyes widened.

Sarah looked about the room as if she were about to share the Queen's secrets. "Ashton Carswell Trewelyn the Third."

The collective resulting gasp turned the heads of the other patrons.

"Casanova . . ." Claire whispered with disdain.

"You saw him?" Faith asked, awe in her voice. "Was he as handsome as they say?"

Sarah nodded. "I can understand the attraction. He has these high cheekbones with hollows beneath and intense dark eyes and lips that . . ." She blew out a breath that lifted the loose hairs framing her face. "I can understand the attraction."

"That man knows no restraint." Claire bent her head closer to the others. "I've heard that because of him, five otherwise decent women have been unexpectedly bundled off to the Continent for an extended stay." She hesitated. "All within two months of each other."

Everyone gasped.

"My brothers told me that he was tossed out of every school in England on moral grounds," Edwina murmured, though she had no knowledge what moral grounds those had been. At the time she had difficulty accepting that news. His name, Trewelyn, so resembled the name of the noble squire from *Treasure Island* that she had trouble separating the two. Even today, she felt as if someone had slowly stroked a feather down the inside of her arm just at the mention of his name.

"Didn't he leave the country?" Faith asked, pulling Edwina from her reverie.

"I thought my brothers said he joined the King's Royal Rifles," Edwina offered.

"He's returned, and he's even more handsome than before," Sarah said. "His years away have given him a harder edge, a sort of dangerous quality that . . . well, I don't recall before." She leaned forward. "Lately when I go to those dinners and dances on behalf of the *Messenger*, the question is always if Casanova will make an appearance. All the single women hope he'll be in attendance. Some of the married ones too."

Claire scowled, then turned the paper around so she could read the ad. "Why would London's most notorious rake advertise for a kindhearted lady who prefers quiet conversation—"

"And enjoyment of a good book," Faith added with a wistful gleam in her eye.

"—over the lively demands of society?" Edwina finished,

a bit envious. Such a notorious rake must live an exciting life, much more so than her own dull routine.

"I can think of only one reason," Sarah said, shifting to the back of her chair. Her sober face studied each of them in turn. "Debauchery."

"Sarah!" Edwina straightened, drawn back into the conversation. Faith merely mouthed the sinful word without giving it voice. "You don't know that."

"Think of it," Sarah insisted. "Gentle women, quiet women, respond to his ad in pursuit of love and affection. He lures them to his lecherous lair and seduces them into trading their innocence for a life of scandal and degradation." Sarah rummaged through her reticule for a handkerchief and dabbed at her eyes. "That's how it happened with my sister."

"Ashton Carswell Trewelyn the Third?" Faith's jaw dropped.

"No, not him," Sarah said with a shake of her head. "But someone like him. He got her in the family way and then abandoned her. My dear sister didn't live long enough to hold little Nan in her arms."

They all knew the sad story. Sarah was raising her niece as her own child and had sought her current position at the *Messenger* as a means for her support. As much as they derided Morrison for failing to publish Sarah's serious articles, they were grateful he'd offered her employment in her time of need. The friends sat in silence to allow Sarah time to gather her composure.

Ashton Carswell Trewelyn the Third. Edwina remembered him from her own two failed seasons years ago, before she gave up the illusion of a man falling at her feet and pleading his undying devotion. Trewelyn had been dashing back then, debonair in his evening tails, and desired by all the young women. He had smiled at her once, but she hadn't the coquettish looks, or the charm, or the connections to draw men like honey to her side. She certainly hadn't the allure to attract Casanova. After that brief moment, he returned to his wealthy friends . . . and one beautiful woman in particular . . . what was her name? She remembered watching them on the dance floor; they had moved so eloquently, so full of grace as if they were one person. Edwina recalled the woman had the smallest waistline she'd ever seen, and a strange sort of laugh. Trewelyn hadn't glanced Edwina's way again. He'd ignored her, just like so many others.

"I wrote a poem about him once," Faith admitted. "I fancied him an angel cast to earth."

"From hell, more likely," Sarah grumbled.

"We can't let this occur," Claire insisted. "We can't let him take advantage of innocent women." Ever since Claire had become involved with Women for a Sober Society, Edwina had noticed her passion for platforms. Sometimes the cause didn't matter, just the related call to action.

"How can we stop him?" Sarah asked. "I had to run the ad even though I suspected it was a deception. I have Nan to consider."

Faith patted her hand in sympathy. "Casanova's lecherous actions are not your fault."

"Surely we can use your connections to the *Messenger* to thwart his scheme of seduction," Claire said, gathering a head of steam. "Think, ladies."

"Will you see the responses to his ad?" Edwina asked.

"Only the envelopes," Sarah replied. "I'm not allowed to open them. I could lose my position."

"Some of those envelopes will have the return address on the back," Faith said. "We could at least warn those women."

"He may not have set his sights on all the replies," Edwina said thoughtfully. "It would be better if we knew which responses interested him the most, then concentrated our efforts there."

"And how are we to do that?" Faith asked. "It's not as if we can sneak into his residence and see which responses he favors. We might as well follow him about London to see whom he meets." Faith laughed at the absurdity of her suggestion.

Follow Casanova about London? Edwina brightened at the thought. While she wasn't as convinced as Sarah that the ad was for evil intent, the diversion of following a rake about

London had an appeal. Surely this would pose an adventure more stimulating than simply transcribing her brothers' exploits. "I'll do it," Edwina stated. "I'll follow him."

"You can't follow Trewelyn around London!" Sarah exclaimed. "What would your family think?"

"I can," Edwina protested. By far this would be the most daring feat she'd ever attempted. Jim Hawkins from *Treasure Island* must have felt a similar twinge of anticipation before boarding that ship. The lure of adventure was just too tempting to resist. "My father is so involved with the Perkins case, he won't know that I'm not about. My mother is barely home as it is with all her clubs and organizations. I could be Trewelyn's shadow, and he won't even know I'm there." Given that she escaped his notice at the ball two years ago, she could state this last with an air of confidence.

"What about your Mr. Thomas?" Faith asked. "Won't he disapprove?"

"I don't know," Edwina replied, defiance in her voice. But she did know. Walter would not approve of anything that involved risk or adventure. Handpicked by her father from among his employees to squire her around town, he thought of himself as her beau. And why not? She hadn't a host of other men competing for her attention. If it weren't for the fact that being in Walter's company allowed her a certain measure of freedom, she would have ended their relationship. "I do know that Mr. Thomas has binoculars that he uses to watch birds. I'm certain he will let me borrow them."

Sarah's skepticism showed in her eyes.

"I'll watch him from afar, Sarah. No harm will come of it."

"She could try," Faith said. "What is there to lose?"

"I don't know, Edwina." Sarah gave voice to her uncertainty. "I'm not certain this will work, and it could prove dangerous. Besides, your actions could anger Mr. Thomas. While you may not appreciate it now, a potential husband is nothing to gamble away. One never appreciates security until they have none."

Edwina took her hand. "If we save one woman from the

fate of your sister, it would be worth the risk." Admittedly she had her doubts that her secret observations would lead to such results, but if they did, London would most assuredly be a safer place. Still, reluctance registered in Sarah's eyes. "I won't do anything foolish, Sarah. I promise."

Edwina held her friend's gaze until skepticism reluctantly turned to acceptance.

"And if we're successful, as I'm certain we will be," Claire said, "we can do this for other questionable personal ads as well. We'll protect innocent women."

"We'll be the Rake Patrol," Faith whispered.

"The Rake Patrol," Sarah said softly, testing the sound.

Edwina lifted her teacup, inviting the others to do the same. "To the Rake Patrol."

The four carefully clinked their cups, then grinned as their pact was formed. After each took a dutiful sip of the cold tea, Edwina replaced her cup on the saucer. "Now, ladies, let us plan how this is to be done . . ."

THE BASE OF HIS NECK TINGLED, A WARNING NOT FELT since his service with the fourth battalion of the King's Rifles. Ashton looked about the stark environs of the *Mayfair Messenger*'s office. He suspected he was under unfriendly scrutiny, and by someone in addition to the woman clerk behind the wooden counter, who kept glancing his way when she thought he wouldn't notice. He remembered her from when he'd initially placed the ad. Based on her reaction to his appearance then, one would have thought that he crawled unbathed from a sewer to place an advertisement in the newspaper. Under the circumstances, he decided to wait patiently for a well-attired young lady to conclude her business before he subjected himself again to the clerk's overt disapproval. The *Mayfair Messenger* had become known for its personal ads, just as the *Pall Mall Gazette* was known for its coverage of social issues, or *The Illustrated London News* for its woodcuts. They each had their specialty, but Ashton had to admit, the *Messenger*'s niche appeared to be a lucrative one.

The young woman turned away from the counter. The instant she'd spotted him near the door, her cheeks had flushed an attractive pink. After a moment's hesitation, she'd patted her hair and issued a seductive smile. Ashton opened the door, then tipped his hat as she passed by, just as any gentleman would. Yet she paused, issuing a brazen unspoken invitation with her eyes. He remembered a time when he would have led the lady to a less public location to explore the pleasures her gaze requested. But today he slowly shook his head. She nodded and continued on her way. Though he never understood why his appearance managed to elicit that almost universal reaction, it was what it was and he'd become accustomed to it. He returned inside, removed his hat, then stepped up to the counter.

"The replies in box eight, if you please." He held the marker he'd been given to claim the responses to his search for a suitable companion for James, the man responsible for saving his life in Burma. Though finding a partner for a man disfigured by his courageous act seemed a small payment for his sacrifice, it allowed Ashton to utilize his one God-given gift, his ability to attract women, for the benefit of another. One far worthier than himself, truth be told. During those dark, pain-ridden nights when the two of them recuperated in a primitive hospital, Ashton had composed a long list of past wrongs that he planned to right, friendships he planned to mend, should God grant him the time and ability to do so. He would make a difference in the world, leave some value behind in case the next bullet struck a vital organ. He could start with this one kindness and work his way forward, so that he might be known for something other than his ability to dance and charm.

"Your ad met with success." The lady clerk smiled, an event so unexpected and transforming of her features that Ashton was taken aback. She stacked a small quantity of letters before him.

Strange. This very same clerk wouldn't spare him the time of day last week. Now she embodied the very symbol of cooperation. "Do you wish to continue your ad for another week?"

"All this resulted from one ad?" There must be twenty letters in that pile. "I had anticipated only one or two responses."

"London is filled with honest women seeking companionship," the clerk said, her eyes warm and helpful. He truly must have caught her on a bad day before. That, or the lady had a friendly twin. A particularly licentious memory from years ago brought a smile to his lips. He'd had some experience with twins.

Did a flicker of disgust just flash in the clerk's eyes? Or was that merely a reflection off the lenses of her spectacles? No matter. The clerk's demure smile obscured any ill feelings. "Responses are bound to be plentiful when the ad is placed by a refined and educated man such as yourself."

"You recall the ad?" he said, surprised. "Given the number of advertisements that must slide across this very counter, you must possess a remarkable memory."

"It is a consequence of my position to associate the faces of the advertisers with the ads they place." She hesitated a moment, then glanced up at him from beneath her lashes. "I assume you intend to interview the respondents?"

"That had been my initial intention, yes." He ran his finger across the edges of the envelopes. "However, I hadn't planned on so many replies."

She brightened. "You may find that some are unsuitable once you read their letters. The others . . ." She pushed her spectacles further up the bridge of her nose. "If I may be so bold, sir, have you given any thought as to where you intend to interview the others?"

Ashton straightened. "I believe that's a personal matter—"

The clerk leaned forward. "I only meant to caution that an honest, respectable woman might have difficulty meeting a bachelor in his own quarters."

"That is true." His lips quirked. He should've thought of that before.

"So you might want to consider arranging a meeting in a public location. Are you familiar with the recently renovated Crescent Coffee Palace?"

He frowned. "Coffee Palace? I thought the Crescent was known for . . . beverages of another nature."

"It has something of an illustrious past," the clerk admitted. "However, Women for a Sober Society has renovated the building, and it now offers a variety of wholesome food and drinks of a more genteel nature."

Teetotalers. He winced. "Have you been to this new Crescent?"

"I have, sir." She smiled. "It is the reason I can recommend the location as perfect for your purposes."

He hesitated, then nodded. The clerk certainly would have more experience and knowledge of such matters than he. He supposed she dispensed this sort of advice with some regularity. Perhaps the Crescent would be best. He began to stuff the envelopes into his pocket.

"And, of course, you'll need a method to identify the woman," the clerk continued.

"Identify her?" Another detail he hadn't considered. Who would have thought finding a woman for James would prove so difficult?

"Of course, sir. There will be many women of quality at the Crescent. You should employ some method to distinguish the lady responding to your advertisement from the other patrons."

It had been Ashton's experience that most women managed to recognize him immediately. Or, if an attractive, engaging woman had only recently arrived in London, he generally knew someone who could intercede with an introduction. This meeting of strange women was problematic.

"Ask her to carry a rose," the clerk said suddenly. "There's a florist near the Crescent. Securing the flower would not be difficult."

"A rose . . ." It was a romantic notion worthy of one of those Austen books. He could place a bud in the buttonhole of his lapel. A woman with a single rose should be easy to spot. "That's an excellent idea."

Delight spread across the clerk's face, again transforming her into a much younger woman. Obviously she hadn't ex-

perienced an easy life or she would not be employed in a
newspaper office. Ashton briefly wondered if his own face
carried the travails of his years in Burma. His aching leg
certainly did.

"Thank you," he said, sweeping the last of the letters from
the counter. He secured some in his inside pocket before
stuffing others in his coat pocket. "You've been most helpful."

All should be fine as long as Constance did not discover
the letters. He'd planned to meet with her and young Matthew
in Regent's Park after this stop at the *Messenger*. While two
letters would have been easy to conceal, twenty or so might
catch her attention. With her sharp tongue, she'd eviscerate
any kind woman daring enough to respond to an ad. Constance
knew a thing or two about "daring."

Ashton removed a few shillings from his pocket and placed
them on the counter. "For your assistance."

Color bloomed in the clerk's cheeks, but as he turned, he
heard the scraping of metal across wood. As he suspected,
times could be difficult. He left the office, leaning more heavily on his walking stick. A change of weather must be in the
air.

The prickling at his nape resumed even as he left the newspaper office. Pausing a moment, he searched for the unseen
assailant. He'd foolishly thought he'd left combat behind
when he departed the Royal Rifles with a bullet in his thigh.
Instead, he'd returned to a household riddled with conflict.
He hadn't sorted out all the issues as yet. No one really spoke
except young Matthew, and his governess hushed him at every opportunity. One didn't need words to sense the powder
keg of tension, or the feeling that somehow he might be the
match to ignite it all.

Scanning the street, he noted nothing out of the ordinary,
except a lovely young woman with hair the color of sunlight.
She stood next to one of those safety bicycles that seemed to
be the latest craze, angling her binoculars toward a copse of
trees. What the devil was she studying there—pigeons? It was
not as if the grays of London were disturbed with colorful
birds like those of Burma. A smile tipped his lips with the

memory. Some of Burma's heat would be appreciated on this cool spring day. London may not have been the best choice for his recuperation, but at the time, he had thought it was the easiest. He'd been mistaken there as well.

He glanced back at the girl. Surely a comely bird enthusiast posed no threat, especially one that should be the object of study rather than some feathered creature likely to end up on a dinner plate. He couldn't imagine danger coming from that quarter. No, the warning must be something else. Something not visible, not yet.

He patted his pocket, feeling the packet of envelopes tucked there, then climbed into his carriage. Constance and her son were waiting. He'd promised Matthew he'd show him the tigers, at least the ones behind bars. If nothing else, Matthew had been a delight in Ashton's homecoming. Perhaps as the boy matured, Ashton would be able to teach him how to spot the predatory tigers who didn't wear stripes to warn of their ferocity. Tigers that hid behind serene human faces but had the ability to carve out one's heart with a single swipe. Tigers like Matthew's mother.

· *Two* ·

ONE MORE CUP OF TEA AND EDWINA WAS QUITE
certain her skin would turn scaly and gills would form
on her neck. Sarah had instructed her to watch for a woman
carrying a rose. But as they weren't certain when exactly the
dashing Casanova would begin to interview women for his
sordid affaires, the ladies of the Rake Patrol each took turns
holding afternoon vigilance at the Crescent Coffee Palace.
Today marked Edwina's turn.

Their strategy to foil Trewelyn's plan had its limitations.
What if he rejected Sarah's suggestion and interviewed women
at another location? Edwina had thought to continue to follow
Trewelyn all over London, tracking his every movement, and
learning his unique patterns, but the others forbade her such
foolishness. In the end, she had to agree. Even a determined
modern woman on a bicycle was no match for a man in a
carriage. Her one attempt to follow him had proved that. The
downpour that ended that day and continued the following
made her plan ludicrous.

So they'd adopted a different approach. Faith would call

on the women on Sarah's list who so kindly included return addresses on their replies. Edwina and Claire alternated the days they would wait in the Crescent in case Trewelyn still managed to lure someone into his seductive snare.

Excitement tingled to her toes at the thought of being seduced by someone the likes of Ashton Carswell Trewelyn the Third. Sarah had been correct. When viewed through the lens of Mr. Thomas's binoculars, Trewelyn had appeared more seasoned and more earthly sinful than during his earlier days as a debonair rake. He'd almost caught her studying him. She recalled the panic and the excitement of the near discovery. He'd glanced in her direction, but then quickly lost interest. She sighed. How would it feel to be regarded in his eyes, or anyone's eyes, as someone worthy of attention and value? More often she was an object of curiosity, or, as with Walter, a means to secure ties to her father's business. What if Casanova saw her, truly saw her for all that she was? Would he still turn away?

And what of the women Casanova planned to interview? What if he had decided that none of the replies were suitable for his purposes and he'd chosen to abandon the whole plan without interviewing any? Disappointment that their mission might end before it ever had a chance to begin left a heavy weight in her stomach, or maybe that was just the countless tea cakes she'd consumed waiting for Trewelyn to appear. She really shouldn't hope that a nefarious scheme might unfold in front of her, but Edwina hadn't had this much excitement since decoding her brother's last letter. She sighed. Just once she'd like to experience a true adventure. Spying on Ashton Trewelyn and his innocent victims was as close as she'd come, and even that wouldn't extend beyond the confines of the Crescent.

The Rake Patrol didn't know when the interviews were to begin, nor when they were to end. Would she be waiting in the Crescent for weeks on end? She pulled a copy of the *Messenger* from her satchel. At least she had the personals for company.

She started reading an article on Menie Muriel Dowie,

who had recently married and was traveling down the Nile with her new husband for a honeymoon. The Scottish woman explorer was living the life that Edwina so desperately desired. She could never imagine Walter taking her on a cruise down the Nile. She doubted he could even be persuaded to cruise the Thames. That blasted bell rang, drawing her attention to the door.

Finally! A lady, similar in age to herself, stood with a red rose firmly clutched in her gloved hand. Not a woman of adventure, Edwina assessed. The poor fragile thing looked in need of a fortifying cup of tea, but if Edwina was successful in convincing her of her peril, the quivering rabbit would depart before she'd consumed two swallows of the hot brew.

"Excuse me." Edwina approached her with a wide befriending smile. "Are you here to meet with Mr. Ashton Carswell Trewelyn the Third?"

The girl's eyes widened. "Is that his name? His letter simply said to bring a rose to the Crescent and all would be revealed."

Edwina guided the woman past the painted mirrors toward her table. "I doubt he would reveal the nefarious purposes for which he lured you to this place."

The woman gasped. "Nefarious purposes!"

Edwina tilted her chin and set the *Messenger* aside. Her eyes narrowed. "Does his name mean nothing to you?"

The woman hesitated thoughtfully and shook her head. Edwina sighed. The woman really did need the patrol's assistance. "Ashton Trewelyn is a well-known rakehell, a rogue, a debaucher of women, a libertine of the worst nature. He's often referred to as Casanova. Have you heard of that name?"

"But he had the most beautiful penmanship," the woman protested, "and his words sounded so sincere and . . . trustworthy."

Edwina nodded in sympathy. "That's how they do it. They charm their victims into a never-ending web of despair." She studied the woman's trembling lip. "May I ask your name?"

"Miss Grimwood," she replied, her eyes dazed in disbelief.

"Well, Miss Grimwood," Edwina continued, adopting an

authoritative tone, "I've been waiting here just to warn you to run away from this place as fast as you can, else you'll meet the devil incarnate. He beguiles women with his charm and seduces them down a path of destruction. Don't make the mistake of so many other poor unfortunates."

The woman stood abruptly, her eyes wide with terror. "Thank you. Thank you so much." She clasped Edwina's hand. "The world would be a better place if there were more concerned women such as yourself." Before she fled the Crescent, she tossed her vivid red rose on the table, whereupon it rolled to the table's edge and fell to the floor.

Victorious, Edwina pushed her back to the chair. How gratifying to be the one who saved another's life. Her pride and self-satisfaction pressed the restraints of her corset. The Rake Patrol had protected an innocent from ruin. Like truly modern women, they had recognized a problem and taken action to resolve it. How fortuitous to be part of such an illustrious group!

The discarded rose lay inches from her feet. Edwina placed a hand on her new straw hat to hold it in place while she bent to retrieve it. The hat featured a jaunty ostrich plume, which seemed to have a mind of its own, so she held it stable while she reached just a few inches beyond her feet . . . just a few . . .

The bell above the door jangled. While her retrieval efforts kept most of her face hidden by the tablecloth, she was still able to peek at the newcomer above the tabletop. She froze.

The very man who had haunted her dreams of late and titillated her with visions of adventure stood near the entrance, sporting a neatly clipped rosebud on his lapel and a handsome silver-topped walking stick in his hand. The steady hum of conversation in the Crescent suddenly dropped to near silence, and then slowly resumed. He was even more handsome and charismatic in person than when viewed through Walter's binoculars. Her cheeks heated, her pulse raced. What to do? Would he recognize her from that near discovery when she'd followed him about London? Was there nowhere to hide?

The *Messenger* lay nearby on the table. Her fingers crept toward it until she had it in her grasp. She waited till Trewe-

lyn scanned the room in the opposite direction, then she
quickly lifted the newspaper to cover her face. Only the feather
of her hat bobbed above it. Straightening in her seat, she tried
to kick the visible rose stem under the table before Casanova
thought she might be an innocent waiting to be ravished. Her
cheeks heated anew and something akin to butterflies batted
at her rib cage.

She should have anticipated his appearance, she supposed,
but she really hadn't thought much beyond warning the
woman. So what was she to do now? Would he recognize
her? She'd been discreet chasing him about London that first
day. Trying to keep up with the carriage had certainly proved
taxing on her legs, and she'd lost him in the vicinity of Regent's Park. By the time she'd spotted him near the zoo, he
was assisting a beautiful woman and a darling little boy who
looked remarkably like Casanova himself into his carriage.
Maybe not so remarkable. Her lips shifted into a frown. That
was, after all, one of the reasons she was warning women
away. So there wouldn't be any more darling little boys growing up to look just like Casanova.

Edwina peeked around the edges of the *Messenger*. He had
taken a seat at a table between hers and the door. Heavens!
He was so close she could see the pattern on his pale gray
waistcoat and the fine shadows thrown by his long downcast
eyelashes. Her mouth dried to the consistency of newsprint,
making her wish she hadn't drained that last cup of tea. Sarah
hadn't exaggerated about his attraction. Though tempted to
flee, Edwina supposed she should wait to see if Casanova met
with someone else. If nothing else, she could observe how Mr.
Casanova dealt with frustration when his plans met with defeat.

A waitress hurried to his table. Edwina had waited several
minutes before anyone had noticed her or taken her order, but
for Casanova, service was instant. Not that she could blame
the waitress. Trewelyn looked up, eyes large and pleading,
impossible-to-refuse eyes, much like those of a cocker spaniel Edwina had spoiled as a young girl. Trewelyn's lips curved
into a smile that managed to turn the mature waitress into a
giggling, blushing schoolgirl. The man certainly had charm.

Just then, his gaze shifted and his smile turned toward her. Panicked, she ducked back behind her trembling newsprint, but not before the force of all that seductive allure blasted through her with a heat that warmed her more than those countless cups of tea. She couldn't trust her hands to keep the paper still, but she couldn't risk letting the barrier fall to expose her to his mesmerizing gaze.

She reminded herself to be strong. If Trewelyn could affect a woman bent against him with just a smile, how much more devastating would that smile be to someone who hoped to form a relationship? She thought of the young boy who had looked up at Trewelyn with those exact same adoring eyes. While she should find Casanova's obvious trysts abhorrent, thoughts of sharing illicit intimacy with a man of his persuasions sent that titillating flutter in her rib cage spiraling lower. He would be one to cruise the Nile. Of that, she had little doubt.

"Excuse me, ma'am." A waitress with a charming Irish lilt loomed over the edge of the newsprint. "The gentleman at the next table sent over this warm pot of tea." She replaced the near-empty pot with a fresh steaming one. "He thought you might be cold, as your paper trembled so."

Edwina lowered the *Messenger* just enough to see Trewelyn. He smiled and nodded his head. Her lips tightened and she issued a quick head bob as a means to acknowledge his generosity.

She supposed now she was committed to sit there and drink at least one cup of tea. There was no need to hide behind the paper, now that he'd seen her face, which was just as well. It would be entirely too difficult to pour a cup of tea and hold the paper upright at the same time. She poured the steaming liquid into her cup, added one lump of sugar, idly stirred, and tried very hard not to stare at Trewelyn waiting for a woman who, thanks to Edwina's interference, would never show up. Surely he would tire of waiting and leave. Meanwhile she observed the flow of people outside the Crescent through the large plateglass window lettered with menu options.

Time passed. Trewelyn checked his pocket watch but remained at his table, writing on a small pad of paper, giving her an opportunity to steal discreet glances. She supposed there was no reason she couldn't leave, but her legs refused to spring into action. She gazed out the window and noted another young lady clutching a rose, standing outside the Crescent as if hesitant to enter.

No wonder the man was so patient waiting in the Crescent— he'd lined up multiple interviews. This would never do! Edwina abruptly stood, then crossed to the door, determined to talk to the woman before she entered. Trewelyn's head lifted briefly from his notes. Edwina hurried to the door to intercept the woman before he spotted his next victim through the window.

The bell jangled at her hasty exit. She dashed toward the stranger. "Don't," she cautioned, not even waiting for the door to close behind her. "Don't go in there."

The woman stared as if Edwina had escaped from Bedlam.

"You're here to meet a man, aren't you?" Edwina asked, then waited for the tentative answering nod. She took the woman's elbow and turned her away from the Crescent. "You appear to be a decent woman. Do you truly believe a respectable man would advertise in the paper for a life mate? Do you?"

She searched the woman's eyes, noting cold disappointment settle over a glow of desperate yearning.

"How did you know?" the woman whispered.

"The rose." Edwina nodded to the flower in the woman's hand. "All of his targeted victims carry a rose."

The emphasis on "victims" did the trick. Although almost a year had passed since Jack the Ripper's last attack, the Whitechapel tragedies were not far from memory. The woman gasped and dropped the offensive flower.

"Go," Edwina said gently. "Go quickly and don't look back."

The woman obliged, her brisk pace swiftly putting distance between them.

Edwina barely had time to feel the pleasure of her accomplishment in saving yet another from Trewelyn's clutches, when the door opened behind her.

"Miss? You forgot your flower," an Irish voice called.

Edwina turned to see not only the waitress holding the rose, but Trewelyn standing behind her, his gaze focused on her.

"Allow me," he said, carefully removing the stem from the waitress's hand. His smile almost reduced the woman to a puddle at his feet.

Edwina remained frozen in place, half wishing to run, half wanting to stay. Her heart raced as he advanced, tapping the rose against a small cleft in his firm masculine chin.

"Were you scaring off the competition, Miss Grimwood?" An eyebrow lifted, as did one corner of his lips.

She shook her head slightly, unsure what to say.

"I hadn't expected a woman of action, a woman of strategy when I advertised for someone quiet and refined." Interest sparked in his eyes, while his low tantalizing voice mesmerized. "I'm not certain why you didn't make your presence known earlier, but I do admire a woman who is unafraid to take a risk now and again."

His gaze slid down her length in a slow appraising perusal. She should run, just as she had suggested to the others, but her feet refused to obey. She felt weightless, as if she might rise from the ground like a hot air balloon, but his voice kept her firmly tethered to his expressive lips. He had managed to upset all her patterns, wiping them clean. Which must explain why she stared like a wide-eyed child.

"Let us return inside to sit and talk." He reached for her elbow to guide her back into the Crescent, just as she had moments earlier guided others away. "I have many questions for you, Miss Grimwood. Shall we?"

"I should warn you," Edwina managed, annoyed that under his influence her feet obeyed his wishes and not her own. "I'm not—"

"Edwina!"

Rats! She'd forgotten Walter normally passed this way after leaving his clerking position at her father's law office.

"Unhand her immediately!" Walter demanded, marching toward the Crescent entrance with the stride of an angry bulldog.

Trewelyn released his hold on her elbow, but raised a brow. "Edwina?"

Her lips wouldn't move. It seemed her entire body refused to function in a normal manner with Trewelyn's brown eyes turned her way—brown with the most interesting flecks of green. Trewelyn turned toward Walter and calmly extended an arm. "Allow me to introduce myself, I'm—"

"I know who you are," Walter snarled, his face an unbecoming red. "You're a womanizing blackguard who has no business placing his hands on my fiancée." He harshly gripped Edwina's other elbow.

She supposed she should be flattered by Walter's possessive posture, but her annoyance left no room for trumpetry. Walter didn't have the right to interfere, especially when he hadn't been presented with all the facts regarding her presence with Trewelyn.

"Fiancée?" Trewelyn's eyes widened a moment before narrowing at her in censure. "Is this true, Miss Grimwood? If so—"

"Miss Grimwood?" Walter's lips quirked.

Her head swam. So many misconceptions, so much manly posturing. "No, it is not," she said, trying to pull her elbow free from Walter's grasp. "I can explain—"

But Walter didn't give her the opportunity. He tugged her toward the street, away from the most handsome man she'd ever laid eyes upon. What must Trewelyn think of her? Embarrassed, she tried to look back while holding her hat to keep the bouncing feather intact. But Walter's speed made it difficult enough to just stay on her feet, much less try to judge Casanova's reaction.

ASHTON WATCHED HER GO, PULLED AWAY BY THAT LIP-curling stick of a man. He'd thought to interfere, to stop the cad from using brute force to drag her away. However, if she was his fiancée, the man was right to remove her from Ashton's presence. Lord knows he should have used whatever force was necessary to drag Constance away from his father so many years ago.

At the time, he had thought of Constance as his fiancée, though he hadn't gotten the nerve to ask her the all-important question. Little did he realize that his very own widowed father had similar intentions. His father had announced the impending nuptials one evening, and Ashton had left the next day to join the King's Royal Rifles. That was four years ago. Yes, he should have dragged her away the moment his father laid eyes upon her.

But that was yesterday's news. Constance had made her decision and chose to become his stepmother, not his wife. Now they both had to deal with the consequences of her decision.

Somehow though, he wasn't surprised that Miss Grimwood wasn't satisfied with the man who wished to claim her as his own. She had a spark of life in those inquisitive soft blue eyes, a vitality that would most likely be smothered by that suffocating fiancé. Her bright hair would fade, the perky tilt of her nose would be at odds with downturned lips that rarely smiled. Women trapped in misaligned marriages readily displayed their woes to those who could read the signs. That Miss Grimwood would become one of those sad victims was unfortunate; she had such potential. For a moment, he thought she had seemed somehow familiar, almost as if he'd seen her before, but that would hardly be likely.

Still, she wasn't the sort of woman he had in mind for his friend. Miss Grimwood was like an exotic parrot, while he envisioned something more of a quiet field mouse for James. He shook his head. Funny, he hadn't thought Miss Grimwood had listed her Christian name as Edwina. He couldn't exactly remember what Miss Grimwood had listed, but he would have remembered Edwina. It was the unusual sort of name that one wouldn't forget. Not that it mattered now. Her fiancé would undoubtedly take steps to ensure she was properly prohibited from meeting Ashton again, and that was a pity.

He checked his pocket watch. Time to meet James at the

club. He had hoped to have surprising news of an introduction, but it appeared that must wait.

EDWINA STRUGGLED TO KEEP PACE WITH WALTER, BUT then decided she'd had enough. She planted her boots firmly on the pavement and braced herself. Fortunately, Walter stopped before his fast stride pulled her to her knees.

"I am not your fiancée, Walter," Edwina scolded. "You must stop telling people that we're betrothed." She pulled her arm free of his grasp. "I have a say in this matter, not just my father."

"An inexperienced woman like yourself shouldn't speak to men like that Trewelyn," Walter grumbled, easily dismissing her complaint. "You have no idea of the sort of man he is."

"Neither do you." She tried to pin her hat more securely to her hair. "He was quite the gentleman in the Crescent."

"I know things about him." Walter scowled. "He has a reputation, you know. I've heard the men talk about his exploits at my club. I'd tell you, but it's not suitable for innocent ears."

Walter's standard reply to any question she might raise on a topic of interest was that it was inappropriate for innocent ears. A respectable woman, in his opinion, must never discuss anything beyond the weather and fashion. Where was a woman with a natural curiosity to find answers if not through discussion?

Walter glowered at something in the distance. "Besides, he may have been the one."

"The one?" She frowned up at him. "What are you speaking of?"

"Why were you there by yourself?" he asked suddenly. "Your bluestocking friends won't be meeting until tomorrow." Though she was surprised he knew her schedule so well, the sneer in his voice left no question about his opinion of her friends.

"I was . . . conducting research." He wouldn't leave her alone unless she provided some purpose for her activity.

"Research? Research for what?" He narrowed his eyes.

"You don't fancy yourself a newspaper writer like that friend of yours."

"I was researching for the suffragettes." It was the one topic that she knew would bring an instant end to his questions.

"You know your father and I don't approve of that group." He averted his gaze, and hastened his pace toward her residence.

"You don't approve of any of my interests," she murmured. "Why is it that you attend your clubs with pride but ridicule mine?"

"Because men are expected to go out in the world. Women are expected to stay at home." His voice softened as if he were talking to a child. "Once you have your own house and children to care for, you won't have time for that suffragette nonsense."

She didn't reply, as she suspected that he was right. She'd be trapped into a life of caring for the needs of everyone else except herself. She'd be like the women who sent those coded messages to the personals. Women longing for someone else, something else that would be forever denied once they traded their freedom for the security of marriage.

Not that the alternative was much better. She didn't want to be a spinster forever clinging to the charity of her parents and, once they were gone, becoming a burden to her brothers.

Why wouldn't society allow her to be like her brothers? Free to travel the world and experience other cultures? Why must she always be under the protection of some man who obliged her to keep a tidy house and mannerly children? It just didn't seem fair.

"Here you are, Edwina. Safely delivered to your doorstep." Walter beamed as if he had single-handedly fought off an entire tribe of marauding Zulus, just to escort her down the avenue. "Be sure to tell your mother that I inquired about her health."

Did he? She hadn't been listening. He had that look in his eye again. The one that suggested he was debating whether to kiss her cheek.

"We're not engaged, Walter," she said with one hand on the doorknob.

"But we will be." He smiled. "I've been saving every week. Soon I'll have enough to lease a small house, then I shall ask permission of your father."

The impulse to ask her permission never seemed to enter his thoughts. Edwina sighed and went inside.

THE NEXT DAY AT THE CRESCENT, EDWINA REPORTED HER experiences—including the kindness of a hot pot of tea—to the rest of the Rake Patrol, except for Sarah, who was unable to join them that day. Edwina pointed to the table where Trewelyn had planned to interview the women he'd selected from the stack of responses, and shared how a fallen rose had led to Trewelyn's misconception.

"Then what happened?" Faith asked, hanging on every word. "Did Casanova really believe you were one of his correspondents?"

"He did until Walter arrived. I'm . . . I'm not certain what he thinks now." But she was afraid she did. His pattern change hadn't gone unnoticed. When he thought she was one of his respondents, he appeared interested, perhaps even appreciative. She recalled the flutter beneath her corset when his eyes warmed as he took her measure. Then Walter referred to her as his fiancée and that very appreciation faded into derision. Yes, she could very well guess what he thought of her now, and none of it was complimentary. She gazed at the open *Mayfair Messenger*, hoping the others didn't notice her discomfort. She ran her finger down the personals. "Now that he's seen my face, it will be more difficult to warn others without his knowledge."

"Do you think he'll continue to meet women here?" Faith scanned the customers almost as if she expected a wide-eyed innocent to be clutching a rose at one of the tables. "I talked to several women who had responded to his ad. Most had not received an invitation to meet Mr. Trewelyn." She hesitated. "I suppose I could take Edwina's place for watching for future meetings held here. It's an important kindness we are doing and—"

"No!" Edwina exclaimed, pointing to an ad. "Look at this!"

Claire peered sideways. "It's just a series of numbers. What does it mean?"

Edwina scrambled in her reticule for her journal and pen. "It's in code, but if I'm not mistaken, this portion of the series is the address for Trewelyn's residence." Her brothers varied the codes they used for their letters as a form of sport. To hasten the translation when they used a number code, Edwina kept a conversion table that listed the letters of the alphabet and their numeric components. She untied the ribbon on her overstuffed journal and quickly transcribed the code. "Casanova's arranging a meeting at his residence." She decoded another sequence of numbers.

"Why would he send a coded message to his intended victims?" Faith asked. "How would they know to transcribe the code?"

"This message isn't for the ladies." A sense of foreboding settled deep in Edwina's stomach. Based on her brief encounter with Trewelyn, she doubted that the man was as dissolute as the others inferred. Else why would he have been disappointed when Walter said they were engaged? A truly dissolute man wouldn't care about the commitments of their conquests, would he? But this . . .

She glanced at Faith. "The message is for a group called the Guardians. He's arranging a meeting for them at his residence."

"For what purpose?" Claire asked.

"No one uses a coded message for philanthropic purposes," Edwina said in hushed tones. Even her brothers had initially started using code to hide their activities from their governess and parents. She bit her lip, not sure she wanted to give voice to her fears.

"Perhaps we didn't interfere in all of his appointments," Faith whispered. "Perhaps he already has women installed in his residence, and now he's inviting his friends to participate in a night of debauchery."

Edwina had to agree they could have missed warning some of the women. They had assumed Trewelyn would follow Sarah's advice about meeting at the Crescent. But he could have arranged to meet women at other places as well. The Rake Patrol simply didn't have the means to follow all of Trewelyn's activities. Following him for one day had been difficult enough.

"Those poor women," Claire said. "They'll have no means of escape."

Edwina hesitated. In spite of all the stories of his womanizing ways, Trewelyn just didn't seem as evil as the others insisted. She'd need additional proof.

"Edwina, buying you a pot of tea doesn't make him less of a rogue," Faith said, sensing her indecision. "He could have been trying to ferret his way into your good graces so as to seduce you into becoming one of his women."

The word "seduce" tingled through her rib cage. She supposed it was wrong of her to wonder . . . but what would it be like to be seduced by the likes of Casanova? A delicious warmth stirred deep in her belly, unlike anything she'd ever experienced in Walter's company.

"If only we had a way to know what these Guardians intend," Claire mused. "Maybe we should watch Trewelyn's residence in advance of the meeting."

"Why?" Edwina asked.

"I'm not certain," Claire admitted. "We'd at least learn the identities of the Guardians."

Edwina wasn't convinced.

"We simply can't remain silent and do nothing," Faith argued. "We are the only chance for those poor frightened women."

Though reluctant to connect Trewelyn with evil intent, the existence of the coded message proved problematic. Why have a coded message if not to meet in secret? And why meet in secret unless for wicked intentions? Perhaps she needed to see Trewelyn's evil exploits for herself. Then perhaps she could embrace the others' opinion of his dire intentions. Maybe she would even be able to appreciate Walter's protective tendencies rather than lapse into annoyance. "I'll go," Edwina said quietly.

"What?" Faith's head turned toward her. "Where will you go?"

"To Trewelyn's address," Edwina said with conviction. "They're meeting tomorrow night. I'll go and see if women are being lured for a feast of debauchery."

"Walter would take you?" Faith's lips formed a small moue of surprise.

"No." Edwina almost laughed at the thought of Walter escorting her to a gathering of ill repute. "I'll go alone. I'll watch the entrance from the confines of a hansom cab and if I see an innocent, I'll do my best to warn her so she can flee."

"Your father will not let you go out alone at night without an escort," Faith warned.

"My father won't even know I'm gone." Edwina smiled. "When they lived at home, my brothers routinely left the house without anyone knowing."

"How?" Claire asked.

"They climbed the rigging of the *Black Spot*." Edwina's lips turned with the nostalgic memories. "The boys read the story *Treasure Island* to me when I was still in the nursery. We used to pretend the old oak in the back garden was a pirate ship, the *Black Spot*."

"I thought the black spot was a pirate's note of impending punishment," Claire said.

"It was, in the book," Edwina explained. "Richard thought the name would inspire an amount of fear and trepidation among our imaginary enemies."

"And how does an oak tree in the garden assist you in escaping your room in the house?" Faith asked.

"We referred to the tree branches as the rigging. We could climb to the crow's nest near the top of the tree, and back down rather easily. One of the branches reaches close to the boys' room." She didn't mention that obtaining that branch would require a jump from her window ledge. She was too small when her brothers were at home to attempt such a feat, a fact the boys had routinely taken advantage of. They would race away for adventure while she remained behind, watching them disappear into the night. Little did she realize that was to be their pattern as they grew. She was always to be the one left behind to translate the stories of their adventures.

"And you've climbed this rigging before?"

"Not recently," Edwina replied. She could have said "never" and been just as truthful. By the time she'd obtained the sufficient length to make the jump, the boys had moved away to school, leaving her home alone without the proper incentive to do so.

Faith shook her head. "You'll break your neck."

"Perhaps," Edwina said, but she doubted that would be the case, though she wouldn't rule out a torn dress or even a broken arm. A sort of excitement began to build. An excitement that she hadn't recognized since she waved good-bye to her brothers so many years ago.

"It might be a little dangerous," she said, glancing up at her friend. "I'm not a coward. Besides, it's an adventure."

"It's unnecessary," Faith said, shaking her head. "I'm coming with you. Make some excuse for your absence. There shouldn't be complaint from your parents. Nothing bad could possibly happen if we're all together."

· Three ·

🌺 ANTICIPATION THICKENED THE AIR, MAKING IT DIF-
ficult to breathe. The driver had positioned the brougham
so that they had an unobstructed view of the Trewelyn town
house without being directly across from the front entrance.
Even so, they left the carriage lamp unlit to avoid detection.
All three of them speculated early in the evening about which
depraved individuals would constitute the Guardians. Edwina
and Faith kept their noses pressed to the windows, waiting to
confirm their suspicions.

They waited . . . and waited. Claire broke the silence by
lecturing about the latest political scandals revealed in the
Pall Mall Gazette, a subject Edwina found tiresome at best.
Only an occasional hansom passed their position, and none
of those slowed to allow passengers to disembark. Soon Edwina's initial excitement mellowed to something akin to bore-
dom.

"What if the girls are already inside?" Claire asked. "If
they are, we won't be able to prevent them from succumbing
to Casanova's web."

While Edwina couldn't actually see her clearly, she could sense Claire's disappointment. How odd to be disappointed that acts of depravity were not taking place, but then that sort of news wouldn't appear in the political papers. "The ad said that the meeting of the Guardians doesn't begin till eight o'clock," Edwina reminded them. "I would guess it's barely seven now. We shouldn't have arrived so early."

"Suspicions would have arisen otherwise," Claire insisted. "Think of it, Edwina. If the purpose of the Guardians is to use a woman in some deviant conception of pleasure, wouldn't Trewelyn be certain of a woman's availability before advertising the party? If so, wouldn't he already have one or more women confined in the house?"

Faith gasped and lowered her voice. "They could be drugged and not able to refuse."

"Drugged?" Edwina couldn't imagine Ashton Trewelyn would need to drug any female to gain her cooperation. All he would have to do was look at her with those eyes, speak with that voice, smile with those lips . . .

"Opium, Edwina. That's what they do. They force an opium pipe on an innocent so she can't object. She won't even know what has happened until it's too late."

Edwina's head swam with talk of political scandal, opium, and innocents, all of which was phrased in context with Trewelyn. While her mind accepted the possibility of her friends being correct, especially given Casanova's reputation and the existence of the coded message, something still felt at odds with their perceptions. She opened the carriage door.

"What are you doing?" Faith asked, grasping her arm.

"I've been sitting too long," Edwina replied. "I thought I could walk a little to clear my head." And escape the close confines of the carriage, she thought, but kept to herself. The windows made the cramped interior of the brougham tolerable, yet she was still uncomfortable. She had never been at ease in confinement. Not since her brothers had locked her in a chest when she'd tried to follow them in her early years. She breathed easier with the carriage door open.

"If you walk on the pavement, the Guardians might see

you. They could sweep you up into their web of decadence," Faith admonished.

Edwina smiled to herself, believing such an occurrence unlikely. Something about time spent waiting in a dark conveyance must heighten the imagination. She glanced down the solid row of fashionable London town houses. "We don't even know if any women are inside." She turned back to Faith. "No one has arrived for the festivities. I'll just take a peek around back." Faith began to protest, but Edwina was insistent. If she stayed in that carriage another minute, she'd scream.

Faith rose as if to follow into the night. "You stay here," Edwina insisted. "It could be that the girls just haven't arrived as yet. If you stay here, you might be able to intercept them."

"But what if the Guardians catch you? What if you don't come back?"

"If I'm not back in an hour, then you can find a policeman to make inquiries," Edwina said. "Not any sooner, though. I don't want to be arrested in the mews as a potential thief." She smiled and pulled the hood of her cape over her hair. "Most likely I shall return in plenty of time."

Faith handed her parasol to Edwina. "Take this. It makes an effective weapon if necessary." Then she settled back into the cushions. "You be careful, Edwina."

THE GUARDIANS HAD PICKED A MOONLESS NIGHT FOR their meeting. A few well-lit lower rooms cast a soft light to the pavement. Edwina silently rounded the row of well-heeled dwellings to access the collection of carriage houses behind them. She counted her way down the lane to discover the back entrance to the Trewelyn residence.

A well-attired footman stood just outside the door, smoking a cigarette. He would be impossible to pass. Just as she had concocted what she hoped was a plausible reason to be admitted inside, the door flew open and a woman servant called out.

"Henry, come quick! They're having at it again!"

The footman tossed the remains of his smoke into the kitchen garden and hurried inside.

A fight . . . That would absorb the attention of the servants. If ever there was an opportunity to sneak undetected into a residence, this would be that time. She dashed forward and quietly entered, taking care to go upstairs toward the more intimate areas of the household and away from the popular— and from the sound of it—painful diversion belowstairs.

She managed her way to the first floor without discovery. Now what? If indeed there were women being held captive in the house for the amusement of others, where would they most likely be confined? She hadn't time to fully consider this question when she heard footsteps advancing from the opposite direction. Edwina slipped into the first open room and cowered in a corner, waiting for the footsteps to pass.

The familiar fragrance of old leather and musty paper teased her nose, pulling a smile. A library! Her fingers slipped along the binding of shelved volumes to her side and back. Did a rake stock a library with tales of adventure and piracy on the high seas? Would she find Robinson Crusoe and his marvelous tree house here, or Ivanhoe, or perhaps Shakespeare's sonnets? This was not the time to consider such things, she scolded, pressing her back to the shelves and holding her breath. The footsteps hurried past, affording her a sigh of relief.

Suddenly, a spark flashed with a sizzle of sulfur. She gasped, turning her head to the source of the light. She felt her life's blood fleeing her face. *Casanova!*

"I wondered who crept into the room." He lit a gas jet on the wall, flooding the library with a yellowish light. "So you're a thief, Miss Grimwood, as well as a liar and some poor fool's fiancée."

His insults, though not unjustified, stung. "What are you doing here?" she hissed.

His brow lifted. "This is my home. I ask the questions." He walked toward her, his stick leading the advance. "I hadn't anticipated such an attractive thief would steal into my house this night." A wicked gleam sparked his eyes. "Searching your person for missing candlesticks will be a delight I hadn't anticipated."

Her heart pounded with a ferocity to rattle the books on the shelves. She wrapped her cloak more tightly around her. "I'm not a thief," she protested. "That's not why I've come." He stepped around a large table situated in the center of the room. With each step toward her, she felt her confidence erode. "I'm . . . I'm searching for someone."

He drew up short and cocked his head. His eyes narrowed in accusation. "You followed me the day I picked up the responses from the *Mayfair Messenger*."

The man continually surprised her. "You knew?"

"I thought you looked familiar when we met earlier but I hadn't put it together until just this moment." He pushed the hood of her cape back, then slid a strand of her hair through his fingertips. "Your hair gives you away, Miss Grimwood. It's the color of sunlight. I thought it unusual to see this particular shade on so many women about London that day, but it was you all along. Only you."

She tried to shrink back from him, but there was little room for retreat in the corner.

His voice turned gruff. "Why were you following me?"

"It was your personal advertisement," she admitted. "We thought—"

"We?"

"There are others, yes." She looked up into his eyes. A mistake. She instantly felt her confidence draining, so she quickly glanced away. "We thought it unlikely that a man of your reputation would need to advertise for companionship, unless it was for . . ." She paused.

"For what, Miss Grimwood?"

She winced. "Please don't call me that. It's not my name. The real Miss Grimwood left the Crescent before you arrived."

He hesitated. She heard a swift intake of breath. Apparently she had the ability to surprise him as well. That knowledge restored some of her confidence. "Then what should I call you?" he asked.

She thought she heard a smile in his voice, but she could

have been mistaken. More likely it was a sneer, not a smile. The tips of his fingers gently guided her face back toward his. She couldn't avoid his eyes now.

"Who are you?"

The time for fabrication had passed. "Edwina Hargrove," she replied. He stood so close. His body trapped hers in place, keeping her close enough that she noted the scent of sandal-wood soap on his skin, close enough that he most likely could hear her heart racing.

"Then, Miss Hargrove," he said, his voice low, tantalizing, and seductive, "please explain for what purpose you believed I would advertise for companionship?"

She shrugged and averted her gaze, not wishing to admit their suspicions.

"Do you believe that a man such as myself does not deserve companionship?"

A slight catch in his voice, a slight shift in his speech pattern, alerted her to a possible vulnerability, but she had no time to consider that now.

"No, not at all," she replied quickly. "We thought that a man such as yourself had ample opportunity to secure companionship through the more traditional methods."

Demand was in his eyes as he gazed down a straight nose, past expressive lips and the dark shadow that covered his chin and defined his cheeks and, inexplicably, incited in her a desire to touch. The moisture in her mouth evaporated, making speech difficult. She grasped Faith's parasol more firmly. "You . . . you don't need to advertise."

His lips—lips that were rumored to be quite experienced in all sorts of decadent acts—pulled into a half smile that resonated in places it really shouldn't. "I suppose I should be flattered," he said. "But I fail to grasp how that would lead to your need to spy upon me."

"We thought that Casanova—"

"Casanova?" He drew back, faintly amused. "Do they still whisper that name?" She nodded slowly. He shook his head. "I thought that had died years ago."

His demeanor lightened, and she took a welcome breath. Glancing down the unbroken row of books in something akin to nostalgic revelry, he chuckled softly then returned his focus to her. "I don't recall seeing you at any house parties, Miss Hargrove. I would have remembered you. How would you know of Casanova?"

"The social column of the *Messenger*—"

"Ah, yes," he interrupted with a smile. "That ridiculous column about who is wearing what. As if the matter of jewelry flashed at one's tête-à-tête would make the slightest difference in the outcome of world affairs." His smile faded, but his eyes continued to search her face, his black pupils large in the dim light. "But go on . . . you thought Casanova would have no need . . ."

"No need to advertise unless . . . unless . . ." It was difficult to admit the Rake Patrol's suppositions to his face, especially as they now seemed frivolous and unsupported. But she drew herself up tall. "Unless he was planning to lure an innocent woman for unconscionable purposes."

He pulled back. "Unconscionable purposes?" He stared at her a moment and then chortled. "I suspect you have me confused with my father."

Such an odd response, her nose crinkled in annoyance. "No. I don't believe—"

"The ad was placed to benefit another, Miss Hargrove," he said without listening to her protest. "Someone who is truly worthy of the love of a good woman, as it appears in your estimation I am not."

Confused, she fumbled mentally for a moment. "I did not mean to imply . . ." He stood close, too close to discuss his worthiness for anything other than the sort of delicious unease he caused within her. She slipped past him, freeing her back from the uncomfortable press of the shelves. "Still," she insisted, "you lied in your advertisement. Those women thought you were the person with interest."

"The ad did not identify me," he protested. "I would have explained my purpose had I received the opportunity to actually speak to the respondents." A wicked smile spread across his face. "I had no idea there existed an entire corps of women determined to thwart my purposes."

She was tempted to believe him, if only for the humor in his eyes. But his words didn't explain the reason for this evening's venture. "What about the Guardians?" she asked. "Why did you call them to a meeting this evening?"

"The Guardians?" His brows lowered. "What are you talking about?"

"A coded message appeared in the *Mayfair Messenger* that announced a meeting on this very night in this very house."

"Coded?"

He certainly appeared flummoxed, but it could be more of his cat and mouse game. "It wasn't a particularly difficult code to break." It was her turn to sneer. "If you don't want strangers to read your secret invitations, you should use a more complex coding methodology."

He looked at her as if she spoke in scrambled text. "I didn't place a coded message in the *Messenger*."

"There was no mistaking the address," she insisted. "The Guardians are to meet here at—"

They both heard men's voices in the hallway. Panicked, she glanced at Trewelyn. He immediately ran his fingers along the top of a series of books on a shelf far to her left. "Good. It's still here," he murmured.

His fingers tugged on one of the books and an entire section of the wall with bookshelves swung forward. A hidden door. Just like those she'd read about in adventure novels. Curiosity tingled down her backbone, but with it a cautious uncertainty.

"You can't be discovered here." He grasped her arm and tugged her toward the door. "You'll be safe inside."

"But—"

He didn't listen to her protest, but pushed her through the opening. He followed and once on the other side, he pulled the bookcase door behind him.

The space was devoid of light, but she could sense his presence even without seeing him. It was as if he extracted the air from what she envisioned to be little more than a pantry. She backed up slowly, attempting to put distance between them. Confined in a dark closet with a man known as Casanova, with only a parasol for protection. How did she go from protecting vulnerable women to becoming one herself?

Her bustle bumped something that rattled.

"Be still," he rasped. "This is not an empty room. I wouldn't wish you injured."

She heard the click of a second latch. "There," he said. "They can't hear us or see a light with both doors closed."

"What is this place?" she whispered.

"It's a place you shouldn't be," he stated. His harshly spoken words, combined with the total darkness, lifted gooseflesh on her arms. After a moment, she heard a resigned sigh. "Miss Hargrove, I would not have brought you here if there had been another option. You understand that, don't you? Your reputation would suffer greatly if you were to be discovered alone with me at this time of the evening."

"Yes. I understand, but—"

"Since I'm not certain how long we will be detained here, I'm going to light the gas jet so we might safely negotiate the limited space. But in all fairness I must issue a warning."

"A warning?" Alarm rattled her already jittery insides. Had she escaped the stewpot only to be sacrificed in the fire? She slipped her hands behind her to investigate what she had backed into. She discovered what felt like chess pieces that wobbled and fell to the floor. She withdrew her hands before she did more damage. "What kind of warning?"

"If you value your innocence"—he struck a match that flared a moment, casting his face in stark, somber shadow—"keep your eyes tightly closed."

· *Four* ·

EDWINA STRAIGHTENED HER SPINE. "I'M A MODERN woman, sir, and in no need of your condescending platitudes." Insulted by his guileless inference that she was little more than a schoolgirl and not a full-grown woman, she lectured his back as he fumbled with the screw for the jet. "I cannot believe there is anything in this servants' closet that requires . . ."

The fumes ignited and the room opened before her. Far more than a pantry or a closet, the long narrow space in which they stood approximated the size of her parents' bedroom. In fact, if she wasn't mistaken, a mattress lined the far wall. Her breath caught. Dear heavens above, had she erred in her assumption that Trewelyn was not the rakehell her friends believed him to be? Was she truly trapped in the debaucher's den? She attempted to swallow the rising lump in her throat and gripped her parasol tightly. Perhaps it would serve as a weapon yet.

"If you plan to ravish me," she said stiffly, her gaze glued to the mattress, "I will fight you tooth and nail." No need to mention that her tendency to chew her fingernails had rendered them useless as weapons. "My eyes shall be open the entire time, and you shall witness in them my utter repugnance to your actions."

Trewelyn followed the direction of her gaze, then chuckled. The low sound rattled her more than the sight of the bed.

"My dear Miss Hargrove." His warm breath and soft seductive voice managed to titillate her breasts by way of her ear. Was there no part of her that wasn't receptive to his charms? She pressed her lips together to block an escaping sigh. "Fisticuffs will not be necessary. I assure you, I pose no threat."

If he believed that, then it must have been a long time since he looked in a mirror. She watched him move toward the gas jet in the back of the room.

"This is my father's gallery, where he keeps his art collection of shunga woodcut prints." He tilted his chin toward the opposite wall. "It's the nature of the collection that required a warning."

Curious, and strangely disappointed, Edwina allowed her racing heart a moment to settle before further investigation. As soon as she moved, the shelves behind her shook again, causing the additional tumbling of tiny objects. Something hit the floor and rolled. She glanced behind her. A series of shelves, the sort her mother used to display her delicate Parisian snuffbox collection, lined this portion of the wall. These shelves, however, held tiny carved wood and ivory figurines, the sort that normally would require close scrutiny. But she gave them little more than passing notice. She was far more interested in this shunga about which she'd been warned. She stepped toward a better angle from which to view the prints.

Initially she saw no reason for his concern. A series of bold prints adorned the walls, while small boxlike compartments rose from the floor to knee height. The compartments were filled to overflowing with bound papers. Nothing out of the ordinary there. The prints on the wall were Japanese, judging by the pattern-draped figures with slanted eyes and unique hair arrangements. She recalled the pattern of intricate letter characters raining from the top of the print in parallel lines from an exhibition of Japanese art and industry at the Crystal Palace. Unlike the European paintings that decorated most households and museums, these Japanese prints had no depth, no subtle shadings to denote distance or rounded curves. The renderings appeared to be pen and ink drawings with bold swatches of color. She moved in front of the first print, a man hovering over a woman reclined on steps, and gasped.

"Is that . . . ?"

"Yes." Trewelyn stepped behind her. She imagined even there he could sense the heat burning her cheeks. "Now you understand why I suggested you keep your eyes closed."

The print contained detailed depictions of a man's genitals. She should look away. She should verbalize her shock and disgust, but her eyes wouldn't move. Surely the print was not realistic. This man's huge member was easily the length and thickness of Faith's parasol. While Edwina knew something of a man's physique—she had, after all, accidentally spied on her brothers jumping into a stream—she had no idea that a man could be so gigantic. His female companion's delicate hand could barely circle the appendage. *A woman's hand? Why would a woman have her hand just there?* A lump formed in her throat at the prospect of being introduced to such a . . . weapon on her wedding night. How could men hide such an encumbrance in their trousers? How could Walter? She fought the urge to look behind her at the junction of Trewelyn's trousers. To do so would expose a lack of knowledge that she supposed a modern woman would have in abundance. Just knowing, however, that Trewelyn stood behind her with an encumbrance of his own . . .

She swallowed, hard. "The man is so . . ."

"Exaggerated?"

Relief flooded her body, easing tension from her shoulders that she hadn't realized existed. Knowing he couldn't see her face, she closed her eyes and said a quick prayer of gratitude that this massive instrument would play no part in her future. She smiled to herself. "Yes . . . exaggerated."

"The purpose of shunga is to show the pleasure of a natural union." The hesitancy in his speech caused her to question if he was experiencing a difficulty articulating. She knew she was. "The prints illustrate the many ways gratification can be achieved. Thus the artist . . . embellishes . . . both the male and female for instructional purposes."

Female? The prints illustrate female anatomy? She followed the direction of the bulbous tip of the man's member, but the drape of a flowing sleeve obscured its intended destination. "Instructional?" Her voice sounded strangled even to her ears. Now that she could look at other aspects of the print beyond the obvious fat sausage punching the air, she noticed the bodies in the print were flat and nonproportional. "I don't think such positioning is even possible." She glanced over her shoulder toward him. "For what purposes could one call this instructional?"

That was a mistake. She could clearly see his tantalizing eyes crinkle with humor, causing her to feel silly and ignorant. Perhaps she was in this particular area, but she didn't wish to be so obvious. Her cheeks heated. His lips parted as if to say something, but he caught her gaze and coughed into his fist instead. All traces of humor had vanished when he looked at her again. He led her to the next print.

"The prints were often contained in a 'pillow book,' as you can see here."

Following on his heels, eager to leave the intimidating illustration in front of her, she focused on his words, hoping to ignore her embarrassment. "The pillow book provided guidance to a new bride as to what would be expected within the marriage. The books also provided inspiration and ideas for experimentation for couples. You can see this couple consulting such a book."

Though tempted to ask what he meant by inspiration and experimentation, she remembered his attempt to hide his laughter at her last question, so she remained mum. Turning her face toward the woodblock print, she noted several square books on the floor surrounding the couple. A fully clothed man intensively studied an illustration, while the woman looked discreetly down at the blurred page. Curiosity led

Edwina to twist her head to see if she could make sense of the contorted couple depicted in the pillow book, but the details escaped her. As there were no exposed genitals in this print, just beautiful flowing robes of multiple patterns on both of the participants, she relaxed a small bit—as much as an inexperienced woman could relax when surrounded by explicit depictions of copulation.

The man, propped up on his elbow, had his back to the viewer. His gown, a dark blue with a sensuous swirl of light blue and white dots, left his legs exposed. The subject was so finely rendered that she could count each toe on his feet. Though the woman's mouth was hidden by an equally impressive printed cloth, something about her expression as she gazed at the pillow book gave Edwina the impression that she was hiding a smile. The blues and grays of her clothing worked well with the open sky of the background and with the intricate pattern on a nearby tray of food. It was a very pleasing nonthreatening print, and she supposed she must have studied it overlong.

"You seem enthralled with the pillow book," Trewelyn observed. "My father has several such books in his collection that you could study in some detail." He pointed to the overflowing cubbyholes below. His voice took on a hint of disdain. "But then, I'm sure you're well aware of what to expect, as a soon-to-be bride yourself."

She kept her focus on the print. "Mr. Thomas likes to suggest we are engaged, but we are not. I have not given my consent."

"No?" He sounded surprised. After a moment of hesitation, he continued. "You are a rare woman indeed, Miss Hargrove. The one woman in all of London, in fact, who doesn't rush for the promise of security that comes with marriage. Why is that?"

She glanced toward the secret door, hoping to avoid his question. Surely they'd been trapped a sufficient time. He followed her gaze.

"Don't worry. My father has been known to meet with industrialists to discuss business issues," he said. "I imagine those are the men who interrupted our conversation in the library. Hardily a secretive society—"

"I know what I read," she insisted. "How else would I know those men would gather here this evening?" He did not appear convinced. "Did you think my appearance on the same night as them is a coincidence?"

His lips pursed as if in consideration. "I'm certain you will agree that nothing good would result from exposing your presence in this room. I'll look into this matter of . . . Guardians, if you will, after you have safely left the premises. However, the gentlemen"—he nodded toward the door—"have barely begun their discussions. We've time yet to wait." He motioned toward the next print. "Shall we continue?"

She followed his lead, though she thought they had less time than Trewelyn imagined. How long would Faith wait before she called the police? Would they discover this chamber and her presence when they came? How embarrassing that would be. She almost wished she hadn't made the suggestion that Faith involve the police. Her thoughts left her unfocused even as they moved toward the next print. She harnessed her wayward thoughts to concentrate on the print before her, when the images registered with a jolt to her senses.

The man in the picture used his hand to explore the woman's "embellished" parts, thus coaxing some sort of liquid from them. The woman showed no form of protest; in fact, one would think she enjoyed this strange probing.

Trewelyn's voice warmed her ear and, truth be told, other parts hidden from his view. "This print shows there's more than one way to coax ying from a female."

"Ying?" She stared at the depiction of a woman's privates. Dear heaven, what manner of art was this? When the Rake Patrol thought Casanova was abusing innocents, they hadn't considered he was doing it by means of a secret art gallery. She attempted to swallow her surprise and maintain her composure. She needed her wits about her, that much was certain.

Taking a calming breath, she looked at the print anew. Was that how all women looked in that area hidden from inspection? Or was this unique to Japanese women? European paintings suggested a woman was devoid of tresses in the nether regions. She knew from her own ringlets that those depictions were not correct. While she hoped she didn't resemble this gaping orifice surrounded by tufts of black hair, she suspected that the Japanese print was the more honest. If that were true, was the depiction of pleasure at the act of probing true as well? While the two caricatures were crass and common in their actions, they still remained somehow fascinating.

Trewelyn nodded beside her. "The Japanese believe that a balance of ying and yang is necessary for the health and longevity of both genders. The more they can collect, the better. A woman produces ying in her body fluids, a man produces yang. A man can obtain ying through sexual congress or"—he pointed his chin to the print—"in a more direct fashion straight from the heavenly gate."

There was nothing heavenly or even angelic in this depiction of a woman, but the term was less embarrassing than some of the other words she'd heard used for that particular area. "I suppose that woman in the first print holding the man's . . ."

"Jade stalk?" he offered.

Edwina tried unsuccessfully to keep from smiling. "She was collecting yang?"

He turned toward her, a devilish lift to his lips. "I believe she was priming the well to receive yang in the more traditional approach."

Why had she considered this room large? It seemed to be shrinking at a precarious rate. She glanced about, looking for windows. Anything that could bring relief to the heated air. But there were no windows. That surprised her. Normally, just being in a room without windows would be terrifying in itself, but Trewelyn's presence made her fear dissipate.

"Is something wrong, Miss Hargrove?"

She shook her head. "How do you know so much about this aspect of the Japanese culture?" She had attended some of the popular Japanese exhibitions with her mother, but the sort of information of which Trewelyn spoke had not been presented. That he should be so knowledgeable about the intimacies of a foreign land intrigued her.

"I suppose my father taught me at an early age, or perhaps it was . . ." His brow wrinkled. "Or perhaps it was . . ." He hesitated. "It was my father," he said emphatically. "Yes. My father taught me."

She had apparently broached an uncomfortable subject and so followed him as he moved quickly to the next print. This time the man's outrageous jade stalk was partially embedded in a woman's magnified heavenly gate. The woman was not terrified or disgusted. The few lines used to denote her expression showed she was a complicit partner, if not anxious for the act. *Strange.* The grotesque exaggerated depictions no longer shocked her as had the first print. Somehow that made her feel worldly.

"They're still dressed," she said, though why this seemed unusual was beyond her. The rich patterns of the garments flowed with almost sensuous curves around the exaggerated portions of the copulating couples. The patterns were lovely and caught her eye more than the activity depicted. She moved on to the next print on her own and the one after that. Both showed a couple involved in some form of sexual congress. The first showed the couple observed by another woman who explored her own heavenly gate while spying. The second depicted a beautifully dressed woman with a lute who sat on a man who appeared to be her music teacher. Their robes had parted to show his stalk engaged in her gate. She had no idea there were so many ways to accomplish that basic function. After viewing such a multitude of prints depicting similar scenes, their graphic sexual nature proved less shocking. Still, she concentrated on the beautiful patterns and avoided the baser components of the print.

"The fabrics are lovely," she said, refusing to comment on the illicit activities. "How interesting that the parties are fully clothed." She turned toward Trewelyn. "Is there a meaning in the patterns?"

He seemed surprised at her question. *Good.* She liked surprising him for a change. He considered her a moment. "The patterns indicate the social class of the man or woman. The more intricate the pattern, the higher one's station." His mouth quirked. "I suppose it's not dissimilar to an English ballroom in that regard."

She smiled. "Actually, I wondered if a message could be embedded into the pattern of the cloth." Using her hands as a guide, she indicated the curve of the cloth as it broke over raised knees and exposed limbs. "The message would be interpreted by the folds and sways."

"I hadn't considered that possibility," Trewelyn said in a contemplative tone. "There are several symbols that convey meaning in the print, and some say the sensuous parting of the fabric is to suggest the feminine—"

"Symbols?" she interrupted, her interest piqued. "What symbols?"

He pointed to various images in the prints. "Note the upright branches in the vase, the ones without leaves. Those represent an erect male. The fans, cherry blossoms, scraps of paper on the floor, knot holes in the wood, umbrellas, they all have specific meanings."

She brightened. "You mean like Holman Hunt's narrative paintings. A discarded glove on the floor or a cat playing with a bird are all clues to the moral message of the painting. Meanings within meanings. The symbols are like that?" Or just like the "every other word" code in the personal ads, but she kept that to herself.

She didn't look at his face, but she heard a sort of astonishment in his voice. "Yes. Something similar to that."

"I've noticed many of the prints have cherry blossoms," she asked. "You said they have a special meaning?"

His voice returned to normal, his astonishment short-lived. "Cherry blossoms denote the ephemeral nature of existence. They suggest we should experience life to its fullest today, as only death and decay await tomorrow. Thus the couples are encouraged to find pleasure while they can." Trewelyn tilted his head, scrutinizing her carefully. "Do these prints not bother you at all, Miss Hargrove?"

"While rather rudimentary, they are still items of art, Mr. Trewelyn." She tapped the point of her parasol on the floor, not wishing him to see exactly how the prints had affected her. Granted they were shocking at first, but they also spurred her curiosity and inexplicably set certain body parts to hum. She smiled tentatively. After all, even she recognized her reactions wouldn't be considered appropriate by most of society. "These are not the sort of images I'd hang in the family gallery, but they have a certain quality . . ."

She attempted her best modern woman expression of open-mindedness, hoping to fool him into believing she was worldly and sophisticated, and not the naive miss she truly was. With her head held high, she took the lead in moving to the next print and gasped.

A woman, devoid of clothing, lay on her back with an octopus at the juncture of her legs. The beast's tentacles wrapped around one of the woman's breasts and even slipped between her lips. The beast's mouth sucked at the woman's nether parts, while the woman's head was tossed back in an expression of ecstasy.

"This cannot be considered educational," she said, shocked at the image. Yet even as she protested the print's depiction, her entire body pulsed with awareness. "Surely, the Japanese do not employ creatures in such a fashion."

"No. This represents the dream of a fisherman's wife," he said slowly. "By her expression I'd say that this is a pleasurable dream." He hesitated, then his voice lowered in a sort of teasing intimacy. "Wouldn't you enjoy being caressed in such a fashion?"

He must be joking, though her cheeks heated with his baiting comment. "That is not a suitable question, sir." Yet her body tingled in a manner she hoped was not evident.

"This entire viewing would hardly be considered suitable," he muttered beneath his breath.

She glanced toward the door, anxious to escape this awkward situation. "How will we know when it's safe to leave?"

He followed her gaze. "If my father is still conducting a meeting in the library, I should be able to hear their voices in the passageway. Even if they've left, I'll need to find a way to smuggle you outside without notice. It may take some time for my return."

"You're going to leave me alone?" Panicked, she glanced nervously about the confined space. "In here?"

His eyes narrowed slightly. "Is that a problem?"

She didn't want to admit her fear. She was a modern woman, after all. Modern women weren't afraid of small windowless rooms filled with illicit paintings. She tried to keep the panic from her voice as she spoke a lie. "As long as the jets remain lit, I should be fine."

ASHTON STUDIED EDWINA FOR A MOMENT. SHE WAS A strange one. Unlike any other woman he'd met before. While he had fully expected his father's shunga collection would shock and perhaps frighten her, she'd been strangely fascinated. She was full of surprises, including her admission that she could decipher seemingly indecipherable messages. How would a young lady develop such a trait? Based on her curiosity, he thought she might prefer being alone in the chamber so she could study the prints without his presence. Yet now she appeared nervous and frightened, the very traits he'd expected her to exhibit earlier. There was more to Miss Hargrove than the simple innocent he had imagined.

"Are you quite certain there are no windows?" she asked, a nervous smile attempting to form on her lips. "Maybe if you turned a knob or pulled a lever, a window would appear . . . just like the door?"

"No secret windows, I'm afraid." He crossed the room, then opened the inner door and slipped into the tiny passageway. She followed close on his heels. Pressing his ear to the outer door, he listened. "All's quiet," he whispered. "Stay out of sight until we know everyone has left."

He opened the outer door slowly. There was no response. He peeked around the edge. No one was in the room. A new shunga book, however, lay upon the table. That must have been the reason for the meeting of the so-called secret society. He smiled. A secret society of old men who enjoyed Japanese erotica. The gathering sounded fairly harmless.

No sooner had he cleared the passageway door when Miss

Hargrove eagerly emerged. Once she stood fully in the library, she took a deep breath. Even in the soft light of the room he could see tension flee her face. *Interesting.*

"I need to check if the way is clear. It might be safer if you wait in the chamber room," he said, playing a hunch. Terror instantly crossed her eyes. "Or you can stay in the library, as long as you're quiet." She sagged in relief, thus supporting his supposition. She was . . . what did they call it? *Claustrophobic.* The thought that he knew this small thing about her pleased him somehow, like a shared secret. "I'm going to close the door to the library," he warned, "just in case someone should pass by. Is that all right?"

"Of course, that is fine," she said. If he wasn't mistaken, her nose rose just an inch in the air. He noted her discreet glance to the library window. "I'm a modern woman, you know."

He smiled. "Yes. So I've observed."

He closed the door to the library softly behind him. Such a twist of events. He'd come to the library earlier to sort out his thoughts over Constance, his father, and his stepbrother. Unlike Miss Hargrove, he preferred the solitude afforded by the dark. Lighted rooms offered too many distractions, and in this residence, too many memories. He certainly hadn't expected to encounter the charming Miss Hargrove. If he wasn't mistaken, for a self-proclaimed modern woman, she was as innocent and naive as a new dawning day, which was delightfully refreshing given his most recent female acquaintances.

He quickly ascertained that the back steps would provide the quickest exit for Miss Hargrove. If no servants were about, she should be able to slip out unnoticed, which in retrospect, would explain why she stumbled into the library in the first place. He, however, was apparently not as fortunate as Miss Hargrove as he barely made it to the steps before being intercepted by a footman.

"Sir, your father has been asking for you. Something about the police, sir."

"The police?" Now, that was a message he hadn't been anticipating.

"Yes, sir. They're looking for a young lady, and they thought you might know her whereabouts. They're talking to your father now, sir." The footman had difficulty hiding the slight smirk that threatened. *Lord Almighty*. Now that he was back in London, was his earlier reputation going to cause him to be suspect in every young woman's disappearance?

Ashton felt his brow furl. "Where is my father?"

"Everyone is in the foyer, sir."

The commotion near the front entrance greeted him before he could approach. One uniformed bobby restrained two determined females who seemed oblivious to his father's pronounced displeasure and the butler's silent but obvious vexation.

"Are you certain the young woman is not here, Mr. Trewelyn?" the bobby addressed his father. "These ladies seem to think—"

"My son is most likely off enjoying himself in a most inappropriate manner, but I assure you, he's not doing so here. These young ladies are mistaken in—"

"There he is!" One of the ladies, a harsh-looking young woman with an unfortunately predominate nose, pointed a finger in Ashton's direction. "Casanova! He's the one!" Everyone turned to look his way. "He and his friends have taken Edwina for their own sordid purposes."

His father's anger found a new target. He turned toward Ashton. "You'd best have an explanation for this accusation! I'll not have that sort of violation under my roof."

Ashton pretended to look about him as if the allegations were meant for someone else while he scrambled for a solution. He couldn't very well admit that he had Miss Hargrove sequestered in the library. Given their lustful imaginations, that would not do at all. Someday, he vowed, he'd have a frank discussion with the engaging Miss Hargrove about what sordid activities these women imagined occurred on a nightly basis. He leaned heavily on his walking stick. "Who exactly am I accused of violating?"

"Miss Hargrove, sir," a soft-spoken woman with a compassionate air replied. "She is one of our friends."

He liked this woman. She was far more agreeable than her harsh companion. He directed his reply to her. "What makes you believe she might be here?"

"We were in the area for . . . a recital. Edwina . . . expressed an interest in this residence." Lying apparently was difficult for her. That failing spoke well of Miss Hargrove's friends.

"It sounds as if you simply misplaced Miss Hargrove," Ashton said with what he hoped was a meaningful glance. "I suspect she is probably looking for you at this very moment."

The soft-spoken woman smiled lightly then nodded her head. Message received. Ashton discreetly nodded as well, not surprised that Edwina had intelligent as well as compassionate friends.

"Yes," the harsh one insisted. "She is looking for us to save her. Don't be fooled by him, Faith. He's the devil." She pushed forward. "Edwina!" she shouted. "We've come to save you! Cry out if you can!"

"Now see here, Miss—" The policeman tried unsuccessfully to restrain the irritating woman, but she brushed by Faith, causing her to knock the policeman off balance. Ashton moved to catch Faith before she fell. Unfortunately, this provided the determined woman the opportunity to surge down the passageway.

"I'll save you, Edwina!" she called. "Even if I have to search the entire house!"

"Young lady, stop this!" his father yelled ineffectively.

The policeman righted himself and gave chase to the intruder. The one called Faith regained her footing and murmured her thanks to Ashton. After a quick nod, Ashton dashed after the others to stop the madness before they reached the library and his curious intruder. If discovered, not even a self-proclaimed modern innocent like Miss Edwina Hargrove would survive the ensuing scandal.

· *Five* ·

❧ EDWINA GLANCED AT THE FLOOR-TO-CEILING BOOK-cases surrounding her and sighed. If circumstances were different, if she had been an invited guest rather than a snooping annoyance, being abandoned in such a library would be akin to a fantasy. She could spend hours curled up on the alcove window seat lost in a swashbuckling adventure. However, after her unsolicited appearance this evening, she imagined this was the last she'd see of this room.

Her gaze fell to a square book with a plain cover on the center wooden table, nested in paper wrappings. She was fairly certain that this table had been empty when Trewelyn pushed her into the secret chamber. Curiosity carried her closer. She tentatively lifted a few pages at a corner and noted the bright flat colors and pen and ink technique of the books in the gallery. *What had Trewelyn called them? Oh yes, a pillow book, used to teach young wives what to expect in a marriage.* A tremor of excitement slipped through her. She hadn't had a very good opportunity to closely examine the books in that chamber, not with Trewelyn watching her every expression.

Cautiously, she opened the pillow book more fully, hoping to spot some of the symbols Trewelyn had mentioned, meaning within meaning. The sight of the exaggerated sexual genitals—*and please God, let Trewelyn be telling the truth about that*—did not shock her as they had earlier. Instead, she was able to focus on the entire print, the setting and the emotions. If the prints were to be believed, "having a bit of bum" as her brothers called it, was not limited to a private room or to a single couple. Some prints depicted what she would describe in whispered conversation as an orgy. A shiver slipped down her spine. Yet, in all the prints, the women had soft reassuring smiles, which made her wonder. Perhaps the act of coupling was not as tortuous as she had been led to believe. She turned a page and noted a slip of folded paper had been tucked into the binding of the book. She started to remove it when she heard voices. Loud agitated voices. Someone was coming, and she suspected the library was their destination.

There'd be no hiding under the table as there was no cloth to provide privacy. Certainly the attractive alcove would be no help; she'd be spotted immediately. Her only recourse was to find the latch that unlocked the secret chamber. With the pillow book in the crook of her arm, she attempted to duplicate Trewelyn's moves. She tugged on books in succession, praying for the sound of an opening latch. Unfortunately, the only sounds beyond the pounding in her ears were the approaching agitated voices. *The latch must be here*, she prayed. *Please. Please. Please . . .*

"STOP HER!" THE SENIOR TREWELYN SHOUTED. "DON'T GO in that room!"

The policeman caught the noisy meddler just outside the library door. She was a fighter, that one, swinging her arms and grabbing everything she could to free herself from the policeman's grasp.

Ashton sagged with relief. He could well imagine poor Miss Hargrove trying to press herself into the corner of the bookshelves, attempting to make herself invisible. His lips tightened. As if that could happen. If she hadn't been able to make herself unnoticeable on the crowded streets of London, she certainly couldn't escape notice in an empty room.

Just as the policeman was attempting to pull the feisty intruder forcibly away from the library door, she grabbed the doorknob and pushed the library door open for all to see.

"There!" she cried out triumphantly, pointing to the interior. Ashton's stomach clenched hard as a rock. There could be no saving Miss Hargrove now.

The policeman paused and peeked cautiously into the room. The senior Trewelyn pushed his way forward, causing both the policeman and his captive to enter the library. Ashton followed behind the others, trying desperately to think of some logical explanation for a woman to be secluded in a stranger's library at this hour of night.

But there was no need. The library was empty.

Ashton quickly glanced at the secret door and noticed a slight, almost unperceivable crack. The door wasn't closed completely. He moved deeper into the library, placing himself directly in front of the opening, hiding it from sight. "I hope you're satisfied, miss." He used his best glare. "As you can see, there's no one here."

"You could have her sequestered upstairs," she replied. She opened her mouth so as to shout again, but Faith clamped a hand over it.

"Enough, Claire. At this rate, you'll have all of London on the Trewelyns' doorstep. She's not here." She glanced at Ashton. "I think we should follow Mr. Trewelyn's advice. Edwina is most likely waiting for us at the carriage right now, wondering what happened to us."

"But . . ."

"She's not here," Faith insisted. She turned to his father. "My apologies for the intrusion on your household, sir. We were obviously mistaken in our information."

"Would you like to press charges against this one, sir?" The policeman scowled at Claire. "She's guilty of disturbing the peace, she is."

His father stared at the empty table as if Edwina herself sat there wrapped in a flowing Japanese robe with a beckoning smile. Ashton shook his head, wondering why imagination had conjured that particular image. "No," his father said. "Just take her out of here. I don't wish my wife to witness this disturbance."

The policeman escorted the two women out of the library. As their footsteps retreated up the passageway, his father turned toward him. "That was quick thinking on your part. I must admit I panicked when that chit flung the door wide open. I would have had a difficult time explaining the pillow book." His lips quirked as if he wasn't quite certain . . . "You did move it, did you not?"

Ashton suspected the talented Miss Hargrove waited on the other side of the secret door, pillow book in hand. "Yes," he replied. "At the moment, it's well concealed."

"Good." His father closed his eyes and sighed. "I should have placed it in the chamber myself once the Guardians had left, but then that commotion erupted."

"Guardians?" Ashton asked, silently thanking the powers that be that his father didn't stumble upon the both of them in the chamber. Edwina was correct about the meeting. His admiration for her talent increased tenfold. "Who are the Guardians?"

"Did I . . . ?" His father's eyes widened a moment before he looked away. "Perhaps one day I shall be able to introduce you, but for now it would please me greatly if you just forget you ever heard that name." He fumbled about for a moment, as if he'd misplaced his pocket watch, then he glanced back to Ashton with a weak half smile. "I'd best make sure those women have left. Wouldn't do to have your mother discover them here."

"Stepmother," Ashton corrected.

"Yes . . . yes . . . of course. I meant to say that." His father turned for the door. "With Matthew in the house, referring to Constance as 'mother' has become something of a habit. I'm sure you understand."

No. Ashton was quite certain he would never understand why Constance occupied that particular role in this house.

His father, framed by the library doorway, looked back toward him and frowned. "You don't know anything about that missing woman, do you?" His father shook his head. "I had hoped after your stint with the Rifles you would abandon these frivolous romantic interludes." He didn't wait for Ashton's reply but kept talking as he walked down the passageway. "It's small wonder that every time a woman goes missing, the police appear on my doorstep."

ASHTON FELT A PROTEST FORMING DEEP IN HIS BELLY. Perhaps if his father had acknowledged his presence in the slightest way in those early years, he would have traveled a different road, and not one that earned him this Casanova title. He stood in the library fuming, when the press of the door to his back reminded him he wasn't alone. He pulled the secret door fully open and Miss Hargrove tumbled out, the missing pillow book in her arms.

"I'm sorry," she managed in between gulps of air. "I just picked it up to look at it. After you had shown me the others, I was curious. I should never have taken it."

"Actually, you did my father a service, not that you can ever tell him." His lips lifted in a smile. So the contents of the chamber had intrigued her after all. Enough to study the new arrival for his father's collection. He would have liked to discuss that interest further, but now was not the time.

"Allow me to put the pillow book away. Then we need to get you out of here and reunited with your friends." She placed the book in his hands with downcast eyes and a bit of color high on her cheeks. She blushed very sweetly, that one. It made him wonder what else beyond embarrassment would cause that rise of color. He mentally gave himself a shake. Most likely he'd never see her again. Sweet innocents did not travel in his jaded circles. "I'll need to douse the lights. This may take a moment or two."

He returned the book to the secret chamber, then paused, sensing a faint scent of oranges in the room. Funny that he hadn't noticed her scent earlier. His attention must have been focused elsewhere. He turned off the gas jets and returned to the library to discover Miss Hargrove studying a piece of paper. "What is that?"

She folded it and handed it to him. "I found this in the pillow book. It must have fallen when I gave you the book. It was lying here on the floor."

He slipped the note into his pocket. "I'll read it later. Let's get you safely away before my father returns, looking for his latest purchase." Ashton peeked down the corridor and spotted his father involved in conversation at the far end. Constance must have returned home. All the more reason to get Miss Hargrove out of the residence. He turned toward Edwina. "My father is busy at the front of the house. I'll distract the servants from the back entrance. Wait here a few minutes, then slip out the back door. Understood?"

She nodded.

"I'll meet you outside," he said. She began to protest, but he silenced her with a quiet hush. "I'm not about to let you wander unescorted in the dark. Just wait for me outside and I'll see you safely returned to your friends."

EDWINA WAITED FOR TREWELYN AS INSTRUCTED, GRATE-ful for his promise of escort. The hour had advanced beyond that for which she had confidence. Even Faith's frilly parasol would prove no match for the sorts of miscreants that might be out at this hour. While she and her friends hadn't uncovered the sort of debauchery they had suspected when they embarked on this adventure, she had enjoyed an experience she hadn't anticipated. Could she . . . would she . . . describe the contents of the secret chamber to the Rake Patrol? Or would that cause them to think less of Trewelyn? For some reason, their opinion of him held importance to her.

He appeared a moment later as promised. "Shall we?"

She had to admit, the mews was less ominous with Trewelyn at her side. "Thank you for this," she said. "I suppose I'm not as brave as I'd like to believe."

"Given tonight's discoveries, I would disagree," Trewelyn

said, his voice companionable and warm in the dark. "I'm sure those Japanese prints were rather shocking to you."

"I've not seen anything like those before." It was easier to talk like this, in the open, in the dark. "They were certainly lewd and . . . common, but at the same time"—she shook her head—"I don't know how to explain it."

He laughed, a soft sound that vibrated deep within her. "So tell me, Miss Hargrove, have I passed inspection? Will I be able to continue to look for a suitable companion for my friend without interference?"

"Will you do that?" In light of all the recent activity, Edwina had forgotten that a personal ad had started it all. "Will you continue to advertise for a companion?"

"I haven't decided," Trewelyn acknowledged. "For the most part, the responses I received from that first advertisement were not exactly what I had hoped. Perhaps I should employ more traditional methods, or"—he laughed— "perhaps I should leave James to search for himself."

Once she reported back to the others, she was certain the Rake Patrol would no longer question Trewelyn's intent and would thus terminate their intervention. That he passed their inspection was a disappointment, as it meant she'd have no valid excuse to spy upon him. If nothing else, the research had proved an adventure.

"Are your friends waiting in that carriage?" he asked.

She nodded. It was the only carriage pulled along the curb. So much for discretion.

"Then I'll leave you here." Trewelyn turned toward her. "You'll be safe under the driver's gaze, and while I admire her loyalty, I'd prefer not to encounter your friend Claire."

Edwina smiled. "She can be an acquired taste."

"Good night, Miss Hargrove." He took her hand in his. Edwina's heart jumped a little at the contact. "Though it was accomplished through unconventional means, I must say I enjoyed making your acquaintance." He smiled down at her. "I can understand why your Mr. Thomas is so protective of you. I think he might have his hands full with that endeavor."

"He's not *my* Mr. Thomas," she insisted.

"Good night, Miss Hargrove." He hesitated a moment then kissed her hand. She thought her knees would melt on the spot. He turned to walk back the way they had come.

"Mr. Trewelyn?" she called.

He stopped and turned.

"Should you need my assistance, I'll be at the Crescent Palace about three o'clock tomorrow afternoon."

He chuckled. "That sounds a bit presumptuous, Miss Hargrove. Why do you believe I shall have need of your assistance?"

"Because the note that fell from the pillow book, the one you placed in your pocket. . . . it's in code." She smiled sweetly. "Good night, Mr. Trewelyn."

· Six ·

SHE COULDN'T VERY WELL TELL HER FRIENDS THAT she'd been sequestered in a secret chamber of lewd Japanese prints with the most lascivious man in all of London. Claire would most likely storm the Trewelyn residence again with loud protests of the secret gallery. No, Edwina would have to keep that information to herself. But then how to explain her absence? She didn't wish to lie to her friends, but she saw no other recourse.

"I miscounted," she said as she climbed into the carriage. "I waited a long time, but when no carriages came down the lane, I decided to sneak into his house."

"Edwina!" Faith admonished her. "That's dangerous! You shouldn't have done that!"

"But I entered the wrong house," Edwina explained, unaffected by Faith's outburst. "I had to remain hidden a long time before I could sneak back undetected. Did I miss anything?"

"Only my near arrest for trespassing." Claire glared. "I thought you were being held hostage. I thought you were being compromised."

"Fortunately, none of that was true," Faith said quietly. "So you didn't see anyone? You didn't see the Guardians?" While her voice held no accusations, Faith's steady gaze did, as if she could see through Edwina's lie.

Edwina shook her head. At least that part was true. She'd heard the voices in the hallway and then that book appeared on the library table. Someone had come to the Trewelyn residence as a result of that ad. She was sure of it.

"Not even Casanova himself?" Faith quietly persisted.

Edwina glanced up. Faith knew something. She could see it in the set of Faith's shoulders. Edwina just held her gaze.

"Perhaps you misread the coded message," Claire said with a determined air. "It was probably just another agony lamenting over a failed tryst or improper attraction."

Edwina clenched her teeth. Claire had never accepted Edwina's abilities in that regard. Under the sting of incompetence, Edwina mustered a false smile, then shifted her gaze to Claire. "I should thank you," she said. "Had I truly been in danger, it's good to know that my friends would rush to my defense." Claire's lips tightened in acknowledgment, then she nodded and resettled in her seat.

"We should consult with Sarah," Faith interjected, "but now that I've had a chance to speak directly to him, I'm not certain the younger Mr. Trewelyn is as intent on debauchery as we supposed. In light of this evening's events, maybe we should turn our talents to other ads. Do you agree?"

"He seemed kind enough at the Crescent," Edwina said to justify her response. After all, she couldn't very well admit to having spent an inordinate amount of time locked in a gallery with him. Still, she was grateful Faith had come to the same conclusion as she had. Casanova just wasn't the Casanova of his earlier reputation. "Yes, I think we can assume Mr. Trewelyn is not as evil as we had imagined."

"Good." Faith settled more comfortably in her seat. "I'm certain Mr. Thomas will be pleased that we are no longer pursuing the charismatic Mr. Trewelyn. He seemed to take offense at Mr. Trewelyn's interest in you."

"Interest? It was a misunderstanding," Edwina said, recalling the incident outside of the Crescent. "That was all."

But was it? She couldn't deny the way her spine tingled whenever Mr. Trewelyn's brown eyes, with that interesting pattern of green flecks, turned her way. Her pulse still raced from his close proximity in the chamber. She was, after all, female. Still, she'd no reason to suspect he had any interest in her.

Edwina let the resulting conversation flow around her. She certainly hoped she hadn't seen the last of Mr. Trewelyn. There was the matter of the coded message in the pillow book, which piqued her curiosity, and the matter of the man himself, which certainly piqued . . . other areas. She shifted uncomfortably on the leather cushion.

She smoothed her hand over Faith's parasol, intending to return it, but her fingers encountered a hard lump beneath the fabric. A lump that shouldn't be there. Given her recent activities, she didn't wish to alert her friends to the item's existence. Her finger drew a tiny inconspicuous circle on the surface of the parasol fabric, but her senses noted a distinctively curved surface and a cavity such as one might find in a bead. The shelves! She couldn't recall exactly what the items were on the shelves, but they were small and had toppled when she bumped into them in the dark. One must have fallen into the parasol. "Would you mind if I borrowed this just a little bit longer?" she asked Faith, raising the parasol slightly in her lap. "I wish to show the fabric to my mother. The color suits me, don't you think?"

"Of course, keep it as long as you like." Faith looked at her curiously. "I don't recall your interest in colors before."

"Colors." Claire snorted. "Women should wear either black or white. Colors are so impractical. If one considers the unhealthy dyes utilized to produce . . ."

But Edwina had ceased to listen, concerned instead about this accidental souvenir of that secret chamber. At least, she was assured of one thing. Whether Mr. Trewelyn was interested in her abilities or not, she'd be obligated to call upon him once more to return whatever had fallen into her possession.

• • •

THE NEXT DAY, AFTER THOUGHTS OF MR. TREWELYN HAD
caused a sleepless night of tossing and turning, she almost
hoped he wouldn't seek her assistance at the Crescent. As
much as she longed to take a crack at deciphering that note,
the fear of discovery by her friends had left her a jittery mess.
No one of her acquaintance was currently in the Crescent at
this hour, but that could change in a moment. Faith tended to
meet with fellow women poets at Hastings House most Thursday afternoons, and Claire only visited the Crescent for the
weekly Women for a Sober Society meetings and for the Rake
Patrol gatherings. Sarah would still be at the *Messenger* at
this time of day, and Walter wouldn't expect her to be here
at all. The choice of time she'd given Trewelyn wasn't without justification, but one never knew who would forfeit the
norm and drop in unexpectedly for a cup of tea. She checked
her locket watch once again. Yes, perhaps it would be better
for all concerned if he didn't come.

But then what would she do with that strange wooden
object she discovered in Faith's parasol? After she'd arrived
home last evening, she'd gathered a lit candle to guide her
upstairs and then opened the parasol in the safety of her room.
A carved wooden bead the size of a large walnut fell to the
floor. Upon close inspection, the bead resembled a naked
woman sitting in a small wooden barrel. She turned the bead
to discover the artist had carved the view from the underside
of the water, which depicted the woman exploring herself in
a similar manner as the prints. A hole tunneled through the
sides of the figure, which explained the cavity she'd felt earlier while in the carriage. Why on earth would someone carve
such a thing and in such intimate detail?

A knock at her door had startled her, causing the bead to
slip from her fingers and fall to the floor. While she heard it
roll, she hadn't a chance to look for it when her mother opened
the door.

"Edwina? I just wanted to see how you enjoyed your evening." Her mother, with her neatly plaited hair down the front

of her white nightgown, stood with a candle in hand. Edwina's black kitten, Isabella, named for the famous woman explorer Isabella Bird, took advantage of the open door to stroll into the room. She chirped a welcome before leaping on the bed. Edwina prayed the pool of light from her mother's candle didn't illuminate her souvenir. Before she could respond, her mother's eyes widened. "What a lovely parasol. Where ever did it come from?"

"Faith allowed me to borrow it. Walter invited me to the theater next week and I thought perhaps this might accompany one of my gowns." Dear heaven, she could weave a thick carpet with all of her recent lies. Now she'd have to convince Walter to take her to the theater, an entertainment he generally despised. She worried her lip. Her soul must be becoming as black as Claire's wardrobe.

Her mother had seemed impervious to her daughter's distress. If anything she was elated at the news. "The theater? How lovely!" She winked at her daughter. "I imagine Walter wishes to show you off to society. I'm certain we can find something tomorrow that will nicely accompany Faith's parasol. Meanwhile you need your sleep. I'll send Kathleen in to help you ready for bed."

She disappeared before Edwina could protest, then Kathleen arrived before she'd discovered the bead's hiding place. After Kathleen left, Edwina was too exhausted to look further and fell asleep with a thought to search in the morning. But then she'd slept too late and after reviewing every item of her wardrobe with her mother, no longer had time to look for the bead. Her plan to return the object to Trewelyn would have to wait until she found where the blasted nuisance had rolled.

A tingling at the base of her neck roused Edwina from her thoughts. She looked up to see Trewelyn by the door, sweeping the room with that accessing glance of his. When it rested on her, she smiled, and all her earlier concerns dissolved like a sugar cube in a cup of hot tea.

"I wasn't certain you'd be here," he said, once he had negotiated the labyrinth of tables and chairs to where she sat. Raised heads and interested glances followed in his wake.

She wasn't the only one affected by his smile, she thought, perversely pleased that he came to *her* table. For the first time in her life, she imagined she was the envy of other women, even though they might have the advantage of society position, appearance, or intellectual pursuit. He came to *her*. Her rib cage fluttered.

He lowered himself to the chair opposite. "I was afraid that once you'd reflected on my father's passionate pursuits, you'd have nothing further to do with me." His eyes crinkled almost in question, and her lips lifted immediately in response. "Or this mysterious message."

He pulled the paper from his pocket and laid it on the table. Her fantasies about being desired for her feminine attributes crashed about her. He was here for her abilities to decipher code. Nothing else. Her hopes—dreams really—that something else had passed between them last night were obviously a product of the late hour and unusual circumstances. She swallowed past the sudden lump in her throat.

"May I?" She reached for the paper, just as he pushed it across the table. Their fingers briefly touched. As if to verify her suspicions, there was no sudden arcing of heat at the contact, no passionate flare of awareness, just his fingers encased in a butter-soft glove briefly touching hers. She was disappointed, of course, but also immediately aware of her unrealistic expectations. He was here for a translation. Nothing more.

As before, the waitress appeared immediately after Trewelyn arrived. He ordered a beverage, and the waitress suggested he supplement his order with a selection from their pastries. He raised a brow. "What do you suggest?"

The girl flushed. "The éclairs are very popular. Custard tarts, almond brioche . . ."

Trewelyn turned back to Edwina, a wicked twinkle in his eye. "What tempts you, Miss Hargrove?"

"I shouldn't," she replied. They all sounded wonderful, much more so than the dry tea cakes she'd sampled a few days ago, but her mother's lectures about eating too much in the company of men held her back.

"Please, Miss Hargrove? I owe you something for last night's ordeal."

The waitress's head swerved her way with a bit of a smirk twisting her lips. Just her luck to have one of the former barmaids as a server. Edwina pressed her lips shut.

"One éclair then, but with two forks," Trewelyn told the waitress. Once they were alone again, he leaned across the table toward her. "Oscar Wilde once said, 'The only way to get rid of a temptation is to yield to it. Resist it, and your soul grows sick with longing for the things it has forbidden to itself.'"

Edwina scoffed. "That sounds like an excuse for misbehavior, sir."

He smiled. "And isn't misbehavior the largest temptation of all." His face sobered. "At least it was when I was younger. Now it hasn't the allure that it once did, so you see, Mr. Wilde was right in this."

The luscious cream-filled pastry arrived. Edwina tried to resist sampling, but the spread of rapture across Trewelyn's face when he tasted the chocolate convinced her otherwise. Soon they were both licking chocolate and sweet cream from their lips, the dessert devoured. Trewelyn smiled at her indulgently. "Watching you enjoy yourself is as much a pleasure as the sweet itself."

Flustered, Edwina quickly picked up the folded note to hide her heating cheeks from his view.

"It appears to be gibberish," he said. "Random letters in no perceivable order." He paused a moment. "Do you really think this has some meaning?"

"Yes, of course," she said. "You can tell by the break and repetition of certain letters that this is a code."

"You can make sense of that?" he asked with an incredulous air.

"I could make sense of it if I had the key," she replied.

He looked confused.

"There are many kinds of codes," she explained. "Some are based on numbers, some are based on letters. Some involve inclusion of extra words and phrases, or a reordering of letters.

Some use different types of inks. Based on the grouping of letters, I would guess that this uses a line or phrase from a particular book known to the intended recipient and sender that transcribes the nonsense letters into the intended message. It's an easy code to use but challenging to break unless you know the key." She glanced up at him. "In fact, my brother uses this type of code in his letters to me."

Trewelyn's face twisted into a curious expression, but she wasn't inclined to explain her own family's eccentricities at the moment.

A woman unknown to Edwina passed the table and dropped a lacy handkerchief near Trewelyn. He retrieved it from the floor and stood to return it, earning a softly murmured thank you and what Edwina would call a sultry glance in exchange. He lifted a brow, then returned to his seat.

"Let me show you." Edwina set her annoyance over the interruption aside and pulled her brother's most recent letter from her journal. "My brother uses *Treasure Island* to code his letters to me." She pointed to the top of the letter. "You'll note that he begins with the numbers seventy-three, slash, two, another slash, then one." Using her finger, she pointed out the various components of the code. "The first number represents the page number. It tells me which page in the book to use."

She handed her copy of *Treasure Island* to him, indicating that he should open the book to the directed page. It was fortunate that she'd thought to come prepared just in case Trewelyn needed to see an example. While she'd fretted earlier about his presence, suddenly she was pleased he'd come. "The second number tells me which paragraph to use and the third number tells me which sentence within the paragraph. As Harry—"

"Harry?" he interrupted.

"My brother," she explained. "As he listed the number one, that would mean the code phrase is the first line in the second paragraph."

"'*Hawkins,*'" Trewelyn read aloud. "'*I put prodigious faith in you,*' added the squire." He looked up. "Is that sufficient?"

"Perhaps," Edwina said. "It really depends on the alphabet my brother requires for his letter."

"I don't understand." He shook his head, looking as helpless as a stray pup. Funny how their roles had reversed from last evening. Now she was the one with the knowledge and he the shocked innocent. She hid her smile.

"That's because there's another step." She lifted her journal and untied the scarlet red ribbon that held it closed. "I keep a list of all the letters of the alphabet in a column down a page just for this purpose. Like this." She opened her journal to the page where she had created that very list on the left page. "Then, I list all the unique letters of the code phrase next to it. See, the 'A' of the alphabet lines up with the 'H' of 'Hawkins.' The 'B' of the alphabet lines up with the 'A' of 'Hawkins,' and so forth until I have a unique letter equivalent for each letter of the alphabet. I use this chart to transcribe the letter's code to its English equivalent and then write the decoded message on the opposite page."

"I see," he said. His eyes scanned the page while his brow lifted in a form of admiration. His appreciation of her abilities warmed her as if a purring Isabella had curled up in her lap. She basked in that unexpected pleasure for a moment before suddenly realizing that his gaze was not on her alphabetic listing but on the transcription of the letter itself. She pulled the book abruptly from his hands, then securely tied the ribbon that held the journal closed. "That letter is personal, sir, as is my journal," she scolded.

"Forgive me," he said with wide-eyed contrition. She suspected he was not sorry at all.

She bit her lip, experiencing once again the pull of his soft smile. What had Faith called it? *Charismatic.* She placed the tied journal on the table between them. "It's nothing important," she said, wondering how much he had read. Hopefully, he had only read the beginning of her brother's letter and not her impressions of last night. "It's just private."

"It seems to me that you and your brother must retain the same edition of *Treasure Island* for the key phrase to function properly. For example, while I'm sure you both have copies of the Bible, the various translations and editions would make it unsuitable for a key."

"Exactly." He truly did understand the nature of the code. She tapped the coded message that had fallen from the pillow book. "This is a code with an unspecified recipient. Someone wrote it so that only the correct individual would be able to translate it."

"So there's no way we can decipher this message?"

"I wouldn't say that," Edwina said.

Another embroidered handkerchief fluttered by the table. Trewelyn returned that one as before, with much the same results. Softly spoken words, an exchanged glance, and then he lowered himself to the seat.

"I'm sorry. You were saying that you can perhaps make sense of this message?"

Edwina lowered her gaze to her fingers fidgeting with the red ribbon on her journal, attempting to keep her annoyance in check. Beautiful women with greater talents at attracting a man's attention than she must besiege him on a regular basis. She took a calming breath before continuing. "The messages are written to be decoded . . . just not by the wrong people. If we had the key, it would be easier to decipher, but it's not impossible to translate without it."

He leaned forward, intrigued. "How do we do that?"

Encouraged by the use of "we" and the implied continued association, she leaned forward as well. "In the English language, certain single letters, like the letters 'e,' 't,' 'o,' and 'a,' are used more frequently than others. Thus we can attempt to decipher the note by trying to identify what coded letters are used the most frequently."

"I wouldn't think that would help very much," he said, a frown pushing his lips. "Knowing one or two letters in a word wouldn't give us the full word."

"There's also common two-letter combinations. We can search the coded letter for the repetitious use of the same two-letter pattern that might be 'th' or 'he'—"

"How about the combination 'i' and 's'?"

"Yes, 'is' would be one. It's also a common two-letter

word, beyond the mere combination." She smiled. He was starting to be caught by the challenge. "There are common reversals and three-letter words. If we can determine the pattern by isolating the combinations, we might be able to unlock the other combinations." She leaned back in her chair. "It's a time-consuming affair, but not impossible."

"Can you do it?" he asked, enthusiasm evident.

She hesitated, considering. While she relished the possibility of working with Trewelyn, one concern kept her from accepting the challenge. She held his gaze. "Who are the Guardians?"

His brow lowered. "Why do you ask?"

She softened her tone so as not to be overheard. "A coded message from the Guardians brought me to your library last night. Now we're attempting to decipher another message, perhaps from them, perhaps from someone else. Still, it seems to me that the two events are related. If I'm to assist you in this, I want to know it's for a worthy cause, or if it's for . . . something not so worthy." As much as she wished to embark on this adventure, she needed to know the purpose was just.

He tapped his fingers on her copy of *Treasure Island*. "You wish to know if we are the pirates or the righteous crew."

She nodded, pleased with his analogy. "You've read it?"

"I believe I proved last night that I'm familiar with many books and many cultures." His finger slowly stroked the well-worn binding of the novel. Something about the timbre of his voice and the repeated motion reminded her of the prints of men stroking parts of a woman's body. His simple gesture assumed a more intimate nature, as if he were stroking her intimate places. A shiver slipped down her spine.

"While I can't speak for the nature of the note," Trewelyn said, "or the recipient for that matter, I can assure you that I'm not involved in any nefarious purposes. I would think that if anything, we may have the opportunity to stop wrongdoing, not participate in it ourselves."

He pulled his hand away from the book, severing that intimate connection. Yet he seemed impervious to her thoughts. "For all I know," he continued, "this note could be a listing of the week's menu prepared by my stepmother for the cook."

"Menus are rarely written in code, sir," she said. She narrowed her eyes. "You are avoiding my question. Who are the Guardians?"

Another delicate bit of embroidered linen floated past the table. This time Edwina retrieved the handkerchief, then slapped it into its owner's hand. There were no words or appreciative glances in response.

Trewelyn appeared to suppress a grin before he grew serious again. "Would you care to go for a walk, Miss Hargrove?" he asked. "I believe the fresh air and open space might better serve our purposes."

· Seven ·

THE SLANT OF THE AFTERNOON SUN BEYOND THE
Crescent's windows suggested she should really leave
now to avoid uncomfortable questions when she arrived
home. However, the lure of a potential collaboration with
Trewelyn proved too tempting for a hasty retreat. She accepted his invitation, then collected the bicycle she'd left
outside.

"You rode that contraption?" he asked, his eyes creased
with a grin.

"It's a very practical means of transportation," Edwina
explained. "The modern woman shouldn't need to rely on a
horse and carriage to tend to her affairs."

"That is true," he said, though his expression implied otherwise. "I don't think I'll abandon the carriage just yet."

She carried her journal and book while he pushed the bicycle along as they walked. Something about Trewelyn in
possession of her journal, even to just carry it, seemed unset-
tling. Some things were just too personal.

Hyde Park was resplendent. Even though they remained

in the public eye, they were able to talk without fear of being overheard, or interrupted due to stray handkerchiefs.

"I can't tell you definitively who the Guardians are," Trewelyn finally admitted. "I'd heard of a secret group by that name when I was stationed in Burma. I had no idea that my father was connected in any way to them until you appeared in my library yesterday evening."

"Your father is a member of that group?" She hesitated. "I thought it might have been . . ."

"Me?" He chuckled low beneath his breath. "No, Miss Hargrove. I am not a member, but I believe I may have recognized some of the voices before circumstances called for our hurried removal last night. My father was among them. He and some of his business associates . . . captains in industry, you might say . . . were walking down the passageway toward the library."

She tightened her grip on the books, remembering her near discovery last night and Mr. Trewelyn's swift action to prevent her imminent ruin. "Did I thank you last night for protecting me from detection?"

This time he laughed outright. "Given the means of protection, I'm not certain gratitude is in order. Those prints are explicit at best and hardly suitable for such a respectable and attractive . . . modern woman."

She felt a blush spreading. It was an awkward conversation, but it provided the opportunity she needed. "There was something else in that room besides the woodblock prints . . . ?"

He looked at her in question.

"On the shelves?" she prodded.

"Oh." Awareness brightened his face. "I didn't realize you'd noticed the collection of netsuke."

"Netsuke?" She tested the sound on her tongue. At the rate she was learning about ying, yang, and netsuke, she could be a docent at the Crystal Palace.

"They are fancy carved toggles that can be attached to the obi"—he gestured toward his middle—"the sash. Small boxes or cords attached to the netsuke could be used to carry personal needs."

"Something like a woman's chatelaine?" she asked, recall-ing the contraption her mother sometimes wore with keys and scissors and other household necessities.

"I suppose, although both men and women use a netsuke. They're decorated for various purposes. Some are quite beau-tiful. My father only collects a certain type of netsuke." He leaned closer and dropped his voice. "I can show you an example the next time you visit the gallery that—"

She pushed him back. "Mr. Trewelyn, please! My presence in that chamber was purely accidental. I'm certain proper women never venture into that room."

"You'd be surprised."

Her gaze snapped to his face. "I beg your pardon?" He just smiled in response, and her heart flipped like a fish on a wharf. She glanced away, flustered.

"I'm not one to engage in needless gossip, Mr. Trewelyn." Another lie of a sort. Other women had been to that gallery? She would love to know their names. Not to whisper about, of course, but just to know in whose company she stood. She studied the far trees that bordered a stream in this portion of the park. "These netsuke things, are they expensive?"

"Many are not, but my father's collection is unique, as you can imagine."

She could imagine very well, having studied one of the items from his collection at close range.

"Yes. I suppose compared to the newer, more common netsuke," he said, winking at her, "my father's would com-mand a high price."

Her heart sank. If she could not find the missing piece, she wasn't sure how she could pay for its replacement.

"Why do you ask, Miss Hargrove?" His brow creased. "I don't recall you studying those shelves last night." His brows lifted, and his lids lowered with an invitation to sin. "Are you interested in purchasing one for your personal collection? I'm certain we can come to terms."

She stopped dead in her tracks. Her jaw fell and she stared in disbelief. Had he just made an inappropriate suggestion? She would have slapped him if her arms weren't full with her books. Instead, she placed the books on the seat of the bicycle then jerked the handlebars free from his grip. She pushed the bicycle steadily ahead.

Laughing, he trotted after her. "Forgive me, Miss Hargrove. I forgot with whom I was speaking." She kept her focus straight ahead and refused to look at him. "Please, Edwina. May I call you Edwina?"

She glanced to her side. "No. You may not."

"Edwina, please." He wrestled the handlebars from her and stopped her progress. She might have continued her determined departure if not for the lure of the coded message. Such a challenge and opportunity might not come her way again. She couldn't risk looking at his pleading eyes, not yet. So she turned her back toward him.

"I apologize for my inappropriate humor," he said to her back. "Edwina, please look at me. I'm truly sorry."

That blasted indecent netsuke had placed her in a particular bind. If she admitted to having it, he'd want its return, which she couldn't accomplish at the moment, nor could she pay for it. Her only option would be to thoroughly search her room, then return it unnoticed to the secret chamber, and to do that and test her abilities on the coded letter, she'd have to continue her association with Mr. Trewelyn.

She turned begrudgingly. His finger tilted her chin so she couldn't avoid his eyes. "I promise to be on better behavior, but I need your help with the coded message and I value your friendship too much for you to be angry with me. Please forgive me."

She couldn't resist that pleading expression and suspected he knew as much. She nodded, which earned his wide smile. His fingers lingered on the sensitive skin a moment before he moved his hand.

"Friends?" He waited for her nod again. "Good. Then you should know that friends call me Ashton. Mr. Trewelyn is my father's name."

"Ashton," she repeated. Though she tried to hide her pleasure at being afforded this intimacy with such a notorious character, her lips turned upward nonetheless. She caught his gaze; it was clear he noticed. She cleared her throat. "It appears we have drifted away from the original topic . . . the Guardians?"

"Yes." As her irritation lightened, his smile deepened, and he immediately assumed the task of pushing her bicycle forward once more. "I have gathered from certain innuendo that a secret organization exists that is determined to maintain the superiority of the Crown against all challengers. They have tentacles of smaller groups scattered throughout England. The Guardians may be one of those tentacles, or perhaps it's the larger organization."

Tentacles! An image of that woman and her octopus sprang forefront in her mind. A frisson of sensation shot from her core to her breast and required she exert a conscious effort to keep walking in a cohesive manner.

"I'm relieved the Guardians are a group of good intent," she managed, albeit with difficulty. "Though I'm not certain how a purchase of a book of *that* sort would benefit the Crown."

"What one considers 'good works' often proves inappropriate to everyone else," he counseled. "I would not sing the praises of the Guardians based on a few rumors. We don't know as yet if they are truly involved. This note was meant most likely for an individual, not the entire group. Otherwise, why would it be hidden?"

"Shall we assume then that the note was intended for your father? Wasn't the package addressed to him?"

"But it was opened in the company of others. If the note had been meant specifically for my father, and if he expected such a note to be hidden in the book, wouldn't he have opened the package in private?" He grimaced. "The note conceivably could have been intended for anyone in that room and have slipped their notice. No, I believe to truly understand what is transpiring under my father's roof, we will need to transcribe the note and ascertain for certain for whom it was intended."

"That's liable to take some time," Edwina cautioned. "Without a key, breaking the code will become to a certain extent a function of trial and error. Granted, there are certain letter combination frequencies that may help, and patterns or shapes of letters, but still . . ." She shook her head. "While I'm intrigued by the task, I must warn you that success may not be obtainable. My experience has been limited to translating the very basic sort of coded messages that appear in the personals and those codes to which I already possess a key."

His face brightened. "Could the pillow book itself be some sort of key?"

She shook her head. "I suspect it is only the vehicle. You, of course, are more familiar with such things than I, but I don't recall a single English word on any of those pictures. Of course, I did not look overly long." Her cheeks warmed. She dared to glance at him. "If I may be so bold, why not just ask your father about the note? It may be that he was expecting it. That certainly would provide an opportunity for answers."

"My relationship with my father is . . . difficult." His eyes narrowed on something in the far end of the park. "I thought the distance and time spent with the Rifles might resolve our differences, but it appears I was mistaken."

She could hear strain in his voice. Whatever wedge existed between his father and himself he wished to remain private. "I understand," she sympathized. "You barely know me. I didn't mean to pry, I just wondered—"

"Ashton Trewelyn! Is that you?" A fashionable open landau carriage rolled to a stop beside them. A woman with a stuffed hummingbird on her bonnet addressed him while fairly buried beneath squirming little spaniels. "I thought I'd heard rumors that you'd returned to London, and here you are!"

"Miss Marsh." Ashton doffed his hat.

"It's Lady Sutton now." She laughed. "Much has changed since you left. I've married a viscount." She turned her gaze to Edwina. "And who is this? The two of you were speaking as if you were thick as thieves. I'm not sure you even heard my horse approaching."

"Lady Sutton, may I present Miss Hargrove. We were just discussing the far-reaching influence of certain aquatic creatures." He turned, and unseen by Lady Sutton, winked at her.

Edwina almost bit her tongue to keep a straight face.

"Aquatic creatures! Surely you can aspire to a better conversation than that. Apparently much has changed with you, Ashton, unless, of course, you were discussing mermaids. I can understand your participation in a lengthy discourse on that topic." She laughed gaily at her own humor, then turned toward Edwina. "They call him Casanova for a reason, Miss Hastings. Best you keep your hatpin at the ready."

Edwina felt a subtle change in the man next to her as if he'd tensed, yet she noted he maintained that lazy smile. Perhaps if she hadn't been standing so close, even she would have been fooled to think that the teasing comment had missed its mark.

"Now, Ashton," Lady Sutton continued, "I believe you'll hear more relevant conversation if you attend my little soiree tomorrow evening. Lord Fitzhugh is coming, and I do need someone to lighten the mood."

"Ah my lady, I'm certain the moment you enter the room, the conversation will be light enough to compete with the clouds."

Lady Sutton tittered while Edwina reached to pet the silky smooth head of one of the lapdogs eager to escape the carriage. "They're adorable," she said, allowing another to lick her hand. "What sort of dogs are these?"

"Japanese spaniels, of course," Trewelyn replied with a grin.

"That's right!" Lady Sutton exclaimed. "They're all the rage."

Edwina almost retracted her hand. *Japanese. Again!* Was everything to remind her of last evening and those prints?

"Good. Then I shall see you tomorrow evening. Your Constance is coming. I'm certain she will be grateful of your escort." Lady Sutton glanced at Edwina. "You must come as well, Miss Hardin. It's just a small gathering of friends. Aquatic creatures, indeed!"

"Thank you . . ." Edwina managed, surprised by the sudden invitation. "However, I believe my schedule—"

"Till tomorrow, then." Lady Sutton waved her fingertips and instructed the driver to move on.

Edwina bristled from the snub. Not that she wasn't used to it. She'd heard disdain and soft laughter in others' murmurs at the Crescent about "bluestockings" and "modern women." She didn't fit with the fashionable crowd. She knew that, but it didn't lessen the sting from their words.

Ashton watched the carriage roll away. "It appears we shall be able to continue our conversation tomorrow evening."

"I don't think she truly intends for me to appear," Edwina said. "She couldn't even remember my name." She shook her head. "She was only trying to be polite."

He looked at her. "An invitation is an invitation. Unless her memory has improved substantially during my absence, Lady Sutton most likely mangles everyone's name, except those of her dogs."

She suspected he was just trying to make her feel better. She appreciated the effort but she didn't take him at his word. He had always been accepted by the social strata, had he not? What did he know of the discomfort of appearing in the wrong outfit, or with the wrong companion, or even being born to the wrong family?

"I would have thought that someone brave enough to trespass my father's town house would not let a silly soiree intimidate them," he teased.

"I'm not intimidated," she snapped, though she knew it to be another lie. She was curious about the soirees of the fashionable set. Sarah had told stories of such events, but reading an account in the *Mayfair Messenger* was not the same as attending. Still, she had no wish to be a laughingstock. "I don't wish to impose where I'm not wanted, that's all."

"Then that is easily resolved. I want you there. I find these affairs boring and wearisome." His lips quirked. "I will say this for you, Edwina. You are most definitely not boring."

She wasn't sure how to respond, but the heat in her cheeks might have done that for her. He looked at her as if he expected some response, though. The distant Westminster chimes tolled the hour, reminding her she needed to hurry if she was to arrive before her father and avoid awkward explanations.

"It's getting late," she said. "I must go."

He held her bicycle immobile. "Give me your address."

"My address?" she asked, shocked.

"My stepmother and I will serve as escort. I'll bring the carriage about eight? Just tell me where you live."

She wanted so much to accept, if only because it would give her an excuse to see him again. Pride, however, brought the necessary response to her lips. "That will not be necessary. Good-bye, Mr. Trewelyn. It has been a pleasure making your acquaintance."

She tugged the bicycle free and pedaled off before she yielded to temptation.

ASHTON WATCHED HER RIDE DOWN THE STREET. BLASTED contraptions, those bicycles. They enabled one to arrive and depart much too fast and, for all that, lacked the fine personality of a horse. He wished he was sitting atop one now so he could follow her. Her refusal to give him her address had him flummoxed. He could not recall a time when a young woman refused such essential information. However, if she truly had no wish to see him, knowing her address would be of little value.

He spotted a hansom idling at a nearby stand and made his way toward it. While his leg seemed to have appreciated the exercise, he was loathe to overdo it. As he reached in his pocket to procure some coins for the coachman, his knuckles brushed paper—the coded message. He was no closer to deciphering it now than he was last night. Worse off, he supposed, as he had managed to scare off the only person who could have been of assistance. He had to admit, she was most impressive in her knowledge of deciphering coded material. Now that she had shown him the basics, perhaps deciphering the message was something he could attempt on his own. How difficult could it be if an otherwise ordinary girl could accomplish such a feat?

He gave the driver the fare and climbed into the well-used leather bench seat while thoughts of his recent conversation plagued him. There was something about Edwina that was not ordinary. He couldn't exactly put his finger on it, but no ordinary girl would have responded with such calm to his father's gallery—that much was certain. She even quizzed him about netsuke, something he didn't even think she'd noticed in the chamber. She was most perceptive, this Edwina. To complicate matters, he had never encountered someone so immune to his normally highly effective charm. His teasing fell on deaf ears, forcing him to reveal more of his private circumstances than he was normally wont to do, just to get back into her good graces. Was that what made him jittery in her presence? Was it because she saw past the role everyone had assigned to him? An unexplored territory, that. He half-snorted, alone in the hack. Perhaps that was why she hadn't committed to helping him.

Well he wasn't going to think about her anymore. Not if she was determined not to aid him in this project. He would just put her out of his mind and decipher the message himself, and if that proved impossible, he'd call upon some of his old friends for assistance.

Of course, he'd been surprised to discover that some of his friends from his wild Casanova days no longer roamed the streets of London. Their pursuit of pleasure had brought them to an untimely end. Others had taken a wife, or a mistress, or both, and withdrawn from the wild parties of their youth. The human landscape had changed in his years of self-imposed exile. One name, one old friend, bubbled up through his sad nostalgia. A powerful name. In fact, the name of one of his school chums, who had decided to pursue political aspirations. He might have the sorts of contacts that could shed some light on this mysterious letter.

Ashton used his stick to rap on the roof of the hack. He shouted out a new address to the driver, then settled back for the quick jaunt to one of the more prestigious clubs in London.

· Eight ·

🌿 EDWINA TURNED HER BICYCLE, NOT TOWARD HER home, but toward the offices of the *Mayfair Messenger*. Sarah would still be there. Sarah could help her decide what to do.

"You were invited to one of Lady Sutton's soirees?" Sarah's eyes gleamed with delight. "That's wonderful. I've been hoping she'd send the *Messenger* an invitation. Not everyone does, you know."

"Then you think I should go, even though she couldn't even remember my name for five minutes?"

"She invited you, that's the important thing," Sarah said, inadvertently echoing Ashton's words. "I'm sure she'll remember your smile."

Edwina couldn't remember if she'd actually smiled at the woman. She was too besotted, in awe that someone of an elite social standing was actually speaking with her. "If I had such difficulty in the park, how will I be able to converse with her at a soiree?"

"You won't have to," Sarah assured her. "Be sure to thank

her for the invitation when you arrive and thank her again for the pleasant evening when you depart. The rest of the time you can converse with other people."

Edwina inwardly sighed. As if that wasn't intimidating as well.

Sarah studied her a moment. "How was it exactly that you were introduced to Lady Sutton?" Her eyes narrowed. "Did it have something to do with your activities of last evening?"

That was a heart-stopper. News had apparently traveled quickly. "You know about last evening?"

"Faith told me that the three of you stationed yourselves outside of the Trewelyn household, hoping to discourage some women who never materialized. She mentioned that sometime in the course of the evening you disappeared." Sarah peered down at her through her spectacles. "Really, Edwina. You must be more cautious. Respectable women cannot go traipsing about at all hours of the night without proper escort. Faith and Claire naturally assumed the worst. As would I. I'm not certain of the connection between that disappearance and today's invitation, but I suspect one exists."

"I managed to speak briefly with Mr. Trewelyn last night," Edwina admitted quietly. "I was walking with him in the park when Lady Sutton saw us."

Sarah's lips tightened. "How could you? You know what kind of man he is." Her eyes narrowed, and her voice dropped. "Did he try anything? Have you been compromised?"

Tempted to roll her eyes, Edwina just shook her head. "Nothing happened of that sort. We just talked, that's all. He explained that the ad he placed was for the benefit of another, not himself." She caught Sarah's gaze. "So the Rake Patrol has no reason to discourage respondents."

"And you believed him?" Sarah asked incredulously.

"Yes. I do." And she truly did, she realized. He certainly had the opportunity to take advantage of her in that secret gallery, but he didn't. She didn't wish to admit it to Sarah, but she felt disappointed that he didn't even try. Perhaps Faith's parasol discouraged him . . . although she suspected that Casanova would not let a mere parasol keep him from what he wanted. Which left only one conclusion; he didn't want her.

"Be careful, Edwina," Sarah cautioned. "Many women have been lured to ruination because they believed what a man told them."

"It was not like that." Edwina's lips quirked. "He's not interested in me in that fashion."

Sarah's eyebrow raised in disbelief, bless her heart. At least her friends believed she had allure, even if Ashton did not.

"We talked about breaking codes," Edwina explained in a huff.

"Codes?"

"So you see, nothing happened. He's not interested in anything beyond a mere curiosity about my ability to read codes." The admission hurt. When they were trapped in the secret chamber, she thought she detected a sort of physical attraction, but their afternoon together proved how foolish her imagination had been. "I'm certain Lady Sutton invited me because she didn't wish to appear rude in front of Mr. Trewelyn." She looked away. "After the way I left him in the park, there's a good chance he won't talk to me either."

Sarah just stared at her for a few minutes and shook her head. "Nonsense. Pure nonsense." She fished about behind the counter, then produced a small writing pad, the sort that would fit easily in a reticule. "If no one talks to you, then just take notes. Write down what food is served, how many people attend, what they're wearing, all the little interesting things that can be turned into a story for the column."

"A newspaper story? Won't that make Lady Sutton angry? It seems so . . . imposing."

"No one is angry when an event is reported in the *Messenger*. It adds a certain swagger to the occasion." She waved her hand in the air to indicate the event was frivolous. "Now, tell me, what do you plan to wear?"

THE HANSOM STOPPED ON PALL MALL IN FRONT OF THE Reform Club, one of the largest political clubs in London. Ashton went inside, produced a card, and inquired after Lord Rothwell. He didn't wait long before his old friend appeared.

"Trewelyn! I can't believe it's you. I'd heard you'd gone off with the King's Royal Rifles, and quite frankly, I thought I'd never see you again." He pumped Ashton's hand, then stepped back. "Let me look at you!"

Ashton smiled thinly. "I almost didn't return. If it hadn't been for the heroic action of a man in my squadron, I might not be standing here now." He glanced at his walking stick that helped bear the weight of his left side. "Or rather, leaning here right now."

The comment drew laughter from Rothwell, which was the point. Ashton really preferred not to talk about those days in Burma. Some things were best kept to oneself, or only discussed with men who had survived similar events.

Rothwell waved him forward. "Come in, come in, have a drink. There're others here you might remember."

"Thank you for seeing me. I wasn't certain of my reception," Ashton said hesitantly.

Rothwell laughed. "You can't be serious, man. Everyone remembers Casanova with great fondness." He leaned close to Ashton's ear. "Or envy." He smacked Ashton's shoulder. "Oh, the parties we had!"

Ashton grimaced, preferring people forgot about those lost years of wild abandonment. In the end, they were causing him more pain than any lasting delight. He stopped his forward progress, causing Rothwell to turn back with surprise. "Perhaps I can meet the others another time," Ashton said, deflating some of Rothwell's buoyancy. "Is there someplace we can speak privately?"

"Yes, of course," Rothwell said with a more serious demeanor. He ordered two glasses of brandy to be placed in the small library, a favored private meeting room. Once the drinks were delivered and the door closed, Rothwell turned to Ashton. "So what is it you wish to talk about?"

"Are you familiar with a group called the Guardians?"

Rothwell's brandy snifter paused midair. His lips thinned. "Why do you ask?"

Ashton found a comfortable chair so as to rest his leg. "Answering a question with a question is never a good sign." He sipped his drink. "Let us say that the details of my discovery of the group's existence aren't important. I need to know of their workings."

Rothwell tipped his head as if considering the consequences of sharing information. The scale must have weighed in Ashton's favor. "Have you ever noticed how all the riches and treasures from the world over find their way to London? Statues from ancient Rome, jewels from Egypt, portions of temples from Greece?"

"England has far-reaching explorations and political concerns. I supposed someone collected those objects, like you at one time with your butterflies and plants."

Rothwell smiled. "You remember that? Those days were long ago. However, the comparison is a good one. The Guardians are collectors, but they are a secretive bunch."

"Then there's nothing illegal or wrong about their activities," Ashton said, relieved.

"I didn't say that," Rothwell corrected. "Not all collections are harmless. Every garden has a poisonous species."

"What are you trying to say?"

"That there are rumors that more than artifacts travel the established trade routes to the Guardians. It's said that an abundance of information travels as well."

"I would imagine that some information naturally would—"

"Not this kind of information," Rothwell interrupted. "I really can't say more. But in light of our history, I will warn you of this. The Crown has an interest in the Guardians' activities, a very close interest. If you suspect you are talking to a member, be careful of what you say." Rothwell swirled the liquid in his glass, a half smile lifting his lips. "Even you couldn't charm your way out of prison."

"I appreciate the warning," Ashton replied, though he felt as if a stone's weight of concern settled on his chest. Could the message Edwina discovered be a communication between spies? Was his father involved in some treasonous action?

Rothwell studied him a moment. "I must say, Ash, you

seem a changed man since your military service. Far more serious than before, I believe."

"Bullets have a way of making one reassess their priorities." Ashton's lips tightened. "If not for the act of another, I would not be standing here today."

Rothwell seemed to consider this before he placed his snifter on the fireplace mantel. "I suppose I could say the same of you."

Ashton frowned, confused.

"If you hadn't taken the blame for that incident at Eton, my life would have taken a decidedly different turn," Rothwell said. "You wouldn't have been tossed out on your bum had you told the truth about who took the pound notes from Professor Melachor's desk."

"Perhaps," Ashton agreed. "They certainly had no difficulty believing it was me."

Rothwell frowned. "Why did you do it?"

"What?" Ashton scoffed. "Allow a boyhood prank to destroy the record of our future prime minister?"

Rothwell laughed. "My ambitions were never that high."

"Well, they could have been. Even then everyone suspected you had a grand and glorious future in the parliament. No one had grand allusions for me." Not even his father, who accepted the news of another school ousting with little more than a dismissive wave. "I correctly assumed there would be no repercussions for me." One would have had to care for there to be repercussions.

"Perhaps they knew you would land on your feet like the proverbial cat." He chuckled low. "I've never forgotten your generosity that day, so consider this advice a small repayment on that debt. Stay away from the Guardians."

Ashton nodded, but he knew, under the circumstances, that piece of advice would be impossible to follow.

THE MOMENT SHE RETURNED HOME, EDWINA STOWED her bicycle in the back of their house—modest in comparison to the Trewelyn town house—then slipped quietly inside so as to change for dinner before her absence was noted. She hadn't counted on her father's keen hearing.

"Edwina, my dear, would you step inside my study for a moment?"

This did not bode well. For the most part, her father ignored her except as it related to a possible match with his highly prized clerk. She removed her hat and hung it on a peg, then smoothed her skirt and hoped that his summons was not to report of the progress of marital arrangements.

Her father sat behind his desk flanked by walls of law texts and history books. Not an adventure novel or explorer biography to be had, not in that library. While her father maintained an interest in medieval artifacts, his books on the period focused on wars and weapons and nothing as fanciful as the Arthurian legends. "I want to show you my latest acquisition."

She saw a paper with a design of a circular labyrinth on his desk. "Are we putting a maze in the garden?" she asked, quickly ascertaining that only two of the four entrances would lead to the center.

"Not that." He hastily removed the paper to a drawer, then held up a brass circular disk with an assortment of letters and numbers etched into the outer ring. As she looked closer, she noted a second ring with letters and numbers.

"Do you know what this is?" her father asked. "It's nearly four hundred years old." She could feel his intent study, but she wasn't certain why she would generate his interest.

"I don't know what one would call it, but I know how it would be used," she said. "The letters would make it a transcribing device. May I?" She took the disk from his fingers, feeling the heavy weight of it. The rings did not turn as easily as she imagined they once had. Some sort of lubricant might return the artifact to a working order.

"What do you suppose it was used for?" he asked.

"Sending secret messages," she replied instantly. "One letter on each ring would be the key. Once they were aligned, a coded message could be deciphered." *Christopher!* She hadn't considered that Ashton's coded message might require the use of such an instrument. "Of course, both the person sending the message and the person receiving it would have to have the same device, and both would need to know the key letters." The key. It always came down to the key.

He looked at her in amazement. "Then it is true. Walter told me you could unscramble the coded messages in the agonies."

She laughed lightly. "Most of those codes are very basic, just like the ones the boys and I used when we played pirates. Of course, we thought they were brilliantly difficult back then." She attempted to twist the outer ring. "This, however, would generate a very difficult message to decipher." She glanced up. "Walter knows I read the personals?"

"Something one of your friends said alerted him to your abilities."

She grimaced. "I imagine he didn't approve." She handed the coding device back to her father.

He smiled benevolently. "The idea may have frightened him initially, but he'll adjust." He glanced at his pocket watch. "Dinner should be ready shortly. You should go along and change."

"Thank you, Father." She left the study, relieved that nothing along the lines of a pending engagement had been mentioned. Yes, Walter would be frightened by a pursuit that he didn't share. Perhaps her deciphering talent would keep her free just a little bit longer.

THE FOLLOWING NIGHT, SHE PREPARED FOR LADY SUTton's soiree.

"Edwina, perhaps you should try this." Her mother laid one of her own gowns on the bed. "While your gowns were appropriate for your season years ago, fashions have changed. I suppose I have been deficient in not insisting your wardrobe stay current with the times," she said, looking askance, "but there hadn't been a need before."

It was true. The academic affairs Edwina preferred— lectures, exhibitions, and poetry readings—had not required the same apparel as a society soiree. Walter had no interest, or time it seemed, to suggest they attend fancier venues. In reaction to the invented theater invitation, her mother had ordered new gowns, but they would not be ready in time for this evening's event.

"This is so beautiful." Edwina fingered the delicate pink silk gown with leg-of-mutton sleeves. "Are you certain you won't mind?"

Her mother shook her head. "The beading on the bodice is designed to catch the light and emphasize a more youthful bosom than mine. The waist is too tight to be comfortable for me, but may be too large for you. That doesn't matter. Kathleen can pin the excess so it won't show."

But it did, which would not have bothered Edwina at all, but managed to cause a world of concern for her mother.

"I have a solution," she exclaimed and dashed off to her room. Meanwhile Edwina studied herself in the mirror. She had to admit she'd forgotten the thrill of dressing for a special evening. The creamy silk had a luminous sheen that bloomed in her cheeks. The high neckline had a V-plunge in the center front that exposed a small bit of skin. Hardly anything scandalous, as ball gowns would have exposed much more, but to a young woman who wore nothing but high-collared blouses, the flash of skin felt decadent. More astonishing than that was the realization that she liked it.

"Here it is." Her mother returned with a colorful array in her arms. "I purchased this at the Japanese exhibition last year. The fabric is exquisite and the pink in the cherry blossoms matches the dress perfectly." She draped the light-as-a-feather scarf over Edwina's arms in such a manner as to hide the pinched gathers at her waist. "As long as you don't raise your arms overly much, that should do nicely."

Edwina laughed. "If I raise my arms, I'm liable to be stabbed with Kathleen's pins."

"I also found this." Her mother draped a necklace around Edwina's neck. "Your father gave this to me several years ago." Small cherry blossoms flashed in the V-opening of the dress. "At the time he told me cherry blossoms stood for something . . ."

"The ephemeral nature of existence," Edwina murmured, almost hearing Ashton's voice in her ear, whispering about the need to experience pleasure before it became too late. A shiver unrelated to the temperature of the room teased her rib cage. She recalled his observation that the clothing worn by the people in the prints revealed much about the individual. What did the colorful scarf and the delightful necklace whisper about her?

Her mother looked at her strangely. "I just thought it was pretty."

"The flowers look lovely on you, miss," Kathleen said. "Just the thing for that dress."

"Mr. Thomas will be most impressed, dear," her mother observed. "He must be taking you somewhere special." Her eyes glistened.

"Mr. Thomas is not my escort this evening, Mother. Lady Sutton has invited me to an evening party."

Her mother gasped. "Lady Sutton! However did that transpire?" Her gaze narrowed. "You must have been with that newspaper woman."

"Sarah?"

"That's the one. An invitation at this late conjuncture is not one issued in sincerity. You should have refused," she lectured.

Her mother wasn't saying anything she didn't already know. The proper thing would have been to decline the invitation and suggest she had other obligations, but Edwina knew another invitation wouldn't be forthcoming. If she was to have a glimpse of high society, this could well be her last chance.

"Am I to assume you didn't decline?" her mother asked.

As the answer was obvious, Edwina didn't respond.

Her mother sighed. "I can't really blame you. I'm rather curious about those society affairs myself." She fussed about the dress. "You'll be sure to tell me all about it—the clothes, the topics of conversation, who looks to be wearing a wig . . ."

"Mother!" Edwina laughed, recognizing that as much as her mother disapproved of Sarah's occupation, she still read her columns.

"Just because I'm older doesn't mean I'm less curious," her mother replied, studying her own reflection in the mirror. She patted a stray hair in place. "Now, who will be escorting you to this affair?"

"I'm a modern woman, Mother. A modern woman doesn't require a man to take her anywhere. Sarah attends parties on behalf of the *Messenger*, and she hasn't an escort."

"You might be a modern woman, but I don't think it's safe for a young woman to be traipsing about the city without protection. If Mr. Thomas won't accompany you—"

"He wasn't invited, Mother. He can't very well escort me if he wasn't invited—"

"Then I shall be your chaperone." After one final glance, she tugged on her bodice before turning toward Edwina. "There's no reason for that shocked expression. I'm certain Lady Sutton knew you could not attend without accompaniment. To think otherwise would be . . . improper. I'll blend in with the other matrons and make sure you aren't approached by the wrong people. You won't even know that I'm there." She dashed out of the room, but her voice drifted back down the passageway. "Lady Sutton! Oh, the possibilities!"

Edwina sincerely doubted her mother would go unnoticed. And she could accurately predict Ashton would be designated as not suitable. So the only man with whom she wished to converse would be denied to her, while there'd be no restrictions on the men who held no interest. Her stomach already simmered with turmoil. She wished she could stay home with the agonies.

· Nine ·

THE MOMENT ASHTON CROSSED THE SUTTON THRESH-
old, nostalgia rushed at him with the force of a cavalry
charge then wrapped about him like a prodigal son. Little had
changed from his Casanova years, except then he felt honored
to have Constance by his side. Now he was embarrassed.
Everyone in this room knew of their earlier entanglement. He
could almost hear their sneers behind his back. If it weren't
for little Matthew, he'd leave this all behind and go somewhere
where he had no history, and no stepmother to remind him
of what he'd once been.

The current crop of society beauties turned at his entrance,
then tittered behind lace and feather fans. The matrons, the
lovelies from past seasons that had successfully snared a wedding ring, were more blatant with their unspoken invitations.
Ashton grimaced, remembering having read an article in the
Mayfair Messenger about some secret language of fans. No
secret dialogue was needed here. Not while women understood the power of a bold smile and a seductive stare.

He inhaled sharply, letting the combined taste of flowers,

perfume, and sweat settle on the back of his throat. "I need a drink."

"Your father would have insisted you dance the first dance with me," Constance murmured, before adding discreetly, "had he thought of it." She held out her gloved wrist, presenting him with a dangling dance card.

"Even in your self-absorbed existence, I would have assumed you had noted that my stick is more than a nod to fashion," Ashton grumbled. "I've accompanied you out of respect for my father's wishes. That should be enough. You'll have to hawk your wares to some other fool blinded by your finery."

She pushed out her lower lip in a pout. "Ashton, I'm hurt that you should say such an awful thing. Your father—"

"Do not play the martyr with me, Constance," he interrupted. "I have no delusions that yours was a love match. You might have convinced my father that you've come for the female entertainment afforded by this gathering, but I know better."

He surveyed the crowd. Unlike earlier years, Ashton discovered he had no interest in the seductive matrons. Though he had no doubt that he could play with the best of them, he'd lost interest in flirtatious games. Instead he longed for conversation, serious conversation, not suggestive banter. An image of Edwina flashed in his mind, but she had already said she wouldn't attend. Pity that. However, judging from the omnivores disguised in fancy silks and satins, hers was the prudent decision. Already he craved the distance alcohol would bring. He descended a few steps into the ballroom. "If you'll excuse me, I'm in search of Lord Sutton's brandy."

"Go on," Constance sneered, "ruin some willing innocent's reputation. That is your special talent, is it not?"

Ashton stopped midstep on his descent. Five years and still he shouldered a rake's reputation. He had thought that a rich wife would resolve his current residence situation, but he found he hadn't even the desire to pursue that. He glanced back at Constance. "I suppose it is. However, after so many years away from this den of vipers, I'm shamefully out of practice."

• • •

So many patterns, repetitions, consistencies — all viewed from the steps above the ballroom. Colors met, converged, dispersed. So many feathered headdresses bobbed in a choppy rhythm that Edwina thought an aviary cage must have been opened to a field of grain. The men clumped in groups, as did the women. Even age seemed to play a part. All this she saw with alarming clarity, because as anyone who was familiar with patterns would note, she did not fit a single one. She did not belong in this particular gathering.

Their clothes were different. Jewels suspended on sparkling gold decorated their necks and arms, not simple cloisonné flowers. No scarves draped the arms of the other guests. Edwina touched the fresh roses tucked in her coif, not the more popular ostrich plume. Another reminder that she was an outsider. So be it. She patted her reticule, feeling for the small notebook. Even if she were an outsider, she could at least be a productive one.

"Edwina, are you certain we were invited?" her mother whispered harshly. "They don't seem particularly friendly."

"No," Edwina agreed, wondering why she had wanted to come. "They don't."

She spied Ashton on the far side of the room, speaking to a woman who seemed anxious to press up against him as if he were a tasty morsel and she one of Lady Sutton's dogs. The woman fluttered a somewhat distinctive fan, holding it as if it were a barrier to separate them from the rest of the crowd. There was something familiar about that fan, but the sight of Ashton in an elegant morning coat chased all logical thoughts from her mind. Her throat tightened even more than her snug corset.

Lady Sutton separated from a group of guests and approached Edwina. She smiled as if she were welcoming a long lost cousin.

"I'm so pleased you could join us, Miss . . . ?"

"Hargrove," Edwina supplied, embarrassed about this verification that she was truly not expected.

"Hargrove. Thank you. I'm so horrid with names, you know. But faces . . . faces I remember. And I shall always remember yours as one of the many connected with dear Ashton."

A little twist of the knife—yes, that's how it felt. So she was "one of the many," was she? But then she was familiar with his reputation. *Casanova, indeed.* She reminded herself that if she were here with romantic aspirations then that little comment might indeed hurt. But she was here to observe, she reminded herself, to experience a lifestyle beyond her reach— and Walter's, she added absently. Yes, this was bound to be her only high-strata social gala and she wouldn't let her host spoil it. Lady Sutton snapped open a fan that, Edwina noted, had a remarkable resemblance to the one the woman held across the room.

"And I see you've brought . . ."

"Lady Sutton, may I introduce my mother, Mrs. Hargrove."

"I'm certain you understand," her mother explained. "A young unmarried woman should never travel about without a chaperone. Don't you agree, Lady Sutton? I knew that you'd be one to observe the proprieties one expects at affairs of this sort."

Lady Sutton, a woman not much older than Edwina herself, turned to her with a sympathetic look.

"What an unusual fan," Edwina remarked. "Are those Japanese figures?"

Lady Sutton smiled. "This fan? Not so unusual, I would think. I've had this for about eight years now. Japanese is all the rage, you know?" She leaned close. "I would imagine you'll have one yourself before long."

She stepped back before Edwina could ask for an explanation, then motioned to one of the older women for an introduction. She left the three of them alone while she attended to a new arrival. Edwina smiled and made small talk. Her mother launched into enthusiastic conversation with everyone she met, allowing Edwina to be quiet and observe. One person would introduce them to the next and in such a way she navigated the room.

An ancient man passed Edwina on to a beautiful woman with the tiniest waist she'd ever seen and . . . a Japanese print fan. "Mrs. Trewelyn, allow me to introduce Mrs. Hargrove and her lovely daughter. I'm certain Miss Hargrove would much prefer conversation with someone closer to her own age than myself."

"Mrs. Trewelyn?" Edwina repeated, recognizing the woman she'd seen with Ashton when she spied upon him in the park. It was true then. He was married, after all. She could almost see Sarah gloating while her own heart sank.

"Yes," the woman responded absently while searching the room beyond Edwina's shoulder. "Have we met? I don't recall."

"We've not been introduced before, but I have made the acquaintance of your—"

"Constance, there you are." Edwina recognized Ashton's voice. He joined their circle and smiled at Edwina. "And Miss Hargrove. I see you've met my stepmother."

"Mother?" Edwina repeated with a gasp. The woman appeared to be decades younger than her own, even with the frown she'd directed toward Ashton.

"Stepmother," Trewelyn repeated, emphasizing the first syllable. He turned toward the wasp-waisted woman. "The current wife of my father." Edwina detected a tone of derision, as apparently had his stepmother. Her eyes narrowed slightly.

The censure left Ashton's voice as quickly as it was initiated. "You won't mind if I steal Miss Hargrove away for a moment, will you? I have a private matter to discuss."

Edwina glanced toward her mother, but she was distracted by another acquaintance.

"Be careful, Ashton," his stepmother said. "This one does not have your experience. You may find yourself caught in a trap from which even your father can't extricate you."

Edwina's ire rose. They spoke of her as if she weren't standing in front of them, and the woman's insinuations were less than flattering. Ashton gripped her elbow with his strong fingers and guided her to a less populated part of the room. The stares of many of the women they passed burned into her back, and the tittering behind raised fans found its way to her ears. She could hear their censure. She didn't belong here.

"I'm pleased you changed your mind," Ashton said, the strong odor of brandy scenting his breath. "We have unfinished business." His eyes crinkled at the corners while a smile played about his lips. "Business begun in a most provocative setting."

In spite of her efforts to appear worldly and cosmopolitan, she felt heat rise in her cheeks at his reference to their meeting in the secret gallery. His eyes downcast and hidden from view, he fingered the smooth silk of her scarf. "Perhaps my stepmother is mistaken about your lack of experience."

She stiffened. At the moment, she wished she had one of those Japanese fans; she had a strong temptation to whack him with it. "I'm a—"

"Modern woman. Yes, you've told me as much." He raised his gaze, and she was struck by the flattering and captivating heat in his eyes. This was not the Ashton she'd become accustomed to. This, she imagined, was the rake of whom she'd been warned. He moved a fraction closer. "I see that you're wearing cherry blossoms. Only we know the meaning of that fragile flower. Are you telling me you wish to embrace life's pleasures?"

His gaze held her transfixed while her knees melted like fresh butter on a warm muffin. If he moved his hand from her elbow, she would collapse about his feet in a puddle of pink silk and rose petals. She should run from him. She should signal her mother. This was the seductive power the Rake Patrol had decided to fight, but at the moment, she hadn't a fighting bone in her body.

His eyes widened, and he shook his head lightly as if he had been captured in a similar trance as herself. "Nevertheless, this is neither the time nor place to discuss such . . . accommodations." He locked his fingers behind his back, while Edwina suddenly mourned the loss of his touch. "Will you join me on the terrace? I thought we might resume our discussion of this afternoon to solve the cipher in the note you found."

It was a letdown, shifting from that magical moment when he held her enthralled and spoke nonsense, to this more ordinary conversation about a topic she knew too well. While she had always enjoyed a certain stimulation in the solving and sharing associated with the secret of a cipher, she enjoyed discussing the process less so. She shouldn't be surprised Ashton had rescued her from that uncomfortable conversation with his stepmother to challenge her talents in this area. While his interest in the cipher and not herself was disappointing, she was grateful for the opportunity to escape the censure of so many eyes. Looking about the room for her mother, she found her happily chatting with a group of matrons. Even though she knew her mother wouldn't approve of her leaving the room, she nodded her consent. "I don't belong here."

His lips tightened as he surveyed the room. "Little has changed since I left five years ago. I would have preferred not belonging so well."

It was a strange reply that made little sense to her. He was so readily accepted in this gathering; why would that displeasure him? He led her toward the veranda door. "Why did you leave so many years ago?" she asked.

"You met my stepmother?"

She nodded.

"Five years ago, I thought Constance was to be my fiancée. Before I had the opportunity to propose, my father announced she had accepted his offer of marriage." They stood on a stone patio in view of the occupants of the ballroom.

Edwina gasped. "Your fiancée married your father? Why would she do such a thing?"

"I have my suspicions, but didn't stay around to ask. I left immediately and joined the King's Royal Rifles." He gazed up at the skies overhead. "Five years . . . I thought my reputation would have been forgotten in five years."

"You wanted them to forget?"

"Bullets change a man." He continued to stare at the stars. "Have you ever studied the stars, Edwina? I studied them through a spyglass until I took it apart."

The man was full of revelations. "Why did you take apart a spyglass?"

He stared at the stars, lost in the heavens. "Hmmm . . . ?

I wanted to see how it worked. It wasn't very useful for look-ing at stars, you know. Not enough light to collect in the lens, but it did add a certain character to the moon." He smiled, letting his fingers circle overhead, as if they were stirring the heavenly brew. "The constellations are known by different names in India and Burma, and their placement is altered, but they still appear with the same reassuring regularity." His hand paused. "That one is called—"

"The saucepan," Edwina completed with pride. "My broth-ers taught me how to use it to locate Polaris, the North Star." She followed the line established by the star pattern, and pointed with her finger. "There it is."

"Well done." His breath warmed the back of her neck. With her head tilted toward the heavens, she hadn't noticed that he'd moved behind her. A delicious heat pooled in her rib cage. He reached from behind her and tenderly directed her arm toward two sparkling stars near Polaris. "And do you know what those two are called?"

She could barely breathe, much less think. His touch on her bare skin reverberated with delectable intensity all the way to her throat. She simply couldn't form the words. He might be interested in her solely for her knowledge of ciphers, but his touch still made her pulse race.

"The brightest one is Kochab, but together they are referred to as the Guardians," he said, a wistfulness in his voice. "An older and more benign group, I'm afraid, than the one you encountered in my father's library."

She turned to search his eyes, which had assumed the weightier seriousness of earthbound objects. "Have you learned something?"

He shook his head, the magical experience of shared star-gazing clearly faded. "Just that there might be reason to sus-pect the note contains secrets of interest to the Crown, or it might be something of a more personal matter. Either way, you need to know that transcribing that letter might place you in jeopardy."

"What sort of jeopardy?" Edwina asked, a new flutter in her breast. The very word encompassed excitement, adventure.

"I'm not certain," he said, exasperation clear in his voice. He toyed with her fingers, his eyes downcast. "I don't know what the letter contains, of course, but if it's national secrets"—he glanced up, capturing her gaze—"you need to be aware of that."

Did he honestly think she wasn't already in a form of jeopardy? Perhaps not of the sort encountered by translating state secrets, but jeopardy nonetheless. Her heart raced to be standing with him on a shadowy veranda while the ladies of a higher social station seethed with jealousy on the other side of the wall. She'd recognized their dagger glances as he led her outside. Would her involvement with Ashton jeopardize the rather boring yet secure future her parents had planned for her? Would she be able to repair any harm to her reputation? While she realized his suggestion of danger related to a more physical variety, her involvement with him was dangerous in and of itself. Dangerous in ways only a woman, dependent on a man for her future, could appreciate.

The hands holding hers offered acceptance. His eyes pleaded for her assistance, while his words dangled an enticement of adventure as if it were a scrumptious chocolate-covered éclair offered as a treat. Within his gaze, thoughts of security and reputation vanished and, as she had before, she assaulted the sweet with her fork waving. How could she not?

"I understand," she said. "Whatever we discover, I promise I shall keep your secrets safe."

She tilted her head as if she had just exchanged a vow of a different nature. He stepped closer, exchanging his grip on her hands for her waist.

"Then we'll meet again?" he asked, his lips close enough to press a whisper to her own.

"The Crescent. Tomorrow at two," she replied. "You should understand. This could take months."

"Then I shall meet you for months," he managed before his lips met hers.

•   •   •

HE SHOULDN'T BE DOING THIS, KISSING SWEET EDWINA with a nest of vipers and gossipmongers so close at hand. But he couldn't help himself. If there was one thing he knew how to do, it was to kiss a woman senseless. She offered her lips, and instinct took over. After he pressed her pliant lips in a gentle marriage of breath, he had intended to withdraw, but her soft moan pulled him closer. He almost wished she'd push him back as she had earlier, before his rakish talents had completely engaged his sensibilities. Edwina had values. Edwina had morals. She saved women from the likes of rogues like him. Yet his tongue gently parted her lips, then deeply sampled all she offered. And offer she did.

Her tongue timidly stroked his, sending a jolt of heat straight to his groin. He gripped her tighter to deepen the kiss, but then felt the jab of a pin . . . or perhaps it was the prickling of Constance's voice.

"I thought I'd find you out here, luring some innocent to her ruination."

Interrupted, he slowly withdrew, trailing the tip of his nose lightly up Edwina's cheek. "Go away, Constance."

"Did he tell you about the constellations?" the intruder continued. "Did he tell you your eyes rivaled the stars?" His stepmother laughed, a sound full of spite and little humor.

Ashton rested his forehead on Edwina's, then snapped at Constance, "Go inside. I'll be there momentarily."

The sound of her retreating footsteps faded before he stepped away. While Edwina's unexpected response to his kiss made him yearn to continue his exploration, the cool night air shocked him back to reality.

"Don't worry. Constance won't say anything." His finger followed the path of her gold chain and lifted the cloisonné cherry blossom on his forefinger. "Not that such an indiscretion would concern my Mistress of Cherry Blossoms." He smiled. "I know you, Miss Hargrove. You are a modern woman who rides bicycles and breaks conventions as easily as breaking my poor devoted heart."

Edwina stepped back, covering the necklace with her hand. Her lip trembled. Did he just call her a mistress? Was that the result of dropping her guard for the sake of her curiosity? That was not her intent. While she wasn't rushing into marriage the way others felt she should, she had no intention of being anyone's mistress.

"I need to go," she said, backing away. "My mother will be worried if she doesn't see me inside."

She turned and fled back to the ballroom, reminding herself that her future did not lie with the likes of the Trewelyns of the world. He would eventually choose a woman with a tiny waist and a feather in her hair. Edwina's future would be a stable sort of imprisonment with Walter. She pressed her fingers to lips that still tingled from Ashton's kiss. At least she'd have the memory of a kiss from the most handsome man in Mayfair to sustain her in that incarceration.

"Don't be deceived, my dear." Edwina turned to discover Ashton's stepmother had moved to her side. "Ashton has no interest in anything other than stealing your virtue. Believe me, I know." She stepped closer. "I'm telling you this for your own good. He's known as Casanova for a reason. Ashton Trewelyn is nothing but a rake, and he will break your heart."

Edwina paused for a moment, appreciating the irony that she was being counseled to avoid a rake and not the other way around. When had her life become so twisted? "I appreciate your concern," Edwina said, not wishing to offend the woman. "But I believe there is more to your stepson than you perceive."

"Has he presented you with a fan?" Her brows lifted. "A Japanese fan?"

That was the second mention of a fan. Edwina shook her head, pondering the repetition. "It is of little concern, though. I'm not so foolish as to believe my future lies there."

Victory flashed in the woman's eyes. Edwina spotted her mother at the far end of the ballroom speaking to Lady Sutton. She excused herself from further conversation with the disagreeable Mrs. Trewelyn, then crossed the room to rejoin her mother and thank Lady Sutton for the invitation.

It took several moments to extricate her mother from various conversations. Eventually, they climbed the stairs, only to encounter Ashton standing in the foyer. Edwina made the introductions and watched as he teased a smile from her mother with his observations of her youth and beauty. Edwina felt her own lips lift in a grin. Ashton Trewelyn could charm the stars from the sky. Was it any wonder that he had managed to charm a kiss from her? He pulled her aside, a short distance from her mother. "Tomorrow then? At the Crescent?" He took her hands in his.

Before she could reply, a commotion at the door pulled their attention. Walter marched toward her with a rage she'd rarely seen. His brows pulled together to form one thunderous line. "You . . ." He glowered at Ashton with icy accusation. "You filthy, lecherous scoundrel. Unhand her immediately."

· *Ten* ·

ASHTON SHOVED HER BEHIND HIM IN A HEROIC EF-fort to shield her from Walter's reach. But Edwina knew Walter posed no threat. Not to her. She stepped out from behind Ashton's protection. "Walter. What are you doing here?"

"Stay out of this, Edwina. You don't know what sort of man he is. You shouldn't be here, and most certainly you shouldn't be with him." His finger shook as he pointed at Ashton. His voice dripped with acid. "If you've injured her in any way—"

"Walter, stop this," Edwina hissed. "Your accusations are more injurious than his actions. People are starting to notice." With her mother's assistance, the two of them managed to push Walter out the front door.

"I commend you for your concern for Miss Hargrove," Ashton said from the open doorway. "I have no intention to harm her in any way. You have my word on that."

"From what I've heard, your word has little value," Walter yelled before the door closed.

"How dare you!" Edwina punched his arm. "I receive an invitation to an affair the likes of which I could only dream of attending, and you rush in hurling insults with absolutely no basis."

"I have basis," he grumbled.

"Rude behavior never has basis," her mother scolded. "Why are you here and not my husband? He was to escort us home."

"He sent me instead." Walter glared at Edwina. "And it's a wise thing he did."

Edwina took a breath. "I understand Mr. Trewelyn has a reputation, but I think much of what is rumored about him are exaggerations and untruths."

"He certainly acted the gentleman to me," her mother insisted before accepting Walter's assistance into the waiting carriage. Edwina shrugged off Walter's hand and followed her mother into the dark interior.

"Perhaps the gossip is true and you refuse to see the truth of it," Walter said, settling opposite her. The carriage lurched forward, then gently swayed with the pull of the horses. After a few moments, the lulling motion seduced her mother into soft snores.

"Tell me," Edwina whispered so as to avoid waking her mother. "Tell me what you think you know."

"I know my sister is dead and he's the cause of it," Walter replied, keeping his voice low as well.

"He's the cause?" Her voice squeaked. "How can that be? You told me your older sister died in an accident . . . alone."

"It wasn't an accident. She committed suicide."

The words had the impact of a slap in the face. She heard her own gasp, then tried to see Walter's face in the dark. She couldn't make out specifics. Her voice mellowed. "I'm so sorry. That must have been devastating."

Walter turned his face to the window. "It was. We don't speak of it. Margaret always wanted to make the acquaintances of her betters, the young lords and their fancy ladies. She stole out of the house one night to attend a party at the invitation of a fellow who'd been sweet on her. Her clothing was torn when she came home, and she never acted the same. Two months later her body was fished from the Thames."

A chill raced down Edwina's spine. It hadn't even been a decade since the courts ruled self-murder either criminal behavior or insanity. Such designations as those could ruin a family. It was surprising Walter confessed this to her as even he would certainly carry a stigma from the event. A lump solidified in her throat. For Walter to mention this must mean . . .

"Was it Trewelyn?"

Walter shook his head. "But the bastard did his dirty work at one of Trewelyn's parties, that much is certain." He scowled at her across the confining interior. "That's why you can't be in his company."

The lump dissipated. She could draw breath again. Ashton himself was not at fault. "I don't think he's the same man he was then, Walter. People do change."

The carriage slowed and rocked to a stop in front of the Hargrove residence, jarring her mother awake. Walter helped her exit the carriage. This time Edwina accepted his offer of a steadying arm in her own departure.

Walter held her in place momentarily, while her mother made her way to the front door. He tightened his hold, then crushed his lips to hers. The kiss, if one could call it that, was wet, painful, and generated none of the reaction she had felt with Ashton.

Walter pulled back, a glint in his eye. "Don't be a fool, Edwina. This isn't a game."

AFTER A QUICK STOP AT THE SHOP OF THOMAS HARRIS & Son, Ashton headed toward the Crescent, eager to rise to the challenge of deciphering the letter. Eager, he corrected, to use his mind for something other than finding ways to utilize the passing days. He missed the structure of the military, the purpose. It was clear he had no purpose here at home, other than to alleviate his father from escorting Constance to

various insipid social functions and engaging Matthew in
games and offering him advice. After all, someone had to
show the boy the best way to bait a hook, thrust and parry
with a blunted stick, and throw a rock to skim across the
water, all things Ashton's father had never found time to teach
him.

Last night had shown how easy it would be to fall back
into the inconsequential life he'd known before his military
experience. It only helped to reaffirm his desire to acquire
enough funds to establish himself outside of his father's influence. But before that, he needed to make sure the coded message didn't contain anything to threaten Matthew's future or
his father's.

Of course, it didn't hurt that deciphering the message
would require close conspiracy with his sweet-lipped little
code breaker. Who would have suspected that a bluestocking
such as Edwina would have charms of her own?

While he had to admit his need to sample her lips was a
hasty gamble, which could have earned him a slap across the
cheek for his attempt, he found he couldn't help himself.
Unlike the other women of his acquaintance, there was nothing false about Edwina. She was engaging, interesting, and
unusual in her insistence of being a "modern woman." But it
was her sincerity and compassion that drew him like a lode-
stone. He patted the gift in his pocket that he'd brought to
show his appreciation for her assistance in this endeavor.

Even the pain in his leg faded as he approached the familiar establishment. A fine omen for a fine day. He stepped into
the coffeehouse and scanned the tables. Edwina was nowhere
to be seen. His lips tightened while he dismissed a niggling
concern that his kiss might have frightened her. Not Edwina,
he reassured himself. A woman who rode bicycles and broke
into houses would not be frightened by a kiss, but still . . .

Remembering the interruptions of the dropped handkerchiefs from their earlier rendezvous, he chose a table in the
rear, and selected a seat that would place his back to the wall.
That way his full attention would be directed to Edwina and
not to any passerby. He placed an order for tea from the

waitress who followed him to the table. While tea was not his beverage of choice, it was what Edwina preferred and thus his beverage for the day.

She arrived soon after with the two loyal ladies who had threatened to storm the house in search of their friend. The memory brought a smile to his lips. A smile only faintly returned by the one called Faith. Something had changed. He could feel it in Edwina's stern expression and her ramrod straight posture.

She spoke a word to her friends, then walked toward his table while the other two sat somewhat removed.

He stood. "Miss Hargrove. I was afraid you'd been dissuaded from coming today." The jest inspired by her tardy arrival failed to solicit a returning smile. Strange, he would have thought she'd have some reaction.

Instead she quietly untied the ribbon to open her journal. "I assume you brought the note."

She was avoiding his gaze, an action that did not bode well. He removed a folded paper from his vest pocket and handed it to her. "Has something changed since last night?"

She smoothed the paper and placed it on the side of her journal. She picked up her pen to copy into her book, all in silence. His earlier good humor soured and congealed in the pit of his stomach.

"It's that kiss, isn't it?" he said, keeping his voice low. "I won't apologize, Edwina. It may have been ill-advised. It may have been presumptuous on my part, but it was the loveliest moment of the entire evening." He altered his voice to what had always been an effective seductive purr. "One that I hope will be repeated."

Her pen stopped its motion. She frowned at him, her expression as stern and formidable as the high collar on her stiffly starched blouse. "I would not count on that occurring, Mr. Trewelyn. In fact, I must insist that if we are to work together on this project you will not attempt such familiarity again."

His eyes narrowed. "Has that brute that caused the ruckus last night turned you against me? What was his name?"

"Mr. Thomas was concerned about my reputation." This woman, overly formal and annoyingly polite, was not the Edwina whose company he'd so anticipated. Her pen continued to copy the nonsense words into her journal.

"Just keep the note," Ashton said, irritated. "It's probably safer in your hands. No one would think to look for it with you."

She glanced up. "Someone is looking for this?"

"No." He considered his answer. "At least not yet. My father hasn't mentioned a note, and Constance seemed no more agitated than usual last night. That woman, however, has the talents of an actress on Drury Lane. There was a time I thought I knew her thoughts. Now I wonder if she shows a true face to anyone."

She returned to her task. "I don't require the original to work on the code. I'll copy the letter so a second copy exists. You can keep the original. You may wish to keep it for—"

"Bait?" He leaned back in the uncomfortable chair. "That's an interesting thought. I see you have a mind for espionage, Miss Hargrove. I would not have expected as much." Though he had noticed a wicked little gleam in her eyes on occasion.

"My brothers and I fancied ourselves spies on occasion," she said. "Although I think they were more interested at times in torturing me for any secrets I might have."

"Torture?" His stomach clenched.

"Spiders and garden snakes . . . harmless things."

And something maybe not so harmless based on the hesitation of her pen. His code breaker had secrets of her own, it seemed. He decided to carefully explore this area, but not now. She was so tight-lipped at the moment, he would consider himself fortunate if she gave him the time of day.

Once she'd copied the mysterious correspondence into her journal, she proceeded to list the letters of the alphabet in several long horizontal lines on a different page of her journal. With her finger moving along the line of coded text, she recorded a mark under the corresponding letter on her alphabet page each time that she encountered it in the message. Even as she efficiently tallied the frequency of the letters, he had the sense that something was still amiss. She paid little more attention to him than the cooling cup of tea near her hand.

"Is it true," she asked suddenly, "that a woman committed suicide after attending one of your parties?"

"What?" Another blow to his gut. "Who told you this?"

"Someone with a personal connection to the young woman," Edwina replied, keeping her head down in her task of recording letters. "A man took advantage of her at one of your parties seven years ago. When she discovered she was with child, she threw herself into the Thames."

Dear God, was it true? The devil knew it could have been. While he'd never experienced difficulty finding a willing woman to share his bed, he knew that was not necessarily true for others of his acquaintance. Back then he had tended to turn a blind eye to the others, preferring to place his full attention on his *amore* of the moment. He raked his hands over his face. Had the devil come to collect his due? "I don't recall that such a thing had occurred. It might have. There's much about those parties that I don't remember or . . . avoided." He looked askance. "I was often involved in other quarters."

"Do you remember Sarah from the *Mayfair Messenger*?" Edwina asked, her pen poised in the air. "Her sister has a similar tale."

"She committed suicide?"

"No. The sister died giving birth to a beautiful little girl. A girl who Sarah now raises."

"Was that the result of one of my . . ." The burden on his shoulders intensified.

"No. But the outcome is similar."

His eyes narrowed. "It is true that for a period in my youth, I gave little thought to the consequences of my actions, or those of my acquaintances. I found it difficult to ignore the . . . opportunities presented to me." How else could he explain the surprising number of women, married and otherwise, who were desperate for companionship and attention? That they'd enjoyed the physical pleasure he gave them only added to the demand for his favor. "Why are you asking me this?"

"Because I'm finding it difficult to trust your sincerity in the midst of such stories." She glanced up from her pages, meeting his gaze head-on.

"Those tales are from years ago."

"Last night was last night," she countered. She quickly looked right and left and lowered her voice. "Why did you do that?"

"I couldn't help myself," he replied. In that moment he knew it was the truth. While he recognized that kissing her was not the wisest course of action, it was a most pleasant one. "You looked lovely wrapped in cherry blossoms, standing in the moonlight."

She harrumphed and returned to her deciphering task.

Suddenly, her aloofness made sense. Between her departure last evening and now, someone had filled her head with stories from long ago. Hadn't he already explained that his time in the King's Rifles had changed his ways? "Is that the reason for the company of your friends? Are they protecting you from my alleged dubious grasp?"

She didn't respond immediately, but her pen had stopped its forward progress. "Are you going to just sit there and watch me?" she hissed.

"If there is some other matter in which I can be of assistance . . ."

She glanced up. "No. In fact, I believe you've done enough. The work is quite tedious and is probably best if done with a certain element of privacy. Let us meet in two weeks and I'll report my progress."

"Two weeks? I had thought you'd be able to unravel the mystery before then." *Two weeks!* He'd have to live in his father's residence not knowing if he lived among traitors and spies for two long weeks?

"You must not grasp the difficulty." She placed her pen down and appraised him without humor. "Some codes are never broken. I did mention last night that it could take months."

He looked out a window, gnawing at his lip. "I thought you meant that as an invitation."

"An invitation?" Her eyes widened in surprise. "How could you interpret such a statement as an invitation?"

Now who felt the dullard? "I thought . . ." He tried to think of a way to explain without sounding like a presumptuous fool, and came up empty. He had no choice but to admit his error and hope for mercy. "I thought you were encouraging me to meet with you on a frequent basis." His lips raised at the corners. "And you'll recall that I agreed most urgently."

She stared at him with disbelief for a moment, then her eyes crinkled with humor. Her shoulders relaxed, which, in turn, lightened his mood.

"Perhaps it would help if we knew from whom or from where the letter originated," Edwina said. "What became of the brown paper that wrapped the pillow"—color heightened in her cheeks—"the purchase?"

He had to think for a moment. "It may still be in the chamber. I haven't returned since that night." Something akin to panic flashed in her eyes. His focus narrowed. "Is something wrong?"

"No," she answered quickly and studied her journal, but she was hiding something. A silent warning sounded in his head. He thought he'd finally found someone he could trust, only to discover this. Strange that his mention of returning to the chamber spooked her.

"Your father's freight business would have delivered the package," she continued. "Would there be a record? Some sort of journal that would indicate the individual who sent the package? Their origin or route?"

Not only was she hiding a secret of hers, but she thought nothing of asking the impossible of him. "You wish me to speak to my father about the coded message? What if he is the recipient?"

"You don't have to mention the message," she explained quietly. "Just the package. Perhaps if you'd expressed an interest in the process . . ."

Gloom shaded his thoughts. "You don't know what you're asking."

"I'm not certain what you mean," she said, obviously innocent of the relationship between himself and his father. A relationship not enhanced by his father's choice of bride.

"My father wishes that I join him in the drayage business. If I were to approach him—"

"Is that such a bad thing? Working alongside your father?"

Now that was unexpected. Most of the women he had met would shrink from the idea of his working anywhere. His father's allowance allowed him to live sufficiently, so in their minds, there was no need for him to actually earn a wage. Truth be told, though, he wasn't comfortable living on his father's coin. He'd much prefer to have his own means . . . but without any discernable skills, that possibility led nowhere. If he were to join his father in drayage . . . ? "I'm not certain my interests follow that pursuit," he quickly replied.

"If your interests include discovering who sent that letter, I would think learning its route would provide the proper start," she challenged.

"How could studying the backside of a Clydesdale possibly assist our discovery of the initiator of that note?" He couldn't keep his irritation from his voice.

"Think. You would be privy to the inner workings of the business," she explained. "If books of record exist notating the senders of packages, you would know where they were kept. Perhaps you'd even know if similar packages were sent to your father's business associates, or to your father? You'd learn the delivery routes taken in the event that the note was inserted in the pillow . . . purchase . . . while en route. As you don't wish to approach your father with questions, you'd be able to find the answers yourself."

Damn the woman! Need she be so determined? While he could appreciate her logic, he wasn't certain he appreciated her conclusion. "You wish me to drive a freight cart?"

She tilted her head just a fraction and just looked at him. It was answer enough.

"There's no guarantee you'll be driving a cart," she said. "Your father's respect for you—"

"Respect." He snorted. "Therein lies the difficulty. He considers me a dandy whose only apparent skill was in the selection of his future wife." He'd even failed at that if one considered the tension that simmered at home.

"Perhaps this would give your father an opportunity to appreciate your other talents," she counseled.

That was unlikely. His father had ignored him for most of his life. Why would he take an interest now? Still, should his father insist he drive a cart, he'd escape Constance's attempts to reinsert him into a social structure for which he had little use. He'd escape the powder keg of his father's household. He'd have time to think about the future. And while it would be unlikely that he'd earn the respect of his father, the set of Edwina's chin suggested it might earn hers.

"I suppose if it will help in deciphering the purpose of the message, it is necessary," he said, though he wasn't entirely convinced. "Most likely I won't be in London to hear of your deciphering progress." He glanced at her face, but even that pronouncement did not earn him sympathy. Then it occurred to him that traveling the length and breadth of England must seem a reward and not a punishment to one whose soft blue eyes lit inexplicably at the mention of adventure.

This certainly wasn't the conclusion he'd anticipated when he arrived at the Crescent in such high spirits. Which reminded him . . . "I've brought something for you."

He removed the cylinder wrapped in brown paper from his pocket. Her eyes widened, but not with appreciation. "Do not assume I'm one of your conquests, Mr. Trewelyn." She regarded the package as if it were a poisonous viper. Her journal closed with an audible thud and she hastily retied the ribbon. "I didn't fail to notice the number of fluttering Japanese fans last evening." She stood, gathering her belongings. "Keep your fan for your next paramour." Her eyes narrowed. "Your next Mistress of Cherry Blossoms."

"Edwina, wait!' But she didn't. She hurried to the table where her friends lingered. Then after a shared glare in his direction, the three turned as one and headed for the door.

He looked at the small spyglass wrapped in brown paper. Fan? Why did she believe the package contained a fan? In light of their discussion of the constellations, he had thought she'd enjoy the spyglass. It had been at least six years since he'd given a woman a fan, and that was for . . . Damnation! His jaw set. He'd forgotten that a Japanese fan had once been considered his unique personal gift to women with whom he'd enjoyed a special relationship. He hadn't paid attention to the women's adornments last evening, but clearly Edwina had. Obviously, the path to Edwina's respect was not to be paved in gifts. He supposed he should be grateful for that. *No*. She demanded a higher price that required humiliation and self-sacrifice.

CLAIRE GLARED AT EDWINA ONCE THEY HAD LEFT THE Crescent. "You still intend to work with that man after what Mr. Thomas told you about his sister?"

"I don't think Mr. Trewelyn was responsible for that," Edwina replied.

"He's a rake, Edwina, and he's leading you down the garden path." Claire shook her head in disgust. "How can we protect innocents from a rake's grasp if we can't even protect our own?"

"Enough, Claire," Faith quietly scolded. "You've always championed women's rights, now champion Edwina's right to choose her own course of action."

Edwina smiled her gratitude.

"You do know what you're about?" Faith asked quietly. "You've given consideration to Mr. Thomas's wishes in this matter?"

"I'm assisting in decoding a note," Edwina insisted. "Nothing more." Though she wondered if that were true. The lure of testing her abilities against the letter was strong enough that she was determined to honor the agreed-upon rendezvous this afternoon, but not without the support of the Rake Patrol. The presence of so many Japanese fans last night, which she suspected was connected to Casanova, combined with Walter's suggestion that Trewelyn was attached to his sister's untimely death, had kept sleep at bay half the night . . . or perhaps it was that kiss that caused her to resist sleep. She sighed at the memory.

"Did you say something?" Faith asked.

Edwina shook her head. "Just tired from the late evening, I suppose. I was just reminding myself not to be swayed by Casanova's abundant charms."

Faith nodded. "Good advice."

ASHTON ASSUMED HIS FATHER WOULD BE IN HIS STUDY. Ever since Ashton had returned to his father's residence, he'd noted it was the one room his father rarely left. A knock on the doorframe caused his father to pause in rolling an inked stamp of Falcon Freight's trademark—a falcon head enclosed in a circle—across an envelope. "It's our *mon*," his father had explained when he was a boy. "An emblem the Japanese use to distinguish a family or organization. Falcons are fierce fighters that fly at high speeds, like us," he had said, patting his chest. Strange that even as a young boy, he hadn't asked why his father had adopted a Japanese symbol for his business. At the time Ashton seemed to recall many Japanese influences in the home. More so than now.

Two Japanese swords with elaborately tooled hilts hung on his father's study wall: a *katana* and its shorter companion sword, a *wakizashi*. Both were suspended by four fiercely decorated netsukes. He'd have to show these to Edwina so she could see that not all the netsukes were as . . . stimulating as those in the gallery.

His father flitted his gaze briefly over Ashton before he intently returned to applying the *mon* to papers scattered across his desk. "What is it now?" he asked.

Ashton's lips twisted. Nothing had changed. He was as ignored now as he had been in earlier years.

"Is the night watch at our door searching for another missing female?" his father groused. "Have the servants not procured enough wine and spirits to meet your entertainments?" He glanced up, annoyance in his expression. "I'm a busy man,

Ashton. I haven't much time to invest in your exploits, or those of your stepmother."

"Yes. I know your time is precious." Too well, Ashton was tempted to add, but refrained. "I realize I've had a working relationship with most of the vices known to man, but you may have noticed that those days are behind me." Ashton straightened, planting his walking stick securely by his side. "While in the King's Royal Rifles, I became known not only for my shooting abilities but also as a man of courage and honor."

"And a talented figure with the ladies, I've no doubt," his father sneered.

Ashton lowered himself to a chair opposite his father's desk. "I suppose you're as much to blame for that. I'm told the acorn doesn't fall far from the tree." He used the tip of his stick to tap the pillow book on the corner of the desk.

His father chortled, the first sign of humor Ashton had seen in far too long. "I was young once myself, you know." His father lifted the pillow book and placed it out of sight in his desk drawer. "Shouldn't leave that out for the servants to find."

Ashton noted that he hadn't mentioned a concern that Constance discover the book. Then again, he imagined the book held no surprises for Constance. Edwina, on the other hand . . .

"I appreciate your assistance in hiding the book earlier. Questions about it would have been awkward." There was something about the set of his father's lips that suggested the awkwardness had not been totally avoided. "You didn't happen to notice a note or letter that might have come with the package?"

"A note?" Ashton drew his brows together. "What sort of note?"

"Nothing to be concerned about," his father said, turning his attention back to his papers. "There often is a letter that comes with these acquisitions, that's all. Business details. Nothing to concern you."

Business details would not likely be set in code. His father's anticipation confirmed he, and not some other member of the household, or member of the Guardians, was the targeted recipient. Ashton quickly scanned the room, looking for something that might serve as the key for the coded text, but saw nothing beyond the paintings of frigates on the wall and papers scattered about the desk. Remembering Lord Rothwell's cautionary advice, Ashton was even more conflicted about placing himself in the employ of someone possibly disloyal to the Crown.

"I didn't interrupt your work to discuss your collection." Ashton took a breath, preparing himself to step off the precipice. "I've been considering your advice about my future, sir. I believe I would like to know more about the movement of freight."

His father's jaw slackened a moment before he studied Ashton as if a stranger had wandered into his study. "Are you certain, lad? There'll be no fancy parties or fawning women in my world."

"Yes, sir." Ashton winced while he lightly tapped his walking stick on the floor. "I believe you said my options were limited. I suppose I should count myself fortunate that you have opportunities for a cripple."

"A whole man would have been better, that's for certain. Lifting a heavy load requires the cooperation of both legs." His father stopped his work, then shifted back in his chair. He scrutinized his son like one assessing a horse. "With all those schools you attended, I'm hoping you learned something. I could put you in the yard. You could schedule the freight with the railroads . . . or maybe I should put you in a cart. You won't need your legs to snap the reins of the Clydesdales. The men might even appreciate your skill with a rifle. Bloody robbers are everywhere." He squinted at his son. "It's hard work. Are you sure you're up to it?"

Ashton nodded.

"Good." His father smiled. "I'm sure I can find a position for you."

It was without a doubt a candle-snuffing moment.

· Eleven ·

"EDWINA, YOU'VE BEEN WORKING ON THAT LETTER for days. When are you going to tell me about the boys' mischief that has kept you so occupied?"

Startled, Edwina glanced up from her sequence charts and attempted translations to discover her mother pulling at her gloves in the doorway. Edwina's kitten, Isabella, prepared to pounce on the fringe trim on her mother's skirt before Edwina scooped her up into her arms. "I'm sorry, Mother. What did you say?"

"Don't look so shocked, dear. I've known for some time that your brothers like to keep their secrets by writing in code. I was just wondering when you planned to tell me of their latest exploits."

She'd been working on Ashton's coded message for weeks, not days. Relieved that her obsession with cracking the code hadn't been noted, she released the struggling kitten to the floor while she gathered up her charts and translations before her mother could see that the handwriting was not that of one of the boys. That gave her pause. Why hadn't she thought of that earlier?

"If there was anything significant, I'd be sure to tell you," Edwina replied. "Mostly they write about the scenery." She'd have to view the original coded letter again to be certain, but if she recalled the slant of the letters and their shaping correctly, the original had a decided feminine nuance. She'd have to mention that to Ashton when she saw him next—whenever that may be. Since she'd refused his gift of the Japanese fan, labeling her in a sense as one of his women, she hadn't heard from him at all. At least the intervening weeks had given her time to find the missing scandalous netsuke. For the moment, it lay buried deep in her bureau. Hiding it there was only temporary until she managed to return it to its proper owner.

She slipped the gathered papers into the drawer of her writing desk, then turned to her mother. "Are we making calls this afternoon?"

Her mother adjusted her hat. "Not today. Mrs. Farthington is addressing the gardening society on all matter of pests among the perennials." She met Edwina's gaze. "I don't suppose she will include herself in that category, but she really should. She has nothing but criticism for my hydrangeas."

Edwina smiled. The animosity between her mother and Mrs. Farthington had been years in the making and would most likely disappoint the both of them if one or the other refused to participate. There was little doubt that her mother enjoyed the bickering, but only with Mrs. Farthington. Such arguments with her father did not have the same effect. Which made her wonder . . .

Edwina studied her mother's face. "Are you happy, Mother? Truly happy?"

Mrs. Hargrove cocked her head while dangling a handkerchief just out of reach of the kitten's batting paws. "That is a strange question from you, dear. Why do you ask?"

"I just wondered if you had regrets." Edwina wasn't sure how to ask the question that was on her mind. "I know you didn't know Father well when you married, and I wondered—"

Her mother sighed and put the handkerchief away. "You're wondering how you and Mr. Thomas will suit, aren't you?" She moved deeper into the room.

That really wasn't what was on her mind, but Edwina knew enough to keep that to herself. Better to just listen to what her mother had to say.

"I knew what I needed to know about your father. I knew his prospects were sufficient to provide an adequate household. He came from a respectable family, and my father approved of him. It was a good match."

"But you loved him, did you not?" The kitten hopped into Edwina's lap and purred contently.

Her mother smiled softly. "I was too young then to know of love. A good wife tends to the hearth and home. Then, if she is lucky, in time she will learn to love her husband." She patted Edwina's hand. "You'll see. Your father says Mr. Thomas is a studious clerk and will sit for the boards soon. His income will rise accordingly and be of a sufficient nature to allow him to ask for your hand. You are a very lucky young woman to have caught his attention. Any number of women would be thrilled to have an offer from such a fine prospect." She tapped her hand on the bed. "I must be off. Do not strain your eyes unduly on that letter, dear. Oh!" She patted her cheek. "I almost forgot to tell you what I came in to say. There's a package downstairs. I believe it may be a gift from Mr. Thomas. Gifts from a suitor are always an encouraging sign."

Edwina could not imagine what Walter could possibly have sent her. A book, perhaps? One on the proper deportment for a traditional wife? She sighed, remembering her mother's words. She certainly didn't feel lucky. She felt . . . trapped. Yes, much like a beast in the zoological park, denied the freedom to explore beyond the bars that defined the cage. Thinking about being trapped made her long to dash out of the house and into the sunshine, perhaps even ride her bicycle, just to remind herself that she was a modern woman, and not just a decorative object like so many of the women she and her mother had called upon in their fifteen-minute visits.

Her mother continually assured her that those calls would ultimately benefit her in an improved social status, but Edwina had her doubts. She'd agreed to participate in the practice, as it made her mother content and, in the long run, might improve her mother's social status. While that might be her mother's dream, it certainly wasn't Edwina's. She looked out the window at the beckoning sunshine and thought of all the places beyond that window, all the places she would one day love to explore. A whimsical fantasy, that! While her brothers were encouraged to explore the world, her father had made it perfectly clear that it would be a waste of money for a woman to do so. Her future was to be a wife and mother, here in England, where all respectable women resided. She'd live in a stuffy little house, with a stuffy little husband, and entertain calls in a stuffy little parlor. Excitement would be experienced only through reading the writings of others, like those of Isabella Bird, her kitten's namesake. A cloud slipped in front of the sun, dimming the sunlight, dimming her dreams, dimming her future.

Her concentration interrupted, she glanced at her lap writing desk, hesitant to pull out all the papers to return to her code-breaking efforts. Instead she put the box on the top of her bureau, the same bureau that housed the scandalous netsuke. She had found it in a far corner under her mattress, then hid it in a silk stocking tucked in a deep corner of a drawer. Now she just needed a way to return it.

Just thinking of the scandalous artifact made warmth expand in her private areas. While she kept it hidden by day, sometimes she took it out at night when she knew she wouldn't be disturbed. The carving reminded her of her adventure closeted away with Ashton in the secret gallery with prints of men and women performing intimacies with no sense of shame. After a week of resisting, she'd even explored herself in the manner of the woman on the netsuke. Her finger discovered areas so sensitive to touch, sensation rippled from her chest to her toes. If her slim finger unleashed such sensation, she marveled what a jade stalk could do. A delicious shiver tingled through her.

Her gaze caught on the cherry blossom necklace curled near her lap desk. Ashton had called her the Mistress of Cherry Blossoms that magical night at Lady Sutton's soiree. The mistress of fleeting pleasures, she almost wished that was true, as it appeared any opportunity for pleasurable pursuits was rapidly disappearing. She should cast concerns aside and live each day to the fullest. Well, Christopher, that was precisely what she was going to do. No stuffy houses today!

She stood, dropping Isabella to the floor, then grabbed a wide-brimmed hat to shield her from the sun. She slipped down the stairs, the kitten in close pursuit, but she stopped in the foyer. A familiar cylindrical package wrapped in brown paper sat on the table where mail was placed for her father's perusal. Edwina collected the surprisingly heavy package as she escaped into sunlight, fresh air, and the freedom of her Victor safety bicycle.

Perhaps it was her earlier maudlin thoughts of caged animals, but she was drawn to Regent's Park. Rather than visit the zoological gardens, though, she found a quiet bench that faced one of the green commons and contemplated Ashton's gift. She was surprised he had sent it, after her rather triumphant refusal at the Crescent. Trewelyn was nothing if not persistent. She hadn't anticipated, however, that a fan would be quite so heavy.

She quickly removed the paper and string, discovering she had erred in her assumptions. This was no Japanese fan but a spyglass. Her mind instantly turned to their conversation the night of the Sutton soiree when he told her of the stars and constellations. A bit of shame rose to her cheeks. It was a thoughtful gift, and one for which she would have thanked him profusely, if she hadn't been so intent on criticizing him. She raised it to her eye and discovered she could see nannies pushing perambulators on the far side of the green as clear as if they walked in front of her bench. She saw birds flitting from one tree to another, where before she would have just seen green. Delighted with the gift, she felt she was back playing pirates with her brothers, climbing trees, dueling with sticks. She stood, imagining she was the captain of the *Black Spot*, studying the horizon for . . .

A familiar, though vastly more tanned, face appeared through the lens. She lowered the spyglass to confirm. Yes.

She recognized his awkward gait. Ashton walked beside a much smaller replica of himself, carrying a boat almost as large as the child holding it. Their appearance presented her an opportunity to correct her earlier rudeness. Yes, she told herself. Holding both the spyglass and the handlebars of her bicycle proved challenging, but she felt she couldn't pedal across the green fast enough. She needed to thank him and speak again of codes and constellations, secrets and adventure. Once more, before it was too late.

"ARE YOU SURE SHE'LL SAIL, ASH?" MATTHEW ASKED BESIDE him.

"Most certainly," Ashton replied. "That's why you'll have to hold on to the string. Otherwise, she just might sail down the stream, then into the Thames, all the way to the ocean."

He smiled down at the boy, whose enthusiasm at the simple task of putting a boat in water proved infectious. Ashton had to believe his father was a fool for not spending time with his own son. Foolish, but not unexpected. After all, Ashton recalled a similar dismissal himself as a young boy. He supposed he'd spent a goodly part of his youth trying to capture that attention. When polite, obedient behavior failed to garner notice, he tried the other extreme. That approach failed as well, but at least he managed some fun in the process. For all intents and purposes it appeared the process of avoidance and dismissal was beginning again, only with Matthew as the victim.

Would you do any better as a father? The question loomed in his mind. According to society, child rearing fell in the realm of a mother's responsibilities. If no mother was present, the father made arrangements with governesses and schools. A father's primary responsibility was to provide for all under his roof. His father had indeed done his duty in that regard. No one was wanting of clothing, food, or shelter. If providing for a family required continuing in the same sort of drudgery that Ashton had faced the last few weeks, he wondered if he could do as well.

"Good afternoon!"

Ashton turned to discover Edwina barreling through the grass in their direction with determined accuracy. Her bike wobbled and bounced over the ruts in the grass like a drunken lord, but Edwina appeared nonplussed. Edwina always appeared nonplussed. Never was a woman so headstrong about taking on the world. She had the heart of a tiger, that one, and the countenance of . . . a disheveled, chaotic, laughing angel. Ashton reached out ready to catch her if she were to fall in his arms.

"Whoa," he called out as he steadied the wobbling wheeled death trap.

"A bike is not a horse," Edwina advised. "It does not respond to spoken commands, though at times I wish it did."

"I've never seen a lady riding a bicycle before," Matthew marveled.

"That's because Miss Hargrove is a modern woman and not an ordinary lady," Ashton replied. No, there was little ordinary about Edwina. He'd forgotten how much he'd missed her. Even though his father had kept him traveling the drayage routes, he'd received invitations from agreeable women to dawdle a bit in taverns and fine manors alike. In his prior life, he'd have been tempted to accept those invitations, but this time around he hadn't. He wasn't sure why until he saw Edwina jostling across the grass like a knight on a charger. Unlike Edwina, those women were disinterested in life, and they had no curiosities or talents beyond the bedroom. They had assumed he was little more than a handsome face driving a team of horses. In spite of many assurances to the contrary, Edwina believed he was capable of more. Just seeing her made his chest expand with pride, and his determination to prove her correct grow stronger.

"Allow me to introduce my brother." He tousled the boy's head. "This is Matthew, the proud owner and captain of the good ship *Impatience*."

Edwina curtsied as if presented to the Queen herself. And Matthew, after Ashton relieved him of the burdensome ship, bowed like a proper gentleman. Ashton beamed, proud of his little half brother.

Edwina nodded to the young lad. "Very pleased to meet you, Master Matthew. That's a lovely ship."

Matthew squinted at Edwina. "Is that a pirate's spyglass? Can I use it to watch my boat?"

"I think you have enough in your hands as it is," Ashton said, placing the toy ship back in his arms. "Perhaps Miss Hargrove will join us as we take the *Impatience* on its initial launch." He raised an eyebrow in invitation.

"Of course. I'd love to watch the launch." She angled her head toward Matthew. "And yes, you may borrow my spyglass if you're very, very careful not to drop it in the water."

Matthew let out a gleeful squeal and hurried ahead to the stream.

EDWINA SURVEYED HER SURROUNDINGS, KNOWING FULL well that her parents, Walter, even Sarah would chastise her if they knew she was publicly walking with Ashton. Yet, how could they find fault? She felt so much herself when she was with him. The world became an interesting place inviting participation, not a closed box suffocating her impulses. She pushed the bicycle forward, following Matthew's path.

"I see you've received my bribe," Ashton said. "I had hoped it would secure your participation in decoding the message before—"

"I should apologize about that misunderstanding," Edwina interrupted. It was, after all, one of the reasons she'd hurried across the green. Still, she couldn't look him in the eye and instead focused on the turn of the bicycle's front wheel on the trodden path. "I thought the package contained something else."

"A fan, if I remember correctly," Ashton replied with a smile in his voice. "Back in my wild and reckless past, I often presented . . . certain women . . . with a token of my appreciation."

She shifted her gaze to him. "But there were so many of them at the soiree."

His face twisted a moment before he used his stick to knock a stone from their path. "Yes. There were. Back then."

"I'm surprised they all flashed their fans as if members of some secret society." A bitterness seeped into her voice that surprised her. She had no reason to be bitter, did she? Except that so many expected that she'd join their ranks. One would think all they had to do was look at her to realize she was not of their league. Ashton deserved someone of a higher social plane than she.

"In a manner of speaking, I suppose they were," Ashton said. His voice lowered. "It's not a period of time of which I'm particularly proud."

"Still, I would have thought that a woman would have preferred to be thought of as special in that context of intimacies. Unique. Not proud to be one of a group."

"Like you?" he asked softly.

She glanced away. Her inability to conform to others' expectations had been the bane of her existence. She'd hoped that perhaps Ashton hadn't noticed, but it was clear now that he had. The thought dampened her spirit. Her mother had drilled into her time and again the concept that men did not cherish the unique. They walked in silence a few moments.

"Have you attempted to decipher the note?" he asked. "After we spoke last I wasn't certain you'd still be interested."

"I've been working on it," she admitted, grateful for the change of subject. "I haven't made as much progress as I would have liked. I believe I've resolved a few letters. I found two words that fit the pattern for 'pillow book,' so assuming that the author mentioned that vehicle of conveyance, then I may have a few letters. Having the code for the letter 'o' led me to discover the words 'to, it, will, look, and took' in that order, but that's not enough to unlock the puzzle. It would be easier, of course, if I knew the key." She looked at him askance. "I did notice one thing this morning. I suspect the letter was written by a woman. I've been working with the version I'd copied in my journal, which naturally is in my handwriting. I'd like to look at the original again, if that's possible, to see if my suspicions are confirmed. I'm surprised I didn't notice it immediately." Of course, she'd been far too excited about the project at their first meeting to consciously note such a thing. Then, after Walter's revelations, she'd been too uncomfortable in Ashton's presence to notice. Now she wondered what else she might have missed.

"My father has asked if I'd discovered a note on the night of the Guardians' meeting."

Her eyes widened. "Then someone *was* looking for it. What did you say? Do you think he was to be the recipient?"

"Matthew, wait!" Ashton called. "Let me help you with that."

The child attempted to put the boat in the stream, which given his small frame put him in danger of falling in. Ashton quickly took the boat from Matthew's hands and knelt down alongside the boy to place the boat safely in the water. He handed him the end to a string tied to the vessel. Once again Edwina was struck with the similarity of their looks. If Ashton hadn't already told her the family history, she would have assumed they were father and son, not brothers. She imaged Ashton would make a wonderful father, watching him with the young boy. He had even noticed the potential danger before she herself had.

"If you tie that string around his wrist, he won't lose the boat," she offered.

"Good idea." Ashton looped the string around the boy's wrist. The three of them watched the stream's current tug the ship away from the bank. The long string enabled it to drift a distance before the boat turned, fighting the force of the current. Matthew ran down the bank, which in turn allowed the boat to continue its race downstream. "Don't run past those trees and stay away from the water," Ashton called before inviting her to sit with him on a bench along the bank. She leaned her bicycle on the back of the bench, then they both watched Matthew's joyful progress. Ashton's eyes crinkled. "I should have brought another string to keep Matthew from running too far from this bench."

"I've missed talking to you," Edwina confessed. It was probably the wrong thing to admit to a man, but she couldn't help herself. "It feels so comfortable. I kept hoping to see you at the Crescent after that last meeting, or maybe receive a note, or—"

"I've been working for my father," Ashton admitted. "Do you not recall? It was your suggestion. You thought the experience might help us identify the sender."

"And has it?"

"In a way, I suppose it has. Remember when you asked about the paper used to wrap the pillow book?" Edwina felt a moment of panic remembering that Ashton had said earlier that the wrapping was still in the chamber. In the course of recovering it, had he noticed anything amiss? "It had been moved from the chamber and made available to the household staff to use," he continued, oblivious to her distress. "Apparently Matthew's governess had taken it to use for his lessons. I managed to find it in the nursery." He chuckled. "I'd about given up hope of finding the piece when I thought to check on Matthew and noticed the conspicuous brown squares. The paper had a mark on it that I now recognize as the *mon* of Raja Shipping, a company based in Calcutta."

Edwina relaxed. Surely he would have mentioned the missing netsuke if it had been noticed. "A *mon*?"

"It's a mark often used in the Japanese culture to designate a family or an association. My father's company uses a falcon head in a circle to note its parcels. You might've noticed it on the wrapping of the spyglass." He grinned. "I made sure it was placed in the wagon for your area. Raja Shipping uses an elephant's head in a circle." He leaned back and tilted his head at a somewhat rakish angle. "You might recall seeing similar marks on the woodblock prints in the clothing of the participants." A decidedly wicked grin tilted his lips. "Of course, if you'd like to reexamine some of those prints . . ."

"A pattern," she said, noting the similarities. "How interesting that both your father and Raja Shipping would use the same circular pattern. I can understand your father, given his intense interest in the Japanese culture, but how interesting that an Indian company would adopt a similar pattern."

"They both deal with freight and specifically with wheels. I assumed that similarity—"

"But neither company is of Japanese origin, yet the package was," she interrupted. "Curious. It's possible there is a connection. Did you learn anything else?"

Ashton pointed to the spyglass. "May I?"

Edwina handed it to him. He promptly raised it to his eye and watched Matthew tug on the string to drag the boat upstream. "I believe I've made some interesting observations on improvements in the freight operation. While I've learned that I have no passion for moving freight myself, I have more respect for those that do." He lowered the scope to his lap, apparently assured that the boy was in no danger. He showed her the calluses that had formed on his palms. "I'm not opposed to hard work, but my injury makes sitting on a jostling cart for long distances difficult. My leg crumbles beneath me when I attempt lifting heavy loads, but I've been doing so anyway. I've noticed some small progress, even if the men I am sent to work with do not. I imagine they believe I'm utterly useless. My father believes my talents lie with seducing women." His lips tightened. "Perhaps he's right."

"Nonsense," Edwina protested. Her heart twisted to hear the exasperation in his voice. At the same time she found an anger building within her at his mistreatment at the hands of his father. "You have abilities beyond that of a common laborer. How can your father not see that? You were a member of the King's Royal Rifles. Not everyone is admitted to that select group."

"There is that," Ashton said. He smiled. "The demand for a sharpshooter on the streets of London is limited, though, and my wound ended my military service." He looked down at the spyglass and turned it gingerly in his hands. His finger slid over the brass plate of Thomas Harris & Son, the manufacturer. "I've often thought that if a spyglass such as this could be affixed to a rifle, it would improve the accuracy of our corps. It would have to be smaller, though." He hefted it up and down. "It's a bit on the heavy side as it is."

"Your wound has obviously not lessened the use of your mind. Have you tried to find a way to make a spyglass suitable for attachment to a rifle?"

He turned toward her, as if seeing her for the first time.

His eyes narrowed. "You don't let anything get in your way, do you? You see a need and you attack it no matter the obstacles."

Suddenly she wished he had given her a fan instead of a spyglass. That way she could use it to fan the heat rising in her cheeks. *Fan* . . . an idea sparked in her mind.

"Ashton, what if those *mon* marks are also symbols of something else? What if they signify membership in a secret society like the Guardians?"

His eyes widened. "I hadn't considered that, but it would make sense. It would give individual members in different countries a way to recognize one another." They sat silent for a few moments.

Ashton studied her. She truly was amazing. An organization such as the one Lord Rothwell described would most likely have members beyond Great Britain. The members would need a system to locate one another. It was time he approached his father about the Guardians.

"You've copied the message in your journal, correct?" Ashton asked. Edwina nodded. "Then I shall give the original letter to my father. I'll tell him I found it on the floor of the library. Perhaps it'll open up a discussion of the Guardians. We'll still have the copy to determine if secrets exist therein. But in the meantime—"

Their heads turned simultaneously at the sound of a scream . . . followed by a splash.

· Twelve ·

ASHTON FLEW OFF THE BENCH IN AN AWKWARD stride toward the child flailing in rapidly moving water. Edwina grabbed her bicycle, thinking it would be faster than running down the uneven path. Using his stick to great effect, Ashton managed to cover distance quickly and continued until he was slightly ahead of the boy. He shrugged out of his jacket, then plowed into the water.

"Matthew! Grab my stick!" he yelled, extending his walking stick with both hands for greater reach. While Matthew didn't exactly grab hold, his thrashing body bumped into the thin wooden barrier. Ashton's back muscles clenched with incredible strength as he used his walking stick to herd the child out of the rapidly flowing center of the stream. His face contorted with the strain but he manipulated the child toward the bank until he was close enough to reach with his arms. Abandoning the stick to float downstream, he pulled Matthew into the shelter of his chest, hugging the child fiercely. Edwina watched from the bank, her heart pounding fiercely in her chest. How could anyone consider a man of such amazing ability less than capable?

After assuring himself that the child was uninjured, Ashton pushed the boy toward her, and she helped haul the child onto the safety of the bank. Matthew cried, more out of fear than injury, and Edwina did her best to comfort him. Her gaze, however, slipped over to Ashton, who stood doubled over in the stream gasping for breath. She saw the taut lines of pain edged into his face, yet when he looked up and saw her concern, his attempted smile twisted his face into a grimace. He shook his head. "I knew I should have affixed a string to that boy."

He made her laugh, mostly from relief that both man and child had escaped injury. Even though Matthew clung to her skirt, she helped Ashton scramble out of the water, leaving the *Impatience* to bobble in the shallows. For one moment, one magical moment, she stood steadying Ashton with her hands on his waist, his hands on her shoulders. Smiling, she tilted her head up, thinking that he too would be celebrating the moment. Laughter shone in his eyes, even as the water plastering his dark hair to his forehead dripped in cold rivulets down his cheeks and nose.

"Thank you," he said.

Before she could respond, desire replaced the laughter in his eyes. His gaze focused on her lips, warning that he was going to kiss her right out in the open park, and she was going to let him. His arms slipped down her arms, pulling her closer. She reached her parted lips toward his even as droplets of water splattered onto her cheeks. Just as their lips met, a hand tugged on her skirt.

"My boat. It's going to drown."

Ashton muttered something under his breath, something that ended in "hell," before he dropped his hands and stepped back. "When you're older, my boy," he muttered, fishing the boat from the water before collecting his jacket from the ground and draping it over Matthew's narrow wet shoulders, "we're going to have a talk about timing."

THE THREE OF THEM MUST HAVE BEEN A SORRY SIGHT. Matthew and Ashton resembled two muddy rats, while she sported a muddied skirt and blouse from hugging Matthew. She'd quieted him earlier with the promise that he could ride her bicycle home. Now he sat on the hard seat and stretched his body forward to reach the handlebars. His feet dangled above the safety chain. Edwina walked the bike back toward the Trewelyn residence, while Ashton awkwardly strode beside her with the wet boat under one arm and her spyglass, which he had retrieved from the grass where it had fallen, in his hand. She suggested he use the bicycle for support, but he declined.

"They have canes, you know, with inflatable life preservers inside." He winked at her. "I may have to invest in one of those."

"A life preserver?" Her face twisted. "In a cane?"

"You'd be amazed at the things one can store in a cane. It can be a snuff holder, a place to store toiletries when traveling, even fishing poles can be stored inside."

"Fishing poles?" Matthew chirped. "Let's go fishing!" One would never suspect the boy had just experienced a traumatic fall into a stream. "Will you come too?" Matthew asked her.

"You need to dry out first, Matthew. We'll go another time." Ashton looked over the boy's head. "Maybe Miss Hargrove will honor us with her presence when we go?"

She nodded and laughed with them. After they'd walked a little farther, she glanced over toward Ashton. "So, is it possible I could see the mystery note one more time before you return it to your father? I have that supposition about the author I wish to confirm."

"I'm certain that can be arranged." They exchanged a glance that suggested they had to modify their conversation for the young ears present.

"How's your friend at the *Messenger*?" he asked without preamble.

"She's doing well," Edwina said, surprised at the question. "She has a mystery of her own to unravel."

"Oh, and what would that be?"

"She has a secret admirer who sends money to her every week."

"A secret admirer?" Ashton raised his eyebrows.

"Yes. A package arrives without identification every Thursday. She hasn't a clue who to thank for the generosity."

"Money should help her with the expenses of caring for her niece."

"Yes." She glanced at him over Matthew's head. "It will." Something about his expression . . . She decided to ask Sarah if the weekly parcel carried the *mon* of Falcon Freight.

Mindful of Matthew's presence, Edwina changed the topic of conversation. They chatted about Ashton's experiences in Burma and India. Matthew had seen a tiger at the zoological gardens but was most curious about the elephants. Edwina was enchanted with Ashton's descriptions. They reached Trewelyn's town house before the stories were completed.

After Matthew had been removed from the bicycle and divested of Ashton's jacket, Ashton handed Matthew his toy ship and directed him to put it away. Once the boy hurried off, Ashton turned to Edwina. "If you'll wait in the parlor, I'll fetch the note."

She looked down at her skirt. "I really shouldn't. I'd hate for anyone to see me like this."

"I don't know what you mean." Ashton grinned. "You look beautiful."

She could feel a blush creeping up her neck.

"You can leave the bicycle here," Ashton continued. "One of the footmen will tie it to the fender of the carriage when they take you home." She started to protest, but he insisted. "Please. It's the least I can do after all your help with Matthew."

She supposed there was no harm in delaying her return home for a few minutes, and she did want to confirm her suspicions about the coded message, so she accepted his offer.

UNMINDFUL OF HIS OWN APPEARANCE, ASHTON DASHED to his room on the upper floor to retrieve the note he'd secreted away. He removed a box from the back of the armoire and found the note stuffed within. If Edwina was right and the hand was decidedly feminine, what would that mean in terms of the contents? He imagined secrets could be conveyed by a woman as well as a man, but he had to admit the possibility surprised him. He pulled a cane from a floor vase by the door, then returned downstairs grateful for the addition of the wooden support. Just as he worked his way down the passageway between the library and the parlor, Constance slipped behind him.

"Ashton. Where have you been?" She ran her fingers across the back of his shirt. "I'll need you to escort me to the Merton's recital this evening. The girl has no musical ability, but Mrs. Merton has influence. I want you to—" He turned to face her. "Dear heavens, look at you! What happened?"

"I daresay you haven't seen your son, as he looks similar. Matthew decided to take a dip in a fast-moving stream. I had to fish him out."

"You allowed my son in a treacherous stream! He could have drowned! He could have died! Died!" She bristled with anger. "Can't you even manage to keep a small child out of danger? I swear your father is right. Your talents excel at drinking and whoring and little else."

He was about to tell Constance to go to the devil, but Edwina, eyes flashing, burst from the parlor. "How dare you accuse Ashton! It was an accident that the boy fell into the water, but due to Ashton's heroic efforts, we were able to pull him back to land and safety. You should be thanking him. He saved your son's life!"

"Ashton? You call him Ashton now?" Constance raked her gaze over Edwina's soiled clothes before turning back to him. "Is this your latest? This little bicycle-riding hoyden? I've heard about her immodest antics from reliable sources. I thought you had higher standards."

"You will *not* insult Miss Hargrove." Anger slapped Ashton in the gut. "She was instrumental in the rescue of Matthew. She deserves your respect." He should have left it at that, but the fact that Constance would attack undeserving Edwina stuck in his craw. His eyes narrowed. "Can't you leave anything fresh and good untouched by your venom? You should be thanking, not insulting her."

Constance laughed, a caustic sound. Why hadn't he noticed that years ago? "Thank her for setting her sights on Casanova?" She focused on Edwina. "I know he's charming, but he's not the marrying kind. I assure you many have set their cap for him but failed to gain his pledge. Even those with better fashion sense and more money at their disposal." She attempted a weak smile. "I suggest you find some safe young man of values and settle down before you've completely passed your prime."

"Is that what you did, Constance?" Ashton sneered. "Settled with some safe *young* man, as it appears to me you prefer the rich old ones." He turned his back on her and led Edwina by the elbow toward the parlor.

"No one can criticize me for seeking to better my circumstances," Constance called after them.

Ashton didn't reply, but his body tensed as if anticipating an ambush. While he hadn't particularly enjoyed traveling on the road with his father's carters and freight vans, he had enjoyed the reprieve from living in this powder keg of a household. He should count his blessings that he'd learned of Constance's perfidious nature before asking her to be his wife. That hadn't saved him from sharing a household with her. If not for Matthew, he'd pack his things in a rucksack and find other accommodations, but someone needed to be here to protect the boy.

Edwina's face had paled. "I wasn't trying to bind you with wedlock. I never considered—"

"Put her words out of your mind. I've learned that she flatters those that she believes have something to offer her, and lambasts those that don't."

Color returned to her face. "As long as you understand . . ."

"Hush now," he said, stepping closer. "While Constance hasn't the wherewithal to know when to thank someone, allow me. Thank you for your help with Matthew in the park and thank you for your defense of my actions." A smile found a way to his lips. He ran his fingers down the side of her face, slipping a stray tendril behind her ear. Trust and admiration shone in her eyes. Lord, she made him feel ten feet tall and as whole and substantial as any man. It was a feeling he hadn't experienced of late. "I can't say that I recall anyone defending me on the basis of my heroic attributes." Her returning smile warmed him more than the sun had on their travel home. "It's a pleasant surprise."

A blush fanned across her cheeks in a most enticing fashion. Many women only flushed like that when in the throes of sexual pleasure. But Edwina pinked for far more mundane incidents. Would that particular color stain her neck and breasts as he brought her to the pinnacle of pleasure? Would her eyes still shine with generous admiration or glaze over in self-fulfillment? His cock stiffened at his wayward thoughts, but he didn't care if she recognized the effect she had on him. Some women would find it a compliment. Some women would—

"The note?" she asked, pulling him from his thoughts. He took one glance at those wide, blue, innocent eyes and quickly stepped behind a nearby table before the evidence of his attraction scared her away.

Shame that he didn't notice that the table supported an eighteenth-century Japanese incense burner in the shape of a rooster. A golden rooster at that. In retrospect, he thought a chair might have been a better choice.

EDWINA WAITED WHILE ASHTON FUMBLED TO REMOVE folded papers from his pocket. "I brought the paper used to wrap the parcel as well," he said.

She held the letter to her nose and sniffed. She shook her head. "If it had been perfumed, it's long since faded."

"Perfumed?" His brows raised in surprise. "Why would a letter of state secrets be perfumed?"

"It could be a letter from a lover," she replied. "I see coded messages between lovers all the time in the *Mayfair Messenger*."

"This isn't the *Messenger*," he insisted. "And the letter was in a book addressed to my father." He grimaced, placing his hand on the head of the golden fowl.

"You'd prefer to accuse your father of treason than of having a lover?" She tilted her head in consideration. "That makes little sense to me."

"I don't wish to accuse my father of treason." His face twisted. "The implications would prove disastrous."

"To Constance?" she asked, feeling a tug of jealousy. The woman had humiliated Ashton in front of a stranger, and yet he still showed concern for her.

"Yes, Constance, but more importantly to Matthew." He shook his head. "The boy doesn't deserve that burden."

"And yourself? Your reputation would be affected as well," Edwina said, noticing for the first time that he stood by a fowl synonymous with his past exploits.

He barked a laugh, stepping away from the table as if he could read her thoughts. "My reputation has already been tossed to the wolves." He paced in the confined room. "As much as I would wish this note was a harmless exchange between a man and his lover, I can't ignore that it could conceivably be something else entirely. The book came from Calcutta. That's a substantial distance for a romantic relationship." He shook his head. "No. It must be a letter concerning government secrets. Why else would it be in code?"

Edwina kept her skepticism to herself. Tomorrow she'd speak to Sarah about researching past newspapers for clues as to the senior Trewelyn's past. "Have there been other notes?" she asked. "Multiple communications might assist my translation."

"This is the first one I've found."

"That doesn't mean there aren't others," she said. "Others that you weren't here to intercept." He was clearly not accepting the possibility that the notes were of a nonthreatening nature. She decided to take a different tack. "Assuming there are others, do you suppose your father would keep them in his study, or would he have left them in the gallery?"

"I would assume the study, but we should investigate both," Ashton replied. "Just to be certain we find them all."

"We?" Surely this was one task Ashton could handle alone.

"There are too many books and too many places to hide a packet of letters for one person to do a thorough search." His lips tilted in that rakish smile that went right to her heart. "You're the only one I trust to help me locate them."

"I think that's impossible," she protested.

"That I trust you?" His eyebrows raised in a pleading sort of way.

"No," she said, but then regretted the implication. "Of course, you can trust me, but I can't help you search. Not here. Even your stepmother takes exception to my being here. To say nothing of the nature of the chamber." An unanticipated shiver titillated the tips of her breasts.

"You know the gallery is private." His voice dropped to a low tone that managed to make her rib cage vibrate in a most pleasant way. Did all men have that ability, or just this man? She suspected the latter. "You've been there before. The contents can no longer shock you, not anymore."

The truth was the contents of that gallery were shocking at best and the images had stayed with her for days. She wouldn't mind exploring further, but only if she were alone. It would be just too difficult to return to the gallery knowing Ashton would be watching her reaction. "I was lucky to come here and leave without being discovered the last time. I don't think we should tempt fate again."

She handed the original coded note back to Ashton. "I suppose a woman can trade secrets just as a man, but I do think this was written in a woman's hand. Perhaps when you return it to your father, you'll be able to determine where he keeps the other communications, if there are others to keep."

She unfolded the brown wrapping paper while Ashton secured the note in his pocket. Immediately, she noted the Raja *mon*. "I don't recognize any code markings, but it would be best if we could compare this to the markings of other parcels that have passed through Calcutta." She looked up. "When will you return the coded message to your father?"

"This evening if possible. I've noted that ever since I've returned home, my father spends more and more of his evenings as well as his days at his office on the docks. Assuming he spends this evening at home, I'll talk to him then."

Now that she had witnessed Constance from a different perspective, she recognized Ashton's position in the household. "He expects you to entertain his wife."

Ashton nodded. "As Constance inferred, he believes it to be one of my more useful abilities." His hand tapped his injured thigh.

"Then he doesn't know you very well, does he?" she snapped. Ashton regarded her with a sort of gratitude in his eyes.

"No," he said. "No, he doesn't. At least, not as well as you." He maneuvered past roosters, chairs, and a settee to stand before her. He lifted her fingers. "I wonder, Edwina, if I might write you while I'm traveling on my father's behalf." While his voice remained noncommittal, his eyes pleaded with her. She felt her heart soften. "You value your brothers' letters so greatly, I hope you might consider—"

"Yes," she said quickly, then tempered her wide smile so as not to appear overeager. "I'd enjoy hearing of your thoughts."

What a shame Ashton's father didn't recognize all the fine traits that his son embodied. There was so much more to him than implied in that silly Casanova name. In fact, if his father knew his son better, he might even recognize him as an equal. Which inspired a thought. She stepped back so she could focus her thoughts. She glanced at him askance. "You know, Ashton, if you truly believe this note is one of espionage and the Guardians are part of it, there is really only one way to discover the truth."

"I'm afraid I've come to a similar conclusion." His face appeared older, more solemn than moments before. His eyes reached hers with the sad realization.

"I will have to join the Guardians."

· *Thirteen* ·

"YOU SAY YOU FOUND THIS WHERE?" HIS FATHER looked at him skeptically.

"In between the secret entrance and the inner door of the gallery," Ashton replied, working hard to keep his expression blank. "It must have fallen out of the pillow book when I hid it in the gallery the night those vigilantes stormed our doorstep."

His father's brows lowered in confusion. "I thought I checked there."

"It was wedged into a corner," Ashton said, hoping he sounded convincing. He'd never been the best of liars. He'd found no need for it. But this whole coded message incident was teaching him skills he never knew he had. Now he wished he had crumpled the paper a bit to support his story. "I'm not surprised you missed it. I would have overlooked it myself except you mentioned you were missing some sort of correspondence."

"Did you read it?" his father's gruff voice barked.

"It looked like gibberish to me, sir. I couldn't make any

sense of it." He raised his brows in what he hoped was an innocent expression. "Does it have a purpose?"

His father's glare was certainly not one of appreciation or gratitude. Any hope that discovering the missing message would somehow gain him a level of respect in his father's eyes vanished.

"No purpose I'd wish to share." He opened the center drawer beneath his desk and deposited the paper. Ashton tried to see if this was just one of several such notes in the drawer, but his father's action was too swift to facilitate such an observation. Once he'd closed the drawer, he hunched over his desk as if to further protect the coded message with his presence. "Constance tells me you're taking her to some silly recital this evening. I'm not certain how you can stomach that sort of poppycock but—"

"I can't," Ashton interrupted.

"You can't what?"

"I can't stomach that poppycock. I've escorted Constance on these many occasions in deference to you, sir. But I don't enjoy it and I'm having difficulty continuing to do so."

His father leaned back in his chair with a faint glimmer of respect in his eye. "Is that so?"

"It is." Ashton gestured to a chair in front of the desk. His father nodded, and Ashton lowered into it. "You've sent me out on the road on the drayage carts to observe the various districts, and quite frankly, I'd prefer to spend the evening discussing where improvements can be made with you, than standing by Constance while she chatters incessantly about some nonsense."

"Improvements?" His brows lowered. "What sorts of improvements?"

"I've noticed some of the equipment needs a good overhaul to operate efficiently. We could use the railroad lines much more effectively, and I've heard rumblings about a new internal combustion motorcar coming out of Germany that—"

"A motorcar?" His father laughed. "A rich man's plaything. Next you'll be saying we should deliver freight from a hot air balloon." He reached to a crystal decanter to pour himself a snifter of brandy.

Ashton smiled, refusing to take the bait. "Right now the motorcars may be expensive toys used to carry passengers. But this is only the beginning. Reliable motor wagons will be built in time. The sort of motor wagon that can haul freight, and we should be positioned to take advantage of it."

"Freight without horses? I'm not sure I want to see that day."

"Nevertheless, it's coming whether you'll be alive to see it or not." His father scowled at him in response. "It's much like the use of rifles in the military," Ashton said, warming up to the analogy. "The old muzzle-loaders were deadly, especially against enemies armed with knives and stones. But when the breechloaders came into being, the victors of a skirmish became the ones with the better weapons." Ashton formed his fingers into the suggestion of a gun. "The ones who could accurately pick off their enemies at a safe distance."

Ashton watched his father's reaction, hoping the change in conversation from freight to military would give him some sort of clue as to the secrets hidden behind his father's eyes. The old man sat for a moment, considering the talk of rifles. "You're not suggesting I arm my cart drivers, are you?"

Ashton laughed and leisurely picked up the Falcon stamp and slid his finger over the raised edges. "No sir, I am not. I had hoped to prove to you, sir, that I can be of some benefit beyond that of profligate."

His father grunted.

"In fact"—Ashton modulated his tone to convey the serious nature of his words—"I believe I can be of even greater service."

Now he got a reaction. His father ran his eyes over him, considering, then reached for his waiting glass of brandy. "What exactly are you proposing?"

"That you introduce me to the Guardians."

His father nearly choked on his drink. Ashton was about to pound on his back when normal breathing returned. "The Guardians," he rasped in a tight airy voice. "I thought I told you to forget about them."

"When I was in Burma, I heard of a group that endeavored

to bring items of cultural importance of other countries back to England: statues, pieces of temples, small artifacts, that sort of thing." He leaned over and poured himself a glass of brandy. "After you mentioned the Guardians, I've been thinking how that kind of activity would prove profitable to a man invested in moving freight. Now that I've seen the operations of Falcon Freight, I've noted that parcels from all over the world pass through your fingers, in a manner of speaking."

His father's eyes narrowed. "I still don't see . . ."

"If I'm going to be a part of Falcon Freight, then I think I should be a part of the Guardians as well. 'In for a penny, in for a pound,' I always say." He pointed to his father's new Excelsior stamp pad. "May I?"

"You believe you're to be part of the operations of Falcon Freight, do you? The company I started with a horse and a map?"

Ashton simply rolled the *mon* stamp over the ink pad—best to give his father some time to adjust. Eventually, his father's glare weakened. "I suppose if the company is going to outlast me, it'll need some innovations. I'll consider the motorcars."

"And the Guardians?" Ashton persisted.

"That's not up to me. The other members have to vote on any new inductees. It's a secret society you know. We're careful about who we allow at our meetings."

The Guardians' meetings couldn't be that secret if Edwina had already cracked the code used in the *Mayfair Messenger.* Ashton bit back his smile as he rolled the *mon* stamp on a blank piece of paper. "Now that's a nice improvement over the old inks." He blew on the paper to help it dry, then wrinkled his nose. "Hope they can do something to improve the smell." He grinned up at his father. "See. Progress."

"You shouldn't even know of the Guardians," his father continued, nonplussed. "I'll need to talk to the others before I introduce you."

"And when will you do that?"

"We're a secret society, Ashton. That includes the meeting dates and location." His father sighed and shook his head.

"We should meet again within the month. I'll let you know the outcome."

Ashton stood, carefully folding the stamped paper, then placed it in his pocket. "I'll be anxious to hear the results."

THE TRULY WONDERFUL THING ABOUT LIVING IN A MOD-ern city such as London was that mail could be delivered up to ten times in a single day. The truly miserable thing about such a modern city was that the mail often arrived without a single envelope for her. Ever since she had agreed to correspond with Ashton, she discovered that she held her breath waiting for the postman to ring with a delivery. Ashton wrote to her daily, based on the dates he'd placed on the letters, but they didn't always arrive in a consistent pattern. He wrote that he'd approached his father about joining the Guardians, which filled her with apprehension. If the group was involved in the sort of espionage that Ashton felt they could be, she anguished that he would come to regret his decision, all the more worrisome because she felt she had a part in encouraging him to join.

While they waited for a response from the Guardians, she wrote Ashton with stories about the calls she made with her mother. She advised him of Isabella Bird's announcement that she planned to travel next to Korea and Japan. She told him about her kitten Isabella's antics and about the ads being considered for investigation by the Rake Patrol. She shared news of her brothers' travels. Like her childhood, it seemed once again she was left behind while the men around her experienced adventures. But with Ashton's frequent letters, she didn't feel alone at all.

"Edwina, where is your head?" Claire asked. "Normally, you'd have torn through the personals in the *Mayfair Messenger* by now. You've barely glanced at the paper."

"Sorry. I was lost in a bit of whimsy, I suppose."

"It's true." Faith joined in Claire's scrutiny. "You haven't been yourself lately. Ever since that Sutton affair, you've seemed distracted. We barely see you anymore."

Edwina was about to explain her mother's intent to call on

everyone she'd met at the Sutton soiree and the ensuing bore-dom such calls presented, but she didn't get the chance.

"I think she's daydreaming about Mr. Thomas," Sarah said with an air of confidence. "He came by the office yesterday, asking for you."

"Why would he look for me at the *Messenger* office?" Edwina asked.

"He called at your house yesterday. Didn't he leave a card?" Sarah asked. "He said your mother was out and no one knew where you had gotten off to on that bicycle of yours, so he thought he'd check at the office. I think he had something special to ask you."

"Probably not to ride your bicycle," Claire said with a quirk of her lips. "You'd best not take up smoking cigarettes. That would drive the poor man into a fit of apoplexy."

Edwina grinned. Her passion for bicycling was becoming a constant bone of contention with Walter. "I'm certain it's nothing."

"He seemed very serious," Sarah added. "I think he may be looking to secure your future. Where were you?"

"Walter is always serious," Edwina replied. "He is a kind and considerate man, but he's always serious."

"Edwina," Faith said, rattling the paper, "did you see this message in the personals? It's in code."

Edwina pulled the paper closer to her. She recognized the number code immediately. She removed her journal from her reticule and opened to the page with the alphanumeric trans-lation key. Thus she determined the date and address of the next meeting of the Guardians.

"What is it?" Faith asked.

"Just notice of another meeting of the Guardians." Edwina tried to keep the excitement out of her voice. "As nothing untoward occurred at that last meeting I assume . . ."

"What's this?" Sarah picked an envelope from the floor. "A letter from your brothers? It fell when you removed your journal."

"That's a local letter," Claire observed. "Just a regular stamp."

Edwina felt a flush rise to her cheeks as she snatched the envelope from Sarah's hands. That, unfortunately, was her undoing.

"It's from that Casanova, isn't it?" Sarah accused. "There's nothing but trouble down that path, Edwina." Her eyes narrowed. "Is that where you were yesterday?"

"No. I haven't seen Mr. Trewelyn since I discovered him and his brother in the park two weeks ago," Edwina admitted. She knew herself to be an awful liar so she didn't even try. Though recent events had given her lots of opportunity to practice. "They were launching Matthew's model ship."

"Casanova's brother," Sarah sneered. "Do you believe that? Did you not see how closely they resemble one another?"

"They share a common father, Sarah; they should resemble one another." She slipped the letter into her journal and closed it. "I think you're being needlessly cruel."

"And I think you're being needlessly foolish," Sarah replied.

"Enough," Faith intervened. "There's no reason for you two to snip at each other. Even if Mr. Trewelyn is known for his . . . charm, I'm certain Edwina has done nothing that would violate the principles of respectability. Isn't that so, Edwina?"

She bit her lip, not wishing to lie, but not willing to be totally honest either. She'd neglected to mention the secret gallery that night when she'd slipped into Trewelyn's library. Likewise, they didn't know about the kiss, or her discovery of the scandalous netsuke and its influence, or that she'd been in Ashton's parlor without benefit of a chaperone, not that anything had occurred that would require a chaperone's interference. So she nodded in response to Faith's question. Somehow not giving voice to her answer made it less of an untruth.

She turned toward Sarah. "I had hoped to ask a favor of you and Claire, but I can't mention the reason for the request. I'm not certain now if I can count on your cooperation."

"A favor of me?" Sarah replied, her eyebrows rising above the frame of her glasses. "I can't imagine what you would want from someone like me."

"You're a journalist," Edwina replied, leaning forward.

The others followed suit. "You know how to research and have access to the archived copies of newspapers at the Ladies of Print Society. I need Claire's assistance, as she has access to many women due to her involvement in so many political movements."

"That's true," Faith agreed.

"I would like you two to research a few things for me," Edwina said, shifting her position.

"What sorts of things?"

Edwina removed the paper Ashton had sent her with the Falcon Freight *mon* from her journal. She smoothed it out on the table. Sarah gasped. "Where did you get that?"

"It's the symbol of Falcon Freight," Edwina replied. "The Trewelyn family company."

"That's the symbol that has appeared on those mysterious packets of money." Sarah stared at the symbol, then raised distressed eyes to Edwina. "Why would Trewelyn send money to me?"

Edwina hid her smile, pleased that Sarah had confirmed her supposition about the mysterious benefactor. "The day after Walter told me how his sister met her untimely end, I told Trewelyn. I also told him about Nan, just so that he would understand the consequences of those reported orgies at his residence. I suspect the money is his way of making amends for any suffering he may have inadvertently caused."

"Inadvertently?" Claire scoffed.

"Sarah has already admitted that Trewelyn is not Nan's father," Faith scolded. "There's no proof that he was the cause of another woman's violent end."

"Nevertheless, his need to make amends is not the basis of my request," Edwina said, bringing the attention of the group back to her purpose. "I have reason to suspect that other companies here in London use a similar design, a circle"—Edwina traced her finger around the outside of the symbol—"and maybe an animal or some other image in the middle." She looked toward Claire. "I would think your network of women might recognize the symbols as those of their husband's employers."

Claire nodded. "I can make inquiries."

Edwina refolded the paper and put it back in the envelope. Sarah looked up. "What about me? You said you needed my help as well."

Edwina smiled. It seemed the revelation of the Falcon Freight *mon* had altered Sarah's attitude toward Ashton. "Didn't you once tell me that reporting the insignificant facts of a ball or a dance as well as the idle talk of the affairs of the highest classes was a journalistic tradition going back to the earliest newspapers?"

"Well, yes, but I don't see—"

"I want you to research those papers for any female names that are associated with Mr. Trewelyn's father in his younger years. I'd also like to know if any of those women currently live in Calcutta, India."

"Calcutta!" Faith exclaimed. "What are you about?"

"I can't tell you," Edwina replied sympathetically. "However, I assure you it's important."

"Is there nothing I can do?" Faith asked.

"Not as yet." Edwina patted her hand. "Just continue to stand by me when I need a friend."

Their business resolved, the meeting broke up soon after Edwina had requested assistance. Faith walked outside with Edwina after the others had left, and waited while Edwina retrieved her bicycle.

"You're falling in love with him, aren't you?"

She hadn't thought about it in those terms. Perhaps she'd been denying the very thing that was clear to others. "He's very kind, Faith, and smart. He's been to the most interesting places and done the most fascinating things. And he's never said a word against my riding a bicycle, or my desire to explore."

"That's because he doesn't have to live with the consequences. Why should he care about what you do?"

"I feel different when I'm with him. Special and worthy of respect." She looked down and toyed with her handlebars. "I don't feel that way with Walter."

Faith sighed. "He's Casanova, Edwina, known for his

charm where women are concerned. His family is far wealth-
ier than ours are. If a time should come when he must choose
a wife, it won't be from the likes of us, I'm afraid."

"He writes to me every day. You don't think he cares for
me?" she challenged.

Faith smiled. "Of course he cares for you. Why should he
not? I think it's dangerous to assume his affections are more
than that. You're inexperienced with men of his ilk and your
heart thus more susceptible to his charm. Casanova can slake
his thirst with just about any woman. Take care that when the
time comes, you are not merely the convenient one."

Edwina bit her lip, afraid to admit that she indeed prayed
that someday he might consider her to fulfill those sorts of
needs. He was the only one that could take her on the sort of
adventure that she'd witnessed on those forbidden prints.

Faith gripped her arm, demanding her attention. "Don't
do it, Edwina. You'll regret it the rest of your life."

EDWINA MANAGED TO SEND A REPLY TO ASHTON'S LETTER
by the afternoon post, advising him of the Guardians' meeting in one week. Would that mean he'd return to London to
be available for the meeting? She missed him. While she could
almost hear Ashton's voice in his letters, she wished she could
see his face, the crinkling lines about his eyes, the devilish
sparkle that made her knees weak.

He wrote to her about the towns through which the drayage carts passed, and described the people and landmarks
with such attention to detail that she could almost see them
herself. When the weather aggravated his leg wound, he told
her about the circumstances of its occurrence, the pain of the
bullet ripping into his flesh, and the guilt and gratitude toward
the man who suffered a disfiguring scar in the process of
saving him. She recalled it was for this very man that Ashton
had originally purchased the personal ad that led to their meeting. She already felt a debt of gratitude to this stranger. He
wrote as well that he'd given more consideration to their
discussion on rifle scopes. He'd sent inquiries to Thomas

Harris & Son, the makers of her spyglass, for their input. While newer rifles had scoping abilities, the newer rifles were never distributed to the ranks in Burma and India. Had he such a scope on his Martini-Henry, neither he nor his disfigured friend would have suffered injury that day.

His letters were so important to her. It wasn't as if she'd not been involved in correspondence before. Her brothers had written to her for years. They wrote of the scenery as well, but Ashton's . . . his letters were different. They satisfied her in a way never imagined in others. They were personal, intimate, humorous, and compassionate, and receiving one was the highlight of her day. She'd even purchased a map of England just so she could follow his daily progress as he traveled with the drayage cart.

Yes, she had to admit, she could very well be falling in love with their author.

THE DRAYAGE ROUTE WAS SO ROUTINE THAT ASHTON WAS able to tell Edwina the days that he would arrive in each town and village. Even though he'd given her the information on how to reach him, he always worried that her letters would not find their way to the country post offices in time. Her letters were the highlight of his day, and he would mourn missing even one of them.

Given that today had been a particularly miserable one, he needed such a highlight. The morning rain had turned the country roads to muck. The heavily laden cart needed manual assistance twice to free it from the sucking mud. Their last delivery had been refused, which affected the entire packing of the cart, and his leg hurt like hell. But even that wouldn't stop him from coming into the village to check for mail.

The postmaster in Leighton-on-the-Wold also ran a dry goods store. The combination of postal services with other shops or services wasn't all that unusual in the smaller villages and hamlets. Ashton waited patiently for the store's customers to finish their business before he approached the young woman behind the counter.

"I was checking for mail. Falcon Freight? Ashton Trewelyn?" He held his breath while she walked toward the cubbyhole cabinet reserved for mail.

"Falcon Freight? We don't normally receive mail for them here."

"Could you check for a letter sent specifically to Ashton Trewelyn?" Ashton asked. He'd had similar reactions in other small villages. "I know we don't have a box here, but I thought you might hold a letter addressed to the post office." He smiled, hoping enough of his old charm still remained to persuade a little extra customer service.

"Well, I'll be," she said, pulling a letter from a slot. "This must be it."

Ashton let out his pent-up breath. It would be a good day after all.

"Ashton Trewelyn care of Leighton-in-the-Wold post office." She glanced up, bouncing the letter off her fingertips. "How did they know to send it here?"

Ashton gritted his teeth, wishing he could just grab the letter from her hand. It was from Edwina; her handwriting had become as familiar to him as his own. Besides, it wasn't as if anyone else would write to him. Even during his time with the Rifles, no one bothered to post a letter, except Constance. She wrote once, right after he joined, but he never bothered to read what she had to say. He'd simply tossed the letter in the fire. She never bothered to write again.

"I made our itinerary known," Ashton explained. He nodded to the letter in the young woman's hands. "She knows the stops we make along the way and plans the letter's destination accordingly. Now may I have my letter please?" Again he tried an encouraging smile.

"How do I know you're the one to whom the letter is intended?" the lady clerk challenged. "I can't be handing out letters to complete strangers." If he wasn't mistaken, she was making a game out of this. A game he had no interest in playing.

"A complete stranger wouldn't know that this letter is from Miss Edwina Hargrove of 86 Commonwealth in London, would they?" he replied with perhaps a little more annoyance than necessary. "When she writes, she has the unfortunate tendency to get ink on her fingers. There is probably a print of her fingertip somewhere on the envelope." He looked over the counter and down at the woman's hands. "Yes, there it is"—he pointed—"lower corner on the left. And if you sniff the envelope, you might get a faint sweet scent of cinnamon and oranges."

The woman sniffed. Her eyes widened, then she offered the envelope. "The woman is certainly known to you, sir."

Once the envelope was in his hands, it was as if the late afternoon sun had found its way to his soul. "Yes," he said, lifting the envelope to inhale its sweet fragrance before slipping it inside his jacket by his heart. "She most certainly is."

HE FOUND A QUIET SPOT IN THE TINY VILLAGE TO READ his letter, not wishing to have the others on the drayage crew interrupt him in the pleasure. It was not as if this were a love letter, far from it. There was no gushing of affection, no pronouncements of undying adoration or devotion. Just Edwina's unique and immensely enjoyable retelling of events of the day. Through her letters, he began to know and appreciate the other women of the Rake Patrol, as she called them. She told of her brothers' adventures and between the lines he recognized her admiration and yearning to travel as they did. He even had to chuckle at some of the "secret" postings in the personals that Edwina decoded. This letter, though, added the news of a different sort of decoding. The Guardians were to meet next week, which he assumed meant his request for membership would be presented. Traveling at the pace of two Clydesdales pulling the freight cart along country roads, he'd almost forgotten about the Guardians and the threat they potentially posed to his family. Instead he'd spent the time contemplating his future, contemplating Edwina, and realizing that thanks to her, he'd discovered he had the capacity to truly trust again.

•   •   •

EDWINA'S HUMOR INCREASED STEADILY AS IT NEARED
the date of the Guardians' meeting. Ashton would surely be
back in London. Hopefully, she'd have an opportunity to see
him before he returned to the drayage routes. With this in
mind, she watched everywhere for his unique gait, his enticing face and listened for his endearing voice. Even as she
dressed to accompany her parents to the theater, she did so
with Ashton in mind.

After the invitation to Lady Sutton's soiree, her mother had
gone to great lengths to improve Edwina's wardrobe. She'd
received several new dresses, a consequence of her mother's
renewed social obsession, and she relished the idea of wearing
one in public. Tonight she wore her favorite of the new gowns.
Clearly, the print of bright oranges and orange leaf clusters on
a deep blue, almost black, background had Japanese influences.
She could well imagine the silk fabric appearing on a kimono
on a shunga print. The many pleats in the front and back created a particularly pleasing symmetry while the effect on the
fruits gave the gown a kaleidoscope quality that made her think
of Ashton's gift of the spyglass. The neck was designed to be
worn either with a concealing lacey jabot, or without. She
chose without. Thus a small amount of daring skin was
visible—not as much as one might see in a ball gown, but a
small amount nevertheless. When she reviewed herself in the
mirror, she smiled. She looked bold and fearless.

Edwina suspected attending the performance of Oscar
Wilde's latest play, *Lady Windermere's Fan, A Play about a
Good Woman*, was part of her mother's plan to advance their
family's social position. Her father grumbled about the time
removed from work and the need to dress to the nines for a
play, but her mother insisted, and in the end he acquiesced.

She shouldn't have been surprised that Walter was waiting
in their box at the theater; her father's intervention, she supposed. She knew Walter was not enamored with plays and
the theater. He'd made that quite clear weeks ago when she
suggested they see a play to satisfy her story about the need
for Faith's parasol. Of all the new, exciting playwrights, Oscar Wilde was his least favorite, but Edwina assumed he ap-

proved, at least, of the title of *this* play. She settled into the chair next to where he stood waiting.

His eyes slipped almost immediately to her daring neckline. "Did you bring your wrap, Edwina?" He frowned. "You might catch a chill without one."

"I'm quite comfortable, Walter. Sit down." She tapped him with her black feather fan.

"I would gladly sacrifice my jacket for your comfort," he insisted. "I can rest it on your shoulders." He started to shrug out of his evening jacket.

"I'm fine, Walter. Please sit back and enjoy the play."

Her mother, seated on the other side of her and in vigorous employment of a pair of opera glasses, urgently patted her knee. "The Trewelyns are directly across from us. Do you see? Oh, look! Mrs. Trewelyn just nodded in our direction." She lowered the glasses, beaming. "It's a good sign. I knew that following up the Sutton soiree with a round of calls would prove productive. Mrs. Trewelyn wouldn't have acknowledged our existence before then."

Edwina borrowed her mother's glasses and peered across the theater. Ashton smiled in her direction and nodded. Her heart leapt to her throat. He was so incredibly dark and handsome. In spite of her mother's exuberance, Mrs. Trewelyn did not appear pleased with his attention. The house lights lowered before she could see more.

Edwina enjoyed the first two acts more than she had anticipated she would. The play revolved around a young bride who suspected her husband was having an affair. When her husband insisted she invite the mystery woman to her birthday ball, the bride contemplated running off with another man. Unbeknownst to her, the mystery woman was really her very own mother. Her husband's involvement with the woman had only been to assist the mother back into society. When the young bride left a note behind of her intentions to run away with a known rake, the mother intercepted the note and pledged to help her daughter avoid making the same mistake she had made herself so many years ago. The curtain was lowered for intermission.

"I don't know why they call this a play about a good woman," Walter complained. "A good woman would have accepted without question her husband's statement that he wasn't having relations. A good woman would never contemplate running away with another man."

"Perhaps the good woman is the mother, the one society rejected," Edwina offered.

"That can't be right," he argued. "If she had been the good woman, she would be married. Her own daughter would certainly recognize her."

She looked at his face. *Sweet Walter.* The concept of hypocrisy was lost on him. Society's restrictions were necessary and beyond question in his mind. She wasn't certain if that was an admirable trait, but it was a reliable one. "Perhaps we should go to the mezzanine during intermission," she said. "I feel the need to stand and take some refreshment before the next act."

Of course, that wasn't the only reason for leaving their box to stand in the mezzanine, but she couldn't tell Walter that. Her mother, however, understood the social aspects of being seen at such an event. She joined them to make a party of three. Her father remained behind to talk to an acquaintance in the next box.

Edwina spied Ashton immediately on the far side of the mezzanine. He was surrounded by women, several of whom she recognized from the soiree. Ashton immediately broke away from the group and walked toward her, a generous smile on his face. "Mrs. Hargrove and Miss Hargrove. What a pleasure to see you both again." He extended a hand to Walter, who begrudgingly shook it.

"Was that Lady Sutton I saw in your box?" her mother asked. Before Ashton could answer, her mother hurried off. "I must inquire about her health. She had suffered a chill the last I heard."

Ashton waited until Mrs. Hargrove had left, then turned toward Edwina. "You are a vision of beauty this evening." His eyes warmed with his words. He leaned heavily on an elaborately carved stick at his side. Edwina was tempted to ask if it concealed a fishing pole or perhaps a life preserver, but that would have required explanation to Walter. "I imagine the other women are seething with jealousy at your unique style," he said, the wicked gleam in his eyes causing her exposed skin to heat.

He was most likely right about glances of envy—not due to her style, but rather her company. Walter stepped slightly forward, almost as if to shield her from Ashton's appreciative gaze, but not before a thrill rippled through her.

"Are you enjoying the play, Mr. Trewelyn?" she asked. It was not the question she longed to ask, but Walter stood near.

"I'm enjoying the intermission much more." He always knew the right words to make her knees weak, but, she reminded herself, he'd had lots of practice in this area. Walter scowled.

"You remind me of that scoundrel in the play, that Mr. Darlington," Walter said. "He's a charmer much like yourself."

"Mr. Wilde did give him the best lines," Ashton replied. "'I can resist anything but temptation,'" he quoted as he turned to Edwina. "Do you believe that, Miss Hargrove?"

"I believe Mr. Wilde spends considerable thought on the subject of temptation," she said, remembering that Ashton had quoted him before. "I wonder what temptation obsesses him so?"

Ashton laughed, then nodded to her in a sort of salute.

"Walter," she said, turning to her side, "would you be so kind as to bring something for my parched throat?" Walter continued to glare at Ashton. "I'd ask Mr. Trewelyn, but given the stairs and his leg injury . . ."

Walter nodded tersely, then bumped Ashton as he passed. Ashton quickly regained his balance and watched Walter tread down the stairs to the lower lobby with a wary expression.

"That man has no love lost for me," he said.

"No," Edwina agreed. She knew Walter didn't wish to leave her side but she needed the privacy to see if Ashton had received her last letter. Sweet Walter would never deny her such a simple request as a glass of lemonade. "He has his reasons."

Ashton straightened. His lips tightened. "I imagine he recognizes my affection for you." His eyes narrowed. "Just as I can see that you care for him."

She laughed lightly. "Walter has been a friend of the family for many years." She grasped Ashton's arm and turned him slightly to carve out a small bit of privacy in a mezzanine packed with people. "Did you receive my message about the Guardians' meeting tomorrow night?"

He took her gloved hand in his and studied it. "I've received all of your many messages." His finger stroked her knuckle. "Edwina . . . it's difficult to describe how much those letters mean to me."

She didn't know what to say. Strange how she found it easy to tell him of her thoughts through the pages of a letter, but felt tongue-tied now addressing him in person.

"As a result of your encouragement," he said, "I've created a prototype of a rifle scope that may work for the Martini-Henry rifle. I delivered the casing to Thomas Harris this morning. He's providing the optics."

His face beamed with his accomplishment. She wished his father, who was missing in that box across the way, could see his son now. "How exciting! I'm so proud of you," she said. Should the design succeed, no one would think of him in terms of "Casanova" again. Especially his father. Lost in her admiration for Ashton's news, she'd lost track of what exactly he was saying. She refocused.

". . . I hope that even after we search the gallery for more notes, you'll consider—"

"We?" Panic filled her voice. "Surely you don't expect me to assist in your search. I can't go back there."

"Why not? The timing is perfect. You've already seen the collection. You examined it quite thoroughly if I recall."

Her cheeks began to heat. It wasn't the woodprints that she feared, it was her feelings when she viewed them. They made her want to do things, explore things that she knew she mustn't. Not with this man. She glanced at his face. That, of course, was the problem. It was precisely *this man* that made her blood hum with taboo desires. She couldn't imagine doing the things the pictures depicted with Walter, but with Ashton . . .

He smiled, seemingly ignorant of the hot currents flowing through her body. "We'll be able to perform a much more efficient search if we work together. It was your suggestion, after all."

She bit her lip, worried that her voice would betray the improper yearnings that coursed through her veins. "I suggested *you* search for more messages." She cast her voice low, not wishing to be overheard, but that only drew him closer. "Not that I would assist." She glanced quickly to the stairs. While sending Walter off for a beverage had been a ploy for privacy, now she wished she had the cool liquid in her hand. She looked across the mezzanine, anywhere but at Ashton. She spotted his stepmother speaking to . . . her mother! Her gaze returned to Ashton. "How could I possibly explain my presence to your stepmother? She certainly wouldn't allow me in that gallery."

"As luck would have it, Constance is leaving for a stay at a friend's country house. With both of my parents gone for the evening, we'll be able to search undisturbed."

"The servants?" Her voice squeaked as Ashton competently removed her objections one by one.

"A few will travel with Constance. I'll suggest several others take the evening off, as their services won't be needed. There will be a minimal staff, but we should be able to avoid those few. Trust me." He winced. "I have a bit of experience in this."

Edwina glanced at her mother's animated conversation. "I wish you had experience in keeping my mother occupied," she said, half in jest. From the look on Constance's face, Edwina imagined her mother was being more tolerated than encouraged to climb the higher rungs in society. She feared for her mother's feelings if all her efforts resulted in rejection.

"Is that a problem?" Ashton smiled. "I have experience in that area as well. Your mother won't be home tomorrow evening to notice you're missing."

She jerked her gaze to his. "How?"

Walter climbed the final steps to the mezzanine with a glass in hand. Their brief interlude of privacy was quickly coming to a close.

"Seven o'clock," Ashton managed a moment before the bells sounded to return to their seats. He crossed to his step-mother, who waited impatiently on the far side of the mezzanine.

Edwina accepted the glass of lemonade from Walter and sipped at it greedily to refresh her suddenly dry mouth. How did she manage to get into this pickle? She could, of course, decline to participate. It was difficult to refuse Ashton when he turned those expressive eyes her way, but she could refuse. She could stay in her room and, inspired by that netsuke, she could . . . Netsuke! This would provide the perfect opportunity to return that blasted annoyance. Ashton wouldn't have cause to think she stole it, and she wouldn't live with the worry that someone would find it in her room.

Thankfully, Walter took her arm to guide her back to their seats. With her thoughts on returning to the secret gallery, she didn't pay attention to such a mundane thing as a third act. She had managed to escape unscathed from her first unorthodox visit to the Trewelyn library. Would she be as fortunate the second?

· *Fourteen* ·

"I KNEW, I JUST KNEW, SPEAKING WITH LADY SUTTON last night at the theater was the right thing to do," her mother exclaimed, her enthusiasm causing Isabella to jump and pounce with joy. "Why earlier today I received a note inviting me to her town home to play cards this evening. Cards! I wish I had time to brush up my skills."

"Is father invited as well?" Edwina asked hopefully.

"No. This is for ladies only. But your father won't mind. He has another appointment this evening. I hate to leave you alone, but I know you'll be content with your books and letters." Her mother covered her mouth for a moment like a young girl. Indeed she hadn't seen her mother this excited in years. "We're on the verge of stepping up higher in society, I just know it. And it's all due to your chance meeting with Lady Sutton in the park. I'm not certain why she was so taken with you, but she is. She always inquires after you."

Guilt tempered Edwina's enthusiasm. Her mother was so excited over her rise in society, while Edwina knew the invitation was a result of Ashton's manipulation to lure her back into that secret gallery.

"If I'm accepted into Lady Sutton's circle, it will mean improved contacts for your father." Her eyes twinkled mischievously. "And for Walter, as well. We'll be invited to balls and soirees and . . ."

"Won't you miss your meetings at the Perennial Society, or the Ladies Society for Good Works, or Matrons for a Common Cause?"

"I can still participate in all of those groups, dear." She bit her lip. "Maybe not as frequently as before but I'll still participate. Or"—her face brightened—"you can take my place. That's a wonderful idea! I will take you to the next meetings of all of my groups and introduce you. You'll just love the ladies. Love them."

"But what of my friends? The Crescent . . ."

Her mother's face dimmed slightly. "Once you're properly married and established in your own household, I'd imagine you won't have time for those ladies. Associating with that firebrand Claire won't be helpful to Walter. And Sarah . . . well, you just won't have as much time for them as you do now."

Edwina could feel the bars on her cage tighten.

Her mother sat on the corner of the bed. "Edwina, I want you to promise me something."

Isabella jumped onto the bed as well. After accepting a few strokes down her sleek back, the kitten hopped off the bed to set about exploring the room.

"You must admit your pursuits are a little peculiar," her mother said. "I believe it's time for you to stop some of your more radical behavior and conform to the roles society expects of young women."

Edwina heard scratching and a roll from the vicinity of her bureau. Looking beyond her mother, she saw Isabella's thin tail whipping the air from the partially open drawer. Her mother glanced back as well, smiled, then continued with her lecture. "You're not getting any younger, Edwina. Most young women your age have married and are well on their way toward producing children."

The kitten's head popped up out of the drawer with the middle of one of Edwina's white silk stockings clasped in her sharp kitten teeth. The bulge in the closed end of the stocking confirmed Edwina's fears that the kitten had discovered the netsuke. Edwina struggled to keep the panic from her face. She wasn't certain what was worse, that her mother would discover the erotic piece in her possession, or that the expensive artifact would be damaged from the kitten's play. Neither possibility was favorable.

"What sort of radical behavior?" Edwina asked in an attempt to keep her mother's attention focused on her and not the kitten's antics.

"Riding that bicycle of yours to start. Proper young women do not ride bicycles."

"Princess Beatrice was rumored to ride a tricycle."

"And she didn't marry until she was twenty-eight," her mother argued. She shook her head. "One wonders if even that would have occurred if she wasn't a royal. We do not have that in our favor. Your future husband—"

"You mean, Mr. Thomas," Edwina said sadly. The stocking fell to the floor with a thump. Isabella jumped to the floor in pursuit, then dragged the stocking under the bed. At least the netsuke wasn't visible, though that could change in a moment with a well-timed kitten stroke.

"Yes, Mr. Thomas." Her mother sighed. "I'm certain it's your insistence on riding that bicycle that has kept him from offering for your hand." The sound of racing paws and the uneven roll of the carved netsuke filled the silence after her mother's pronouncement. "Whatever has that kitten gotten hold of?"

"I'm sure it's nothing," Edwina quickly replied. "Probably just a thread spool. Something Kathleen left behind, I imagine."

"I don't think so." Her mother frowned toward the floor. "It sounds heavier than a spool. Let me take a look." She began to get down on a knee.

"No." Panicked, Edwina pulled on her arm. "You don't want to get down on the dirty floor. You'll be mussed for your card party." Her mother glanced up, considering. Edwina needed to get her out of the room before it was too late, so she did the unthinkable. "I promise to stop riding my bicycle if that's what you prefer. I'll do better to garner Walter's approval." She glanced toward the door. "You don't want to be late for Lady Sutton's, do you?"

"I suppose not," her mother said, rising to her feet. "I'm sorry to ask you to give up something you enjoy, but once you are married, you'll appreciate the necessity." She kissed Edwina on the forehead. "You have a pleasant evening, dear."

As soon as the bedroom door closed, Edwina took a deep breath of relief, then got down on hands and knees. "Come here, you rascal." She retrieved both the kitten and her prize. "You're bound and determined to get me in trouble, aren't you?"

Cradling the cat in one hand, she emptied the stocking on her bed so she could inspect the erotic carving for scratches or marks. What would her mother think of the small innocuous sculpture if she knew of it? Would she suspect it was something a courtesan may have worn on her person? Edwina ran her fingers over the smooth, centuries-old carving. A small thrill tingled her rib cage. What would the Perennial Society say? The Ladies Society for Good Works? She almost laughed, but she didn't wish to attract anyone's attention. Possession of such an item would not be smiled upon by any of those groups . . . or by Walter.

In fact, if he knew she had it, he might think twice about the engagement that her parents had assumed was a certainty. The man thought riding a bicycle was radical and breaking codes peculiar. What would he say if he knew she'd been in Trewelyn's secret chamber? Ashton's voice whispered in her memory. *"I know you, Miss Hargrove. You are a modern woman who rides bicycles and breaks conventions as easily as breaking my poor devoted heart."*

She certainly was going to break convention tonight. Edwina dropped the netsuke in her reticule, anxious to return it before its absence was noted. So much anxiety over a small carved piece of wood.

Glancing up, she caught her reflection in the small circular mirror suspended on the wall. She was not a striking beauty, not in the manner of those with whom Ashton associated. His reputation had been well documented. He was, as Sarah said, not the marrying kind, not like Walter. A lump gathered in her throat. *Not like Walter.*

An earlier conversation played in her mind. *"What do you wish for me, Mother?"*

"I wish for you to be married and have lots of children. No woman can be happy without marriage. No woman can be secure. That's what I want for you. Security."

Security meant that she must return the troublesome carving to the gallery. Security meant she had to forsake the things in life that gave her pleasure. Security meant that she would ultimately give up her association with Ashton Trewelyn, . . . but not tonight. Tonight she needed to break convention one more time.

Just then her mother opened her bedroom door. "I almost forgot to mention that your father has already left this evening. I'm sorry to leave you home alone, dear, but I know you'll be fine."

"I'll probably just go to bed early," Edwina said, stroking her kitty to induce deep purring. "Enjoy your evening."

ASHTON PACED, LISTENING TO THE CLOCK TOLLING THE hour while he waited for Edwina's arrival. Everything was falling in place. The house was almost completely empty, with the remaining servants cautioned to remain belowstairs. Similar demands had been common back in his Casanova days. He guessed from the slight upturn of lips that the staff had assumed the old Ashton Trewelyn had finally returned. In fact, they had most likely cast wagers on when the event was to occur. Good. Their celebrations would keep them out of sight.

Would she come? Never had he so intensely anticipated a woman's arrival as he had this woman's. Of course, never had he felt such a connection with another, as he did with Edwina.

Until he saw her at the theater, he hadn't really considered using the convenient departure of both of his parents for anything more absorbing than settling down with a good book and a fine brandy while he waited to hear of the Guardians' decision. However, the moment he saw her in the black silk with the oranges that were so reminiscent of her scent, and noted the way her eyes sparkled when their glances met, he knew he had to see her in private. Others may wear fringes and falderal, but Edwina's simple elegance outshone them all. He wasn't certain additional coded messages even existed, or that, if they did, such additions would help in cracking a code that had thus far defied Edwina's talents. However, if using the lure of additional notes would bring her to him in private, and to the secret chamber at that, well—he wasn't above resorting to Casanova's tricks.

On one hand, he didn't like that he was exploiting her innocence and trust, but on the other, he couldn't help himself. He was, after all, only a man, and Edwina was . . . Edwina. He'd lusted for her from the first time she stood in the gallery proclaiming herself a modern woman. His groin tightened with the memory. The promise of having her was far more seductive than he realized, and Walter, fool that he was, had left her alone with an out-of-practice but well-experienced scoundrel.

Of course, she could decline his suggestion that he needed her assistance. Even he had to admit it was a thin ploy. As Edwina suggested, he could search without involving another in the process. Most women would laugh in his face at such an outrageous invitation. If she decided not to come, he would accept that she was wise to his ways and had disregarded his amorous inclinations. He would seek information about the code from the Guardians themselves. He would work from the inside and avoid contact with the fair, delectable, highly desired, yet purely innocent Edwina.

But what if his innocent Edwina came in expectation of actually looking for coded messages? Should she come to his residence, how would he know if she came to search, or to sin?

The answer was obvious.

If she insisted on restricting her search to the perfectly respectable study, then they would look for coded messages and little else. But if she agreed to search the pillow books, then he'd know that she burned for him as he did for her. His heart pounded in his chest in a manner to compete with that bloody clock. He paced to the windows, checking once again if the carriage had returned, and praying that it would return with a passenger inside.

EDWINA COVERED HER HEAD WITH THE HOOD OF HER cloak. She didn't wish Trewelyn's neighbors to see her arrival and assume she was one of *those* women. Still, a thrill titillated her bones at the adventure of it all. She slipped her fingers over the cloisonné necklace of cherry blossoms that she continued to wear even after Lady Sutton's soiree. This would be the last night for the Mistress of Cherry Blossoms. She remembered how shocked she had been thinking that Ashton had intended to make her his mistress. Given that he'd never attempted anything more than a kiss, that supposition now seemed laughable. After tonight she would have to revert to demure, traditional behavior as per her promise to her mother. But for now she could pretend she was the sort of woman who did as she wished for the sole pleasure of the experience. How lovely such an experience must be.

She hurried from the carriage Trewelyn had sent to the front door, which opened before her as if by magic. Then she saw him. Ashton. Waiting with open arms for her mad flight from the carriage to the town house. Without hesitation she stepped into those arms that wrapped about her as if to protect her from the night itself. The door closed behind her, sealing off the outside world. Her hood fell back on her shoulders, then Ashton's lips discovered the sensitive skin of her neck, awakening her body as if from a long sleep.

"You came," he whispered. "I was afraid you wouldn't."

She pulled back, enjoying the delicious sensation of Ashton's stubble scraping her skin. Did Walter ever generate this kind of dark enticing stubble? She didn't think so—all the more reason to revel in it now. "Of course, I came. You said you needed me."

His eyes darkened and smoldered; it was the only way to describe how the heat from his gaze affected her insides . . . or maybe it was the heat of hellfire. She could almost hear Faith whispering in her ear that now that she'd entered the devil's playground, she could expect little else. No, she reassured herself, Ashton Trewelyn could have any woman in all of England. He would not smolder for the ordinary and maybe slightly peculiar Edwina and yet . . . his fingers tightened at her waist, pulling her back to press against his chest. Panic that he might have misunderstood her purpose in coming settled in her stomach.

"Where do we start?" she asked in a rush, hoping to defuse his kisses.

His gaze unfocused, a slight smile pulled at his lips. "I'm more interested in where we stop."

She attempted to pull back, but his hold was strong. "Our time to look for additional notes is limited," she said. When he didn't immediately respond, she added, "To break the code?"

He looked as if she were speaking gibberish, but then his eyes cleared, his lips tightened, and he released her. "Yes." He inhaled deeply. "The notes."

"We should get started," Edwina said, almost wishing she hadn't spoken. Her lips tingled for his return. What would have happened if her decidedly practical nature hadn't interrupted? "We only have a few hours."

"Yes," he agreed. He stepped back, perhaps a bit unsteady on his feet. His eyes closed briefly as if he were offering a prayer. When he opened them again, his face had cleared of all expression except that of a reluctant expectation as if time had stopped and the world held its collective breath for the space of this one moment. "Where would you like to start?" he asked tentatively.

She knew immediately. "The secret gallery."

· *Fifteen* ·

🌿 COULD ANY WOMAN POSSIBLY BE MORE FRUSTRAT-
ing?

One minute she was melting in his arms, enjoying kisses
placed to her intoxicating neck—at least, he knew *he* was
enjoying them. The next minute she spoke of codes and messages as if completely unaware of the passionate heat she'd
unleashed by her mere presence. And then, just as he was
regaining his senses and ability to think without the narrowing focus of rampant lust, she invites him to accompany her
to his father's secret chamber of erotic works.

Dear Lord, with those three words he thought she had answered his dreams. Desire and lust resurged that he might sweep
her into his arms and carry her to the chamber to explore the
wonders and intimacies of their surroundings. But he hesitated . . . something was off balance. Something wasn't quite as
it should be. She had just invited him to that shameless gallery,
yet she remained wrapped tightly in her cloak, hugging that
embellished sack to her chest, gazing at him without the fire that
consumed him. She didn't fit the pattern of his expectations.

He had thought that should she respond to his invitation to come to his residence, knowing full well that no chaperones, no family, no saviors of any sort would be present, then he would know that she was willing to ignore society's rules to be with him. Now he wondered if his reasoning was valid, which was troublesome in itself. However, if she wasn't here to advance the intimacy that had begun in their shared letters and conversations, then why did she insist on going to the gallery?

"Would you like me to take your cloak and your . . . ?" He twirled his finger at the cloth bag that he assumed carried her ever-present journal.

Her eyes rounded. "No," she insisted. "If they were to be discovered, my presence would be known."

"No one is here, Edwina," he reassured her. "There will be no interruptions."

She clutched the bag as if her very life depended on it. "Just to be safe, I'd like to keep them with me."

She led the way to the gallery—led the way—then stepped aside to watch him pull the lever, all with a strange sort of urgency, as if she couldn't wait to get inside. If he didn't know better, he would have thought she was being pursued. The thought of some sort of matrimonial trap came to mind.

"Does someone know you're here?" he asked suspiciously, half expecting that crazy friend of hers, Claire, to come pounding at the door.

"No." She looked at him as if his sanity was in question. "Why would I tell anyone? This is not exactly proper." She looked askance. "I may be peculiar but I'm not—"

"Who said you were peculiar?" He engaged the lever that opened the secret door, then frowned back at her. "I might describe you as many things, Edwina Hargrove, but *peculiar* would not be one of them. I might say you were talented, intelligent, interesting, engaging . . ." He stepped into the small passageway and opened the second door that led to the chamber of erotic prints. "Sensitive, highly desirable, adventurous—"

"Did you say 'highly desirable'?" She looked at him in wonder.

Dear Lord, did she not have a clue that she made his blood turn to liquid fire? How his cock was even now straining to find her heat? How his fingers trembled with the overwhelming desire to pull her close and kiss those softly parted lips into total submission?

He pushed open the second door to his father's illicit and highly erotic gallery, a devil's playground if ever one existed, then looked back over his shoulder to where she impatiently waited.

"Absolutely."

A PLEASANT TREMOR SLIPPED DOWN EDWINA'S SPINE. No one had ever considered her highly desirable before, at least not for reasons unassociated with her father. She watched him lean on his walking stick as he fumbled to light the gas jet. She knew him to be observant and humorous from his letters, compassionate for the way he cared about his younger half brother, intelligent from his observations about the constellations and weaponry, and handsome because the sight of him took her breath away. Heat singed her cheeks. "I find you to be highly desirable as well."

He lit the second jet, then turned toward her with a gleam in his eyes that made the strength in her legs dissolve like sugar in tea. She glanced quickly to the shelves that held the netsuke, reminding herself of the real reason for her visit to this chamber. Now that she'd managed to gain access to the secret gallery, she'd need to find a way to return the netsuke in her reticule to its place on the shelves without notice.

As light filled the room, her gaze slipped to the prints on the wall. They weren't as shocking as they had been the first time she'd seen them. And as the memory of them occupied a good deal of her wandering thoughts, they'd become immensely familiar. Once again she saw the enormous "jade stalks," the open and weeping "heavenly gates," the facial expressions that expressed enjoyment, the beautifully patterned robes . . .

"How should we go about this?" Ashton stepped behind

her and unfastened her cloak, then slipped it from her shoulders. His kiss placed to the back of her neck rippled throughout her entire body. Her breasts lifted; her toes curled. His voice close to her ear generated another wave of deliciousness. "Shall each of us select a pillow book and check for hidden notes, or should we look together?"

He was teasing her, she suspected. He didn't seem to take this evening's mission very seriously, which had her wondering if she wasn't here for some other purpose. "We should be able to look through the entire collection in a minimal time if we both look separately," she pronounced. "It would be the most practical method." Then an idea sparked. She turned to him with enthusiastic expectation. "Perhaps you'd prefer to take your pillow books into the library to check for additional correspondence there?"

He looked at her strangely. Perhaps her functional blouse, skirt, and wide leather belt were not the appropriate attire for an evening of searching for coded messages. She glanced down the front of her outfit and then back to him.

"No," he said. "I believe I'll stay close. You might have questions about what you see. I'd like to explain anything you find confusing."

Christopher! Now how was she going to get him to leave? "You answered all my questions the last time we were here," she replied sweetly.

"But now you'll be viewing new prints, and you might have new questions," he insisted.

She sighed. It appeared that avenue was at an end.

Selecting one of the pillow books from the boxes, she sat on the mattress in the back of the room. It was the only seat and her legs were shaking so much with anxiety that she didn't want to risk standing. Ashton selected another book and sat near. Not near enough to bump against her, but close enough to see the pages she turned. Page after page flashed by with vividly detailed depictions of an activity that she should know nothing about but with which she was becoming exceedingly familiar. No secret notes hid in the binding. She supposed she shouldn't be surprised. The notes had probably been removed before the books were placed in this room. Their activity here as it related to helping to decipher the code would be meaningless. Still, she needed a diversion of some sort so she could return the netsuke.

The repetitious nature of the prints rendered them boring after a short period. She'd gone through five books when she paused at a print that showed a man suckling a woman's breast. Her own tingled and peaked as she imagined Ashton making similar ministrations. No wonder the woman's face clearly revealed her enjoyment.

"Does that print interest you, Edwina?"

His voice, so soft and seductive, teased her ear with such fervor, she wasn't certain if he spoke, or if she had dreamed his words. But his fingers trailing down the outside of her arm confirmed that he wasn't searching for messages.

"Look at the woman's face," he said. "Look at how she enjoys the man's touch. Can you see how her nipple reaches for his lips? Did you know the tips of a woman's breasts are highly sensitive? Have you experienced a man's touch there, my sweet?"

Her eyes closed, allowing the combined force of his mesmerizing voice and his titillating touch to turn her veins into molten honey. "Yes . . ." she responded to his first question. She'd noticed the depiction of the cherry nipples reaching for attention, especially as her own seemed to follow suit. She must have a vivid imagination to envision so clearly the jolt of sensation in that print, or maybe it was Ashton's hand on her breast that made it so real.

She couldn't recall the rest of his questions. Who could when caught in such a maelstrom of sensation? Her answer caused Ashton a moment of hesitation, then a sudden increased urgency. He pressed her back on the mattress, the pillow book slipping to the floor. He kissed her neck, while massaging the rise beneath her silk blouse. Somehow in the confusion of lips and sighs, fingers and gasps, her buttons slipped from their moorings, allowing her skin to receive the direct press of his lips.

"Did he touch you like this?" Ashton asked, scooping her

right breast free of the restraints of corset and cover. His lips
latched onto her sensitive nipple, his tongue and teeth teasing
the sensitive nub in a manner she'd never imagined. She
peeked at him through lowered lashes. Just the sight of him
at her breast unleashed a pooling in the area the woman of
the netsuke knew well. His hand wound beneath her skirts,
slips, and drawers with a determination that implied experience. Something of which she clearly had none. Dear Lord,
she never imagined . . .

She tried to say "no," but the sound that issued from her
lips was more of a moan. His fingers slipped over her nether
hairs and found what they were seeking. How to describe the
feeling?

Her back arched as his fingers urged her to some unknown
conclusion of inexpressible magic. Her own explorations had
been pleasant, but this combined attack on breast and below . . . A sudden blossoming of feeling unleashed from that
region, spreading waves of calming titillation through her
entire body. She sagged back to the mattress, spent, though
she hadn't actually done anything. Her eyes slowly opened.

"Did you shatter so prettily for your Mr. Thomas?"

Ashton stood and moved to unfasten his trousers to relieve
the bulge formed there.

"Walter? What are you saying?" She almost giggled at the
thought. "Walter has never touched me so. I'm not certain he
knows how."

Ashton frowned down at her, his voice demanding. "You
said someone did. Who?"

She pushed her skirts back from around her knees. "I said
no such thing. No one has touched me as you have." She
scowled up at him. "I resent the suggestion that they have."

"Ash?" Matthew's small voice sounded in the library. "Are
you in here?"

They both stilled. The door connecting the gallery to the
library stood open.

Edwina sat up, slipping her breast beneath her serviceable
stays. Her fingers quickly worked the buttons back into their
holes. "You said—"

"Stay here," Ashton commanded. "I'll take care of this." He walked toward the secret door.

This was her chance! Edwina hunted for her reticule on the floor. Once she discovered it, she slipped over to the shelves, fishing in it for the netsuke. Her arm outstretched, she was about to set it on the shelf with the others when Ashton returned.

"Edwina?" His face, at first confused, deepened into a scowl. "What are you doing?"

"I was just—"

"Are you stealing one of my father's netsukes?" He stared at her in disbelief. "Is that why you inquired about their price?"

"No," she insisted, placing the piece on the shelf. "This fell in my parasol the last time we were here. I was trying to return it."

"If that were true you would have given it to me earlier." His face contorted, distaste curling his nostrils. "I thought you were different. I thought I could trust you." He advanced until he stood directly in front of her. "Constance might have her faults, but at least she wasn't a petty thief."

She slapped him. "I'm not a thief. I would have returned it earlier, but it rolled beneath the furniture and I couldn't find it." Her explanation sounded feeble, but she was so flustered. What was she to do? "I came here tonight to help you look for more coded messages and you took advantage of the situation." She struggled to finish buttoning the final buttons of her blouse. "If anyone should be angry, it should be me."

She pushed past him and ran into the library, then began down the passageway. Before she'd reached the end she saw Matthew toting a book, or rather, Matthew spotted her.

"Miss Hargrove!" he cried. "Could you read to me? Miss Jordan is gone and Ash says he can't at the moment and—"

"Edwina!" She spun around. Ashton, the imprint of her hand still red on his face, held her cloak. "You forgot this."

As she returned to fetch her cloak, she heard movement behind her. Ashton lifted his gaze. Instinctively, she turned to see a footman crossing at the front of the house toward the front door.

"Quick," Ashton hissed, shoving the garment in her arms. "Back inside the gallery."

Matthew ran after her. "Miss Hargrove, Miss Hargrove!"

Christopher! How could an empty house be so full of people! The secret door stood open. She ran through it and pulled both doors closed behind her. Ashton knew where she was and she'd have to count on him to release her when it was safe to do so. She slowly backed toward the mattress. The lights were still on, illuminating that she was surrounded by the graphic pillow books, the forbidden woodblock prints, and scandalous netsukes. None of that bothered her as much as the fact that the door was closed, trapping her alone in a windowless room. *Please Ashton*, she prayed. *Don't leave me behind.*

ASHTON TOOK A DEEP BREATH, THEN STRODE FORWARD to greet his father. "You're back early." He scooped Matthew up in his arms along the way. "Did everything go well?"

"We discussed your admission into the Guardians if that's what you are asking." His father looked up and scowled. "Were you making inappropriate advances to the parlormaids again?"

Ashton covered his face with his hand, feeling the heat of Edwina's slap. Perhaps he'd been hasty with his accusations, but that discussion would have to wait.

"What's a guardian?" Matthew asked, rubbing his eye.

The senior Trewelyn glared at Matthew. "Why aren't you in bed?"

"Miss Jordan must be occupied belowstairs," Ashton explained. "Allow me to find her to take Matthew back to the nursery."

His father grunted, a sign of acquiescence. "Join me in my study when you're through. We need to talk."

Damnation! Of all nights for the Guardians to conduct a short meeting. Ashton hoisted Matthew on his shoulders and took him belowstairs to the kitchen where the servants ruled. His appearance meant the curtailment of their celebration, much as his father's early arrival had upset his. Miss Jordan relieved him of the sleepy little boy, then headed up the back stairs to the upper levels, but the others scattered to their duties as well. The resurgence of activity made it too risky as yet to release Edwina. But his thoughts were on her as he walked down the passageway to his father's study.

"Come in, come in. Take a seat." His father poured brandy into two snifters, then handed one to Ashton. "I've talked to the Guardians about your admittance as a member. You know that we aren't some social group that allows you to buy your way."

"I realize that, sir."

"We only accept members of a certain superior caliber," he said, puffing his chest out in self-admiration. "I will admit there were some that are opposed to your membership based on your reputation as a woman-chasing rake of the ninth degree."

Ashton's teeth set on edge. The only person who believed him to be something more than a rake was probably loading all of his father's netsuke collection into her tiny reticule as they spoke.

"There were some, however, that saw you as a worthy member." His father sipped at his drink.

"And on which side did you stand?" Ashton asked, guessing that his father was not in favor of his joining the group.

His father's lips thinned. "You are to be tested."

"Tested? In what manner?"

"You are to be tested on your ability to keep the secrets of the Guardians and on your fortitude to complete an assigned task. You will be contacted at a future time with further instructions. I can say no more than that." He stirred the air with his hand as if to dismiss any questions that were hovering. Ashton was not discouraged, however.

"A future time? Can you be more specific?" He sipped his brandy, hoping to discourage any thoughts that he was worried. However, he was concerned how this "mission" would affect Edwina's efforts. Knowledgeable as she was about his application to the Guardians, he'd like to keep her abreast of his progress.

"No. Even I don't know when you'll be called. You can speak of this to no one," his father warned. "When you receive your instructions, you will leave immediately without notifying me or anyone else. I, naturally, will understand when you disappear, but I cannot make allowances for you or explain your whereabouts. To do so would risk exposure of the Guardians."

Ashton wanted to reply that the Guardians had already been repeatedly exposed, but held his tongue. If they wanted to pretend to be a secret society, he would go along with their demands, for now. Keeping this mission from Edwina would be difficult, but hopefully he could complete the task in short order. All he wanted was reassurance that his father was not involved in treasonous behavior. After that, the Guardians were welcome to their secrets.

"You will have to complete your mission on your own resources. I am not allowed to help you in any way," his father continued. "Once you have satisfactorily completed the mission, you will be initiated into the Guardians."

An initiation! As if this test was not enough.

"You are part of Falcon Freight now," his father said. "I urge you to remember our slogan. 'The falcon's path is swift and bold, courageous and honest with service of old.' I expect your actions to exemplify those qualities and make me proud."

Ashton felt a pull on his chest. His father had witnessed less prideful moments in his past, the many changes in schools, the numerous women, the wild parties, and yet never had he mentioned pride before. Even after he returned from the King's Royal Rifles with a wound in his leg, his father never said he was proud of him. Suddenly he very much wanted to have his father's respect and praise. Still the question had to be asked. "And if I do not adequately complete the test?"

"I will cut off all financial resources and send you out of the country. For you to remain in England would be an embarrassment to the Guardians. Better for you to live with the frogs than disgrace this house." His father scowled. "Are you certain you want to do this, boy? The consequences of failure will be severe."

Ashton carefully placed his snifter on the desk before rising. "I understand." Before he left, he turned back to his father. "I suppose you hadn't noticed. I left my boyhood years ago."

"Then accomplish this task like a man," his father said, "or I shall never look on your face again."

· Sixteen ·

TRAPPED. TRAPPED IN A ROOM WITH NO WAY OUT, or at least, no honorable way out.

She could exit on her own, she'd done it before, but even she recognized that her ability to leave undetected would require a great deal of luck. Somehow, she'd didn't feel so very lucky tonight.

How could he think of her as a thief? The accusation still rankled, though she had considered that might be his reaction when he discovered the netsuke missing. She certainly hadn't expected it when the scandalous annoyance was returned. She glanced at the shelves of carved wood and ivory. Bothersome nuisances. Even if she wanted to steal one of those things for the price it would bring, how could she honorably present such an obscene object for sale? Once Ashton thought about it, and once he realized that the collection was still intact, she hoped they could remain friends. But would they be able to return to their previous footing? She fervently hoped so.

At first she continued to search through the pillow books, placing them in a pile by the mattress after she'd checked for coded messages. But she noted it was a slower task than before. The pictures reminded her of the things Ashton had done to her. How he called forth vibrations from her body that she'd never experienced before. The experience brought with it a realization of why those women did not have an expression of horror and shame at submitting to a man's lust. In fact, the prints suggested that women had similar desires for men. Ashton did not present his jade stalk, but if he could solicit such sensations by use of fingers and tongue, how much more intense would those sensations be if he employed such a large instrument? Her womanly core began to stir at the thought.

She turned the page to see the depiction of a man in a black robe investigating the woman's heavenly gate in a manner as had been presented in other pillow books, but this time she noticed the *mon* on the man's garment. A pattern, similar to the maze she had noticed in her father's office, was enclosed in a thick circle. Though she recognized that the maze patterns were not identical, they were close enough for her to contemplate—was her father one of the Guardians? Like Ashton's father, he attended a meeting this evening . . . could it be the same meeting?

She set the pillow book aside, the page opened to the man with the *mon*. She'd leave it as a reminder to tell Ashton of her supposition. Meanwhile, she would leave the rest of the books for him to search on his own. Her body was too responsive to the suggestive prints for her to continue. She yawned, then stood at the door for a few moments, listening to see if people still stirred in the household, but she couldn't hear anything. It was too soon, she decided, for the house to be at rest, or she'd attempt to leave.

Inexplicably, the room felt smaller, tighter without Ashton's presence. While she might actually be in the middle of a grand house, she felt abandoned and alone. She lay down on the mattress and pulled her cloak over her like a blanket. She'd sleep. Yes, sleep and forget about all those faces staring at her on the wall. She'd sleep and dream and imagine she and Ashton were two figures in one of those prints.

• • •

"EDWINA. WAKE UP NOW, DEAR ONE."

A gentle nudge to her shoulder prodded her awake. She fought to open her eyes, for they clearly wished to remain closed.

"Come on now, love. Open your eyes."

So hard not to obey when the command was whispered by such a lovely compelling voice. She complied with his wishes and saw Ashton Trewelyn come into focus. Was she dreaming? Ashton shouldn't be . . . then she remembered. She was not at home in her own bed. While she should have been panicked, just seeing Ashton, just knowing he didn't desert her made her current circumstances less fearful.

"Is it morning?" she asked.

"It's before dawn," Ashton replied. "I had to wait until my father retired before I could come to you." He helped her sit upright then nodded to the pile of books by the mattress. "I see you were busy in my absence."

She shook her head to chase the lingering cobwebs. "I didn't find anything, but what have I missed? Did you speak to your father?"

He nodded. "I'm to be admitted to the Guardians only if I pass some sort of test."

"What sort of test?"

"My father didn't say. Even if he had, part of the test includes my not telling anyone about it. I assume that includes you, dear one."

"Ashton." She stood, then soothed her hand over that part of his face that she'd slapped. "I'm sorry that I slapped you, but I'm not a thief."

"Hush," he said, a finger to her lips. "I know that."

"You do?" Relief flooded her. His opinion of her was too important for her not to try to correct his misunderstanding. "How?"

"Your letters." He smiled. "And Matthew. Did you not see how his face lit like one of those new electric lights when he saw you? He trusts you implicitly, and I realized, I do too. I believe I knew that even as I accused you." His brows lifted. "I know you, Edwina Hargrove. I've read your letters. I've seen your friends' devotion. You are honest and trustworthy, and I was wrong to have forgotten that." He kissed her fingers. "I've been the victim of some untrustworthy acts by people close to me, but you, my Mistress of Cherry Blossoms, you've not been one. I should be apologizing. I hope you'll forgive me."

"Of course I forgive you." She relaxed, releasing all her worries and anxieties over that carved nuisance. "When I discovered the figurine in Faith's parasol, I was afraid you might suspect that I took it." She turned her face from his. "In fact, my main purpose in coming here tonight was to place the netsuke back on the shelf."

"It wasn't because you burned for me?" he murmured. His gaze drifted toward her lips, causing her to think he meant to kiss her. Though she'd welcome his kiss, she wasn't certain it would stop there.

"What else did your father say?" she asked, hoping to draw his attention away from the inspiration surrounding them.

His gaze searched her face a moment, then his lips twisted. He stepped back, putting a bit of space between them. "He warned me not to fail, though I have the impression that he expects that I will."

"Then he doesn't know you well. You'll show him that you're made of sterner stuff," she said with conviction. How could a father be so ignorant of his own son?

" 'The falcon's path is swift and bold, courageous and honest with service of old,' " Ashton recited, as if from an old lullaby.

"What is that piece of verse?" Edwina asked. A smile tipped her lips. "I don't think it's another of Mr. Wilde's sayings."

"It's something my father said. It's the slogan of Falcon Freight. If I fail the test, I will be a stain on the reputation of the company and the family. I'll be banished from England and all financial resources taken away."

Her mind stalled on the word *slogan*. She didn't really

hear the details about consequences. "Is this slogan something you've heard often?"

"Not so much of late, but as a child I recall him saying that line frequently."

"Say it to me again," she said, scrambling for her reticule. Fortunately her journal was inside as well as her pen. "More slowly this time."

"Why is this important?" His eyes narrowed.

"I won't know until I apply it to the coded text. But a slogan, especially one in verse, might be the key. It would be easy for both parties to remember and record, and it eliminates the need for a page reference or a shared copy of a particular book."

He repeated the line. She copied it word for word, then repeated it back to him. She looked up, excitement glowing in her eyes. "I think this could be it."

Before she could say another word, he kissed her, a quick jubilant sort of kiss. She tasted the brandy on his lips, felt it warm her own. Still grasping the notebook and pencil, she reached to rest her arms on his shoulders in the returned celebratory expression. At least it began that way.

Their lips parted to a point that only a breath existed between them, yet both were hesitant to separate. She looked up, noting desire smoldering in his eyes, and a flutter surged in her rib cage. She so wanted to be desired by a man who knew what he was about. She wanted to experience the excitement that he had brought to her earlier that evening, as she'd likely not have another opportunity. Was that what Mr. Wilde meant? She wished to be the Mistress of Cherry Blossoms before the cage surrounding her fully closed, locking her away from experiencing real emotion again.

Her eyes must have reflected her desire. He pulled her close, kissing her, but this time with hunger and demand. His tongue did not shock her as it had before. She allowed her tongue to stroke his with bold assurance while her fingers reached higher into his hair, lifting her chest to press so willingly into his. Her journal and pen fell from her fingers, the sound absorbed by the carpets on the floor.

Almost immediately, he pressed forward with a low growl of demand and dominance. Her back pressed the wall with a gentle thud, rattling the netsukes on the shelves opposite. One of his hands found her breast, his thumb working the nipple to a tight nub beneath the layers of thin cloth. The other hand worked to remove those layers as quickly as possible, and she wished it so—wanting to experience the awakening she had earlier. She pulled his shirt from his trousers, wishing to feel the warmth of his skin. Once her fingers discovered what her eyes had not, she worked frantically to unfasten the buttons of his shirt.

Suddenly he bent, then scooped her into his arms. She could feel the hard muscles in those arms, and remembered that he said working for Falcon Freight had improved his ability to carry heavy loads, something for which she'd be forever grateful. How wonderful to be lifted off one's feet with urgency and need. Both of which she felt building inside. He carried her to the mattress and lowered her gently.

"Edwina, I think you know my intentions. I want you. I've wanted to bury myself deep inside you since the day you first broke into this house. I want you to experience the sort of pleasure those women know." His jaw pointed to the prints on the wall. "Tell me now if you don't want the same. Once we begin, there will be no going back."

No going back. She liked the sound of that. She felt like the tiger discovering the cage door latch hadn't been securely refastened. A world different from the one she'd known, different from the one before her, beckoned with a lure she couldn't refuse. What was it that Wilde had said? The best way to deal with temptation was to yield to it? She might never experience the many exotic locales on the globe, but she would experience this. Intimacy with someone who had been to such places and would teach her the secrets that he'd learned, intimacy with someone she had come to love. "No going back," she repeated, then pulled his lips to meet hers.

She wasn't sure how they shed so many clothes in such a short period of time, yet they managed. Her shirtwaist, skirt, and petticoat puddled on the floor. She'd tossed her wide leather belt, and it landed on the far side of the mattress. She worked the metal fastenings of her corset, unhooking them until the split busk hung on either side of her, then her breath caught. Ashton, naked from his shoulders to his toes, stood before her.

He was so incredibly beautiful, dark curling hair sprinkled across a chest sculpted by hard labor. The masculine hair formed a dark line from his belly button, passed ridges that begged to be touched, to a nest of curls not unlike her own. However, in the midst of this rose his magnificent jade stalk, long, erect, and threatening. Yet, it wasn't. After viewing the prints and the pillow books, he was as she expected . . . and desired.

He watched as her hand reached out and stroked him from the base to the tip. She circled her fingers around him as she'd seen in the prints. Almost immediately a low growl issued from his throat. He pushed her back on the mattress, lifting her breast away from the cover of her chemise. He suckled there as he had before.

Dear Lord she wanted this. She wanted him. Flames danced in her body. Every part of her reached to get closer, begging for his touch. While he laved her breasts, he pulled the bottom of her chemise till it reached her hips. Without a glance, he untied her drawers and tugged them free, first one hip and then the other. Soon she was open to exploration with his fingers, but he did not stop there.

She guessed his intent as he worked his way down her body, stimulating with his fingers and lips, until he reached the juncture of her legs. He gently pushed them apart to accommodate him as he settled there, just as the octopus settled in the woman's juncture in the fisherwoman's dream print. The moment Ashton slipped his tongue into her nether regions, she understood why someone would dream such a thing. His tongue worked the part of her that his fingers had set to throbbing earlier. Soon waves of intense pleasure rippled through her. Her head thrashed, her fingers dug at the woven covering on the bed. Sensation exploded in rapidly increasing waves until she wanted to cry out, but she wasn't assured that even the secret gallery could confine her screams of pleasure. When her littlest finger brushed the leather belt, she grasped it and placed it in her mouth. Biting and screaming behind clenched teeth, the release exploded within her.

Before the waves had subsided, Ashton directed the head of his jade stalk at her opening and thrust inside her. A flash of pain followed, and she screamed silently again into the leather. Ashton slid inside her, pushing and stretching.

"Are you all right?" He removed the leather from her mouth.

"I didn't want to wake the house," she explained.

He smiled, soothing the hair from her forehead. "Intimacy can be painful the first time, but the worst is over. The next time, I promise it will be better. Does it still hurt?"

"No," she admitted. There was a discomfort, but not as before.

He moved slowly, pressing and withdrawing. Strange to feel this part of him inside of her. After the first few thrusts, her body caught his rhythm. Her hips lifted and surged with him, pulling him deeper and deeper inside. He quickened, moving faster and harder until he stiffened and she felt his explosion deep inside.

He lay very still, while she stroked his wide back. The stories he'd told her of ying and yang came drifting back. While she didn't truly believe the Japanese mythology of the value of the exchange of fluids, she did recognize the value of this intimacy, of holding Ashton so close that she could hear his heartbeat.

While she knew she could conceivably come to regret her actions, she didn't at the moment. She was proud to be his Mistress of Cherry Blossoms this night. She imagined she'd never have the opportunity to experience anything so profoundly beautiful ever again, but she had tonight with a man she loved.

ASHTON GAZED AT THE BEAUTY BENEATH HIM. GOOD Lord, what had he done! He had suspected Edwina was a virgin but somehow managed to ignore the consequences of breeching her maidenhead until it was too late. Even in his Casanova days, he had rules about taking virgins. They were to be avoided at all costs, but Edwina . . . she was different.

Ashton slipped out of her and rolled to her side, pulling her into his arms. He kissed her head as she curled onto his shoulder. He imagined she must be filled with regret. "Edwina, I—"

She placed a finger on his lips. "What we did was beautiful."

He kissed her finger and then moved it away. "Beautiful or not, we still need to talk about what just happened. Now, however, is not the time. The servants will be about soon. If we're to slip you out of the household unnoticed, it should be now." He kissed the top of her head. Lord, it was difficult not to kiss her. While he should be ashamed for taking the maidenhead of such a beautiful, trusting, and responsive woman, he was proud of the gift she'd given him. His substantial, practical, compassionate Edwina had considered him worthy enough of her innocence.

Once they were both dressed, he left her momentarily to wake the footman, who in turn was instructed to hail one of the hackneys that prowled the area this time of night. A hack would be more private and faster than rousting the stables and hitching a team. With her hood up to cover her glorious hair and pert little nose, he assisted her into the hack once it arrived, then climbed alongside.

"You're coming as well?" she asked, surprise evident.

"I couldn't let you travel alone this late at night." The hack lurched forward. "Besides, we need to talk about what will happen if there is issue from tonight. I wouldn't want you to become like your friend Sarah, raising a child on your own."

"Would you send me money as you do to her?" she asked.

"I thought the money came from a secret admirer."

"I know better." He heard the smile in her voice.

The robins and warblers began their early morning birdsong. Dawn would be upon them soon.

"Edwina, I'm serious. No child of mine will grow up without a father. If it appears we planted a seed in your womb, you must contact me immediately. Do you understand?"

The hood nodded, but he wasn't certain that she took him seriously. He shouldn't have taken advantage of her as he had. Perhaps it was a consequence of his later years, or perhaps it was Edwina herself, but he couldn't control his need for her. He had to have her with an urgency that he'd not experienced before, and that scared him. He'd not had difficulty refusing a sexual invitation before. But then she hadn't really invited him, had she? No. He was the rotten rogue who took advantage of her sweet nature. And now he was delivering her, used and soiled goods, back to her parents. He was a complete cad by his own admission.

"Edwina, I will take care of you," he reassured her. "No matter what occurs, you shall be protected."

"And what sacrifices do you require for this protection?"

"Sacrifices?" *What an odd question.* "I believe you've sacrificed enough."

"Must I give up my friends? My freedom to go where I please? My interest in reform societies?"

"No." He drew back. Who was this stranger wearing Edwina's cloak? "I wouldn't ask you to change a thing." He took her hand in his. "I . . . care for you just the way you are."

The hood turned toward the pink in the east.

"Will your parents be upset at your morning arrival?" He'd never concerned himself overly much with a woman's means of departure. He'd assumed arrangements had been made, if needed, to shield the lady's return, but Edwina was another matter. She knew codes, ciphers, and patterns well enough, but he suspected lying convincingly was another matter. In all fairness, it was one of the things he loved about her.

"They probably haven't noticed my absence, but if they have, I'll tell them Sarah's niece was ill and I spent the night so Sarah could get some sleep." The hood tilted toward him. "I'm long past the age when they harbored fears about my virtue."

"Your parents did not strike me as fools," he said, squeezing her hand.

"They're not foolish. They're practical," she insisted.

"Assuming your practical parents did notice your absence, would they accept that you'd return at such an alarmingly early hour? We could drive around London until the sun rises to a respectable height. I don't think the driver would mind the additional blunt."

The hood tilted toward him and he slipped it back so he could see her face. She was exhausted, he could see it in the circles beneath her eyes. At least those circles would support her story if asked. He leaned over and kissed her softly on her lips.

"You would do that?" she asked.

"Edwina, for you I would do so much more."

· *Seventeen* ·

🌱 MORNING HAD OFFICIALLY DAWNED ON THE LONdon streets when the hackney shuddered to stop in front of the Hargrove residence. A soft rain dripped from the gray clouds overhead, causing Edwina to be glad of her hood. She left the carriage where she had slept on Ashton's shoulder until an acceptable time had been reached for her arrival. After agreeing to meet him the next afternoon at Regent's Park, she left the hack and walked to the front entrance. She reached the front door, then peeked over her shoulder to see Ashton in the hack. Already the agreed-upon meeting seemed too far away. The door opened suddenly before her.

"It's high time you got yourself home, girl. Your mother is worried ill."

"Father," she gasped. "You surprised me."

"As you do me, daughter. For what purpose have you been out all night?"

Edwina went inside and removed her cloak. "I received a request from my friend Sarah to sit with her sick niece so she could get some sleep. She's been up several nights with the poor girl."

"Sick niece!" Her father took a few steps back, his eyes narrowed. "And you risked bringing home sickness and contamination!"

"She's not that ill, Father. You've nothing to worry about. The girl had recovered beyond the point of concern, but Sarah was exhausted and needed someone to sit with the child in case there was a relapse."

Her explanation didn't fully mitigate his disapproval. "I'm not certain I would have permitted your departure even under those circumstances, but in either case you should have left a note telling us of your intent."

"Yes, Father. I should have done that." She strode toward the stairs, hoping to escape a lecture. The two hours of sleep with her head on Ashton's shoulder had left her wanting. "I'll remember the next time."

"Next time it'll be a husband demanding to know your whereabouts."

She paused with her hand on the banister. "Excuse me?"

"Mr. Thomas has asked permission to speak to you about an engagement." He puffed his chest out. "Naturally, I gave him my permission."

While this was not unexpected news, she wasn't thrilled that it was coming to fruition. She'd have to decide whether to accept Walter and a guaranteed secure, mundane, uneventful future or . . . what? Pray that Ashton felt as she? He was accustomed to a far grander society than herself. Even their intimate activities of last evening would carry no obligation for Casanova. Otherwise, he would have been caught in the parson's trap years ago.

"If Walter plans to ask for my hand, it would best that I get some rest." She continued on her way up the steps. "Otherwise my response will be the sort of audible breathing that will not meet with your approval."

"Have you forgotten what day it is?" he called after her. "We'll be leaving for church services shortly. You'd best prepare."

•   •   •

WALTER WAITED JUST OUTSIDE THE VESTRY, JUST AS HE always did, so he could share a pew with her family. Reverend Virgil Franklin offered a rousing sermon on the evils of temptation. So much so that Edwina felt the tines of Satan's pitchfork jabbing at her for her recent fall from grace. Upon investigation, however, she discovered her mother was pinching her to keep her awake. She suspected her arm would be black and blue tomorrow, a visual testament to a different sort of awakening. One that she eagerly wished to repeat in spite of the reverend's warnings.

She pleaded a headache when Walter requested that he speak to her alone but agreed to meet with him the following evening. In the time in between she needed to decide what answer would be most appropriate to Walter's anticipated proposal. She had a vague recollection that Ashton had promised something last night in the hackney, something about fathers and issues. She knew he hadn't asked for her hand in marriage, as their association had just begun. However, as long as Ashton harbored feelings similar to hers for him, she would wait.

UPON RETURNING HOME SHE DID MANAGE TO CATCH A few hours of rest, but then the lure of applying the Falcon slogan to the coded message proved too tempting. She woke in late afternoon and straightaway pulled out her writing desk. She recovered her journal from her reticule, noting that the scarlet ribbon that she'd used to keep it closed had disappeared. Odd. She couldn't recall seeing it in the gallery. Still, ribbons were easy to replace. Using the slogan as a guide, she copied each unique letter alongside her alphabet chart. Though the unique slogan letters only took her to the letter "T" on her plain text chart, she had enough to decipher the message and use supposition to complete the chart. All earlier guesses based on the words "pillow book" proved correct, and the missing letters fell into place.

A love letter. There could be no doubt. Much like the coded messages in the personal columns, she could see that this letter spoke of forbidden longings and yearnings that distance could not dissipate. It spoke of the power of a lingering touch, the memory of a kiss. Her heart twisted for the authoress of the letter, as it was clearly penned by a woman mourning the loss of her lover. No identification existed of the authoress beyond the letter "S," and although the letter was directed to "my dearest love," she had no doubt it was meant for the senior Trewelyn. Only the intended recipient would be mindful of its initial absence from the pillow book.

The pillow book! Suddenly the frame of reference fell into place. The authoress had placed this in a Japanese pillow book to suggest the sorts of things they had once shared and wished to share again. She wished she could remember the page that secreted the note. Imagining the sound of Ashton's voice whispering, she recalled that quote from Oscar Wilde. *"The only way to get rid of a temptation is to yield to it. Resist it, and your soul grows sick with longing for the things it has forbidden to itself."* The letter was clear. Yielding led to longing as well. A taste of the forbidden fruit only made one want it all the more.

To that, she could attest. Even though they had been together so recently, she felt the absence of Ashton's arms, the touch of his lips on her breast, the play of his tongue much lower . . . She reached for her fan to alleviate the sudden surge of heat in her face. If one was doomed to be sick with longing, she preferred that it be for something experienced and not merely imagined. She would never have imagined the sensations Ashton released last night. Her hand drifted toward that secret place, but her several layers of clothing denied any attempt to emulate the netsuke. It was indeed unfortunate that the Britons did not adopt the far more sensible attire of the Japanese.

She needed to take this letter to Ashton so he could see that it posed no threat in a political sense to his family. As he was bound to wonder about the mysterious S, Edwina decided to visit the *Mayfair Messenger* in the morning. Sarah's research into Ashton's father's past might be able to provide a clue as to the woman's identity. The two must have shared a connection sometime in their past. Perhaps such a connection would have been noted in the social columns.

THE FOLLOWING DAY WAS A BUSY ONE FOR LOVE, IT seemed . . . or at least the pursuit of love. The *Messenger*'s office was filled with those seeking to kindle a flame. Edwina waited for several customers to finish placing ads before she could approach Sarah.

Sarah squinted at her through her spectacles. "There's something different about you. Is your hair arranged differently?"

Edwina patted the back of her head. "No, nothing's changed." Of course, something indeed had changed, something life-altering, but she was surprised it made a difference in her appearance.

"You look younger, happier," Sarah observed, a bit suspiciously.

"Maybe I'm well rested. I slept away most of yesterday." Sarah wouldn't approve of the real reason, so Edwina kept that to herself. "Perhaps it's my new gown." She twirled in front of Sarah so she could appreciate the printed day dress with a lacy bodice and peplum. Even her hat was new. A straw confection with a wide front brim that both shaded and framed her face. She had dressed for her later meeting with Ashton in Regent's Park. This gown featured an exposed neck as opposed to those stiff high collars that Walter preferred. "But I wanted to stop by this morning to see if you'd uncovered any information on my request."

"Edwina, I have so much to tell you. I tried to research the newspapers, but it was a monumental undertaking without specific dates to mark a starting point. You know the *Messenger* has been published for almost forty years! That's a lot of newsprint to review if you don't know what you're looking for or when to begin."

"But you discovered something, yes?" Her friend's enthusiasm was certainly a good sign. Plus she did say she had something to tell . . .

"No. I didn't find a thing, but Mr. Morrison noticed my difficulty and dedication and offered assistance."

The door bells jingled, announcing another patron had entered the office. Even as she was anxious to hear the rest of the story, Edwina stepped aside so as to offer privacy to the new patron. A privacy she hoped Sarah had extended to her research mission. Edwina certainly didn't wish to expose Ashton's father to any untoward gossip. Even if Sarah found nothing about the mysterious "S" or the Calcutta connection, the transcribed letter itself should alleviate Ashton's fears that his father was involved in treacherous acts. Quite the contrary.

From the back of the office, Edwina observed her friend as she efficiently dealt with a patron wishing to place an ad. If she wasn't mistaken, Sarah seemed happier and more enthusiastic this morning—the very qualities of which she had accused Edwina. Was it possible that Sarah had . . . *No*. She shook her head. To her knowledge Sarah was not keeping company with anyone. As she so often explained, with Nan to attend to, she simply didn't have the time. The patron paid for the ad and left Sarah and Edwina alone once more.

"Mr. Morrison suggested that I would make better progress in this venture if I spoke to the person responsible for writing most of the social columns."

"You could do that?" Edwina was astonished. "One person wrote all those columns?"

"Indeed. Would you believe it was Mr. Morrison's grandmother?" Sarah's eyes radiated excitement and pride. "The *Messenger* was started by Mr. Morrison's father in 1856. At the time he enlisted his mother to write the society column. She never stopped. Well . . . until recently, that is."

"And you can still speak with her? She's still alive?" Edwina asked. Having lost her own grandparents so many years ago, she'd forgotten that others hadn't that same experience.

"He took me to speak with her. Her mind is very lucid, though she tires easily." Her voice dropped. "She appeared exceedingly frail; a stiff breeze could conceivably blow her away. Mr. Morrison is so attached to her, he'll be devastated when her time comes." Her voice trailed off in premature mourning.

Edwina just stared. Was this the same "Old Measly Morrison" that Sarah had fairly lambasted on a daily basis? Now she was sad for the eventual passing of the tyrant's grandmother? "We are speaking of the same Mr. Morrison who won't publish your articles?"

Sarah waved her hand as if that was of little consequence. "He took me in his carriage to his grandmother's house for tea. His parents died when he was very young, you know."

Of course, Edwina didn't know. From her previous descriptions, Sarah seemed to question if Mr. Morrison was born of human parents and not beasts of the jungle.

"His grandmother raised Mr. Morrison, just as I'm raising Nan."

Suddenly, Edwina realized that Sarah regarded Mr. Morrison's grandmother as a sort of contemporary.

"So you had tea with his grandmother . . ."

"Mr. Morrison left us alone to talk. It was the most amazing thing. Mrs. Morrison knew Trewelyn, Sr."

"She knew him!"

"Well, she knew of him," Sarah corrected. "Trewelyn, Sr. would have been a contemporary of her son."

"I see," Edwina replied, even though she didn't. Even if the grandmother wrote the gossip column, it was unlikely the woman would know of everyone in London, unless . . . "Trewelyn, Sr. appeared in the gossip column?"

"Let's just say the acorn didn't fall far from the tree," Sarah said with a bit of smugness.

"Mr. Trewelyn is a handsome man," Edwina reasoned, half to herself. "It would stand to reason that his father would have been as well."

"Oh, it's more than appearances." Sarah shuffled through a stack of envelopes. "Trewelyn, Sr. was said to enjoy women of all cultures and stations in his day," Sarah said.

"Cultures?"

"Trewelyn, Sr. was involved in his father's shipping business and thus had traveled the world over by the age of eighteen. He married a young woman who brought money and connections into the family business, according to the wishes of his parents." She turned and stuffed the envelopes into a wall of cubbyholes. "You're aware that she died giving birth to Ashton."

That information solidified in a lump in Edwina's throat. "No . . . I didn't know that." Poor Ashton. He never knew his real mother, never experienced that deep abiding love a mother feels for her newborn. "I knew she'd died of course," Edwina managed somewhat awkwardly. "But I didn't know of the circumstances."

"Of course, after she was gone, his father retained a series of nannies, nursemaids, and governesses—"

"Was one of them Japanese?" Edwina asked on a hunch.

Sarah stopped her envelope sorting and turned toward Edwina. "How did you know?" She peered over her glasses. "That's where the scandal comes in. It's the main reason Mrs. Morrison remembers Trewelyn."

"Scandal?"

Sarah put the envelopes down and leaned on the counter, lowering her voice. "When he returned from a shipping venture to the Orient, he brought a woman with him and installed her in his house. Can you imagine? It was said she had full authority over the child and the servants, even though she rarely spoke and knew only a little English."

Edwina could imagine very well. The Japanese artifacts scattered throughout the house had to be the result of someone who appreciated the culture, and to appreciate such a thing, one must have had some sort of strong influence. The secret gallery was most likely an indication of the type of influence.

Sarah returned to filing her envelopes. "She would have been a most irregular woman to hire to care for his son, yet he did just that. To make matters worse, he even tried to introduce the woman in society. He took her to plays and refused house parties that would not include her as a guest. One wouldn't attempt that with an English governess much less a Japanese one."

"There were repercussions?" Edwina wasn't certain which shocked Sarah more, that the governess was Japanese or that Ashton's father attempted to elevate her position.

"Of course! His father, Ashton's grandfather, cut his son off from the shipping business. That's how the freight business began. Mrs. Morrison wasn't exactly certain what led to the decision to replace the governess. She seemed to recall some incident at a dinner party where Trewelyn, Sr. brought the woman. Soon after, she left his employ and London, it seems. Mrs. Morrison thought she recalled the girl got mixed up with someone else in the freight trade, but she wasn't certain. She only remembered that the girl refused to adopt proper attire. She insisted on wearing those silk robes wherever she went. That's what made the whole affair so memorable."

"Did she remember the woman's name?"

Before Sarah could answer, the bells above the door jangled again and Edwina reluctantly moved to the back of the room. *Christopher!* These interruptions might be necessary but must they occur at such critical junctures? The patron bent over the counter to write a message on a form. Sarah glanced over the man's head toward Edwina, then silently shook her head in answer. Edwina would have been tempted to bet her journal that the woman's name began with an "S."

It all made a sort of sense. As she decoded the letter last night, she was struck by the expressions of dedication and devotion. Trewelyn, Sr. and the mysterious "S" shared an intimate connection that had survived years. The thought made her smile, thinking of the range of emotions Ashton's letters had brought her. The edgy anticipation whenever the postman made his rounds, the intense pleasure of opening the envelope and reading Ashton's words, the disappointment and longing when the reading was complete. Did those emotions lessen with the passage of time? She suspected the answer was no, placing the correspondents in a heaven and hellish existence. She felt sympathy and a sudden appreciation of Ashton's father that she hadn't felt before. Would Ashton feel the same?

But why were the letters sent in code? Perhaps the answer

lay in Mrs. Morrison's comment of a competitor in the freight industry. Certainly the coded messages she read in the *Messenger* spoke of entangled relationships where one or both were married. It was sad, really. That two people who so obviously loved each other would be separated by more than distance.

The jangle of the door bell pulled her from her thoughts. With the customer gone, Edwina returned to the counter.

"Did Mrs. Morrison mention anything about Calcutta?" It was the puzzle piece Edwina had not yet fitted into the pattern.

"No," Sarah said. "But she did invite me to return for a visit sometime. She was a fascinating woman, and very proud of her grandson, I might add."

From the look on Sarah's face, Edwina imagined that the grandmother wasn't the only one proud of Mr. Morrison's accomplishments.

"So . . ." Edwina's lips tilted in a mischievous smile. "Have you spoken to Mr. Morrison?"

The arrival of another customer brought their meeting to a close. Edwina thanked Sarah for her information and exited from the office. She glanced at her locket watch once she reached the bustling street. It was time to meet with Ashton at the park to tell him of the letter's contents. Even the darkening clouds building in the sky could not lessen her soaring spirits. She waved her handkerchief to signal a hansom. A bicycle could not take her to her love fast enough.

· *Eighteen* ·

✤ THE TIGER CAGE AT THE ZOOLOGICAL GARDENS IN Regent's Park had always been popular among gray-attired governesses and their noisy young charges, so it was hardly surprising that a crowd had gathered in front of the striped Bengal tiger that paced relentlessly behind thick iron bars. The unruly children were silenced, however, when of all the peering faces that day, of all the gesturing hands and awed stares, the tiger stopped its constant movement and fixated its goldenrod stare on none other than Edwina. Without so much as a growl, the beast sat and narrowed its gaze of pure desperation toward her, toward someone who was once a kindred spirit.

Edwina understood how it felt to be trapped, though her bars weren't visible to any but herself. Bars that were slowly lowering, boxing her into a future she hadn't chosen for herself. Bars that would lock in place once her father announced her engagement to Walter. Her dreams of exploring the world would be given as much consideration as her childhood aspirations to be a pirate.

But loving Ashton had changed all that. She laughed to herself, feeling that she had by her very actions flung the door to her own cage wide open. Ashton accepted her for who she was. He understood her desire for adventure. His letters told her as much. Fabulous letters, wonderful letters that she could read and reread when the house was quiet and settled. Each time she found she fell in love with the man once known as Casanova all over again.

She watched couples stroll by. Nannies pushed perambulators. A man pushed a broom to clear the sidewalk of discarded papers from the costermongers selling treats from pushcarts. No one would think twice about a woman resting on the bench in front of the tiger cage. There was another bench that she'd come to think of as "their bench." The one she'd shared with Ashton the day Matthew had slipped into the stream. But that spot would be too secluded for a single woman to wait alone. This public venue was a much better choice.

Granted, Ashton hadn't offered for her hand or even expressed the possibility of such, but she had his letters and she could read in them a connection she'd not shared with another. In time, perhaps Ashton would choose to make that connection permanent. Certainly when he read the decoded letter she was bringing to him, the one between "S" and his father, he would eventually recognize the power of such a connection. She certainly didn't want to be writing coded letters to Ashton years from now, just as she was certain he wouldn't want to experience that kind of agony. As long as she was patient, Ashton would come to claim her. Edwina smiled ruefully at the tiger and slowly shook her head. She wouldn't be confined to a cage of bars, watching life pass by without taking part.

So she waited, watching the shifting pattern of tiger stripes against the vertical bars. Thunder rumbled in the distance. She checked her locket watch. He was only fifteen minutes late. It felt longer, as she'd arrived early. Ashton would arrive shortly, an event that she anxiously anticipated. Meanwhile, she'd entertain herself with memories of their last night together, of the way he made her body feel alive and made her feel important. *The next time, I promise, it will be better.*

Just knowing that there would be a next time made her feel as weightless as the birds in the aviary. She wasn't certain how such a rendezvous would be arranged, but as Ashton was experienced in this regard, she was certain there would be a next time.

A baby cried in a passing pram, reminding Edwina of her earlier conversation with Sarah. Did the mysterious "S" push Ashton as a baby in such a contraption? She tried to imagine.

She searched the faces beneath the tall hats of the passersby, watching to see the smile she loved, the soft twinkling eyes that populated her dreams. She listened for the distinct pattern of his stick on the walk, but time passed and Ashton wasn't among the many people that passed her bench. The skies darkened and the wind increased. The number of passersby dwindled. A copy of the *Messenger* skittered across the walkway, buoyed by a sudden breeze. She caught the paper as it flitted by her bench. The storm will blow over, she thought, wishing she'd brought an umbrella. Perhaps Ashton would have one hidden away in a cane. The thought made her smile. Nevertheless, she shifted her position on the bench to place herself under the protection of a tree. Hopefully, Ashton would arrive before the rain threatened. Though she enjoyed the thought of them trapped together in a shelter while a storm kept others away.

She glanced at the *Messenger*, noting the personal ads on the front page. She quickly scanned the column, noting two that were written in a basic code. Suddenly, decoding the ads was not the amusing game she had once considered it to be. The emotional toll of not being with a loved one and keeping it secret must truly be wretched. Claire once referred to the personal ads as "the agonies." She wondered if Claire truly understood the misery and suffering encapsulated in those ads.

But there was no need for her to feel the torture expressed by others because Ashton, although late—she checked her locket watch—a little over an hour late, would eventually join her at the park to learn the contents of his father's note.

He couldn't have forgotten, could he? No, she reassured herself. The decoded note was too important. She was too important, wasn't she? After what they had shared? Yet a small doubt registered in the back of her mind.

The first raindrop struck her lap, earning her attention. The dull plop of water droplets striking surrounding leaves intensified around her. Thunder rumbled overhead. The few people remaining in the park hid beneath their umbrellas and scurried toward the more substantial shelter of their carriages or home. Even the tiger found shelter beneath an overhang created for that purpose. He stared at her as if she were the most foolish person alive, and at that moment she wondered if she was.

Holding the *Messenger* overhead, she ran to a nearby wooden structure, a maintenance shed of some sort. If she stood beneath the eaves she might stay reasonably dry while remaining in sight of the bench. Ashton would appear at any minute beneath an umbrella large enough to cover them both. Even the animals retreated to the backs of their cages, seeking cover from the downpour. The rich green scent of foliage surrounded her as damp circles grew on her new gown, causing her a chill. While she hoped Ashton hadn't been similarly caught in the rain, as the park emptied and lightning flashed overhead, she had to accept that Ashton was not coming. She watched the empty bench, the walkway that passed the cages, and all was vacant. Just the hard driving rain filled the park. She stood alone beneath the leaky eaves of the shack, her new hat, saturated with the downpour, drooped in front of her, the lovely embellishments of flowers and feathers flattened about her ears.

"You best go 'ome now, miss," a man's voice said.

She turned to see the man with the broom. Rain dripped off his hood and ran in rivulets down his mackintosh. The same rain that soaked through the lace on her dress, causing it to stick to her skin. Even her corset, thick with layers and boning, couldn't keep the rain from soaking clear through to her skin. Fortunately, she'd kept her journal and its precious contents behind her back, away from the elements. The coded letter and her translation were bound to be the only dry things on her person.

"It'll be getting dark soon and this don't look to let up. Go on 'ome, miss. I'm going to lock up."

While the shelter was minimal, it was better than no shelter at all. The *Messenger* she'd held earlier had absorbed so much water as to be worthless. Perhaps he saw hesitancy in her eyes, though with water dripping from her once jaunty brim onto her lashes, she wasn't certain how he could see anything. She was certainly having difficulty.

"You been 'ere before, 'aven't ye? I've seen you on one of those bicycles." His eyes narrowed. "Take this." He shoved an old black umbrella in her hands. "I got me mac. You can bring the brolly back next time."

"Thank you, sir," she managed, blinking the water from her lashes. She pushed the sticky ring to open the umbrella. Two panels sagged from broken spokes, but the others carved out a small dry oasis. "You're very generous."

He grinned and bobbed his head. "I'll take this for ye," he said, taking the soggy *Messenger* from her hand. "Off with ye, now."

She had to remove her hat to see where she was going. By carefully positioning the dips in the waterproof fabric, she managed to keep the bag that carried her journal dry. Thus she stoically walked away from the park, carrying her pride and dragging her wounded heart.

She should have gone home as the kind man had insisted. It was painfully obvious that Ashton was not coming to meet her as promised. In spite of the pain that wound caused, she held her head high and straightened her spine, then walked to the Trewelyn residence. She wanted—no, needed—to know why he hadn't kept his promise. Why had he left her out in the rain with no explanation like day-old rubbish? Sarah's words haunted her with each step. *He'll run off and leave you. A man like that can't be trusted. Don't, Edwina. Just don't.* While Sarah appeared correct in her predictions, Edwina needed confirmation, no matter how painful the knowing would be.

She stood in front of the Trewelyn residence, looking for all intents and purposes like her kitten Isabella when she'd been out in the rain, ready to shake her fur dry. Her mother would disapprove of her desire to confront Ashton. Proper young ladies did not walk bald-faced up to a gentleman's residence. But when one was soaked to the skin, one did not give a fig about propriety.

With her head held high, she knocked on the door. Hastings took one look at her sodden clothes and broken umbrella and rudely gestured to the service entrance set below the pavement. Edwina refused. "Please inform Mr. Ashton Trewelyn that Miss Edwina Hargrove is here to speak with him."

Hastings looked down his rather long nose at her. "Mr. Ashton is not in."

Was that truly the case? Or had Hastings been given orders to lie? The umbrella must have turned at that moment, as a rivulet of water ran directly onto the back of her neck, sending a fresh chill down her back.

"May I wait in the foyer? As you can see, it's very wet out here."

He stared at her, undoubtedly imagining massive puddles on the floor and carpets caused by her sopping clothes. "Mr. Ashton is not in, miss. Perhaps you should come back when it is not raining."

"And will Mr. Ashton be available once the rain ceases?" Edwina said, unable to keep sarcasm from her voice.

"I wouldn't know, miss. He is not in at present."

"Is there a difficulty, Hastings?" a woman's voice interceded.

"A Miss Hargrove wishes to see Mr. Ashton. I have explained that Mr. Ashton is not available."

"Miss Hargrove?" There was a long pause. She imagined the propriety issue was being weighed against curiosity. Curiosity won. "Don't make the poor girl stand out in the rain, Hastings. Let her in."

The door opened sufficiently for Edwina to step inside, though she felt rather the poor cousin dripping all over the carpet. She placed the mangled umbrella and her ruined hat in Hasting's waiting hand.

"She'll need a towel. Several of them, I should think." Mrs.

Trewelyn regarded her with a cold eye, or perhaps it just felt that way, as Edwina was already chilled to the bone. "Send tea to the drawing room. She's going to need something hot."

"I didn't wish to interrupt your afternoon, Mrs. Trewelyn, and while I welcome your hospitality, I have an important message for your stepson."

"You do, do you?" Her lips curled, giving Edwina the impression that she actually enjoyed seeing her in this plight. "As Hastings has informed you, Ashton is not here. However, we can speak privately about it in the drawing room. This way."

Edwina followed, leaving a trail of moisture in her wake. "I know mine is an unusual request—"

"On the contrary," her host interrupted. Hastings entered with a stack of linen towels. Mrs. Trewelyn handed Edwina one and placed the rest on a table. "Your request is not unusual at all. In fact, it is all too common."

Edwina paused in the mopping of her face and neck, suspecting she'd just been insulted, something about hidden meanings buried in pleasant-sounding words. She let the sting of the comment fade, then rubbed her arms briskly.

A maid entered with a laden silver tea tray. An English styling, Edwina noted, not Japanese. So the current Mrs. Trewelyn did not share her husband's passion in that area. In fact, she looked about the room and thought she could have found a similarly furnished room in any well-appointed home in Mayfair. The china was hand-painted, and imported from India, she suspected. Exotic creatures, little brown monkeys and colorful birds frolicked across the porcelain. The pattern reminded her of Ashton and his days spent in such a setting. The maid left, closing the doors to the room with a gentle click. Mrs. Trewelyn placed a towel on a settee and indicated that Edwina should sit. "It's time you and I exchanged confidences."

Though hesitant to sit due to the condition of her clothes, Edwina placed another towel on her shoulders to catch the drips from her hair and then lowered herself to the very edge of the cushion so as touch as little as possible. She scrubbed her lap and skirts with her towel before accepting a much appreciated hot cup of tea.

"Hastings was telling the truth. Ashton is not here."

A memory nudged her brain, perhaps stimulated by the hot drink. Could Ashton's absence be part of that test he'd mentioned? Of course, he hadn't specified the nature of the challenge, or the timing. He could well be detained in another part of the city, proving his worth to the Guardians. She sighed then took another sip. That must be it. He would come to her tomorrow or the next day and she'd share her findings then.

Edwina rose, cup and saucer in hand. "If Ashton is not available, then I've no reason to take further of your valuable time," she said. "I appreciate the opportunity to dry a bit, but—"

"Sit down, Miss Hargrove. There's more you should know."

The back of her neck tingled in warning. Something in the woman's smug expression reminded Edwina of the Bengal tiger in its cage, only there were no bars to separate them. Still she lowered herself to the cushions as directed.

"He's gone," Mrs. Trewelyn said. "I don't know when he'll return, if indeed he'll ever return."

"Ever?" The words knifed through Edwina's heart. "What do you mean?"

"Precisely what I say," the woman raised her brows, then took a slow swallow of tea. "I assume you've slept with my stepson." Edwina's cup slammed to the saucer. "There's no need for such dramatics," Constance said, a smirk on her lips. "You aren't the first, and you most likely won't be the last."

Edwina, mopping up the spilled tea that added to the water damage of her skirt, sputtered, "You have no right—"

"I have every right," the woman insisted. "You see, Ashton did the same to me."

Edwina's hand paused. She didn't really want to listen to this. Constance did not know her stepson the way she knew Ashton, or so she imagined. She should march out of the parlor and not listen to another word, but her feet refused to move. She didn't know if curiosity or fear glued her to the cushion, but like the trapped tiger she listened.

"There now," Constance gloated. "I see I have your attention. Five years ago, Ashton Trewelyn courted me in the manner of which every woman dreams. He was dashing, debonair, attentive, and skilled in a way few men can claim." She closed her eyes as if lost in a memory. "The things he made my body feel. It was as if I'd awoken from a long slumber and come alive in his arms."

A shiver raced down Edwina's spine that had nothing to do with her clinging wet clothes. She knew that feeling, that sense of being awakened and truly alive for the first time.

Mrs. Trewelyn stared at her. "Did he take you to that den of iniquity off the library? Did he show you the pillow books and promise to do every disgusting thing pictured there?" Her eyes narrowed. "I can see from your wide-eyed expression that he did."

The pattern shifted, she could feel it. The awakening she'd attributed to Ashton didn't go hand in hand with words like "disgusting" and "iniquity." Something wasn't quite right. "He never promised—"

"To marry you?" The cold waves of Constance's laughter chilled her more than her wet clothes. "Of course, he didn't. Look at you. You're not in his league. Not that it would matter." Constance sipped her tea as if this were a proper conversation and not a dissection of her stepson's virtues. "Ashton indicated that he wished to marry me as well. I waited and waited." She patted her stomach. "And then I couldn't wait anymore." She smiled grimly, then selected a finger sandwich from the tray. "Eat something," she directed. "You're bound to need more sustenance now."

The turmoil roiling in her stomach wasn't really conducive to eating, but her host did more than insist—she demanded. Edwina selected a small watercress sandwich and nibbled at the edges, mindful of the similarities in their experiences.

"Naturally, I told Ashton, and what did he do? He ran off to play war hero with the King's Royal Rifles."

"Ashton told me that he left because you agreed to marry his father," Edwina said tentatively.

"Is that what he told you?" Again she laughed, then looked

at Edwina. "You truly are a gullible innocent. Have you not seen my son? Is he not the spitting image of his father?"

As Ashton resembled his father, the best answer to this question was no answer at all. Patterns, she reminded herself, listen for the patterns. Patterns don't lie.

"Even Matthew instinctively knows his father. Ashton is the only one who can make him behave."

From her observations, Ashton was the only one willing to spend time with the boy. Matthew looked up to Ashton. Of course he would do as Ashton directed.

"I was fortunate in that Ashton's father agreed to marry me," Constance continued. "I turned to him with my dilemma. He, of course, was anxious to protect the child and the family name." She selected another treat from the tray. "What else was I to do?" Her eyes raked over Edwina. "Society is not kind to a used and abandoned woman."

Edwina needed to speak with Ashton about all this. The turmoil in her stomach seemed to have worked its way up her throat, so that her voice had lost much of its strength. She wanted to trust her heart about Ashton, but there was some truth in Constance's words. Enough truth to make her uneasy. "When did Ashton leave?"

"Sometime last night. He took much of his wardrobe, his walking stick, of course, his razor . . . the sorts of things a man takes when he plans to disappear for a long, long time."

A long time! Would a test from the Guardians keep him a long time, or were Constance's insinuations true? She swallowed hard. "Did he leave a letter?"

"A letter? For you?" Constance laughed again and shook her head. "Ashton does not write letters. He certainly never responded to mine."

One small flicker of hope ignited in her chest, and Edwina carefully nursed it to keep the flame burning. Ashton did write letters, and there was a good chance there was one waiting for her at home. She scolded herself; she should have gone there directly. Ashton must have had a good reason for leaving. At least the time of his departure explained his failure to meet with her at the Park.

Constance's brow lifted in a determined arch. "Your mother tells me that you have a potential match with a Mr. Thomas. As a woman who made a difficult choice to protect my own security, I would suggest that you give serious consideration to his proposal."

That proposal that hadn't even been extended as yet but seemed to have been accepted by many on her behalf. Edwina sipped her tea to give herself time to think. Constance lifted her teacup, reminding Edwina of the tiger painted there. How apropos that she should choose that pattern. Could Edwina trust anything that Constance had told her? Her interpretations made sense, though. Maybe too much sense.

She glanced over Constance's shoulder and saw a small, framed embroidered picture of cherry blossoms on an otherwise cluttered wall. The silk threads were woven with such intricate detail, the flower appeared luminous. In the lower corner, she noted the letter "S." She could understand, if Constance's facts were true, why she had married Ashton's father, but Edwina wasn't certain why Ashton's father had married Constance. Clearly, he loved another enough to hang this small memento in a very public room. Curious, she smiled toward Constance. "Have you had second thoughts about your decision to marry Ashton's father?"

"Not at all," Constance replied. "It was the proper thing to do."

The proper thing. Why did it always seem that propriety took precedence over the right thing to do? Edwina tilted her head, listening for the drum of raindrops, but heard none. "Thank you for your advice, Mrs. Trewelyn. I shall lend it serious consideration."

"Be sure you do." She stood. "Allow me to have my driver take you home." Constance squinted at Edwina. "You didn't ride that awful bicycle here, did you?"

Edwina was about to protest but remained silent. The sooner she left this woman's company the better. She did, however, accept the offer of a ride in a small gig. A letter from Ashton was bound to be waiting at home, she closed her eyes and prayed. *Please let there be a letter.*

· *Nineteen* ·

🌿 No letter waited for her at home.

No letter arrived the next day, or the day after that. Edwina was dizzy and dismal and took to her bed, claiming that being trapped in damp clothes had given her a chill. That was not exactly accurate. She knew the cause of her malady.

She didn't want to think that Ashton had used her and then abandoned her, but all evidence seemed to point in that direction. Regardless of what society might think, she didn't regret losing her innocence to Ashton. That was a temptation well worth the taking. It was his departure without a word, without an explanation, that tore pieces from her soul. Had he been called to perform some task for the Guardians, surely he would have sent her word without actually disclosing his mission. Even if he had sent a letter in code, she would have understood.

Constance's story played again and again in her mind. Had he left her as Constance claimed he had left her five years ago. Given their last night together, his absence was a betrayal of all they had shared.

Her own absence from the Crescent was noted by Claire and Faith, who came to call upon her. They ignored her mother's cautions about contamination and insisted they be allowed to see Edwina in her bedchamber. Faced with Claire's stubbornness and relentless demands, her mother acquiesced and allowed the girls upstairs.

Edwina sat in bed, writing yet another letter to Ashton to tell him how he had hurt her. The letter, like the others, would not be posted, as she had no address to which to send it, but writing her feelings on paper made her feel better for a short time. Then she'd remember that she couldn't tell him how she felt because he'd run off as if she were an ordinary trollop. How ironic, as everyone insisted that she needed to be more ordinary. She had mistakenly thought her uniqueness had appealed to Ashton, but in the end it appeared it was the very thing that scared him away.

"Edwina, are you all right?!" Faith burst into her room and rushed to her bedside. "We were so worried when you didn't appear at the Crescent."

"You don't look sick," Claire observed. "Your eyes are puffy and red, and maybe your nose as well, but sick people don't sit in bed and write letters."

Blast that Claire. She was always too observant for her own good, and too quick to put those observations to words. Edwina quickly slipped her letter into her lap writing desk, then closed the lid before setting it aside. Isabella quickly abandoned attacking her blanket-covered feet with her tiny kitten teeth and claws and investigated the heavy lid on the lap desk instead.

"What is it?" Faith asked. "Is it Mr. Thomas? Did he not ask for your hand?"

The question so surprised her that she managed a sort of sad smile. "I haven't seen Walter since church on Sunday," she admitted. "He sent flowers." She pointed to the colorful bouquet of daisies, carnations, and roses arranged in one of her mother's blue vases.

"How lovely," Faith said, rising to inspect the bouquet.

"It's that Trewelyn, isn't it?" Claire said, her gaze never

leaving Edwina. "That Casanova fellow. He did something to you, didn't he?" It was more statement than question.

"Claire!" Faith admonished. The raised voice frightened Isabella, who stopped rattling the lap desk momentarily.

"Look at her face, Faith." Claire pointed with an extended arm. "She's been crying her heart out." She dropped her voice. "She wouldn't be crying that way over Mr. Thomas."

She was right. Edwina had to admit that as nice of a person as Walter was, he never managed to capture her heart as had Ashton. If Walter disappeared from her life, she'd feel a little sad, but she doubted she would have soiled as many handkerchiefs as she had crying over Ashton's abandonment.

"He's gone," Edwina said, and immediately tears welled in her eyes. "He left and I don't know where he went." She lifted her hands in the air to express her helplessness. The gesture had to work, as her throat had constricted enough to make words impassable. "No letter," she squeaked.

Faith rushed back to her side at the onslaught of tears. "Now, now, Edwina. Don't cry. There's nothing to cry about. You knew his reputation. You knew there was a chance he would do this. It's a good thing that he left now before he took advantage of your sweet nature."

Claire marched around to the opposite side of the bed to offer comfort. As she lifted the kitten to move it from the lap desk, stationery that had snagged on its needle-sharp teeth slipped from beneath the lid as well.

"What's this?" Claire caught the squirming kitten in the crook of her arm and unfastened the paper. She started to read.

Edwina's face heated. "That's personal," she said, trying to grab the letter out of Claire's hands, but Claire stood out of reach.

Her eyes widened. She gazed down at Edwina. "It most certainly is. I can understand your concern over Ashton's disappearance."

Faith looked from one face to the other. "What is it?"

Claire handed Faith the letter with the kitten-mangled corner. "May I read this, Edwina?" Faith asked, with a glance to Claire.

"You might as well. You'll most likely know soon enough."
She stared daggers at Claire while Faith skimmed over the
words. Her hand shook when she handed the letter back to
Edwina.

"Did you expect him to marry you, Edwina? Did he make
promises?"

"No. No promises." While she could honestly say she
didn't think marriage would result from their interlude in the
secret gallery, she hadn't really thought through what would
result. All she knew was that she wanted to feel what it was
like to be intimate with a man like Ashton Trewelyn. She
wanted to know why all those Japanese women were eagerly
looking at the pillow books. She wanted to experience life
just once before . . . before . . . before she was forced to play
the role society had assigned to her.

"It's a good thing the no-good, son of a—"

"Claire!" Edwina admonished. "He's not like that. What
he did . . . what we did," she corrected, "I wanted as much as
he did. I don't know how to explain it. Everything was so . . .
perfect and I wanted to know what a man felt like."

"But you have Mr. Thomas," Faith said. "Won't he be
upset?"

"He doesn't need to know," Claire replied. The other two
turned to stare. Claire dropped the kitten on the bed before
lowering herself closer to the other ladies. "Mr. Thomas wants
to marry you, not your—" She wiggled her fingers at Edwina's
lower regions. "Men have all sorts of intimate experiences
before marriage, why not women?"

"Because we're not men," Faith said hastily. She turned
to Edwina. "What are you going to do?"

"I haven't decided," she said, though that wasn't true. Even
before she'd met Ashton, even before she'd lost her innocence,
she'd planned to marry Walter. She wasn't certain she ever
had another option other than to accept his proposal. After
meeting Ashton, she'd begun to hope for something different.
She'd begun to hope that all her dreams and desires were
actually obtainable . . . that she wouldn't have to sacrifice
them for the sake of security. Now that Ashton was gone, so

were those flights of fantasy. She always thought she'd marry Walter; in fact, it was one of the reasons she did what she did. She just didn't want to admit that her deception was intentional to her friends. She wasn't certain they'd understand she was trying to make the sort of memory that would last a lifetime.

"So . . . what was it like?" Claire asked. "What was he like?"

"Did it hurt terribly?" Faith asked.

Edwina smiled, remembering the innocent pushed into the secret gallery almost two months ago. She'd been curious about those things and more before she became experienced. "It pinched a little. There was some bleeding," she told Faith.

"I've heard that *some* women secret a small bottle of blood on their wedding night, then smear it on the sheets. That way the husband believes his wife is pure." Faith and Edwina just stared at Claire. "What? It's not as if he would actually look down there."

"Walter wouldn't," Edwina agreed. She suspected Walter had very little experience in this particular area.

"You mean Trewelyn did!" Faith said, shocked. "Oh, my! Oh, my!" She looked around the room, then grabbed Edwina's black feather fan from the bureau to wave at her face. Tiny feather filaments lifted in the furious created current.

"He was tender and kind and . . . talented," Edwina said, remembering the way her body exploded in waves of pleasant titillation. Her eyes drifted shut reliving the memory.

"Where were you that you were able to do this in privacy?" Claire asked. "Did he take you to an inn outside of London?"

Edwina didn't want to answer. Fortunately, she was spared when Faith interrupted. "But what was he like? You know, his thing—was it very big? Were you scared?"

"At first," she admitted. "I suppose he was normal." Who was she to compare him to? Trewelyn said the jade stalks in the pictures were exaggerated, thank heavens. So how was she to know about comparisons? "I know that once he pushed inside me, he felt enormous, and powerful, and so much a part of me that we couldn't be separated."

They all fell silent until Faith spoke up. "What are you going to do now that he's gone?"

Edwina felt the lump return to her throat. "I'm going back to my old life. The way things were before Mr. Trewelyn purchased a pot of tea for me because he thought I was chilled." The memory of his thoughtfulness slammed into her chest. Tears welled in her eyes. She couldn't blink fast enough to keep them at bay.

"Can you do that?" Claire asked skeptically.

"I haven't a choice," Edwina answered, dabbing at the corners of her eyes with a bit of the blanket.

"I know how babies are made," Faith said, her eyes downcast. "Is it possible he left one inside you?" She tapped her fingers on the bed for Isabella to attack. Edwina imagined it was Faith's way to avoid looking at her face.

"I don't know," Edwina replied. "I hadn't considered the possibility at the time." Or maybe she had and wanted to keep a piece of Ashton in her life. "Sarah will be so disappointed in me if I have a child out of wedlock."

The three of them sat still, though Edwina suspected they were all thinking the same thing. Marriage to Walter would solve that problem as well as many others. But would a marriage based on a lie really solve anything? Could she keep such a secret from a man she would see every day of the rest of her life? The answer was clear. "I'll have to tell Walter."

Faith's eyes widened. "Will he still have you?"

"I don't know, but I won't live with that sort of lie between us. It would eat away at our relationship." The painful constriction eased in her throat. Perhaps she'd been hiding in her bedroom, not to avoid his proposal, but to avoid telling him the truth. She would always mourn the loss of Ashton in her life and the promise of adventure and excitement they'd shared, but he'd run away, leaving her to face reality . . . and Walter.

A sense of calm and, yes, maturity settled over her. "Thank you," she said, patting her friends' hands. "You've helped me see what must be done." The two exchanged a dubious glance, but neither said a word.

Claire rummaged in her reticule. "You asked me to do some research for you. I'm not certain you're still interested."

"Yes," Edwina said, curiosity chasing away lingering maudlin thoughts. "I am. What did you discover?"

Claire pulled out a small notebook, the sort that Sarah had given her to take notes at Lady Sutton's soiree. She wondered briefly if Sarah had supplied them all with such notebooks for newsworthy opportunities.

"You asked me to check on husbands or businesses that include an image within a circle as a symbol of their business. I discovered there are quite a few of them." She glanced up from her notes. "Including your father."

She shouldn't have been surprised. She had her suspicions, after all, but there was something about the confirmation . . . "May I see the list?"

"Tell me first, what does it mean?" Claire asked. "I have at least twenty men on this list in various industries and all of some financial significance."

"I believe they're all part of the Guardians." Edwina waited, wondering if they'd remember the reason for the evening surveillance of the Trewelyn residence.

Claire's eyes widened. "You mean that group of men who lure innocents to a life of debauchery? The ones who advertised their meetings in code?"

Edwina shook her head. "We don't know that they lure innocents—"

"They did one," Faith said quietly.

Edwina turned toward her. "That was my desire, my curiosity, and my decision. That was not the Guardians. I haven't found evidence that they are a malicious group at all."

"Then why the secrecy?" Claire asked.

"I haven't figured that out yet," she admitted.

LATER THAT EVENING, EDWINA DRESSED FOR DINNER. As she walked down the steps, she checked the hall table to see if any letters had arrived while she was abed. The silver receiving platter was empty. Unfortunately, after so many days of silence, that was not unexpected . . . disappointing, but not unexpected.

"Edwina," her mother called. "You're going to join us for dinner this evening? How lovely. I'm sure Walter will be happy to see your return to health."

"Walter?"

"He's speaking with your father in the library. I'm certain they'll be out shortly."

A bit of fear shot through her, as well as anguish and a strong desire to return to Isabella and her bedroom, but she kept her chin high and walked toward the library. She'd been avoiding Walter long enough; it was time to settle the uncertainties between them. She took a deep breath, then knocked lightly before opening the door.

Her father's scowl shifted to a smile the moment he saw her at the door. "Come in, Edwina. We were just speaking of you."

She glanced to Walter. His beaten expression lifted hopefully. He crossed rapidly to her to place a clammy hand on her cheek. "No indication of fever, but you shouldn't be on your feet. You should sit."

She took Walter's hand between her own and removed it gently from her face. "I'm feeling much better, and I'd prefer to stand. Thank you, however, for your sincere concern." She nodded her head in a sort of acknowledgment of gratitude. Walter's face softened. A gentle smile lit his weary eyes.

Still holding Walter's hand, she turned to her father. "I wonder if I might speak with Walter alone, Father."

His eyes darted from her face to their clenched hands. "Certainly." He beamed. "I suppose the moment calls for privacy, no?" He walked toward the door but paused a moment to kiss his daughter's cheek. "You two take all the time you wish. I shall wait for your news with your mother in the drawing room."

The moment the door closed behind her father, Walter took both of her hands in his. "Edwina, you know how I've felt about you from the day we met. I—"

"Wait, Walter. There's something you should know before

you say another word." She pulled her hands from him and took a few steps to put distance between them. "I'm not the woman you believe I am. More to the point, I'm not the innocent you assumed me to be."

It was amazing how much lighter she felt as the result of her confession. Just as discussing her circumstances with her friends had helped heal her heart, so did this admission. Still, she knew her words would not be accepted with joy and gratitude. She braced herself for scorn and insult.

Walter appeared confused, then a wide grin chased his concerns away. "My dear, I suppose your friend Claire has probably introduced you to some political attitudes of which you weren't previously aware. We can discuss those later if you like, but I should warn you that, in some contexts, the word 'innocent' takes on a different sort of meaning. It implies—"

"I'm aware of what it implies, Walter," she interrupted. "I'm not speaking of politics. I'm trying to say that I've recently become personally acquainted with the intimacies that can exist between a man and a woman."

He still appeared confused, or perhaps shocked. It was difficult to tell the difference. Even so, she needed to know that he understood precisely what she was trying to say.

"For pity's sake, I'm not speaking in code." She walked over to stand in front of him, took his hands in hers, and looked him square in the eye. "Walter, I'm no longer a virgin."

· Twenty ·

🌿 ASHTON SLUMPED IN HIS SEAT ON THE TRAIN TAKING him from Rome to Paris, the final leg in his acceptance test to join the Guardians, with an old beaten rucksack beside him. Everything of importance was packed in that sack, except the one essential he kept in his pocket. Funny. The rucksack reminded him of Edwina's journal, overstuffed and tied with that red ribbon. He imagined her heart and soul were contained on those journal pages . . . and he hoped loving thoughts of him were written there as well. Lord, he could not wait to see her again.

The challenge from the Guardians had arrived nine days ago in the middle of the night. His father woke him none too gently to deliver it. Ashton almost rolled over and ignored the whole trial by secret mission, but his father's gleam of pride and expectation proved enough to roust him out of comfortable slumber. He couldn't recall ever having seen his father look at him that way, as a responsible man with meaningful goals. He certainly had withheld that sentiment during Ashton's Casanova days. Even a bullet wound earned while serving with the King's Royal Rifles hadn't resulted in that paternal slap on the back and hearty wish for success.

He'd been instructed to leave in the middle of the night without telling anyone of his destination or purpose. He could leave no notes nor post any letters. His father assured him the Guardians would know—they had eyes and ears everywhere. For all intents and purposes, he was to vanish. This, he was assured, would be a test to see if he could keep his activities secret, a fundamental element of being a Guardian.

He was to make his way to a small town in Italy to see a farmer who had unearthed several medieval artifacts. He was to purchase what he deemed worthy based on his finances, then report to an address in Paris for an expert to evaluate the items. The mission seemed innocent enough. No government secrets to extract, no threats to make. Just pay a farmer out of his own pocket and return eventually to London . . . and Edwina.

It had been a long, long week, most particularly because he wasn't even allowed to write to Edwina. He had so much to tell her he thought his head might explode. Then all the little details about the scenery he'd passed and the people he'd met would come tumbling out. He'd even ridden a bicycle! How he longed to see her face when he told her that tale. The farmer had lived so far away from the train station and he couldn't find a horse to hire, so he'd rented a bicycle. The bone-jarring ride over earthen roads hurt his leg like nothing else, but somehow knowing that Edwina would enjoy hearing that he'd tried had kept him moving forward.

If riding a bicycle had marked Edwina as a modern woman, did riding a bicycle make him a new man? Lord, he hoped so. He certainly felt new and confident whenever Edwina looked at him. Even his father seemed to recognize the "newness" of him, and approved of the change.

Would his father approve of his choice of Edwina as a wife? Not that it mattered. While he would regret losing the new bond that had developed with his father as a result of his efforts in the family business and participation in the Guardians, both of which resulted from Edwina's suggestions, the new respect and friendship would not stand in the way of his taking Edwina as a wife. He wanted her beside him always, ever into the future. The thought made him smile. Of the items he was able to hastily assemble for this trip, his most treasured were her letters. He refused to leave those behind for fear Constance would find them and destroy them. It would be like her. This way he could reread Edwina's letters while they were apart. Once he returned and made her his wife, they would forge a new path, travel to the places she had dreamed, sample a new life, and join together each and every night.

His groin throbbed just at the thought of seeing Edwina naked on his bed, her arms wide in invitation. He knew from the moment she offered herself to him that she was the one he wanted to be with for the rest of his natural days. Someone to love. Someone he trusted implicitly. Someone he hoped now carried his child.

Edwina would be a wonderful mother; he saw that in her interactions with Matthew. She would be a wonderful companion, mother, lover, and wife. What more could a man ask for?

A man could ask to get this Guardian business over with quickly so he could return home and make her his once again, that's what. He frowned. Three days to get from Rome to Paris, a modern miracle, but not fast enough to meet his needs. He had made this same trip in reverse about a week earlier. The dismal skies and rain slashing across the windows on that journey mirrored his mood at leaving Edwina behind. He knew she'd understand why he couldn't tell her of his quest once he returned home to explain. At least the skies had cleared by the time he reached Rome. He lost a day in traveling from Rome to the countryside, and then renting the bike to travel to the farm and back. He traveled back to Rome and then allowed himself a day to get his filthy clothes cleaned and rest his throbbing leg, the result of his bicycling experiment. Three days ago, he boarded the train for Paris and now glanced out the window while the train slowed into Montparnasse station.

Suddenly, he sensed movement beside him. He glanced

up to see a stranger with a bag that looked remarkably like
his scurrying toward the rail car exit. A quick check to his
side confirmed it was indeed his bag, the one that contained
a few changes of clothing, three artifacts, and all of Edwina's
letters. In a moment, he was on his feet giving chase to the
miscreant. He would have had him had the doors not opened
to the rail station. Fellow passengers were quickly on their
feet, trapping him in the aisle. He forced his way off the train,
then spotted the man attempting to blend into the crowds on
the platform.

"Stop! Thief!" he yelled, pointing his cane in the thief's
direction. A gendarme on the platform blew a warning whistle and gave chase on foot. Ashton would have done the same
but knew that his leg would never keep up. Then he spotted
the bicycle leaning against the station wall. Tucking his cane
beneath his arm, Ashton mounted the bicycle and pedaled
furiously after the thief and the whistle-blowing policeman.
The smooth platform made for fast progress and much easier
steering than had his Italian route. Shouting warning to the
foolish few in his path, he made significant progress toward
his target. Pedestrians dashed and jumped out of his way, and
unfortunately managed to knock the pursuing gendarme into
a stack of luggage. Ashton continued past the commotion, his
bag with Edwina's letters in his sights.

Medieval artifacts were not necessarily light affairs, as the
thief most likely discovered. The sheer weight of the bag
appeared to be slowing him down even as Ashton closed the
distance between them. Ashton caught up with him just as
the smooth train platform ended in an earthen patch filled
with weeds and rocks. Letting the vehicle fly off the platform,
Ashton leapt from the bicycle onto the man's back, shoving
him into the dirt. While the crook struggled to regain his
footing, Ashton used his cane to snag the handle of the bag
on the ground.

Ashton pulled a snub-nosed revolver from his pocket and
aimed it at the thief, who dared to reach for the rucksack
handle. "Don't."

The single confident command was all that was needed.

The thief scrambled down the dirt embankment, leaving his prize behind. Ashton pocketed the revolver before the gendarme caught up to him, huffing from the run.

"Are you hurt, monsieur?" the policeman asked in French.

Ashton shook his head, then accepted the policeman's extended arm to rise. He dusted the dirt from his pants and jacket. "Nothing that a trip home won't fix."

The officer's lips twitched. "English. I thought so."

"At least I fared better than that bicycle." Ashton nodded to where the bicycle lay, its front wheel twisted at an unusual angle. "It must have landed on a rock."

The officer lifted the bicycle, inspecting its wheel. "Nothing that a few francs won't fix. Plus cab fare to return home," he said with a rueful smile. "The bicycle was mine, monsieur."

"I'm sorry about that." He paid the officer more than required. After all, if it wasn't for the use of the bicycle, he might have lost Edwina's letters forever. Afterwards, they shook hands, then walked back to the train station, Ashton with his bag firmly in his grasp, the officer carrying his wounded bicycle.

"I wonder if you might tell me where I might find this address," Ashton asked, producing a paper with his destination.

After waiting for the warning whistle blaring from the steam engine to cease, the officer told him the hotel was within walking distance and gestured the route. Ashton waved his appreciation and started off on this final leg of his "test."

He followed the directions to the front of a fairly nondescript granite hotel that looked as if it had served witness to the wide tree-lined boulevard on which it had stood for centuries. Pedestrians strolled along the sidewalks while horses pulling hansoms and carriages trotted crisply down the boulevard. Good. Once this final piece of his admission test for the Guardians was completed, he shouldn't have difficulty finding a hack to take him back to the station. Indeed, one waited patiently at the curb of the walkway. Just as Ashton stepped toward the door in the recessed entrance, a beautiful woman emerged from the hotel. She paused, tugging on her gloves, and gifted Ashton with a most alluring smile. But he wasn't interested. He held the door open for her as a gentleman should, but he imagined the woman couldn't transcript a single line of code and had probably never heard of *Treasure Island*. She wasn't Edwina, and he wasn't interested.

With a slight shrug of indifference, she moved to her waiting cab, leaving a lavender scent in her wake. Ashton entered the establishment, anxious to conclude this business so he could continue on home.

He climbed three flights of steps to reach the room noted. He knocked and waited. A voice called to him to enter. He turned the doorknob, surprised to discover it was unlocked. Obviously, he was expected. Still, he slipped his revolver in his hand, as he wasn't certain who was doing the expecting.

He pushed the door open. A man stood with his back toward the door at a washstand in the back of the room. A wide bed, rumpled as if hastily made, dominated the small chamber. Not surprisingly, a hint of lavender scented the air. The man turned, drying his hands with a towel. *Rothwell!*

"A gun? Is that necessary, Ash?"

"Did you expect me to embark on this wild-goose chase without one?" Ashton asked, pocketing the weapon.

"I suppose not." He gestured to a small sitting area. "Have a seat. Tell me of your adventures."

"I wasn't expecting to find you here," Ashton said as he lowered himself to a chair by a window. From this height, he could see over the rooftops to Luxembourg Gardens. Edwina would enjoy the gardens' fountains and plantings. In fact, Paris would be perfect for their honeymoon, or at least the beginning of their honeymoon. There were so many places he wanted to show her. "Didn't you warn me away from the Guardians?"

"I knew you wouldn't listen." Rothwell placed a snifter of brandy near his hand before lowering himself with his own glass in hand into the chair opposite. "And I wanted to see how far you would pursue it."

"Is any of what you told me true?" Ashton watched his old friend carefully, not exactly certain which side he was on.

"Everything I told you was true." Rothwell sipped from his glass. "The Guardians are a group of moneyed individuals who use their resources to bring the world's cultural riches to England. Just as you brought back the artifacts. May I see them?"

Ashton moved to the bag he'd left on the bed and rummaged inside. "Are you the expert I was told would evaluate them?"

"No. That would be Hargrove."

His hand paused on the reliquary that he'd wrapped in one of his old shirts. "Edwina?"

"No. Her father is our medieval expert," Rothwell said. His lips twitched. "But I see you've met his talented daughter. I'm not surprised. I imagine some habits are hard to break."

Ashton let the implied reference to his womanizing days slide off his back. His old reputation was what it was. Eventually, it would be forgotten, or at least be as interesting as last year's news. He handed Rothwell the brass reliquary. "The crystal is broken and the relic missing, but with a little cleaning, I think the artwork will be exquisite. You can feel the pattern of a textured design beneath the dirt."

Patterns. Edwina had him thinking of patterns. Ashton hid his smile while watching Rothwell rub his finger across the crusted dirt. Did she know her father was one of the Guardians? His face twisted. "Why do you call her talented?"

"She's a code breaker," Rothwell said. "You wouldn't know it to look at her, but she has a natural talent for breaking codes. The Guardians have had their eye on her for some time." He held the brass reliquary up to the light, while Ashton prepared to hand him a beaker, the second of the medieval artifacts. "This is a lovely piece. Hargrove will be pleased."

"Why would the Guardians have an interest in a code breaker?" It troubled him that a group of well-placed men had been watching his Edwina from afar, as if they had some ulterior purpose in mind.

Rothwell took the beaker with painted enamel and examined it closely. "What I told you before is true. Sometimes secrets that are of interest to the Crown travel with the artifacts. It's one of the reasons I'm a member of the Guardians. Sometimes those secrets travel in code. Access to a code breaker would be instrumental in deciding what secrets are important and which are not."

Ashton thought of his father's coded note. Did the Guardians know of that communication? Were they suspicious of his father? He knew that he had been. Did the slogan for Falcon Freight finally unlock the full communication? Edwina and he were to have met to discuss her findings, but, of course, this test by the Guardians had interfered.

He unwrapped the final artifact, a piece of limestone that had been carved in the likeness of a king, based on the crown atop his head. The nose was gone and significant effacement had occurred in the facial features, but enough artistry remained to make it an appealing purchase, or so Ashton thought.

"So this is what made that blasted bag so heavy," Rothwell said, taking the carving into his hands.

The comment startled Ashton as he retraced his actions since he had stepped into the room. He couldn't recall a time when Rothwell had lifted his bag. He glared across the small table between them. "How did you know of the bag's weight?"

Rothwell smiled. "It was all part of the test. We wanted to be certain that you would protect any items you were assigned to retrieve. It was of particular concern to those who worried that your wound would hinder your abilities in that area. However, Jacques reports that you were both devious and resourceful in your efforts. He said you pulled a gun on him to protect the artifacts. I found that particularly encouraging, given that these trinkets most likely mean little to you."

He was correct in that regard. The trinkets meant nothing, but Edwina's letters meant everything. But Rothwell didn't need to know that. "Are you telling me that I passed the test?"

Rothwell lifted his glass to clink against Ashton's. "Most definitely. Your performance will silence the critics who felt you weren't ready, or weren't committed enough to succeed. There is one more item I wish to discuss with you."

"Critics?"

"There were some who still think of you as a skirt-chasing rake. They weren't certain you'd take your obligations seriously enough and would put the group's secrecy at risk. Thus the need for the test."

While he wasn't surprised that his old reputation had caused skepticism, one possible skeptic concerned him. "Was my father one of the critics?"

"Not at all; your father was outspoken on your behalf. You made quite an impression on the old man while you worked for him."

Surprise jolted through him. His father had kept that impression well hidden. Again, working for his father was another of Edwina's suggestions. The Guardians thought she was talented due to her code-recognition abilities. They didn't know the half of it. He sipped his brandy. "So what was the other matter you wished to discuss?"

"I understand you've been working on a rifle scope."

Not only did he spill brandy down the front of his last clean shirt, but the alcohol at the back of his throat took a different turn. The resulting burning windpipe made it difficult to take a breath. "How . . . you . . ."

"How did I know?" Rothwell interrupted. "You've been working with Thomas Harris & Son on the optics. Harris is one of our members and speaks very highly of you."

Ashton was beginning to wonder who wasn't a member of the Guardians.

"He says you've developed a mount for the Martini-Henry rifle and have been working with him regarding the placement of a modified scope for maximum eye relief—whatever that is."

Ashton's voice was weak, but at least he could form a sentence. "It's a term for the space—"

"Don't bother explaining. It means nothing to me. Given your experience with the King's Royal Rifles, I would imagine it's important to you and the men who use that particular rifle."

Ashton nodded, wondering what this discussion was leading to.

"And as those men who use the Martini-Henry rifle are important to the Crown, I'd like to extend a contract to purchase sufficient quantities of these new rifle scope mounts."

Ashton thought his jaw might hit the floor. Harris had one prototype rifle scope mount. One. "What exactly do you mean by sufficient quantities?"

"I'd like to outfit every Martini-Henry rifle with one of these mounts. Your father is knowledgeable about the delivery of mass quantities. Harris is knowledgeable about the optics and can help you with the production. All you need to do is set up a facility to produce the product." Rothwell frowned. "That is unless you're adverse to being in trade."

Ashton understood the reference. So many of his peers felt it a badge of honor to depend on someone else to finance a life of emptiness and leisure. Ashton had sampled that life for a short time and found it empty and shallow. While the contract Rothwell suggested was a bit frightening for someone like himself who had no experience in manufacturing, the lure of making his own money was intoxicating. He wouldn't depend on his father for financing anymore, except as a business proposition. He would be independent, and that thought was exhilarating. He could understand why Edwina was so insistent on the concept.

"Of course, there are others among the Guardians who will help you. The members include bankers, solicitors, and other industrialists. We tend to favor like-minded individuals who keep the superiority of the Crown at the forefront."

"I don't know what to say." He shook Rothwell's hand. "Thank you. Thank you very much."

"It's my pleasure," Rothwell said. "Let's have a drink to celebrate."

While Rothwell topped off the glasses, Ashton imagined Edwina's expression when she learned of this news. Again, it had been her suggestion that he pursue his idea for a rifle mount. He was beginning to wonder how he ever managed his life before he met her. She was his personal angel sent down to earth.

They clinked glasses and toasted the new venture. Ashton

was more excited than ever to return to London to tell Edwina of all that had transpired. "What do I do with the artifacts?" Ashton asked. "I had thought I was bringing them for an expert to evaluate. Do I leave them with you?"

"No. They'll go to Hargrove. We had you come to Paris because we didn't wish to do the final test, the stealing of the artifacts, in London. We wanted you to have the difficulties inherent in dealing with a different culture and not possibly having friends nearby to assist."

Ashton nodded. "So you didn't tell the others that I'm fluent in French."

Rothwell smiled. "I didn't see the need."

"So you want me to take these into London and deliver them to Hargrove." Ashton smiled, enjoying the thought of appearing at Edwina's door and asking to speak to her father. Yes, there was much the two men could discuss.

"There's no hurry to deliver them. I imagine Hargrove has his hands full at the moment." Rothwell shook his head. "I should tell you that he's the one who was most opposed to bringing you into the fold. I imagine it was due to your reputation, combined with his having a daughter of marriageable age. But that's no longer a problem."

The fine hairs stood up on the back of Ashton's neck. "What do you mean? Why is that no longer a problem?"

"He's been working on a way to keep his daughter's talents available to the Guardians. He's had one of his employees, a hard-working and enterprising clerk, woo her with little result. Apparently Miss Hargrove has reconsidered and has accepted his suit. The two are to be married within a month."

· *Twenty-one* ·

🌱 "HE'S BACK!" SARAH SLID INTO HER SEAT AT THE RAKE
Patrol meeting, her eyes filled with sad portent.

"Who's back?" Faith asked.

"Ashton?" Edwina whispered, interpreting Sarah's sympathetic gaze. Dread filled her. She'd hoped never to experience
this moment. When no letters arrived, no explanations, she'd
hoped he had left forever so as never to remind her of all she'd
lost.

Sarah nodded. "He placed that same ad in the personals.
He said this time it was for himself."

"When?" Her lip trembled so fiercely, her voice sounded
like a death knell. One would have thought that he'd come to
her first, not to the *Mayfair Messenger*.

"Oh, Edwina. He had the most terrifying expression. I'd
suggest we engage the Rake Patrol to stop him if I wasn't afraid
he'd murder one of us first. His hands shook. I don't think he's
shaven for days. He had the most awful scowl. He should be
grateful that the women answering his ad don't require a carte
de visite. The sight of him would certainly scare them off."

Then they'd be the foolish ones, Edwina thought, wishing she were free to answer Ashton's ad. How she'd love to see his expression were she to walk to his table carrying a rose. But she had promised herself to another. Someone who wasn't inclined to run off at a whim and leave her behind to deal with the difficulties.

The bell jangled about the Crescent door. Edwina glanced up and seemingly lost the ability to breathe. There could be no mistaking the man filling the doorway. His gaze swept the room, then settled on her face. Once he had fixed her in his sights, he advanced with apparent disregard for the other patrons until he stood directly opposite her at the table. "Edwina."

In unison the other members of the Rake Patrol stood and vacated the table. Edwina wasn't certain if they left the Crescent or simply moved to another table. The sound of his voice awakened her soul in ways she had wished remained dormant. Her body lifted with expectations, with dreams, with memories.

Her focus narrowed on Ashton's gaunt face. Sarah was right. He didn't look at all like the man she remembered, like the man she'd loved. He looked dark, hard, utterly masculine. She schooled her expression and tempered her thoughts, as in three weeks time she'd be another man's wife.

He sat without waiting for an invitation. "I didn't see your bicycle out front. I didn't realize you were here," he said.

She knew it was a lie. She'd bet he followed Sarah, knowing that her friend would come directly to her with the news. She met his gaze head-on. "Walter doesn't approve of my riding a bicycle. He said it wasn't appropriate for a married woman." His eyes drifted down to her hands. "A soon-to-be-married woman," she corrected.

His lips quirked in that familiar way that twisted her heart. "I see you've gone back to those ghastly high-neck collars."

"Walter prefers that I dress in a more conservative fashion," she replied.

"I'm surprised Walter lets you meet with your friends here at the Crescent," he said sarcastically.

"Walter knows how much they mean to me," she replied. "He wouldn't think of breaking my heart."

Ashton shook his head and chuckled. At least, it appeared that way. No sound actually emerged, as if he'd lost the ability to laugh. "Is that what I did? I broke *your* heart?"

His eyes looked so old, and so jaded. One of the Crescent's female patrons walked by and dropped her handkerchief by Ashton's chair. He didn't notice. "*You* betrayed *me*, Edwina. *You*. Of all people . . ." He glanced away a moment, but when he looked back, his lost expression took her breath away. "Of all people, I thought I could trust you."

"Betray you?" All her sympathy for him disappeared with the accusation in his words. "I betrayed you? You're the one who left with no explanation. I waited for you in the park. I waited in the pouring rain believing that any minute you might appear. I waited, refusing to believe you would abandon me. When it was obvious that you had done exactly that, I dragged myself soaking wet to your house, worried that you might have been hurt, hoping for an explanation. Your stepmother supplied one."

"You spoke with Constance?"

She nodded. "She said you ran off, just as you did five years ago."

"You believed her? I told you what she did. I told you why I left back then. *That* has nothing to do with *this*." He jammed his finger on the table for emphasis.

"Doesn't it?" Her voice lowered to a harsh whisper. "She said you left after you took her virtue. She said she had no choice but to marry your father because you left her with a child in her belly. Is it really so different? What choice did you leave me?"

His eyes widened and a spark of humanity flashed. "Are you . . . ?"

"I don't know," Edwina replied hastily. "I'm not certain. Not enough time has passed." But she had her suspicions. It was the main reason she'd accepted Walter's proposal. Faith thought the stress over the past month might have caused her menses to cease, but Edwina suspected she was just being kind.

"I didn't leave you, you know," Ashton said softly. "I was sent on a mission by the Guardians." Accusation tinged his eyes. "You do remember that you suggested I join them? I was told I could not communicate with anyone. I couldn't send you a letter. They said they would know. I had to trust that you would understand that I wouldn't leave without reason, and that I would return, for you, as soon as I was able. I had to trust in you."

"Ashton, how was I to know?" she pleaded. "After what we did? How was I to know? You left me alone to make some difficult decisions."

"Does he know?" It was spoken as a dare, or maybe— maybe it was a prayer.

She lowered her voice to intimate levels. "I told Walter that I was no longer innocent. He knows that I could be with child."

"You told him!" He looked aghast, then considered. "Of course you would. To others you're as honest as the day is long, but to me . . ." He hung his head. "Does he know that the baby, if one exists, is mine?"

"I imagine he suspects. There were no others. He never asked."

"And it does not bother him to raise another man's child?"

"I told you that he's a good man. He has a good heart."

"Good enough that you chose him over me."

She sighed. "Ashton, you're like one of those rare comets that fly through the night sky. A bright light that flies among the stars, inspiring dreams and wishes. I'm not a comet or even a star. I'm just someone below who is grateful to have spent some time in your world, but I can't live there. I'm ordinary Edwina. You would eventually have been bored with me."

"You're wrong."

"I'm right," she said. "You just don't wish to admit it." She opened her reticule and removed the spyglass he'd given her. "I'd like you to give this to Matthew. It's not really appropriate that I keep a gift from you now."

His eyes pleaded with her. "Edwina."

She removed her journal and untied the white ribbon that now bound it. Opening the book, she removed an envelope with an ink smudge on the back. "This is for you. I finished decoding your father's letter. I had planned to give this to you in the park, but"—her lips tightened—"I can give it to you now."

"Edwina," he said again. "Don't do this."

"I have no choice, Ashton. I gave him my word. I promised I would marry him."

"Did you promise you would love him?" His eyes searched her face.

She bit her lip. Her voice faltered. "I promised I would try."

"Edwina . . ." he pleaded.

She slid her journal back into her reticule. "Sarah says you put another ad in the *Mayfair Messenger*. I wish you luck in finding someone who can appreciate all your wonderful qualities."

"Qualities that you helped develop," Ashton said. "Don't leave me, Edwina. I beg of you. Don't leave me."

She shook her head. "I have to go." She stood, and Ashton immediately followed suit. "Walter is joining the family for dinner. I promised I'd be waiting when he and Father return home."

"Don't let him break you, Edwina. You have intelligence and spirit. Any man who can't see that is a fool."

She placed her hand on the side of his face. The spot where she'd once left a red handprint. His lids cast down, he leaned into her palm, rubbing the stubble against her hand. She wished she could feel that stubble on other more sensitive places on her body, that she could feel Ashton fill her once again and bring her back to life. Her eyes softened. "Good-bye, Ashton."

She started to leave, but his voice gave her pause.

"You're a young woman, Edwina. Can you tolerate being married to a fool the rest of your life?"

She left without looking back. That way he wouldn't see the tears rolling down her cheeks. They'd both be better off this way.

• • •

NOTHING WEIGHED HEAVIER ON A MAN'S SOUL THAN lack of hope. Dragging that limestone bust through three countries was nothing compared to simply returning to his father's town house after Edwina had efficiently eviscerated his heart.

His father discovered him well saturated with brandy in the library, that very room where Ashton had discovered Edwina snooping in the dark on the night that he'd introduced her to the secret gallery.

"It's blazing hot outside, Ashton. Why have you lit a fire? Constance is complaining that her face is ready to melt."

Ashton couldn't see his father, not clearly anyway, but he could still recognize his voice. "I'm as cold as a week-old corpse. I thought the fire would help." His voice dropped. "It doesn't."

He heard the clink of glass and the sound of liquid pouring, but as the level in his own glass remained the same, he assumed his father had poured a drink for himself. "Drink up," he said. "You have a lot of catching up to do."

"What's this?" His father picked up a page of scented stationary from the center of the table. He started to read but he didn't need to read far before he recognized the words. His voice raised in anger. Ashton assumed his face matched the fury in his voice, but again he really couldn't see clearly and quite frankly he didn't care. Not anymore.

"This letter was intended for me! No one else was to see it. How did you get this?" he thundered.

Ashton struggled to lift his eyelids higher. "I found it . . . rather Edwina found it . . . the night the pillow book arrived."

"This isn't Sakura's letter," his father fumed. "Hers was written in code. How did you do this?"

"Edwina . . . do you know Edwina?" Ashton tilted his head back in memory. "Sweet little code breaker, that girl. She figured out the code and transcribed it."

A hesitant curiosity replaced the heat in his father's voice. "Edwina . . . Is that the Hargrove girl?"

"You've met her then?" Ashton held up his snifter in salute. "Sweet little heartbreaker, Edwina."

A chair moved beside him. His father drifted into view. A calmer and sober father. "No. I've not met her, but her father was determined to keep her talents available to the Guardians. I think he talked her into marrying that piece of milquetoast that works for him just for that purpose."

"Walter? That milquetoast has enough spine to marry another man's woman. I should put my rifle scope to good use. If he wasn't in the picture . . ." He glanced to the glowing coals in the grate. "Time for more fuel." He pulled an envelope from a stack of similarly scented envelopes tied with a scarlet red ribbon and tossed it on the coals. The edges of the envelope caught and curled. Flames licked the paper surface, slowly turning it to ash. One tiny corner remained untouched— one with a black thumbprint—then it too disappeared.

"What are you doing, Ashton?" his father asked tenderly.

"Her letters," he replied. "I carried them next to my heart all through Italy. Almost killed a man in France when he tried to steal them from me. But now she's going to marry Walter. She said she's going to try to love him." He turned blurry eyes to his father. "Try to love him when she already loves me."

He reached for another letter to toss on the fire, but his father grabbed his hand and forced it to the table, stopping him. "Don't do it, son. You'll regret burning those memories. Later, when you're sober, you might discover they're all you have to keep you going. Latch onto a dream that one day things will be different and you can be together."

"Sober. I don't ever want to be sober again." Ashton swallowed more brandy, then nodded toward the decoded letter on the table. "Edwina said she thought that was a love letter. I wouldn't listen. I thought you were up to nefar—nefar . . . evil purposes." His tongue must have swollen. Some words were just too difficult to say. He'd done extensive drinking in his Casanova days, but he couldn't recall having this thick tongue before. "Why? You married Constance?"

"A man gets lonely when he's all alone. I thought marrying Constance would make me forget about Sakura. It would make me forget to regret that I didn't marry Sakura when I had the opportunity."

"Sakura?" He liked the way that sounded, so he lifted his glass in salute. "Sakura!" Then he turned to his father. "Who is she?"

"She was the love of my life," his father replied. "I met her when I was far too young to realize how difficult it would be for a Japanese woman to live in this country. I loved her, so I thought everyone else would too. I was wrong." He sipped his drink and leaned back in his chair. "She tried to be like the other women in society. She even attempted to wear English clothes while she pretended to be your nanny. But Sakura was too uncomfortable and couldn't live as if she wasn't her true self. She returned to her native clothing and abandoned the attempt to appear English."

"Pretended to be my nanny?"

"She was never a servant. I never paid her a wage. She just loved you so much, she thought that pretending to be your nanny would allow her to spend more time with you while I traveled on business."

"And when you were home?"

His father smiled. "When I was home she taught me the wonders and wisdom of the pillow books."

"So she's . . ." He swung his drink in the direction of the secret gallery.

"Yes. The Guardians encouraged me to import items of Japanese culture, even if they weren't appropriate for the British Museum. I insisted that we keep the pillow books someplace where you wouldn't find them. Impressionable eyes and so forth. Sakura said it didn't matter, that children should not be protected from that aspect of life, but . . . I built the gallery."

"Why didn't you . . ."

"Why didn't I marry her?" He seemed to contemplate this a bit, though Ashton suspected this wasn't the first time he'd asked himself that question. Ashton knew this because he'd been asking himself the same thing about Edwina.

"I was too young, too stupid, and too cowardly," his father

finally said. "I was afraid of what my business associates would say when they learned I'd married a Japanese woman. So I kept her here without benefit of marriage. Eventually, she decided that wasn't good enough, so she left. The irony was . . . one of my overseas business associates asked for her hand." He shook his head. "We had something special. It was as if we were fated to be together. We were connected at the soul, but I threw it all away because of stupid pride." He swallowed from his snifter.

"She still writes?"

"Yes, but she writes in code in case her husband finds the letters. He's a good man. He's better than me in many respects. He married Sakura, I'll give him that. I've waited for him to die for far too many years, just so I could swoop in and marry my Sakura, my sweet cherry blossom." He sipped his drink. "But I yielded to temptation when you brought Constance home to meet me. She was so young and spirited and beautiful. She reminded me of my Sakura. I didn't think Constance would be interested in an old man like me. I proposed in jest, but when she accepted, I thought she would be the answer to a prayer."

"And was she?"

His lips thinned. "I still pray. Then you ran off and joined the Rifles."

"I was going to ask Constance to marry me, but then learned you had beat me to it."

He smiled. "I wish it had been otherwise. And I imagine Constance wishes it had been otherwise as well."

Ashton shook his head. "She prefers your money to my company. I'm not interested in the social world she finds so interesting."

"That's two of us." His father finished his drink and poured another. Ashton, finding the conversation sobering, placed his hand over his glass, refusing more. "I was pleased that she would have an escort to all those parties and dances and such when you returned."

"With a bullet hole in my leg," Ashton added.

"There is that, but the Rifles seemed to make a man out

of you. You're not the same man now that you were when you left." He shook his head. "Back in those days you were reckless and wild."

"I wanted you to notice me, to get your attention. You were always so concerned with business, you didn't have time for a son."

His father tilted his head. "That's not something I'm proud of. I wanted to spend time with you, but a new business is a harsh mistress, as you'll soon discover. I supported you as best I could, but someone had to mind the store."

"She lied to Edwina, you know," Ashton grumbled, using the tip of his stick to stab at the floor.

"Who?"

"Constance." He looked up. "She said Matthew was my son and that I ran because she was pregnant."

His father shook his head. "Constance was a virgin the night I wed her. I saw the blood on the sheets myself."

"Nevertheless, her lies were enough to persuade Edwina to marry someone else."

"You'd proposed to her?" his father asked.

"No, but I intended to." *She should have waited.*

"Intentions be damned," his father said. "It's the doing that matters."

"I should have told her that night," Ashton said. If only he'd been wiser the night they were together. "I should have told her I loved her."

"Who? Constance?" his father asked, confused.

Ashton just shook his head. "Don't do the same thing to Matthew that you did to me. Falcon Freight is running smoothly. You've got some good men who can make good decisions. Let them carry some of the load, while you spend some time with your son." Ashton smiled. "Otherwise you'll be dealing with another reprobate in ten years."

"You didn't turn out so bad." His father lifted his glass in a toast.

"The credit for that belongs to another." Another who was going to marry Walter.

They sat in silence a moment.

"I propose we strike a barter," his father said. "I won't repeat my earlier mistakes with Matthew if you don't follow in my footsteps with . . . what was her name?"

"Edwina." Ashton smiled. It was a beautiful name. Unique. So perfect for her.

"That's an awful name." His father made a distasteful face. "Whatever happened to the good old-fashioned names, like Mary or Rose?"

"Edwina is a modern woman, a harbinger of the future."

"Well, if you love her, make her yours. It's never too late till the ring's on her finger. Otherwise you'll be reading these letters for the rest of your life. Here." He tied the ribbon that Ashton had stolen from Edwina's journal and pushed the tidy stack toward his son. "Keep them for the lonely times. You'll find them to be little comfort, but better than none. Take this advice from one who knows."

· *Twenty-two* ·

ONCE THE ENGAGEMENT HAD BEEN ANNOUNCED, Walter had practically moved in with the Hargrove family. Every time Edwina seemed to turn around, Walter would be standing there. She even caught him poking through the family mail when she teased him about changing his delivery address to her residence. She sometimes wondered if her parents were so anxious for her to marry just so they could reclaim their house and privacy.

Both her father and Walter were due to arrive from the office. These days they always traveled home together. With only one week to the wedding, Edwina had fallen into the pattern of using the short time before their arrival for personal pursuits, as after Walter arrived, her activities would be predicated on his whims.

She glanced at the *Mayfair Messenger* that she'd picked up at an earlier meeting of the Rake Patrol. A headline on the inner pages mentioned the formation of a new industrial concern, C.B. Manufacturing, determined to make rifle scope mounts. The bold print reminded her of Ashton. Would they manufacture scopes for that type of rifle he'd used in Burma and India? At least his dream would be realized, even if it was by someone else.

Poor Ashton. She hadn't seen him or heard from him since that confrontation last week at the Crescent. The memory of his face when he accused her of betrayal would stay with her till her dying day. Would she ever see him again? What would he say if he knew that she was indeed pregnant from their single night together? She couldn't go to him. Not after she'd pledged her future to another man. She would always hold that night close to her heart, but it was time to move to the next adventure.

She opened her lap desk to compose a letter to her brothers. Their last letter indicated that they'd gone north to America, to a state called Louisiana. They described the most amazing sights and glorious food. Their letter stirred all her yearnings for travel to such exotic locales. She was writing to tell them as much when Walter and her father arrived.

"So what did you do today?" Walter asked in a condescending manner as he crossed the parlor to where she sat by the window.

Ever since she'd agreed to marry him, she'd noted a shift in his patterns. His tone when addressing her had changed and not in an altogether pleasant way. She heard condescension where once there had been respect. She supposed her admission of prior intimacy might warrant a certain lack of esteem, but not to this level, and certainly not from a man she'd agreed to marry. Where once Walter was concerned with her needs and wants, now her needs had become secondary to his. She felt selfish in wishing it were otherwise. Was that wrong of her? Was this a fair exchange for his promise of security?

Though she tilted her face up to accept Walter's greeting kiss, his lips pressed her forehead, such as one would do to a child. It wasn't that she longed for Walter's kisses—his hadn't the thrill that she'd discovered with Ashton—but she had agreed to be his wife, thus she was willing to offer him affection, and accept his offerings in return. She was beginning to think he didn't exactly know how to show affection.

"I met with Faith and Claire at the Crescent," she said. "You'll never guess—"

"I don't approve of Claire," Walter interrupted. He held her fingers in his, and frowned at the ink stain on her index finger. "She's too much of a firebrand and may place you at risk. Perhaps you should consider disassociating yourself from her."

"From Claire?" Edwina echoed in disbelief. "I know Claire can be outspoken, but we've been friends for years. Her beliefs and actions are hers alone, not mine. She understands that."

"Still, people see you together, and they will assume you believe as she does. What people think of you reflects in turn on me." He patted himself on the chest. "No. I think I'll have to insist that you avoid her company . . . hers and that woman at the newspaper office."

"Sarah?"

"If that's her name." He stooped down so as to be on the same level as her. "A woman's place is in her husband's home, not working in a man's world. My mother is anxious to show you all you'll need to know to be a proper wife and mother. You won't have time to spend with Sarah."

Edwina fought to keep the frown from her face at the thought of moving in with Walter and his mother. She'd met the woman shortly after the engagement announcement, and the older widow made no secret of her disappointment in Walter's choice for a wife. While Sarah insisted that Edwina had made the right choice for a secure future, Edwina had begun to wonder if the future would be a pleasant one. At the moment it appeared to be filled with unhappy challenges.

"And what of Faith?" she asked. "Are you going to forbid me to see her as well?"

He smiled indulgently. "I approve of Faith. She is a virtuous woman. I would have no difficulty allowing her into our house, but the other two are a different matter."

"They are not allowed in our house?" Ashton's words came back to her. *Don't let him break you. You have intelligence and spirit. Any man who can't see that is a fool. You're a*

young woman, Edwina. Can you tolerate being married to a
fool the rest of your life?

"It's for your own good, my dear," Walter continued, standing. "I'm the man. I know more about the way of the world
than you."

"Do you believe I'm intelligent, Walter?" she challenged.

"Of course, I do." He smiled. "Your father wouldn't have
insisted that you be available to assist the Guardians if you
weren't intelligent."

She paled. The Guardians had caused nothing but difficulty
in her life. "What do you know of the Guardians?"

"Your father has promised that once we marry he'll propose
that I be allowed membership in that organization. I'm not
certain of their purpose, but if your father is a member, it must
be a very prestigious club." Walter leaned over her shoulder,
presumably to read what she had written to her brothers.

"What sort of assistance do you think they need of me?"
she asked, placing the unfinished letter in her lap desk. She
paused, recalling the time she'd hidden the scandalous netsuke
in this very desk, until she'd moved it to her bureau. What
would Walter have thought had he seen it there now? Though
she was still angry over the Guardians, the thought made her
lips turn in a half smile.

"I'm not certain." Walter frowned down at her. "I suppose
they need someone to take notes and provide refreshments. I
understand that they meet in secret, so perhaps they don't
wish to use servants for such tasks. You know how servants
like to talk."

Take notes! Provide refreshments! While she wasn't certain
why the Guardians would have any interest in her, she knew
it was for some other purpose than this. Could Walter be so
blind as to the nature of a secret society?

"Walter, why did you propose to me?" she asked. While
she knew Walter to be a good and caring friend, she'd started
to wonder if those attributes would translate into a good and
caring husband.

"I must admit, I hadn't really thought we could be a match
until your father suggested as much," Walter acknowledged.

"Then I started to watch you and spend more time with you. While I believe your father has been overly indulgent with you, I can see you have some lovely attributes."

"And what attributes are those?"

"You write letters to your brothers, which is indicative of someone invested in family. You enjoy reading, a solitary recreation. I admire the self-sufficient sort of woman who can exist without the involvement of others."

Isabella trotted into the room, the tiny bell on her collar announcing her arrival. She slipped over to Walter's leg and stretched her paws up to the calf of his trousers, begging affection. Walter shook his leg, dislodging the kitten.

"I've seen the loyalty you've shown your lady friends, and I'm anxious to be the recipient of such loyalty from such an attractive and desirable woman," he added with an indulgent smile. "However, if I may be so bold . . . your father loves you and thus perhaps did not employ the necessary firm hand that you required. I believe as your husband, I can intercede where someone of authority should have interceded long ago. You have the potential to be a wonderful wife, Edwina. I believe together we will have a quiet and pleasant life."

"You mentioned my father's love," she said, lifting the disappointed kitten from the floor. "Yet you've said nothing of your own."

"I do love you, Edwina," he insisted. "I shall love you more, however, when you modify your current behavior to something more appropriate. And in time, I believe you'll come to love me in return." His lips tightened. "It's not as if you have much choice in the matter."

"What do you mean?" Alarms silently registered in the pit of her stomach.

"By your own admission, you've been ruined." He reached over and soothed a hand down the kitten's back. "You're another man's leavings. Do you honestly believe any other respectable man would marry you? You should be on your knees thanking me for overlooking this failing."

The kitten bit Walter's hand. It was a playful gesture, but she saw anger sweep across his face as he shook his hand free, then examined it for teeth marks. "Whatever possessed you to get a cat? You can't train them properly the way you can a dog."

She supposed his next demand would be that she "dismiss" her pet as well. "On my knees, Walter?" she prodded.

"I don't insist on such outward displays of repentance." He set his shoulders back, then raised his brows in her direction. "I'm a bigger man than that. Still, I believe some gratification is in order. And the best way to demonstrate your gratitude is to take to heart the lessons in conduct that I have offered. I'm pleased that you have abandoned that dangerous and unseemly bicycle, and I'm pleased that you've taken to more appropriate attire. I'm certain in time I might request other modifications of outlandish behavior, but I'm certain you will see the wisdom of my experience in such matters."

"Such as restricting my friendships . . ." she said, carefully controlling her voice lest her anger slip through.

"Only if you form alliances with the wrong sort of people," Walter said. "My mother knows of a number of suitable acquaintances. You should be able to replace those old friendships readily enough."

"Doesn't it bother you that I don't love you?" she asked. She hadn't meant to be so blunt, but the warning turmoil in her stomach had grown to fill her with anxiety. Even Isabella's soothing purring couldn't calm her. She placed the kitten on the floor.

He smiled, a cold revengeful sort of twist of the lips. "I don't require affection from a wife. I require obedience."

Her mother chose that moment to enter the parlor in her dinner attire. She greeted Walter warmly. Her father followed behind, then crossed to kiss his wife on the cheek. Neither seemed to notice that Edwina trembled on the chair by the window.

What was she to do? Her parents were overjoyed about the impending nuptials. She had no prospects for another husband. Although Ashton had begged her to see him again, it was not with an offer of marriage. Her parents were unaware of her fall from grace, and if she married Walter, it would remain so. Her pregnancy would be expected, celebrated even. To break an engagement once announced was tantamount to proclaiming oneself a ruined woman. Her entire family would be disgraced.

"Edwina? Are you all right?" her mother asked. "Dinner is ready. Will you not come in with us?" Edwina glanced up, noting her father and Walter had already left the room. Only her mother remained. "Are you feeling unwell?"

"I'm sorry, Mother. I can't," she replied.

"You can't what, darling? You can't eat dinner?"

"I can't marry Walter." Her lips moved as if they responded to another's thoughts. Her own thoughts were too chaotic to form intelligent sentences.

Her mother's face dissolved from caring concern to a knowing understanding. She pulled Edwina to a standing position and guided her toward the dining room. "Of course you can. All brides go through pre-nuptial anxieties. The invitations have been extended. The bans have been read. All is in readiness. Soon you shall be a blushing bride."

"I can't, Mother." Her feet refused to take another step, leaving her stranded midway between the drawing and dining rooms. She could already see Walter impatiently standing on the other side of the dinner table, waiting on her arrival so he could take his seat. He scowled briefly in her direction, disapproving no doubt of her tardiness. She turned toward her mother. "I just can't."

"Why not, dear?" Concern dawned in her eyes and slowly drained her earlier supportive euphoria. Furrows appeared between her brows. "What's wrong?"

"I'm pregnant," Edwina admitted, too late realizing the men in the dining room could hear every word. "With another man's child."

· Twenty-three ·

❧ "EDWINA!" HER MOTHER GASPED.

"Who?" demanded her father. He spun on his heel to address Walter. "Did you know about this?"

"Yes," he admitted. His glare toward Edwina suggested he had intended to keep her child's parentage secret. "Edwina told me, but I agreed to marry her anyway."

"You're a good man." Her father slapped Walter on the shoulder. "I knew as much when I recommended you marry my daughter." He turned back toward Edwina. "You, however, are a disappointment. How could you bring this shame to your family? At least you still have a good man who will marry you in spite of your lapse of good judgment."

"No," Edwina said. Admitting her indiscretion, letting it out into the open, gave her a strength she hadn't anticipated.

"No?" her father repeated. "What do you mean, no? A wedding is expected, and, by God, there will be a wedding."

She turned toward Walter. "I don't love you, Walter. You deserve someone who does, just as I deserve someone who loves me." He opened his mouth to protest, but she interrupted.

"I know you say you love me but . . . I know the difference."
Her hand slipped down toward her belly. "I know what love
feels like. You and I are a poor imitation. You deserve better.
I deserve better."

"You deserve a thrashing by the back of my hand, young
lady," her father said, his face growing redder by the minute.
It was an empty threat. Walter was correct that her father
loved her and had never raised a hand to her. She knew he
wouldn't now.

"You'll be disgraced if you don't marry," her mother said.
"What will you do?"

"I'll go away." Edwina thought of her brothers' letter. "We
can claim that an illness has made the planned wedding impossible at this time and that I'm going away to a warmer
climate to recuperate. In time, I'll be forgotten, as will the
wedding."

"People will talk," her mother said. "They'll assume you've
been ruined, and aspersions will be cast." She glanced at
Walter.

"Walter won't speak of my indiscretion," Edwina said, her
full attention on Walter's face. "He's a good man and Father's
associate. You won't say anything, will you?"

His lips tightened and he shook his head. "I would have
been good for you," he said softly.

"I'm certain you would have tried," Edwina said. "But in
the end, we'd both be miserable."

He acknowledged the last with a nod.

"I've given you every right to call off the wedding. If you
do, society will rightly assume I've been with another man."
Edwina moved into the dining room. Her mother collapsed
into a chair. "However, as I informed you of my situation
before you offered marriage, it does not seem fair to cry foul
now. I propose we let it be known that I called off the wedding. That way it will appear that you have been seeing other
women. Your stature as a man about town will increase, and
you will save my parents from disgrace from my actions.
They and I will be in your debt."

She saw Walter's lips twist at the significance of that statement. Walter was not a man to blackmail another, but he appreciated that her father would be grateful for his sacrifice.

"I will leave London and save my parents from further embarrassment," Edwina said quietly.

"But what of the baby?" her mother cried. "How will you live?"

"What of the father?" her father asked pointedly. "Why isn't he asking for your hand?"

"He doesn't know of my condition." Edwina cast her gaze to the floor. This admission was the most difficult. "He never said he loved me. After I told him of my upcoming nuptials to Walter, he disappeared." *Again*, she thought, but didn't say.

"Have you not considered that if he still wanted you, he would write?" Walter asked.

That was the most painful revelation of all. She had truly hoped Ashton would write. She'd hoped they could remain friends, if not lovers. However, no letter bearing his familiar handwriting appeared at her doorstep. He had severed all communications. She slowly nodded in answer to Walter's question.

"Even with the knowledge that you'll spend your life in ruinous disgrace, alone with no means of support. Even with all that, you'd rather face a life alone than be my wife?" Walter asked quietly. When she didn't respond, he turned to her father. "Under the circumstances, I believe this is a matter for family. I'll take my leave so you can talk among yourselves." He shook her father's hand, then kissed her mother's cheek. He stood before Edwina with a lowered head. "While I admire your courage in confessing your situation, you'll understand if I question your wisdom in doing so."

She nodded, as she had to admit, she questioned her own wisdom. Through her announcement, she'd freed herself from what promised to be a miserable marriage, but she'd also exiled herself from her family and friends. While she had yearned for a life of exploration and travel, she had imagined it would be on her terms. Suddenly, what had once been a dream would become a punishment.

Walter kissed her forehead. "I wish you good fortune."

"Time will tell," she responded with a squeeze of his hand.

"So it shall." He collected his hat and left without a backward glance.

Once Walter had gone, the family sat down at the table in silence. Food was offered but often returned to the kitchen untouched. After the room had cleared of all but the family, her father glared at her. "Who is responsible for this?"

"I am," Edwina said, remembering the cherry blossoms. "I wanted to experience what passion felt like, just once. I hadn't anticipated that one instance would lead to a child."

"I meant who is the father!" He pounded his fist, making the place settings leap an inch from the table.

"He's not the marrying sort, Father." Edwina keenly remembered those very words from Constance's lips.

"He bloody well will be when I'm through with him," her father insisted.

"I won't marry someone who doesn't want to be married," Edwina replied. "Just as I wouldn't marry Walter, who didn't really love me. He only proposed because you asked him to do so too. He'd do anything to please you and very little to please me."

"That's not so. I may have suggested he consider the idea, but he genuinely cared for you, Edwina. He may not be the sort of passionate fool you're obviously attracted to, but he was sincere in his proposal."

"Just as he was sincere in changing my very nature." Yes. The more she considered it, the more she knew this was for the best. Still her father glared his disapproval.

A few more moments of silence ticked by.

"Why do the Guardians require my assistance, Father? Why did they want me to marry Walter?"

His fork clattered to his plate. He cast a quick glance to his wife before he swiveled back to her. "Who told you?"

"Walter. He believed you wished me to serve refreshments, but that doesn't make sense. Why do the Guardians need my assistance?"

"Who are these Guardians, dear?" her mother asked her father.

He threw his napkin on the plate and rose from the table. "I refuse to talk about it. Walter shouldn't have said anything. Forget you heard the name." He hurried from the room, but Edwina rose and followed him to his study.

"Tell me, Father. I have a right to know. What do the Guardians want with me?"

She noticed his office had more medieval artifacts than had been present before. One in particular drew her attention, an ancient limestone bust that stood on the fireplace mantel. She moved closer to investigate, appreciating that by doing so, she could avoid her father's glare.

"What do you know of the Guardians?" he asked.

"I know that they're a secret society and that you and various leaders in industry are members." She raised a brow. "Would you like me to name names?"

"Impossible," her father exclaimed, but she heard the tremor in his voice. "How could you know such things?"

Edwina trailed her finger along the mantel. "There's an ancient Japanese custom of establishing a symbol to represent a group, a family, an organization. They would enclose the symbol in a thick circle. This is called a *kamon*, or *mon*." Her eye drifted to a piece of light paper with charred edges lying outside the grate on the dark mahogany floor. "I noticed when I was here before that you have a *mon*." She stooped to pick it up.

"I don't know about this *mon* business, but I admit I use a symbol encased in a circle to signify my law practice. Many others do something similar. What has this to do with the Guardians?"

The charred piece only had three letters on it—"Edw"—but she immediately recognized the handwriting. Ashton! She looked at the grate and noticed a pile of fresh ash. She spun on her heel. "What is this?"

"Something burned? Cinders?" He winced. "You know how ash flies when paper is burned." He moved closer to her. "About this *mon* business—"

"Father, it's near to roasting outside." She picked up a poker and stabbed at the fresh blackened mass. "Why would you have a fire?"

"Walter had some papers he wanted to burn. Letters, I believe. He said they were personal and best not found again. I assumed they were letters to him from a previous suitor, but I didn't pay much attention. However, we're getting off the subject. What does a *mon* have to do with the Guardians?"

The ash disintegrated beneath the poker. Yellowed, deeply charred papers remained at the core of the mass. She pulled them from the grate, but the ink had faded in the heat. Not enough remained to read intelligently, but she knew the slant of that hand as well as she'd recognize her own. Tears rose in her eyes. "He wrote to me," she whispered.

"Who? Who wrote to you?" Her father's glance shifted from the blackened pieces in her hand to her face. "What are you doing? Look now. Your hands are filthy handling that mess. Put it back where it belongs."

Edwina raised her head defiantly. If Ashton had written to her, he must be open to seeing her, talking to her. She would remedy this immediately and find him. "All the members of the Guardians have those same circle symbols. It's how you recognize one another even if you haven't met. It's a pattern, you see." She clasped the blackened pages to her chest with little concern that the ash would muss the high-neck gown that Walter preferred and she hated. "If you'll excuse me, I'm going to see if I can find a pattern in these remains."

She marched to the door, ignoring her father's angry demands that she return.

ALONE IN HER ROOM, SHE SPREAD EACH OF THE CHARRED pieces on a flat surface, searching for a clue as to where Ashton could be found. It was no use. The damage was too great. All she could determine was that Ashton had written her. Based on the differing stationary, she speculated that he'd written multiple times.

Curses to Walter! Had she known he was even capable of doing such a despicable thing as to destroy letters addressed to her, she would never have agreed to marry him. Thank heavens she'd managed the courage to sever that relationship.

She could see now it was a wise decision, but she wondered, with so many unanswered letters, if Ashton still felt the same way about her as he once had. He might view her unresponsiveness as another example of betrayal.

Her mother knocked on her bedroom door, then opened it. "Edwina, are you all right?"

Edwina selected one piece from the charred puzzle, the piece that clearly contained the word "heart" and set that aside. The rest she swept into a box. "My tears have dried, if that's what you mean."

"I suppose that's part of it."

An overturned basket mewed from the corner of the room. Her mother tipped the basket, freeing Isabella.

"She insisted on playing with the burned pieces. I put her there so I could concentrate," Edwina explained. The kitten immediately jumped into her lap, seeking forgiveness. Edwina lifted her eyes to her mother. "He wrote to me. Somehow Walter intercepted his letters and burned them. But he wrote to me . . . now I'll never know."

"It's Ashton Trewelyn that put you in this predicament, isn't it?" her mother said quietly.

Edwina glanced up, shocked. "How did you—?"

"I saw the way he looked at you at Lady Sutton's affair. Then, of course, there was that play . . ." Her mother sighed. "I was so concerned with climbing the social ladder that I failed to take note of what was happening beneath my nose. I knew you were infatuated with that man, but I thought you had more sense than to let him . . . do what he did."

"I wasn't forced, Mother. I love him." Tears formed again in her eyes. She thought she'd cried them all out, but apparently she was mistaken.

"There, there." Her mother hugged her close, patting her back. "We'll find this Mr. Trewelyn and see what he has to say about all this."

"I don't want Father to force him to do something he doesn't want to do."

"No, of course not. Your Father wouldn't do that . . ." Edwina pulled back and searched her mother's face. Edwina's raised brow left them both laughing. "Yes. Yes, I suppose he would," her mother admitted.

The shared laughter felt good and helped the dismal world to right itself. Edwina wiped the tears from her eyes. Her mother frowned briefly, then moistened a handkerchief with her tongue and dotted Edwina's cheeks. "You've left some black streaks here."

"Don't tell Father that it's Ashton," Edwina said. "Let me talk to him first." She stood and paced about the room. Isabella attempted to snag her hems while following behind. "I'll have to find him, of course. I've been watching the usual places about London that I used to spot him, but he's not been seen. Even Sarah says he never collected the responses to his personal ad. The only clue was in his letters, and now they're useless."

"I believe it's time I pay a call on Mr. Trewelyn's stepmother," her mother said. "She might be able to shed some light on his whereabouts."

Edwina clasped her hands, sincerely doubting Ashton's stepmother would be of valuable assistance. However, her mother wasn't aware of Mrs. Trewelyn's devious nature, and Edwina wasn't in a mood to explain it all. "Thank you, Mother," she said perhaps with less enthusiasm than expected. "That would be most helpful."

Her mother's eyes turned sad. "This isn't a game, Edwina. Even if we find him, what if he refuses to marry you? It's not as if his reputation hasn't already sustained this sort of scandal. What will you do?"

Edwina returned to the bed. "As I said before, I'll go away. I know now that I'm better alone than with Walter. I'll find employment somewhere much as Sarah has. Whatever happens, I'll manage."

"I have a cousin in Yorkshire," her mother said. "I'll write to her and see if you can stay there for the next nine months. I'll make certain you get a small allowance to help you get by."

"And after?" Edwina asked.

"Let's get through the next nine months." Her mother

sighed. "Then we'll concern ourselves with after." She gazed at her daughter in pity. "I know you disagree, but I can't help but believe your refusal of Walter is a sad mistake. You'll be in the world all alone."

Edwina patted her stomach. "Not entirely alone."

A WEEK LATER, EDWINA SHOPPED FOR LUGGAGE AT LE Bon Marche, the largest and fanciest department store in London. These purchases would be the last she'd make in the city, she imagined, as her mother was determined to send her to Yorkshire before her appearance was altered in the slightest manner. Her mother cautioned her to wear a sullen expression as though her life had recently been destroyed and to keep a handkerchief in her hand at all times.

The search for Ashton hadn't proved successful. His stepmother was not forthcoming with an address or location. Her mother said she sidestepped every inquiry with the grace of one of those ballet dancers, as if she purposively conspired to keep her stepson's location a secret.

It was difficult to remember to look sullen when she believed she'd avoided a fate worse than death. While her dreams had carried her to climb the pyramids of Egypt, visit the ancient temples in Persia, and dig for buried treasure in the Caribbean, she was currently content to travel to the tiny village in Yorkshire. She'd miss her friends, of course. Sarah was still angry with her for refusing Walter. She said Edwina had no idea of the monumental task she was taking on alone, which might be true. At least she would be taking it on as her true self and not some hollowed-out shell of a wife married out of necessity and not desire. Faith and Claire were supportive of her decision and promised to write as long as Edwina didn't respond in code.

So now she shopped for the sorts of necessities she'd need in this next phase of her life. The wonderful thing about London was that this new concept in shopping, a department store, had taken root right smack in the middle of the city. So many wonders under one roof! She looked at everything from baby clothes to kitchen equipment, but could only purchase the absolute necessities on the limited budget she'd created for herself. She was looking at infant gowns when she heard familiar contagious laughter in the next aisle. She hurried around the corner to discover Matthew. Unfortunately, the large man by his side was not Ashton.

"Miss Hargrove!" Matthew exclaimed. "Come see. They have boats here. Not as big as my boat. These are my size."

"Miss Hargrove?" the older, dignified man asked. "Miss Edwina Hargrove?"

"Yes." Edwina stared. She knew his eyes, the shape of his nose, but his face was fuller, and older and . . .

"I'm Matthew's father," he said. "I believe you know my other son . . . Ashton?"

Of course! It made sense. She could not contain her smile, no matter what advice her mother had given. "You're Ashton's father."

"We're shopping for fishing poles," Matthew said, clasping hold of his father's hand. "My father is going to teach me how to bait a hook." Two awe-filled eyes gazed up at his father. "Right, sir?"

He stooped to be at the child's level. "But these are toy boats, not fishing poles." He poked the young lad's belly with affection, eliciting a giggle. "Go see if you can find the fishing poles while I speak with Miss Hargrove." The boy nodded and took off on an adventure. The senior Trewelyn rose slowly to his feet. "I understand congratulations are in order. My son told me that you were to be married shortly." He glanced at her finger. "Or has that event already occurred?"

"Due to unforeseen events, that wedding is not likely to occur," Edwina said without a trace of sorrow. "Mr. Thomas and I have parted ways."

His face brightened, though it appeared he was hesitant to show it. His gaze drifted to her hand. "And may I inform my son of your altered condition?" he asked.

"Oh!" She realized he had noted the infant's gown. "This is for my cousin, not necessarily for me."

Perhaps it was the similarities between Ashton and his

father that made the senior Trewelyn charm her so. She had always thought she would dislike him, given Ashton's stories of his neglect. But the coded letter from the mysterious "S" had suggested the man had a softer, more thoughtful side, and Edwina could see the evidence of that in the man's eyes. "I would be forever grateful if you would inform him of my canceled engagement. Could you tell him as well that his previous attempts at communication were intercepted and destroyed before I was aware they existed?"

"Good. He wrote, then." The man chuckled as if this fact were some sort of personal victory. "I thought you might be here shopping for your trousseau, but I'll let Ashton know that is not to be."

Matthew exclaimed that he'd found the poles and his father should come quick. Edwina and Ashton's father turned and strolled down the aisle at a moderate pace as if they were old friends.

"Actually, I was shopping for luggage. I'm afraid I will be departing London for an extended period of time," she said.

"I'm sorry to hear that," he said sincerely. "London will be the poorer for your loss."

Now *that* she recognized as rakish charm. It appeared Sarah's Mrs. Morrison was correct. Ashton truly came by his charm naturally.

"Perhaps there is an address where my son might be able to reach you, that is, if you'll permit my giving him such personal information?"

Oh dear! "That is a problem. I'm not certain of the address myself, as yet," she said, disgruntled. The exact address hadn't seemed important until today. Had she known she'd have an opportunity to pass along a message to Ashton, she would have been certain to have it on hand.

"Father, I found them!" Matthew appeared and tugged on his father's hand. "Come this way."

"That's unfortunate," the senior Trewelyn said, ignoring the child. "However, I'm certain that once my son learns of your altered circumstances, he'll devise a way to find you. Good day to you, Miss Hargrove."

He tipped his hat and turned his attention to his younger son. From the enthusiasm on both of their faces she assumed the whole concept of shopping and fishing were new ones for the both of them.

"Stay out of the water," she called to Matthew, but she didn't think he heard. The two were already off on their own adventure, leaving her behind.

· Twenty-four ·

THE DAY SHE WAS TO LEAVE FOR YORKSHIRE WAS soon upon her, and to her dismay, even after her chance meeting with his father, she hadn't received word from Ashton.

While she'd hoped that he would appear at her doorstep, she had at least expected a letter. None had arrived. Perhaps he truly believed that by not answering his earlier letters she had sent an implied message to him. Then again, perhaps his father had not been able to get a message to his son in time. The result was the same. The wonderful thing about living in London was that the penny post was delivered as often as ten times a day. Which meant she was disappointed ten times each and every day.

Her newly purchased trunks had been loaded on a drayage cart earlier in the morning. With her bicycle strapped on for good measure, the trunks were already making their way to the railroad depot to be shipped north to another rail station. In all likelihood, her trunks would be in Yorkshire before she herself was, but she wouldn't be far behind. Edwina held on to her rail ticket and watched out the front window for Claire, Sarah, and Faith. They'd promised to call before she left, and time was running out.

A hansom flew around the corner of Commonwealth at a reckless neck-breaking speed before jerking to a stop in front of Edwina's residence. Three familiar ladies stumbled out, hats in disarray, fans working furiously. They had arrived barely in the nick of time.

Edwina threw open the door to greet her friends and offer them gentle hugs. Sarah rushed to the door, waving a folded newspaper. "Edwina, have you seen this?" She shoved an edition of the *Mayfair Messenger* in her hands. "Read it."

"Perhaps later on the train." She placed the paper on the table in the foyer, next to Isabella's traveling basket, which looked something like a birdcage, but had ample room for a kitten. "Right now I want to spend all my time with you, my—"

"Read it!" Sarah grabbed the paper and pushed it toward her face. "Read it now! He sent you a message."

Her heart fell. "Who? Walter?" She took the paper and scanned the columns. "He promised he wouldn't say anything, but he's been rather quiet and he—"

"Not Walter," Faith said, squeezing in beside Sarah. "Ashton Trewelyn."

"Ashton?" Her voice turned soft and airy. She tried to focus on the personals, but her hands shook and her voice raised in an urgent pitch. "Where is it? What does he say?"

"We don't know," Claire said, joining the others.

"It's in code!" Sarah fairly shouted.

Faith calmly took the paper from her hands and set it on the table, pointing to a long three inches of gibberish. Isabella reached a black paw through the bars to bat at her fingers. "Here."

"What does it say? What does it say?" Sarah said. "I've been dying to know ever since he handed it to me."

Edwina turned toward her in shock. "You saw him and you didn't immediately send me a message? You know I've been searching for him."

"He made me promise," Sarah said. "He said it was important that you read the personal ad first. It has a clue where to find him."

"A clue!" Edwina said in exasperation. "I don't have time for a bloody clue. I'm expected in Yorkshire and the train leaves shortly. What is this nonsense?"

"Calm down," Faith said slowly, evenly. "We can always send a telegram that you missed the train. Think of the baby."

"The baby is the whole reason I'm supposed to be on that train," Edwina said. But she took a deep breath to satisfy Faith.

"Where's your journal?" Claire asked. "Isn't that where you keep that device to transcribe the message?"

"It depends on the code," Edwina said, her thoughts coming less jumbled now. Faith was correct. They could always send a telegram. If she had the opportunity, she didn't want to leave without speaking to Ashton first. Still, she needed to transcribe the code, and she always used her journal to record the decoded message. It was a pattern. At the moment, she needed those established patterns to help her function. "My reticule. It's in my reticule."

Claire spied the bag on the foyer table. "Got it. What do we do next?"

Edwina stared blindly at the letters and numbers, while the others held their collective breath. She'd never decoded something under such stress before. "Which code . . . which code would he use?" she mumbled. The numbers at the top of the ad registered. It all became clear. Of course! "*Treasure Island,*" she gasped. "He's using *Treasure Island.*"

They all cheered and hopped up and down from her deduction.

"Where's your book?" Claire asked. "You always have that book."

Unfortunately, her copy of *Treasure Island* was packed in a trunk on its way to the train station.

Her friends' faces fell when she conveyed the news, no doubt mirroring her own expression.

"Can't you figure it out from the transcriptions of your brothers' letters?" Claire asked, Edwina's journal in hand.

She shook her head. "No, each code is unique as specified by the page and paragraph. I can't transcribe it without the book." Her lower lip trembled. They had been so close.

"Perhaps there's another copy in the house?" Faith asked.

"Why would they have two?" Sarah said. "Books cost money."

"What is going on down here?" Her mother came down the steps. "I heard cheering and moaning."

Sarah explained that Edwina had received a coded message from Ashton but couldn't decode it without her copy of *Treasure Island*, which was on the way to the rail station.

She turned toward her daughter. "Why don't you use your father's copy?"

"My father?" Edwina repeated in shock.

"Of course, dear. How else were we to know what your brothers were really writing about?"

The entire gaggle of women ran toward her father's study. Her mother quickly stepped on a small stool to remove it from a high shelf. "What page?"

"Ninety-seven," Edwina said, opening her journal to a clean page on her father's desk. She took a pen from his drawer and opened a bottle of ink. "Paragraph one."

The others hovered close while she scribbled the letters of the alphabet down one side of the page, drew a vertical line and then began recording the unique letters of the book passage alongside the alphabet.

"Hurry, hurry," Sarah urged. "I can barely stand this."

Edwina could barely stand it herself. Even as she calmly recorded each letter on the page, her heart raced for the possible message he might be sending her. She bit her lip in agitation. Why couldn't he have just sent her a note in plain English!

After she'd written enough unique letters to satisfy the letters of the alphabet, she began to use her newly created chart to decipher the message. She really didn't have to look at the chart as Claire read the coded text aloud, and Faith called out the transcribed letter. Edwina wrote out the transcribed text, and Sarah called out the full word once translated.

Though they all knew the content of the letter before it was fully transcribed, Edwina stared blurry-eyed through tears at the message she'd written in her journal.

My dearest Edwina, my love. Marry me. Make me the happiest of men. Together we will explore distant lands, distant places, and many, many pillow books. I wait for your answer at our special park bench. Please hurry.

"Pillow book?" Sarah screwed up her face. "What's a pillow book?"

"No time for that." Her mother bracketed Edwina's face in her hands. "Do you love this man?"

Edwina nodded her head, not sure she could speak for the sheer joy and happiness that blocked up her throat. Tears slipped down her cheeks.

"Then your answer will be yes?" she asked sternly. Again, Edwina nodded. Her mother released her. "I just wanted to make certain."

"What are we waiting for?" Claire asked. "Let's find him."

"Where's your special bench?" Faith asked.

"I . . . I'm not sure," Edwina said, wiping her cheeks. "There are two."

"We'll check both," Sarah called, tears streaming down her own cheeks. They ran out of the study ahead of Edwina and her mother. Edwina started to follow but noticed her mother lagging behind. "Are you coming?"

"I'll wait here," she replied, her eyes glistening. "This is your moment. You don't want your mother around when you're accepting a young man's proposal." She turned Edwina by the shoulders to face the door. "Go on now. Tell me all about it when you return. I have telegrams to send."

Edwina turned suddenly and hugged her mother. "Thank you," she whispered. "For everything."

She walked into the hallway where little black kitten paws tried unsuccessfully to catch the air currents stirred by her frantic friends. She followed them outside, where they piled in a sagging overloaded hansom.

• • •

ASHTON PACED ALONG THE STREAM, HAT IN HAND, A ring in his pocket. He checked his pocket watch again. Surely, she had seen the personal column by now. He'd directed her friend at the newspaper office to take it to her first thing in the morning to be certain she saw it. And yet he'd been waiting for well over two hours.

Perhaps she wasn't coming. This wasn't the first time that thought dared to enter his head. Heaven knew he'd given her plenty of reasons for refusing him. There was his reputation, of course, which seemed to matter to everyone else except Edwina. Then he stole her virtue. Granted, Edwina was willing, but he as the man should have known better. He should have been more responsible and less influenced by his overwhelming desire for the woman who so beautifully offered her innocence to him. Then he abandoned her, leaving her to wait in a thunderstorm, not knowing he'd been sent to Rome. While joining the Guardians had been her suggestion, she was worth more to him than any secret organization. He should have gotten a message to her somehow.

That thought inspired another. Certainly she wouldn't go to that spot where she'd waited and waited in the pouring rain. He doubted he could ever visit the Regent's Park zoo without thinking about how miserable she must have been, how heartbroken and disillusioned. Well, he would wait for her here along the stream until the stars came out and then even longer. She loved him. He knew it in his heart. She loved him and therefore couldn't marry another. Dear Lord, when his father told him that, he fell to his knees and thanked God for a second chance. His prayers had been answered . . . even if his letters hadn't.

And so he waited, and paced, and waited, and paced. Suddenly, he heard a commotion begin to rise above the whisper of the wind and the gurgle of the stream. Voices? Shouts? He could sense a rumble in the ground beneath his feet, and if he wasn't mistaken, someone yelled "We're coming!" though it wasn't the voice he longed to hear.

Suddenly, she was there. Standing on the path. She stood all alone, her chest heaving like she'd run the entire way. Her glorious hair had torn loose from its confining pins, as if she'd ridden her bicycle over bumpy country roads to reach him. Sweat glistened on the skin peaking beneath her wide-collared blouse, where a bit of pink flashed. Her cherry blossom necklace, he guessed. He started walking briskly toward her.

Three women suddenly stepped behind her. Her friends from the Crescent. He recognized the two ladies that had stormed his house in search of their lost friend the night he'd secreted her away in the hidden gallery. The woman from the newspaper office was there as well. All three crossed their arms in front of them as if to form a barrier from which there would be no escape. Not that he planned to escape. But he suspected that if Edwina's response was not as he prayed it would be . . . or if his proposal was for anything less than marriage . . . he'd be swimming in that stream with no hope of rescue.

Edwina walked tentatively toward him, while he closed the distance from his end. Dear God, she was beautiful. She had a glow about her, perhaps heightened from what appeared to be a hurried journey to his location. In light of the observers, he'd have to refrain from scooping her up in his arms and kissing her senseless, which truthfully had been his original plan.

"I see you got my message," he said as they approached talking distance. It felt awkward speaking to her like this after only having spoken to her in his dreams for so long. "I understand you are a free woman."

She nodded. Why didn't she speak? Say something?

"I'm afraid I didn't speak to your father beforehand. I thought as a modern woman, you would prefer to make this decision on your own without someone making it for you."

She nodded again. She certainly wasn't making this easy. He reached over and took her hand, smiling at the ink stain on the index finger, but then remembered his purpose and instantly sobered. "I wanted to apologize again for causing you to wait in the rain, and for ever making you think that I wouldn't be there when you needed me."

"I'm supposed to be on a train," she said.

"Yes. My father mentioned you were preparing to leave London. I'm so glad that I was able to reach you before you departed."

"I'm supposed to be on a train right this minute," she said. "But I was led to believe you wished to ask me something."

Somehow he'd thought since he'd already asked in his ad, he hadn't really needed . . . He reached in his pocket, removed the ring, and lowered himself with the help of his stick to one knee. "Edwina Hargrove, the mistress of my dreams, the love of my life. Will you do me the honor of becoming my wife?" He held his breath and offered the ring to her.

"Look, he's talking to the baby," one of the women said, a little loudly.

"Baby?" He pushed on his stick and shot to his feet. "You're pregnant?"

She smiled wide enough to almost stop the tears gathered in her eyes.

"Is it . . . ours?" he asked in wonder.

"Of course," she said, slipping her arms around his waist. "There's never been anyone else."

He intended only a light kiss, given the observers nearby, but the moment he tasted her, he was lost. His arms pulled her tight to his chest while his lips and tongue attempted to brand her in a way that no man would ever dare take her away. He would have made love to her right there by the stream if not for the cheering and yelling nearby. He broke the kiss and leaned his forehead on hers. "Is that a yes?"

"Did you think I'd answer in code?" She nibbled on his lower lip. "Yes," she breathed. "Yes. A thousand times, yes. I love you."

While he suspected that he had her heart, her spoken words nearly caused him to sink to his knees in gratitude. He kissed her lightly. "I love you too."

He sought her hand and slipped the REGARD ring on her finger, so named for the first letters of the gemstones on the band, before she found another man who couldn't resist her sweet charm. "This should keep everyone else at bay until I place a wedding band on your finger."

She studied the six jewels. "Ashton, it's too much. We'll need to be frugal now that a baby is on the way." She took his hand in hers. "I was so sorry to see that someone else stole your idea about the rifle scope. That would have been perfect—"

He laughed. "No one stole the idea."

A furrow settled between her brows, calling for him to kiss it. "But the paper said C.B. Manufacturing—"

"I'm C.B. Manufacturing," he said, slipping his finger beneath the ivory of her necklace. "It's code for Cherry Blossom Manufacturing. I've been scarce these past weeks because I've been—"

He never got to finish. Her lips pressed against his. While he was aware of a great deal of cheering and soft pats on his back, he was focused entirely on the woman in his arms. The woman who had turned his life around, the woman who'd healed his relationship with his father, the woman who made it worth surviving a bullet. He'd come back to London after his time with the Rifles looking for purpose, and she'd given him so much more. Who would have thought a little code breaker could break open the gates of his heart?

Keep reading for a preview of
the new historical romance novel

A LADY NEVER LIES

by Juliana Gray

Coming August 2012 from Berkley Sensation!

· *Prologue* ·

THE DUKE OF WALLINGFORD WAS NOT AT HOME, said the butler, with an upward tilt of his chin.

"Nonsense," said Finn. "We both know very well he's at home. I left him here last night, in the sort of condition that would render impossible his departure by"—he flipped open the case of his battered gold pocket watch—"eight o'clock the following morning. Except, I suppose, in a coffin."

The butler cleared his throat. "The Duke of Wallingford is not receiving."

"Ah, that's better. We deal so much better, Wallis, when we speak the truth to each other. Where might I find the old chap, then?" Finn looked past the butler's head to the wide, high-ceilinged entrance hall beyond, with its floor of checkerboard marble and its profusion of acanthus-leaf plasterwork. Just the sort of entrance a duke's London town house ought to sport, Finn supposed, which made him jolly well grateful (and not for the first time) that he wasn't in line to a dukedom.

"Mr. Burke." The butler straightened to his full height, which was not great in the best of circumstances, and certainly not when interposed against the tall, loose-limbed figure of Mr. Phineas Fitzwilliam Burke, R.S. "I am deeply aggrieved to discover that I have not, perhaps, *quite* made myself clear. His Grace, sir, is not receiving."

"Oh, rot," Finn said amiably. "He'll receive *me*. Besides, we've a breakfast appointment, or hadn't you been told? If you'll excuse me . . ." He executed a cunning side step, agile, really, except that it ended in his chest bumping Wallis's well-oiled forelock and his foot landing squarely on the butler's equally well-oiled shoe.

To his credit, Wallis didn't even wince. "I fear I have been misunderstood once more," he said, voice quavering into the ceiling. His ancient breast strained outward against its natural concavity. "His Grace"—heave, gasp—"the Duke"—heave, gasp—"is *not receiving*."

"Now look here, my good man," Finn protested, attempting another dodge. "I realize breakfast appointments aren't the usual thing in this house, but I assure you . . ."

"Bloody hell, Wallis!" The Duke of Wallingford's voice roared down the profligate curve of the main staircase. "Let the poor fellow in the breakfast room, for God's sake. I'll be down in five minutes."

Wallis narrowed his eyes and issued a faint sniff from his sharpened nose. "As you wish, Your Grace," he said, and stepped to one side.

Finn removed each glove in a single decisive tug. "The trouble with you, Wallis, is that you're a dreadful snob. We can't all be lords, you see. The trade wouldn't bear it."

"Don't harass my butler, Burke," called the Duke.

Finn cast an eye up the stairs and then looked back down, not without sympathy, at Wallis's defeated shoulders. He handed over his hat and gloves in a kind of conciliatory gesture. "I'll show myself in, shall I?" he said, and strode across the entrance hall toward the breakfast room at the back of the house.

"Damned sodding ginger-haired scientist," the butler muttered, just loudly enough for Finn to overhear. "No sodding respect."

The Duke of Wallingford's breakfast room was a remarkably pleasant spot, for a house without a presiding female. Spacious, south-facing, it overlooked the high-walled back garden at such an angle as to block the sight of the neighboring houses and create the misleading impression of having been transported to the countryside, or at least as far as Hampstead. The room's only flaw was its unmistakable air of disuse. The Duke and his brother seldom arose before noon, the natural consequence of seldom retiring before dawn.

Not the case today, however, Finn observed, as he crossed the stately threshold. The sideboard overflowed with all the necessary elements of a proper English breakfast—kidneys, bacon, kippers, toast, eggs without number—and on the chair at the end of the table lay the shipwreck of Lord Roland Penhallow, the Duke's younger brother.

"Good God, Penhallow," Finn said, tossing his newspaper on a nearby chair. "To what do we owe the honor?"

"Haven't a clue," Lord Roland mumbled. "Told to make myself ready by eight sharp, or I should have my estates foreclosed. Though now that I recollect"—he rubbed his forehead meditatively—"I paid off those mortgages years ago."

Finn moved to the sideboard and claimed a plate of bone china, so fine it was almost translucent. "Shabby of Wallingford. Still, it's your own jolly fault, drinking yourself insensible. I've explained to the two of you on any number of occasions . . ."

"Sod yourself, you damned saint," Lord Roland said. "You workaday scientists have no notion of what's expected of idle aristocrats. I'm scarcely keeping up as it is." He hid his beautiful face behind a cup of thick black coffee and drank in gulps.

"Then your luck rides high this morning, old man. I've brought the solution to your dilemma into this very room." Finn folded his long frame into a shield-backed Hepplewhite chair, acquired in a fit of modernization several decades earlier by the present duke's grandmother, and pointed his fork at yesterday's evening edition of the *Times* on the cushion next to him. "Your salvation, m'lord, and your brother's."

Lord Roland stabbed at his kidneys. "And if I prefer damnation?"

"No one asked your preference," barked the Duke of Wallingford, entering the room in a ruckus of booted heels. "Nobody asked mine, to be perfectly honest. But here I am, Burke, your obedient servant. I trust you're enjoying your breakfast?"

"Very well, thank you. I find a brisk morning walk sets one up perfectly for a substantial breakfast like this. Your kitchen is to be commended."

"Sod yourself, Burke," said Wallingford. He made his way to the sideboard, an impressive figure in his morning tweeds, tall and broad-shouldered, his hair unfashionably long and his chin unfashionably clean-shaven. Only the most familiar observer would detect the signs of last night's revelry on his face: the trace of puffiness in his eyelids, the slackening about the corners of his mouth.

"You raise an interesting point," said Finn, "and, in a roundabout way, sodding oneself may have some bearing on the proposal I bring to you this morning."

Wallingford heaped an odd dozen or so kippers onto his plate and dropped the serving fork back into its dish with a significant crash. "I'm panting to hear it."

"I'm damned if I don't detect a note of sarcasm in your words, Your Grace. And yet you were more than curious last night. Curious enough, I'm compelled to point out, to arrange this morning meeting, at vast inconvenience to yourself and"—a glance at Lord Roland's bowed head—"your suffering brother."

"Last night I was blazing drunk." Wallingford dropped himself into a chair at the head of the table. "This morning I'm in my proper senses."

"Shall I cut to the point, then?"

"Do." The single syllable echoed through the room.

Finn reached for his newspaper. "Gentlemen, have either of you two been to Italy?"

"Italy!" Wallingford barked out a laugh. "My good man, I daresay I bedded half the women in Venice whilst you were fiddling around with those damned gadgets in that laboratory of yours, making your sordid millions. What of it?"

Lord Roland raised his head into a shaft of morning sunlight. "Rot. You had that lovely little mistress, the Marquesa Whatsit. Charming gel, jealous as the devil. I should think less than half a dozen genuine notches in the old bedpost, and those only when the little bird was in her confinement."

"Not mine," the Duke said swiftly.

Lord Roland squinted one eye and touched his fingers, one by one, against his thumb. The sunlight formed an incongruous halo about his golden-brown head. "No. No, you're right. Couldn't have been yours. All the same," he went on, looking at Finn, "he isn't half such a devil as he makes out."

"I should hope not," said Finn. "God save us from an Italy populated by miniature Wallingfords. In any case, the Italy I have in mind for us lies at a far remove, a far remove indeed, from the sort of Italy with which I suspect you're familiar." He unfolded the pages of the newspaper, one by one, until he came to the item of interest. "Here," he said, thrusting it toward Wallingford. "See what you make of that."

Wallingford raised one heavy black eyebrow. "My good man. One of my most inflexible rules is the avoidance of all reading before luncheon."

"Again, rot," Lord Roland said, his spirits visibly reviving. He began cutting into his sausage. "Let's have it, then, Burke. You've quite awakened my interest."

Finn sighed deeply and cleared his throat. "An advertisement. *English lords and ladies, and gentlemen of discerning taste*—I expect that's why you missed it, Wallingford—*may take note of a singular opportunity to lease a most magnificent Castle and Surrounding Estate in the idyllic hills of Tuscany, the Land of Unending Sunshine.*"

"Dear me," said the Duke, "does the earth's rotation fail to affect the fair fields of Tuscany? I am amazed."

Lord Roland pointed his knife at the newspaper. "Not much chance of a proper sleep, without at least a few hours of darkness."

"*The Land of Unending Sunshine*," Finn continued, in a

loud voice. *"The Owner, a man of impeccable lineage, whose ancestors have kept the Castle safe against intrusion since the days of the Medici princes . . ."*

"Look here," Lord Roland said, with a thoughtful frown, "I thought all your Tuscan fortifications were in the nature of city-states, eh what? A single castle by itself . . ."

"It's not meant to be a damned geography course," Finn said in exasperation. "It's an advertisement. Oh, blast. Now you've lost me. Impeccable lineage . . . Medici princes . . . Here we are. *The Owner*, et cetera, et cetera, *is called away by urgent business, and offers a year's lease of this unmatched Property at rates extremely favorable for the discerning traveler.* Again, Wallingford, I shall undertake negotiations myself, so he won't smoke you out, ha-ha. *Applicants should inquire through the Owner's London agent* . . . I say, Wallingford, are you quite all right?"

Wallingford, sputtering into his coffee, had been overtaken by a fit of violent coughing.

"I daresay he's a trifle flummoxed." Lord Roland shrugged.

"By what?"

"Presumably by the suggestion that you're taking out a year's lease on an Italian castle, on his behalf."

"Oh no. No, indeed. You've quite misunderstood me. Only a dash of humor, you see." Finn put the newspaper to one side and set to work on his eggs.

Wallingford, coughs subsiding, dabbed at his watering eyes. "Humor?" he gasped out, clearing his throat with a rough hack. "You call that *humor*, Burke? My God, you might have killed me."

"Really, Wallingford. I should never take out a lease on your behalf. I've well enough sordid millions of my own, as you yourself observed." Finn cast a benevolent smile across the table and reached for his toast. "No, the lease will be entirely in my name. You two shall be my guests, nothing more. Penhallow, the marmalade, if you will."

Lord Roland passed him the pot of marmalade as if in a dream.

Really, it was all proving even more amusing than Finn had

imagined. The look of dazed confusion on Penhallow's face. The slow purpling of the Duke's expression, the whitening of knuckles clenched about two-hundred-year-old silver cutlery.

Who would speak first?

Wallingford, of course. "I'm certain, my dear Burke," he said, biting out the *dear Burke* in discrete chunks, "I must have misheard you."

"I assure you, you haven't." Finn spread his marmalade over his toast with neat precision. "My dear fellows, I shall lay my cards upon the table, as they say. I've been concerned about the two of you for some time."

Wallingford's expression grew even blacker. "I can't imagine why. Our poverty, perhaps? Our lack of female companionship?"

"There it is! There's your trouble, right there. You don't even recognize how frivolous your lives have become. You've no purpose, no driving force. You drink yourselves into oblivion, night after night . . ."

Lord Roland set down his fork with a clink. "Now look here. As if I haven't seen you positively legless on more than one occasion."

Finn flicked that away with a brusque movement of his hand. "Once or twice, of course. One's allowed a bit of high spirits, now and again. But you've made a career of it, you two. Wine, women, and song, as the saying goes."

"I object to that. There's been very little song at all," said Lord Roland.

"And that of very poor quality indeed," Wallingford added. "Hardly worth noting."

Finn leaned forward and placed his elbows squarely on each side of his plate. "Three days ago," he said, in a quiet voice, "I came across an old acquaintance of ours, from Cambridge days. Callahan. You'll remember him?"

"Callahan, of course. Jolly chap. A bit thick, but good company on a lark." Lord Roland's brow puckered inward. "What of him?"

"He was dead. Choked on his own vomit in his mistress's parlor in Camden."

In the silence that followed, Finn fancied he could detect the tiny scratches of the ancient ormolu clock above the mantel, counting out the passing of each second into eternity.

"Good God," said Wallingford at last.

"Camden," muttered Lord Roland, as he might mutter *Antarctica*.

Finn removed his elbows and picked up his fork and knife. "I came across his funeral procession, you see. They'd taken his body back to the old family place, in Manchester, not far from a machine works of which I've been contemplating purchase. An only son, did you know? His mother looked quite destroyed."

"There, you see?" Wallingford shrugged. "Our mother's been gone these ten years. Nothing at all to worry about."

Finn went on. "I'm told the body was unviewable. The mistress discovered him in the morning and fled with her cookmaid. Poor fellow wasn't found for a week."

Wallingford sat back in his chair and regarded Finn with a speculative expression. He crossed two solid arms against his chest. "Very well, Burke. A fine point. The dissipated life ends in ignoble tragedy and whatnot. Women are not to be trusted. Forewarned is forearmed. I shall retire instantly to the country, call for my steward, and endeavor to live a life of sobriety and virtue."

Finn had expected resistance, of course. One didn't go about telling dukes to mend their ways without anticipating a certain bristling of the old hackles, after all. He smiled kindly and said: "I have a proposition for you."

"I daresay you do. I daresay it has something to do with castles in Italy."

"I have been corresponding for some time with a man near Rome, who's approaching the same project as I am, only with rather a different plan."

"Do you mean these damned horseless carriages of yours?" the Duke asked.

"Damned rubbishy machines," put in Lord Roland.

Finn's gaze rose to the ceiling. "Luddites, the pair of you. In any case, a few weeks ago, my colleague in Rome, Delmonico's his name, proposed to me the idea of holding a . . . well, I suppose you might call it a competition, a contest, in which the best examples of the machines might be displayed and judged. If enough working engines are brought to the exhibition, he expects to hold a race."

"A race!" Lord Roland began to laugh. "A race! What earthly use is that? I daresay I could walk faster than any of your contraptions."

"The exhibition," Finn said, ignoring him, "is to be held in the summer, on the outskirts of Rome."

"I begin to see your scheme, old man," Wallingford said darkly.

"I shall need the most absolute calm, in order to concentrate on the project without any distractions. And it occurred to me, you see, that a year spent in the peace and tranquility of the countryside, far away from your own circle of degenerates and wastrels, devoting yourself to scholarly pursuits and absolutely proscribing the company of women . . ."

"Wait. Stop. Do you mean to say," Lord Roland said, in incredulous tones, "you mean us to embark on a year of . . . of . . ." He struggled.

"Chastity?" the Duke supplied, as he might say *disemboweling*.

"Why not? There are solutions to hand, so to speak, should one's urges become uncomfortable. Though I suspect, in the manner of monks, we shall soon be grateful for the serenity, and find our own physical needs diminish in response."

"You're mad," said the Duke.

"I pose it as a challenge," Finn said. "If I can contemplate it, surely you can. You're a man of considerable self-control, Wallingford, when you choose to exercise it. And as for you, Penhallow, I can remember distinctly a time when you adopted a far more virtuous approach to living . . ."

"That was long ago," Lord Roland said sharply, "and best forgotten."

"All the same, you were capable then of restraint." Finn paused and looked back and forth between the two men, heads hanging toward their plates, forks picking away at the remains of the noble breakfast. "Think, my friends. Think what we can accomplish in a year, if we forgo idle pleasure. A temporary exile, no more. A few months. Study a new subject, learn a new talent. Sunshine and olives and whatnot. The local wine, perhaps; I'm sure we can make allowance for a glass or two, as we establish the rules of our little society."

Wallingford looked up. "Absolutely *not*. The most absurd scheme I've ever heard."

"You're mad even to suggest it," said Lord Roland.

Finn shifted his gaze to the window. The heavy January sky had begun to shed bits of snow into the yellow air, though it wasn't quite cold enough to stick. London in winter: how he hated it, all brown and tired and slushy, the atmosphere so thick with coal-smoke it seemed to burn the lining from his lungs. "The land of unending sunshine," he said, in a low voice, and turned back to Wallingford. "At least think on it."

"Out of the question," said Wallingford.

"Quite impossible," agreed Lord Roland.

Finn picked up the paper and folded it with care, flattening the creases just so. "A year away from the miseries of London. A year free of vice and obligation, devoted to study, devoid of the distractions of the fairer sex." He rose, tucked the paper under his arm, and smiled broadly.

"What could possibly go wrong?"

· One ·

Thirty miles southeast of Florence, Italy
March 1890

SHE HAD ALWAYS MAINTAINED HIGH STANDARDS. While other young ladies dreamed of finding Mr. Right, Alexandra set her sights on the Duke of Right.

In the end, she had accepted a marquis, but as Lord Morley had been both extremely rich and extremely old, she still considered her marriage a success. Ask and ye shall receive, went her motto. (It *was* in the Bible, after all; she was almost certain.) And never, ever settle for second-rate.

Not even when fleeing from one's creditors.

This room was decidedly second-rate. No, not even that. It was little more than a cupboard, hardly larger than the wardrobe in which she stored her summer nightgowns during the off-season. A narrow cot, wedged against the wall, left no space for even a hatbox; the single coarse wool blanket looked a perfect paradise for fleas. It was fourth-rate, even fifth. It simply wouldn't do.

Alexandra turned to the landlord. "It simply won't do, I'm afraid. *Non possiblo.* Understand? *Comprendo?* It is too small. *Troppo*, er, *petito*. There are three of us. *Trio*. And the boy."

The innkeeper frowned. "The inn, she is full, milady. I make beds in the commons, very warm, very comfort."

"Sleep in the commons! Three English ladies! You can't possibly be serious." Alexandra produced a chuckle to emphasize the idea's absurdity.

"But milady, it rains, the bridge is . . . is flood. The rooms, they are all take!"

"By whom?" she demanded, straightening her spine to an impressive length.

"Is a duke, milady," said the innkeeper, hushed and reverent. "An English duke. His brother, his friend."

"The devil you say! Show me their rooms, if you please. Er, *chamberos*. You see, my good man," she explained kindly, as she herded him down the narrow creaking corridor, "we have, in my country, a darling little custom by which gentlemen are obliged, absolutely *obliged*, to relinquish any present comforts for the benefit of ladies in need. It imposes such a perfect civilized order upon the world, wouldn't you agree, without which we should descend into mere barbarism, like those poor chaps the Romans. This duke of yours, I'm sure, will quite understand. Oh yes!"

She stopped in the doorway and cast her eyes about the room. This was much more the thing. Large, commodious. A plump double bed in the exact center of the opposite wall, with a wardrobe to one side; a fireplace on the other wall, being tended at that moment by an apple-cheeked young miss with that rippling dark Italian hair one couldn't help envying in one's wilder moments.

It was plain, of course. The inn formed a remote outpost along an obscure Tuscan road, far from the civilized refinement of Milan or even Florence, but Alexandra was willing to make allowances for the rustic furniture and lack of proper trim work and so on. And after all, the rain lashed harrowingly against the small many-paned window, and the wind howled down the chimney flue. Really, one couldn't afford to be too particular.

"It's ideal," she said, turning to the landlord. "We'll take it. And the connecting room as well." She gestured to the door standing ajar next to the wardrobe.

The landlord's face had clearly suffered through a long and rainy winter. It hardly seemed possible those hollow cheeks could lose any further color, and yet, before her eyes, every last remaining atom of pigment drained from the face of her host. "But, milady," he said feebly, "the room, she is already take! The duke have her! A very big duke! Very *strong* duke! And his brother, his friend! All very big!"

"Yes, isn't it extraordinary? I often find that large-framed men tend to befriend other large-framed men, and vice versa. One imagines it must arise from one of those clever little laws of nature one reads about from time to time. Indeed, I should very much like to discover why. A large duke, you say?" She cocked her head and turned to walk back to the staircase. "It can't be Wallingford, do you think? Wallingford in Italy? *I* never heard anything about it."

"Wallingford! Yes!" the landlord exclaimed, trotting behind her. "Is Wallingford! He will not like!"

"Oh, rubbish. Wallingford has a sharp bark, I grant you, but really he's as gentle as a lamb. Or perhaps . . . perhaps a sort of youngish ram." She poised at the top of the staircase, nearly flattened by the mingled scents of woodsmoke and wet wool and roasting meat, rising up in a fug from the bustle of the common room below, and went on with renewed determination. "In any case, quite manageable. Just leave everything to me, my good fellow. I shall have it all sorted out in short order."

"Milady, please, is not so bad, the commons . . ."

"It isn't at all acceptable, *non possiblo*, do you hear me?" she said, more loudly, just to be sure he understood. "We are English, *anglese*. We can't possibly . . ." She paused about halfway down the stairs and turned to scan the noisy wood-beamed room, with its long tables and bowed hungry heads. She had little trouble finding the one she sought. "Oh! Your Grace!" she called, infusing her voice with just the proper balance of surprise and gratification.

The Duke of Wallingford seemed to have been expecting her. His lean face wore an expression of deep resignation, and he muttered something to his companions before he tossed his napkin on the table and stretched his limbs to their full forbidding height. "Lady Morley. Good evening. I trust you're well." He seemed, to Alexandra's ears, to growl rather than speak.

She drew in a fortifying breath and continued down the stairs. "Darling Wallingford, you're just the man I was hoping for. I can't seem to make these Italian fellows understand that English ladies, however sturdy and liberal-minded, simply *cannot* be expected to sleep in a room with strangers. *Male* strangers. *Foreign* male strangers." She stood before him now, smiling her winning smile, the one that had laid waste to haughty noblemen beyond number. "Don't you agree, Your Grace?" she finished softly, looking up at him beneath her eyelashes, delivering the coup de grace.

His face remained hard. "Are there no rooms available upstairs, madam?"

She made a helpless shrug. "A small room, a very small room. Hardly large enough for Lady Somerton's boy to sleep in, let alone the three of us." She glanced aside to his companion. His brother, she remembered the landlord telling her, and everyone knew Wallingford's brother was . . .

"Lord Roland!" The enormity of it exploded in her brain. Her thoughts fled outside, to the sodden innyard where she'd left her sister and her cousin to see to the disposition of the baggage, not a quarter-hour before. "I'd no idea! Have you . . . my cousin . . . Lady Somerton . . . good God!"

Lord Roland bowed. Thank goodness, Alexandra thought, thank *goodness* he was a charming well-bred rascal, nothing like his arctic brother. Society had decreed the younger man the handsomest of the two, though in fact their features were clearly cast from the same symmetrical mold. Perhaps it was his coloring, which was lighter than Wallingford's, his eyes a friendly hazel next to the blackened orbs of his brother, and his golden-brown hair giving him the air of a particularly enthusiastic retriever. He spoke, however, with subdued formality. "I had the great honor of meeting her ladyship outside on the . . . the portico, a moment ago. And her charming son, of course."

Something caught in Alexandra's throat; she wasn't quite sure if it was a laugh or a groan. Lord Roland and Lilibet stumbling into each other on the portico, after all these years! Good God!

"Charming! Yes, quite," she got out at last. She felt hideously wrong-footed, with several pairs of fascinated male eyes witnessing her confusion. It was intolerable. She rallied and cleared her throat, hoping the motion would cause something more rational to tumble out into the thickening silence.

Nothing did, however, and she was forced to turn back to the Duke. "Look here, Wallingford, I really must throw myself on your mercy. Surely you can see our little dilemma. Your rooms are ever so much larger, palatial really, and *two* of them! You can't possibly, in all conscience . . ." A thought occurred to her. She turned back to Lord Roland and fixed him with a beseeching smile. "My dear Penhallow. Think of poor Lilibet, sleeping in . . . in a *chair*, quite possibly. With all these strangers."

Lord Roland's expression turned stricken. She opened her mouth to pursue her advantage, but before she could speak, a voice intruded to thwart her.

"Did it not, perhaps, occur to you, Lady Morley, to reserve rooms in advance?"

For an instant, she was confused. That resonant timbre could only come from a singularly spacious chest, and the clipped tones and rumbling impatience could only come from an Englishman. But it was not Wallingford, nor was it Lord Roland.

Oh, of course. The third man.

She knew better than to acknowledge him at once. She was not the Dowager Marchioness of Morley for nothing. She counted off one second . . . two . . . three . . . and then turned in the direction of the voice.

He was not at all what she expected.

Wallingford's friend. Who the devil was he? He was tall, of course—extraordinarily tall, topping even the Duke by a good three or four inches—and broad-shouldered. She'd known that already, Wallingford and his pack of goons. But a voice that dark, that silky, that *weighty*, ought to belong to one of your saturnine characters, your brooders: all black hair and eyes, like Wallingford himself. This fellow was ginger-haired, with lawn-green eyes and *freckles*, actual freckles, an unmistakable dusting of them around the bridge of his nose, descending across the strong wide wedge of his cheekbones. A damned leprechaun, if leprechauns had blunt bones and stern eyes and ran to nearly six and a half deuced feet in their curly-toed stockings.

Surely she was equal to an overgrown leprechaun.

"As a matter of fact, it did, Mr . . ." She dropped a devas-tating pause, a pause that might have brought lesser souls to their knees. "I'm so terribly sorry, sir. I don't *quite* believe I caught your name."

His expression didn't change, not by so much as an iron-ically elevated eyebrow.

"I beg your pardon, Lady Morley," said the Duke of Wall-ingford. "How remiss of me. I have the great honor to present to you—perhaps you may have come across his name, in your philosophical studies—Mr. Phineas Fitzwilliam Burke, of the Royal Society."

"Your servant, madam," Mr. Burke said, with a slight in-clination of his head.

Alexandra's brain took a moment or two to absorb this information. "Burke," she said numbly, and then, with effort: "Phineas Burke. Of course. The Royal Society. Yes, of course. Everyone knows of Mr. Burke. I found . . . the *Times*, last month . . . your remarks on electrical . . . that new sort of . . ." She found herself stammering again. Bloody Wallingford. Bloody Wallingford, to be traveling in the Italian countryside with a man of exalted genius and near-divine eminence. How on earth had he come to know Phineas Burke?

She rallied herself and attempted a smile, a friendly smile, to make amends for her earlier haughtiness. "That is to say, of course we reserved rooms. I sent the wire days ago, if memory serves. But we were delayed in Milan. The boy's nursemaid took ill, you see, and I expect our message did not reach our host in time." She flashed the bemused landlord, who stood a few deferential feet away, a shaming expression.

"Look here," said Lord Roland, unexpectedly, "enough of this rubbish. We shouldn't dream of causing any inconvenience to you and your friends, Lady Morley. Not for an instant. Should we, Wallingford?"

The Duke folded his arms. "No, damn it."

"Burke?"

The scientist made a noise of agreement.

Lord Roland grinned his dazzling grin. "You see, Lady Morley? All quite willing and happy and so on. I daresay Burke can take the little room upstairs, as he's such a tiresome misanthropic old chap, and my brother and I shall be quite happy to make ourselves comfortable downstairs. Will that suit?"

Relief flooded through her. Good old Penhallow. She could have kissed him, except for propriety and Lilibet, which were almost the same thing. As it was, she pressed her hands together in an elegant kidskin knot. "Darling Penhallow. I knew you'd oblige us. Thanks so *awfully*, my dear; you can't imagine how thankful I am for your generosity." She said it with gushing gratitude, really *quite* sincere, and yet she became uncomfortably aware of Mr. Burke's assessing gaze along the periphery of her vision.

Why *had* Wallingford brought along a scientific gentleman? Really, it was intolerable, having the man look at one with such thorough eyes, as if one were a *subject* of some sort. As if he understood all one's secrets.

She returned to the landlord, steeling her voice back into its usual tone of brusque efficiency: "Do you understand? *Comprendo?* You may remove His Grace's luggage from the rooms upstairs and bring up our trunks at once."

The landlord made a sullen bow and hurried off, just as the thick wooden door swung open and two bundled figures hunkered through, sodden and dripping.

Alexandra turned to the entrance and felt a warm glow of mischief evaporate her discomfort. "Ah! Cousin Lilibet! There you are at last. Have you sorted out the trunks?"

Lord Roland reacted with near-instantaneous haste. He wheeled about to the doorway and stepped in Lilibet's direction, before he remembered himself and froze on the spot.

Most satisfactory.

Even more satisfactory, Lilibet gave no sign of noticing him. All her cousin's attention focused on the little boy before her: she had already knelt down and was helping young Philip with the buttons on his wet woolen coat, the picture of concerned motherhood. "Yes, it's all been unloaded," she said. "The fellow's coming in the back." She glanced past the three men to Alexandra, as though they didn't exist at all; not an easy thing to do, when the gentlemen in question might have made up a side of rugby without bothering to recruit another player.

Almost *too* unconscious, Alexandra thought, but then who needed wiles with a face like Lilibet's? Her cousin straightened and began to unbutton her own coat, and Lord Roland seemed even more transfixed than before.

"Oh, for God's sake," someone muttered behind her. Wallingford, from the tone.

"I take it they know each other?" the other—Burke—asked dryly.

It was better than a play.

Alas, just as Lilibet reached the bottom of her coat, and Alexandra held her breath to see what would happen next, Miss Abigail Harewood swept through the door and ruined the scene.

She shook the droplets from her hat like a careless young spaniel and rushed up to her sister. "Alex, darling," she said, shattering the silence, "you won't believe what I've found in the stable!"

Alexandra heaved a disappointed sigh and wrinkled her nose. "What on earth were you doing in the stables, darling? Oh, do leave off that gesticulating and remove your coat. You're showering me, for goodness' sake. Here. Your buttons." She unfastened Abigail's wet coat with efficient fingers. "Now come along with me to the fire and warm yourself. We've a lovely hot dinner waiting for us at the table next to the fireplace.

You can tell me all about what you've discovered in the stables."

She slung the coat over her right arm, grasped Abigail's hand with her left, and steered a course directly to the massive hearth, where Lilibet hovered, hands outstretched: a sight to enrapture the heart of any English gentleman, and particularly one that had belonged to her for years.

Alexandra would have to keep a close eye indeed on Lord Roland Penhallow tonight.

As she passed the gentlemen, however, those eyes did a vexing and unexpected thing. They observed not Lord Roland's lovestruck gaze, nor even Wallingford's thundering scowl.

They lingered, instead, on the way the warm ginger hair of Mr. Phineas Burke kindled into red-gold flame in the light from the fire.